SMALL RAIN

SMALL RAIN

— A NOVEL —

GARTH GREENWELL

FARRAR, STRAUS AND GIROUX

NEW YORK

Farrar, Straus and Giroux
120 Broadway, New York 10271

Grateful acknowledgment is made for permission to reprint the following material:
Lines from "Injunction," by Frank Bidart, from *Half-light: Collected Poems
1965–2016*. Copyright © 2017 by Frank Bidart. Reprinted by permission
of Farrar, Straus and Giroux. All rights reserved.
Lines from "Ilusión de permanencia," by Luis Muñoz, from *Guadarrama*.
Copyright © 2023 by Luis Muñoz. Reprinted by permission of the author.
Lines from "On Home Beaches," by Les Murray, from *New Selected Poems*.
Copyright © 2007, 2012, 2014 by Les Murray. Reprinted by permission of Farrar,
Straus and Giroux. All rights reserved.
"Stranger's Child," by George Oppen, from *New Collected Poems*.
Copyright © 1962 by George Oppen. Reprinted by permission of
New Directions Publishing Corp.

Library of Congress Cataloging-in-Publication Data
Names: Greenwell, Garth, author.
Title: Small rain : a novel / Garth Greenwell.
Description: First edition. | New York : Farrar, Straus and Giroux, 2024.
Identifiers: LCCN 2024008333 | ISBN 9780374279547 (hardcover)
Subjects: LCGFT: Novels.
Classification: LCC PS3607.R4686 S63 2024 | DDC 813/.6—dc23/eng/20240222
LC record available at https://lccn.loc.gov/2024008333

Designed by Gretchen Achilles

Our books may be purchased in bulk for promotional, educational,
or business use. Please contact your local bookseller or the Macmillan Corporate and
Premium Sales Department at 1-800-221-7945, extension 5442,
or by email at MacmillanSpecialMarkets@macmillan.com.

www.fsgbooks.com
Follow us on social media at @fsgbooks

1 3 5 7 9 10 8 6 4 2

for Luis Muñoz

To have turned away from everything to one face
is to find oneself face to face with everything.

—ELIZABETH BOWEN, *The Heat of the Day*

1

They asked me to describe the pain but the pain defied description, on a scale of one to ten it demanded a different scale. It was like someone had plunged a hand into my gut and grabbed hold and yanked, trying to turn me inside out and failing and trying again. Like that, while somebody else kneed me in the groin. For eight hours on Saturday, I said—On Saturday, someone interrupted, I was surrounded by people at this point, some busy with IVs or electrodes but most, it seemed, just looking at me, asking me to answer questions I had already answered, wanting to hear everything afresh. In my own words, they said, not the words they had heard from others, the words that had summoned them here, from all corners of the huge hospital I was lucky to have almost in my backyard, just a mile from my house—on Saturday and you waited until today to come in, the voice said, you must be the stoic type. Stoic or stupid, I thought. For eight hours I had lain on the sofa in the room where I write, where I spend most of my time, reading or writing, though really I hadn't lain, I had crouched on all fours, I had curled into myself, clutching my stomach, I had held my balls as if to shield them in my hand. It didn't occur to me to go to the hospital, in part because for months I had thought of hospitals and doctors, of medical offices of all kinds, as the last places one would go for help, as dangerous places, in the pandemic the likeliest places to get infected, everyone I knew felt the same. Only if you were dying would you go to the hospital and it didn't occur to me that I could be dying. I wonder if anyone ever imagines they're dying, even as it happens, or if anyone imagines it without being sick for a long time, people like me, I mean, who have always been more or less healthy and more or less strong, hale, as my grandparents said, as my mother sometimes says, or said until now, counting her blessings, all of her children hearty and hale. I didn't imagine anything as I lay there, as I crouched or curled, nothing occurred to me, when I try to remember my thoughts they come broken and scrambled. I became a thing without words in those hours, a creature evacuated of soul. I spoke only once, when L came down from his office upstairs—we both work during the day, we're used to hours of silence, our life together depends on measuring out solitude and company—and tapped on my door and receiving no reply opened it slowly, gingerly, until he saw me where I lay and spoke in alarm. What happened, he said, what's wrong, he was speaking Spanish though it was an English day, we alternate days, each of us likes living in the other's language. I must have grunted or moaned, made some sound, because he said But tell me, please, what is it, and I told him I was sick, it was the most I could manage, I said I was sick through gritted teeth, taking shallow breaths; if I breathed too deeply the pain was worse, the fist in my gut twisted at the wrist. Vamos al médico, L said, his tone resolute, stern, he knelt by the sofa and put his hand on my back, right now, vamos. When I shook my head no he began to argue, an argument we've had often, anytime I feel even slightly unwell he insists we go to the doctor; in his country the health system works as it should, he has a European sense of what it means to be ill. Always, nearly always, I refused, even

4

before the pandemic; I've always hated doctors, a sense I got as a child, I suppose, that things usually pass, that doctors waste your money and your time, you wait for hours and they send you home the same or sicker. An American attitude or a Kentucky attitude maybe, most of my siblings share it. But I couldn't argue with him now, I said Please, guapo, I can't, and when he started to speak again I said please, I love you, I can't talk, I need to be alone. I knew it would hurt him but it was true, I couldn't be considerate, pain had sealed me off from sociability. Okay, he said, standing up, okay bello, these were our names for each other, guapo and bello, silly lovers' names, and then he left without saying anything more, closing the door quietly behind him.

For eight hours the pain lasted and then, not all at once but slowly, gradually, I couldn't have said when it happened, it began to ease; the fist relaxed its grip, I could breathe again and think. The pain didn't go away, I told the doctors, but it felt manageable, I could bear it, I could stand up and talk with L, who had been beside himself with worry, he said; he had looked in on me many times over the hours but I hadn't noticed, once he had called my name but I hadn't heard. It was something I ate, I told him, food poisoning, and when he said again I should go to the hospital I said it was passing already, it was nothing, it would go away on its own. And the fever, one of the doctors said, when did that start, and I said The same day as the pain, I don't know what time it started but that evening I had chills and aches in all my limbs, so of course I thought it was Covid, a Google search found that sometimes people did have stomach pains, it was a rare symptom but not unheard of. Basically nothing is unheard of, the nurse said to me days after the pain started, when finally I did want to go to urgent care and they insisted I get a

Covid test first, six months into the pandemic and we still know so little about this disease. The fever was highest on the first day, I said to the doctor, about 102, then it fell off, on the other days it hovered around 100. The pain never went away, I went on, but for the next two days it was bearable, it felt like a normal stomachache almost, indigestion and bloating, and the pain in my groin faded too, I could walk and talk, I didn't have much appetite but I could read and work a little. And then yesterday it got worse again, the pain in my stomach but especially a new pain in my lower back, I thought maybe I had wrenched it on the first day when I was in so much pain. It got so bad that I couldn't sleep, even fitfully, I couldn't sleep at all, so finally I called urgent care. L had made me call, was the truth of it, he got so upset finally I couldn't bear it, and the morning after the Covid test came back negative (the hospital had set up a drive-through clinic, I rolled down my window and they stuck the long swab up my nose) I drove—You drove, the doctor said, and I said What else was I going to do, of course I drove—to urgent care. L wanted to come but it wasn't permitted, there were new policies in the pandemic and patients had to come alone. He was in the kitchen when I left, still in his pajamas—he wore real pajamas, not just a T-shirt and sweats but actual clothes for sleeping: he likes a sense of ceremony about things, for each moment to be considered; a day should be a work of art, he likes to say. The ones he wore now had a pattern of little deer; he ordered them after we moved into our new neighborhood, where there were many deer, we both gasped in wonder to see them in our yard on winter mornings, it seemed magical to us and especially to L, who had never seen them before coming to America. I laughed the first time I saw the pajamas, he came to bed in them and we both laughed, his pijama de ciervos. He hugged me before I left. It's good you're going, he said, you'll find out what it is and they'll make it better, and he stood at the door as I pulled out of the drive, watching me leave.

It was very early, I was the first person at the clinic when it opened. The woman at registration asked me to wait at the door while she pulled on her face shield, not the flimsy almost disposable kind I had seen around town but made of a thick hard plastic, black, almost military. It was open in the back but otherwise it resembled the helmets police were wearing at the demonstrations that filled the news, protests that were largely about the militarization and brutality of the police, brutality that began, I sometimes thought, with the helmets and armor that sealed them off from the people they faced. The nurse who saw me was tired and kind, patient as I told for the first time the story I would soon tire of telling. She took a urine sample and did an exam, palpating my stomach, listening to my lungs. She called in another nurse and asked to examine my testicles, then told me to lean against the bed while she inserted a finger in my ass, the first humiliation, I thought, a visit to the doctor is always humiliating, but she was quick about it, efficient. The second nurse ducked out as I pulled up my pants and the first nurse gestured for me to sit, not on the examination table but in the chair near the computer, so that I was a person again, not just a patient. There were things she could rule out, she said, based on the urine sample and the exam, there wasn't a bladder infection or a hernia, or any of a long list of maladies she recited, I don't remember everything she said. We could do blood work that might rule out other things, but really you need imaging and that we can't do here. The obvious worry is appendicitis, and even if the blood work ruled that out I'd want a CT to see if something else showed up. So I want you to go to the ER, she said, I'm sorry, I know it isn't what you hoped to hear but I think it's the best course. There were two options in town, the huge university hospital and a much smaller, private facility, where the wait would probably be shorter. It was up to me where I went but since the urgent care was run by the university her notes would automatically be transferred to them, they could see the tests she had run and the things she had ruled out, they wouldn't have to call to be briefed. She looked at the computer. And you have university insurance, she said, are you faculty, and I said I wasn't, my partner was, I had insurance through him. It was expensive, they took hundreds from L's paycheck each month; we were lucky they had domestic partner insurance at all but it cost twice what it would have if we were married. We complained about it every month but we didn't want to be married, we both hated marriage. I had thought about dropping it and finding something cheaper, or even going without for a while, I was healthy and still thought of myself as young, young-ish; I thought of myself as lucky is what I mean, I guess, though really I didn't think of my health much at all, which *was* the luck, the privilege of health. Okay, I said to the nurse, I'll go to the university, and she nodded and stood, moving on already to the next patient, of which there were many now, when I stepped into the sitting area there were a dozen people waiting.

There were many more people waiting at the ER, where nearly every seat was taken, all the seats that hadn't been blocked off by tape, signs with the words Social Distancing warning people away. At the entrance, in a cubicle behind plexiglass between two sets of sliding doors, a woman took my name and date of birth, then instructed me to stand on an X marked on the floor, so that an instrument mounted above could scan my temperature as she asked if I had any symptoms of Covid, in which case I would have to go to a different part of the hospital. It was the end of August, students had just come back to town, to everyone's dismay; the summer had been calm, without a huge number of cases, but now the bars and fraternity houses were packed, as though nothing were wrong, and of course there was a surge, a second wave people said, though really I thought the worst was still to come, in winter when all the parties would move inside. Already the rooms the university had designated for quarantine were full, the hospital had sent up flares about scarce resources and few beds, already it was worse than it had been in the spring, when the students were sent home and the city became its summer self, relaxed and nearly empty, a calm that felt like siege but also we sensed we were spared. The state was being aggressive about ending lockdown and insisted on in-person classes, all thirty thousand students were called back to town. It's like watching a car drive straight off a cliff, a friend said, but slowly, deliberately, a slow-motion suicide. Everywhere in the ER there were signs reminding us to wear masks but not everyone did, or they pulled them off to talk on the phone, to eat or drink, or they didn't cover their nose. I wished I had more protection than the surgical mask I was wearing, I would have liked a face shield of my own, I would have liked not to be there at all. The room was large and open, but there was a section somewhat sheltered by a kind of partition, wooden slats framing a medium-sized aquarium, of the sort I associated with cheap restaurants with pretensions to class; it was the part of the room farthest from the door where nurses appeared to call people's names, maybe that's why I found an open seat there. The aquarium was meant to be soothing, I guess, like everything else in the room. The TVs were cycling nature images, a purling stream, grain swaying in sunlight; later this switched to a montage of high school choirs from around the state, singing hymns and spirituals and patriotic songs, which didn't calm me at all actually, which did the opposite, as did the fish: one huge bottom-feeder, too large for the tank, which lumbered from one corner to another, gumming the pebbles at the bottom, and a dozen or so smaller fish, bright and hyperactive, zipping miserably back and forth.

A screen mounted at the front of the room said the wait was two hours, so I was surprised to be called back so quickly, after fifteen minutes or so; maybe I wouldn't be there all day, I thought. I moved slowly, the pain wasn't debilitating but it was bad enough. I moved too slowly for the woman who called my name, who had let the door swing shut and retreated to the interior before I could reach her, then opened it again after I had waited a minute or two, motioning me impatiently through. I only had time to glimpse the main area, the department or ward: there was a central bank of what looked like cubicles, plexiglass partitions behind which doctors and nurses and technicians sat at computers or leaned on desks, all in masks but many with their face shields lifted, and then corridors of examination rooms stretching back, some with doors and some with drawn curtains. There were patients in the corridors as well, people lying on stretchers pushed against walls, all of them alone—it seemed terrible to me that they were alone, as I was alone; even if we didn't have the virus it had still cut us off, whatever we were facing we would face it alone. Seeing them made me frightened, for the first time; my sense that everything would be all right faltered. But I was being dramatic, I chided myself, I wasn't really cut off, my phone was in my pocket, I had already texted L with updates, he had texted back his love. Even if it was appendicitis that wasn't a disaster, it would mean surgery but a routine surgery, it was something that could be fixed. The woman led me to a scale, then asked me my name and date of birth before fastening a plastic bracelet around my wrist, which had a barcode that would be scanned dozens of times each day, with every medication and procedure, every vial they took of my blood. We were in a little alcove with a curtain she left undrawn, I sat in a chair while she took my blood pressure and temperature, she stood at a computer mounted to a wall taking notes while I spoke. Mm-hmm, she hummed at regular intervals, which seemed less encouragement than skepticism. I disliked her, I realized, I felt an antipathy she hadn't earned. Probably she was exhausted; I can't imagine it, day after day seeing people in pain, at their worst moments, over years; how could you protect yourself from that, I wondered, there was some human regard I wanted from her that I had no right to demand. You can head back out now, she said, turning from the computer. We're a little full at the moment, as you can see, you're going to be waiting for a while. Oh, I said, they sent me here for a CT scan, can you schedule that, but she made a dismissive sound. She couldn't schedule anything, a doctor would have to see me first, and for a doctor to see me they would need to put me in a room, and who knew when they would have a room available, she said as she ushered me back through the door, you can see how many people are waiting already.

My seat was still free, far from the entrance to the ward and facing the sad aquarium. I had a book with me and tried to read, but I was distracted by discomfort—hunching over eased my stomach but aggravated my back, which nothing could soothe, not standing or sitting or walking to the little alcove with vending machines—and also by the noise and shuffle of the people around me, the drama of the place. Shortly after I sat down again there was a bit of commotion, a security guard appeared in front of the doors leading to the main hospital, not far from where I sat, and turned away anyone who tried to pass from either side, patient or staff, saying they had to walk outside to another entrance, that the ER was on lockdown. A man entered shortly after, cuffed at the hands and feet and with a chain around his waist, an elaborate restraint, and further restrained by two guards, one at each side. A kind of shudder went through the room, the noise quieted as people looked and quickly looked away, then looked again, as I did. The guards weren't hospital employees, they had guns strapped to their waists, they wore uniforms from the state prison. The man between them was a convict out of central casting, huge with fat and muscle, maybe 6′5″ with a shaved head and tattoos up both arms. We all watched as he shuffled to the registration desk and then to a seat; the guards removed the tape and social distancing signs to sit on either side of him. He kept his eyes on the floor, looking at no one. He didn't wait long, he must have been given priority, almost immediately he was on his feet again for the triage nurse and didn't reappear. There was something terrible about watching the people around me, terrible and irresistible, I wanted to see into their lives but I had no right to; it was an intrusion, like looking into the lit windows of houses at night, which is something else I can't resist, when L and I take walks through the neighborhood after dark my eyes are drawn to every lit pane. Most of the people in the waiting room were like windows left dark, blank or withdrawn, scrolling on their phones or staring into space.

A nurse brought a man into the room from the ward, and stationed him in a corner of the area where I sat, a spot left free of seats to accommodate wheelchairs. Immediately he started talking, not to anyone in particular but not to himself, either. I can't stay here, he said, I can't wait so long, I need my wife, he began saying, please, I need my wife. The hospital's policy was that adult patients should come alone, it was a precaution against the virus, but exceptions were made for those needing assistance, you could call and make your case, surely they would have allowed his wife to come. He had begun moving his head in a strange, distressed way, throwing it back and then rolling it from left to right, Please, he said, his mask had slipped beneath his nose but he didn't replace it, please, I need my wife, I want to call my wife. I felt a tension I've grown familiar with, between desire to help and inhibition, I've felt it all my life; there's a kind of moral paralysis I sometimes feel, a moral weakness I mean, one stands by and so is culpable. Maybe if it weren't for the pandemic I would have offered him my phone; in general I felt like my social instincts, my sense of sociality, my humanness I want to say had atrophied in lockdown. For months I had hardly left my house, I had touched no one but L. We were forgetting how to be with one another in physical space, I thought, how to be creatures living with other creatures, the long transition to virtuality had been sped up by the virus. But then I remembered the student parties, the protests and the president's rallies, I shouldn't generalize; plenty of people still wanted to be together in a way I never had. Finally a woman stood, another patient, and went to him and spoke, simply, matter-of-factly, not with any particular solicitude, asking him if she could help. I need my wife, the man said again, I need to call my wife and I don't have a phone, I need my wife. Well, the woman said, there's a phone in that other corner, and she pointed across the room, if you want I can help you get over there. But the man didn't want this; he would push himself, he said, and then quickly he got stuck, when he tried to maneuver around the wooden partition he couldn't manage the turn, and without saying anything more the woman took hold of the handles on the back of the chair and pushed him through. It wasn't hard, I thought, watching as people in their path made room for them, pulling in their legs, rearranging bags; decency wasn't hard, you saw someone in trouble and you helped them out of it. The man spoke loudly into the phone, You need to come get me, he said, I can't wait here all day. I need to lay down, he said, there's nowhere for me to lay down. He raised his voice to say No, repeating it, no, no, you need to come, you need to come, and then after a moment he dropped the phone back in its cradle. She won't come, he said to the woman, who had remained beside him, and then fell silent, only shaking his head when she asked if he wanted to call anybody else. The woman returned him to his corner and he closed his eyes and let his chin drop to his chest. She stood beside him a moment, hesitating, now she too was unsure what she should do, and then returned to her seat. Maybe he would sleep, I thought, wondering if the woman he had called had been cruel or if she was acting in his best interest; maybe it had been difficult to get him here, maybe she knew he needed to stay. I didn't hear him say anything else;

he became another darkened window, not a story anymore but a blank page.

Two hours had passed when my name was called again, and a different nurse took me to the same alcove, where she drew blood before sending me out to wait some more. I was texting L every fifteen minutes or so, and as time passed he grew more indignant, I don't understand this country, he said, you wait so long and you pay so much. But his indignation didn't help. I was spending more time with my arms wrapped around my stomach, my eyes closed; the pain still wasn't as bad as it had been on the first day but it was getting decidedly worse, it was all I could think about. I stopped answering L's texts as they came, only after he had texted a second or a third time did I reply. It had become engrossing, the pain, it had become a kind of environment, a medium of existence; I wasn't impatient or bored, there was something fascinating and dreadful about the experience of my body. I began negotiating with it, with the pain or with my body, I'm not sure which, or if a meaningful distinction could be drawn: if it stays here, at this level, if it doesn't get worse, I can bear it, it isn't unbearable yet. I was surprised, when I was called into the ward a third time, to see that four hours had passed. It was as if the room were exempt from time, a little enclave outside its regime: many of the people I passed, as I walked toward the woman holding open the door, were the same people, the room was more crowded but it seemed hardly anyone had moved. I hadn't seen this woman before; she led me to the alcove and told me she was the nurse practitioner on the ward, a distinction I didn't understand except that it marked some degree of authority, a rank in a hierarchy, we still don't have a room for you but we want to keep the ball rolling. She was friendlier than the first nurse I had spoken to but the friendliness didn't mean anything, it was just her way of bearing up. The news was full of nurses and doctors who weren't bearing up, there were too many patients and too many of them were dying, and not just dying but dying alone; videos circulated of nurses, still in their scrubs, in tears recounting how they held phones or iPads so patients could say goodbye to their families, how even then they had to ration the time, five minutes and no more, so many patients were dying and waiting for their chance to call. It was her way of enduring, I thought of the nurse and her grating cheer, who was I to judge it. She asked me to repeat the story of what had happened but kept interrupting, wanting me to speed things up. When I said that the urgent care nurse had been concerned about appendicitis she cut me off, saying they weren't too worried about that, my blood work had come back and there weren't any indications of appendicitis, we'd expect your white blood cell counts to be higher; but she wanted me to have a CT scan anyway, to see if they could figure out what was going on. Her tone suggested there was no reason to worry, it dismissed all doubt, and I thought of the things I had said to L over the past days, that it would be a waste of time to go to the ER, that they would just send me home and tell me to wait it out; I felt vindicated by her tone.

She had drawn a curtain across the front of the alcove, making a private space, and now it fluttered, someone on the other side had taken hold of it but waited to pull it open until the nurse said to come in. A short broad woman in a set of green scrubs entered—the scrubs were part of the hierarchy, too, I realized, a code I would try to decipher. She pulled a small metal cart behind her. You'll need an IV for the scan, the nurse practitioner said, we'll get that in and then imaging will come get you when they're ready. And then she was gone, closing the curtain behind her, and the new woman and I were alone. She asked me how I was and reflexively I said fine, and then after a pause we both laughed a little. Yeah, she said, she spoke with a South American accent, Colombian maybe, I guess if you were fine you wouldn't be here. She took her time, opening drawers and pulling out various supplies, unfolding a pad over the top of the cart, on which she set her instruments as she asked me if I had had an IV before. Many times, I told her, though it had been years; I had never spent the night in a hospital before but I had had a couple of surgeries when I was young, normal childhood things, and then when I was desperate for money in graduate school I had taken part in a study that required me, once a month for six months, to spend an afternoon sitting with a line in my arm. It was an HIV study, research for a vaccine, there was a bag of medication followed by a bag of what they called fluids; I don't remember the drug but I was paid a hundred dollars for each day I spent there. Sometimes they have trouble with my veins, I told the woman as she tied the tourniquet on my left bicep— she had asked which hand I used more, whether I was a righty or a lefty—and she hummed noncommittally, turning my arm so she could examine it. She ran her gloved fingers from the crook of my elbow to the wrist, pausing about halfway, where the scars began; this always happened, sometimes doctors ask about them and sometimes they don't, sometimes they ask about mental health, about depression, ideation, and I say it was decades ago, a quarter century, ancient history—she paused but just briefly, she didn't say a word. I liked her, I decided. She made a noise of disappointment, then started tapping my arm with three fingers, asking me to make a fist and release several times. She sighed then, They weren't lying to you, she said, they are a little hard to find, let's try the other arm, and she drew my right hand toward her. She repeated the same motions up and down, tapping the veins while I made a fist, and then she returned to the crook of my arm and pressed again with her fingers. There you are, she said, why were you hiding, and it made me like her more. Then there was a quick swipe of alcohol and she asked me to release my hand, to breathe deep and relax, and the needle slid in. It hardly hurt at all, she was good at her job, but then as always happens she had to adjust the needle, pushing it in more deeply and moving it side to side, that's the real pain. Her head was tilted forward and I looked at her hair; it wasn't long, maybe shoulder length, but it was thick and brown, and she had bound it with a pink elastic, something a schoolkid might wear, frivolous, needlessly pretty, I liked her very much. This is just saline, she said, screwing a syringe into the IV, and as she pressed the plunger there was a taste or smell at the back of my throat, something like rubbing alcohol, a kind of ghost impression. She saw me sense it, Weird, right, she said. We call that the taste of victory, it means the IV's working, I thought I lost the vein for a minute but it behaved. She placed a broad piece of transparent tape over the needle with its two wings, another narrower piece of tape securing the plastic tube she coiled beneath. Okay, she said, you're all set. She told me to go back to the waiting room, someone would call me for the next step; I wondered how many steps there would be. How long have you been waiting, she asked as I stood, and I shrugged, Five hours or so, I said. She sucked her breath between her teeth. It's been bad the last few days, she said, I'm sorry. I hope you can go home soon.

There were no seats in the waiting room now, people were sitting on the floor and standing in corners, it was like an airport in bad weather. In the spring there had been stories in the news about hospitals reaching capacity, about protocols for turning people away to die, not just patients with Covid but other patients, too: people with heart attacks, crash victims, all the myriad ways people approach death, but not just them; pregnant women, too, or people with conditions that should be simple matters, like the appendicitis I might have had, all of them turned away because at a certain point the system breaks down, it was unthinkable and also it was true. In the early months of the pandemic it had been terrible in Spain, there were stories of old people being turned away, of a terrible calculus, scarce resources saved for younger patients, likelier to survive. Hijos de puta, L had shouted, streaming the Spanish news, hijos de puta, and again when Republicans here began arguing against shutdown, saying the elderly would make the sacrifice willingly, for the good of the nation, it was a patriotic duty; hijos de puta, he shouted at them through the screen, los mayores *son* la patria. He was thinking of his father, I knew, who had died the summer before. L had been devastated but also he knew they had been lucky, the family had been together, they had cared for his father in his final weeks, they had fed him and bathed him, they had been together when he died. A year later and he would have died alone. A la cárcel, he said, about the politicians and the doctors, too, though the doctors didn't have a choice, I thought. About the politicians I agreed, I wanted to see them all in prison, every last one, but what choice did the doctors have, they weren't politicians, they couldn't bluff or bully their way through, they were slammed against the rock of reality, and when all choices are unacceptable one still has to choose. In the spring that hadn't happened here, it hadn't been like New York or Seattle, even with cases flown in from across the state they had never filled all the rooms. But now it had come, I thought, perched in the well of a window in the waiting room, and it was still only August, in the winter it would be worse. I couldn't imagine more people fitting into the ER, already people were disregarding the signs placed on seats. A tall thin man was trying to clean the floor, riding some kind of motorized vehicle that swept and mopped, but it was useless, he couldn't find a path through, even as he repeatedly said Excuse me, too loudly, either in frustration or because of the earbuds he wore. The sound he made competed with a woman's moans, a woman in a wheelchair not far from where I had been sitting earlier; at first they seemed like wordless moans but in fact she was saying I can't, repeating it again and again, the words drawn out and broken by sobs. I had thought she was an old woman but glancing again I saw she wasn't, she was in her midthirties maybe, and pregnant; I hadn't noticed her belly at first because she was hunched forward in the chair. She wasn't alone, a man was with her, she must have gotten special dispensation; a young man I thought, his face was young though he was nearly bald already, maybe that was why at first glance I had thought that they were old. He was holding one of her hands in both of his, or trying to; she kept twisting her hand free and he kept taking it again, stroking it, letting go only long enough to push her hair out of her face. She was obviously in distress, in pain, but no one came, she wasn't triaged out. She had to wait like everyone else.

Not much time had passed, maybe half an hour, when my name was called again, not from the ER ward but from the door to the main hospital, the door that had been locked while the prisoner was present. The CT was quick and efficient, two minutes on a slab that moved in and out of a plastic tube, the flush and warmth of the contrast in the vein. In the waiting room the mood was changing, people were getting angry; new patients seeing the screen on the wall—the wait was four and a half hours now—groaned in disbelief. Several of them left, they couldn't wait that long, they said; weeks later there would be an article in the local paper about people leaving the ER without being seen, on the worst days of August and September a quarter or a third might give up on waiting, it was a crisis of care, the article said. L's texts were becoming more outraged, he couldn't believe I hadn't seen a doctor yet, how could the system be so dysfunctional, why did we put up with it. I didn't have an answer; for years I had wondered at American irrationality, and never more than during the pandemic, when the most basic facts had been called into question, when calling them into question had become for much of my country a kind of declaration of allegiance, an identity. Not that it was anything new: I remembered my outrage, in middle school or high school, when Congress passed a resolution declaring global warming a myth; what assholes, I thought, these men who were like children, thinking wishing makes it so. But it had become impossible to ignore, American unreason, it had come to seem less aberrant, less a thing of the margins than at the heart of what we were, it had corroded the idealism that had always also been part of my sense of my country, I mean my sense of myself; corroded it not just for me but for nearly everyone I knew, for nearly everyone altogether, it seemed, for that weird intellectual weather we had taken to calling the Discourse, the amorphous impersonal sense of things that came from scrolling through social media, from watching fifteen-second video clips on YouTube. It was like we had outsourced consciousness, turned inwardness inside out, we thought now in other peoples' memes. It made me despair for my country, not just my country, for the endeavor of humanness—something it had become impossible to think of unironically, an idea that could only be mocked. L was outraged but I couldn't muster much indignation, I felt weirdly detached, engrossed by pain and also by a strange relief, the relief of being a patient, of being passive; I had made my decision to come and now, for a while, there weren't any decisions, other people would decide, and so long as they hadn't decided I could relax in their not-yet-deciding. What I mean is that I was scared of what they would say, it was my own irrationality, as if so long as they hadn't spoken whatever was happening wasn't real, as if there could be no catastrophe so long as the catastrophe wasn't named.

And then it was named. The woman I had spoken with earlier, the nurse practitioner, called me into the ward again, but this time not into the alcove; she had parked a wheelchair just past the door and motioned for me to sit. But I can walk, I said, there's no need—but she cut me off, she said she would prefer I sit, a room was ready for me now. She was a heavyset woman, middle aged; her dark hair fell to her shoulders in curls. I did as she asked, it would have been impossible not to; that was part of the passivity I had taken refuge in, to do as I was told, and as I sat I felt a terrible dread. Nothing in her demeanor had changed, her voice was still bright, chipper, a word I had always hated, a Midwestern word, she even laughed as we started off. Well, you

are not what I was expecting at all, she said, you are certainly
a surprise, I thought I was going to send you home with some
antibiotics but you are much more interesting than that. We
were moving quickly through corridors, there were more banks
of cubicles, all blocked off by plastic partitions, more rooms with
doors open or shut, stretchers with patients sitting upright or
laid out, thin white sheets clutched to their chests. It was cold,
I realized suddenly, the air was aggressively cool, I wondered
why they kept the temperature so low. We were moving too
quickly for me to see anyone, really, to notice them or be caught
by them, to imagine anything about their lives. But what is it,
I asked the woman, or tried to ask her, what's wrong with me,
where are we going. She only answered the last question, saying
a room had opened up and doctors would come to see me, a lot of
people want to talk to you, she said, still in a tone that suggested
this was happy news, a privilege; and then Here we are, she said,
stopping at an open door, a room where a young man, a college
student maybe, was still unfurling a sheet over the bed. The
nurse walked around to the front of the chair and looked down
at me. She told me then what was wrong with me, in the privacy
of the room—that was what she had been waiting for, I realized,
maybe she wasn't allowed to explain anything while pushing
me through the halls—but the words didn't mean anything, I
only understood one of them, aortic; there sprang into my mind
a scrap of a poem, the blown aorta pelting out blood, which I
couldn't place and was of no help at all. I would have asked her
to explain but someone else entered the room, a man pushing a
cart, a computer of some kind. He's going to need a minute, the
woman said, and she picked up a folded garment from the bed;
the other man, the college student, must have left it there, he

had slipped out of the room without my noticing. You'll need to change into this, the nurse said, you can keep your socks and underwear on but everything else comes off. Can you stand up, she asked, and I said I could, of course, and she wheeled the chair out, pulling the door shut behind her.

It was a small room, with just a couple of feet of clearance around the bed; the walls were scuffed and marked, they hadn't been painted for years, and in general the room was in poor repair, like a room in a run-down hotel. I undressed quickly, stuffing my pants and shirt into the tote bag I had carried on my lap in the wheelchair, clutching it as though it contained something more valuable than the novel I had failed to read, the notebook I carried everywhere, where I scribbled lines for poems, the charger for my phone, which seemed more precious than anything else at the moment, I would have been lost without it; all day, even when I hadn't been using it, I had kept my phone in my hand, a line to my life outside the emergency room, my real life. The gown was thin cotton, white with a blue pattern, not quite floral, and ridiculously short, barely extending past my groin; without my underwear I would have been exposed. I felt exposed enough as it was, comical, pathetic; I had drawn my arms through the front and was fumbling with the ties in the back when there was a light knock and the door opened slowly, a man's voice, jocular, asking if I was decent. All right if I come in, he asked, peering around the door, and I nodded. He was older, pushing sixty, older than the other staff I had seen, medium height, with broad shoulders and the thick torso of a lapsed athlete. He wore a simple disposable plastic shield over his face, not one of the helmets like the registered nurses and doctors wore; this was a sign of hierarchy as well, I realized, how durable one's PPE was, personal protective equipment, everyone had learned the acronym that spring when there was a rush on masks and gloves. For months you couldn't find them, and even if you could it would be irresponsible to take them away from hospitals and first responders, that was the discourse anyway in the early days of panic; and they wouldn't help in any case, people said, they didn't offer protection, even the surgeon general said it, though it turned out to be a lie, something they said because supplies were so low. But we believed the lie, and it became a sign of virtue to scold people, Twitter was full of admonitions not to buy masks or gloves, to give any you had to hospitals. L and I had had a terrible fight when he told me he had ordered masks online, that he had scoured the internet and finally found some from a store in Japan, the price had been exorbitant but he had paid it. I had been outraged, it had seemed selfish to me, a failure to care for the greater good, we had raised our voices at each other. How can you talk to me about the greater good, he had said, I have to think about what's good for us, I want to protect my family, and obviously masks would help, anywhere there had been any success against the virus everyone had worn masks, he didn't care what the CDC said, and it turned out he was right.

The man told me his name was Frank, he would be my nurse in the ER, and the first order of business was to get me connected to their machines. There was an elaborate cabinet in a corner of the room, and next to it a small sink with a counter, on which he placed the bags of IV medication he had carried in, before taking a line of adhesive pads out of a drawer. I just need to put these on your chest, he said, is that all right. They were circular, each with a metal piece in the middle, a kind of snap or clip where now he attached wires from a monitor beside the bed. He had left the door open and the man from earlier came back in, stepping over to the cart he had left behind. I'm going to have to do this first, Frank said, and his voice had a kind of warning in it I thought, insisting on a prerogative. The man didn't challenge him, No problem, he said, though it was clear he outranked Frank, he had on the blue scrubs of a doctor. You've had a day, Frank said to me; things are going to get busy quick, everybody wants to see you, you've got them all excited. He asked me to raise my left arm, the one with the bracelet, and he leaned over me to scan it with a barcode reader, a plastic device like you'd see in a supermarket, connected by a coiled cord to the computer station mounted to the wall behind the bed. Then he scanned a barcode on a machine attached higher on the wall, beside and below a large screen that began showing my heart rate, the alarming peaks and valleys I've never understood. He was moving slowly, methodically, unconcerned by the doctor waiting as he took the two bags of fluids and hung them from a stand beside the bed. He scanned my wrist again, then barcodes on both the bags, then another barcode on one of several machines that were attached halfway down the stand, titrators, I would learn, which controlled the flow of the fluids. He was busy with these machines for a moment, opening panels and arranging tubing, then pushing several buttons, and then he flushed my IV with a saline syringe and connected the bags to my arm. One of these is just fluids, he said, and the other is—, and here he said the name of a drug that meant nothing to me; I can never remember the names of medications, they might as well be nonsense syllables. It was to control my blood pressure, he said, they wanted my blood pressure and heart rate down.

Once this was done—he pressed the skin around the needle, satisfied it was working—he nodded to the doctor, who had been waiting; You can get started, he said, circling to the other side of the bed to fit a blood pressure cuff around my arm. The doctor pushed the cart closer to me and introduced himself, he said he was there to do an ultrasound, one of his colleagues would be joining us—And here she is, he said as a woman entered the room. They were both very young, they must have just finished medical school, maybe they were doing their residencies. Have you ever had an ultrasound before, the man asked, and then, as I hadn't, he said something about how ultrasounds work, that there would be no pain. He asked me to lift my gown to my chest, above my sternum, while he opened a plastic packet of gel and spread it across the head of an instrument he held in his hand, a kind of wand attached by a cord to the computer on his cart. He warned me it would be cold and it was; I sucked in my breath and he apologized. He started just below my rib cage and moved slowly down, turning the wand slightly one way and then another. I looked at the screen but it was incomprehensible, I couldn't make any sense of the patches of light and shadow. The cuff on my left arm began to whirr and inflate, the pressure becoming intense, then painful before it released and a number appeared on the screen. The doctor with the ultrasound was having trouble, he couldn't find what he wanted, it seemed; he kept returning the wand to my sternum and dragging it down. He and the woman conferred quietly, like classmates with a difficult task. That's the spine, right, I heard him ask, and she said I think so, and then, maybe you need to push a little harder. Now a third doctor entered the room, an older man, bearded and lean, wearing a white coat over his scrubs, his name embroidered in blue thread at the chest. I just wanted to pop in, he said, speaking to the other doctors, not to me, and when they said they were having some trouble getting a good image he joined them at the machine. The first doctor put more gel on the wand, it was cold again on my sternum. Is this, the woman started but the older doctor cut her off, placing his finger on the screen and saying Here, this is the artery, can you get a better image of this. I'm trying, the young man said, twisting his hand slightly and then, suddenly petulant, I've lost it again. I wondered if the older man was their teacher or supervisor; when he said Do you mind the two doctors immediately gave way, stepping aside to give him room. The young man relinquished the wand, maybe with relief, I thought. Only now did the older man acknowledge me, he told me his name and said he wasn't part of my team, he was just curious to see such an interesting case. Why, I asked, as he was applying more gel to the wand, what makes it such an interesting case? He paused. Well, he said, and then, as if interrupting himself, he asked if it was all right for him to scan my abdomen, and I said it was. Well, he said, your age, for one thing, usually we see this in people in their sixties or seventies, and basically you're a healthy guy otherwise, and—he paused again and pressed the wand harder into my sternum, here it is, he said, satisfied, speaking to the younger doctors. Follow it down from here, he said, and then to me, I'm going to press a little harder now. He moved the wand down as the other man had, but pressing much harder, and when he reached a point just above my navel I cried out. Are you sensitive there, he asked, and I said I was, but he could go on, it wasn't unbearable. He pressed even harder than before, I set my jaw against the pain. Here, he said, you can see it here, and the younger doctor said

Is this it here, this flapping thing, and the older man grunted assent. Grab that for me, he said, and the woman quickly made a couple of strokes on the keyboard, taking a screenshot. Usually I just fan out like this, the doctor said, pressing harder and moving slightly from side to side, all the while telling the doctors to take several more shots. I had pulled the sheet up over my underwear and he asked my permission to scan a little lower, then asked me to push the elastic band of my briefs down just slightly so he could scan a bit more of my pelvis.

We'll get out of your way now, he said then in a louder voice, not speaking to any of us in the room but to the three figures I saw waiting just outside. You can clean him up, the doctor said, handing the wand back to the younger man, who used a paper towel to wipe first the wand and then the trail they had made down my torso, gathering the gel in brisk strokes, an intimate act stripped of intimacy. There was some confusion at the door, the doctors coming in had to make way for the doctors heading out, and then the new doctors took up stations around the bed, two women and a man, all older, all in white coats. The woman who began speaking introduced herself and the man as surgeons, and the other woman as a nurse practitioner. They were all from the vascular surgery team, she said, and my dread deepened, there must have been some sign of it on my face. This must be really scary, she went on, her voice quieter. Do you understand what's happening, has someone explained it to you? They hadn't, I said, not really, I knew it was something to do with my aorta but beyond that I didn't understand. Is it very bad, I asked, and she took a breath. What you have is called an infrarenal aortic dissection, she said, and I asked her to repeat it before she went on, then I repeated it myself. Right, she said. What that means is that there's a tear in your aorta, in the inner layer, part of the inner wall of the artery has detached. So that was what caused the pain, I asked, the terrible pain I felt on Saturday, and she said Yes, probably, that could have been the moment it tore. It was here the man broke in. This happened on Saturday, he said, you've lived with the pain for five days, and I said it had gotten better; after the first eight hours the pain hadn't been as bad. He asked me how I would rank the pain I was feeling now, on a scale of one to ten. I thought for a moment and said seven maybe, eight, though really I had no idea what the scale meant; but when he asked about the first pain, the crippling pain, I just shook my head, the question didn't make sense. I had never felt anything like it, I said. Frank was in the room again, doing something with the titration machine, and I felt relief at seeing him, maybe just because I had seen him before; he wasn't a stranger exactly, and I could trust that I would see him again. Based on your scan I wouldn't expect you to be walking, the male surgeon said, you should seem sicker than you do, you shouldn't be sitting up. Maybe my face brightened at this, because it felt like praise, or like a promise that whatever was happening was still in some category north of terrible, that maybe my case wasn't so grave. His own face turned grim. It's a serious thing, he said, you could die from this, and I saw or felt the two women stiffen, I sensed Frank stop whatever he was doing beside the bed. The woman who hadn't spoken yet, the nurse, said Oh, a little reproachfully, and the other surgeon spoke quickly, You're not going to die from this, she said, not today, we're going to take care of you. But it's a rare thing, she went on, and especially rare for someone like you, young and healthy. You've never smoked, right, never used intravenous drugs; these were questions I had been asked earlier and I shook my head. Usually we see this in older people, with other problems, with very high blood pressure, with other comorbidities, we need to find out why this happened to you. Now another nurse walked in, someone I hadn't seen before, she apologized for interrupting and said she was there to place a second IV. You'll have to double up on the right arm, I heard Frank say, on his way out of the room. The vascular nurse moved to the foot of the bed to make space, standing beside the male surgeon. Is there a history of this in your family, he asked, and I said no as the new nurse lifted my arm to place the tourniquet, asking my permission first. And is it all right if I take a look at you while she does that, the female surgeon asked, and I said yes again, feeling a little tired already of the way they kept asking me for permission, seeking consent; I suppose it isn't meaningless but it felt meaningless, I would have preferred just to be a body they worked on. I felt the nurse tapping, seeking a vein on the inside of my forearm, while the surgeon asked my consent again to lift my gown, which I helped her do, with my left hand; together we pulled it to my chest, stopping just below my nipples. She leaned over me slightly to do this, and I saw the identification card clipped to her coat. In the picture she was a younger woman than she seemed behind her face shield and mask, maybe late forties, with long dull very straight blond hair. Her name was Ferrier, she had mentioned it before but it hadn't registered, I was surprised by it now. It was the name of one of my favorite singers, Kathleen Ferrier, whose recordings I had listened to endlessly; one of the first CDs I bought as a teenager, just after I discovered music, classical music I mean, was a recording of Mahler's Das Lied von der Erde and three of the Rückert lieder, the first of which became a kind of talisman for me, important in a way I was only just beginning to understand art could be important. The song articulated something that had been inarticulate before, but it did more than that, too, it created something; it didn't just light some chamber of myself that had been dark, it made a new chamber, somehow, it made me capable of some feeling I couldn't have felt before. It humanized me, I want to say, it was part of that humanization art has been for me, which is something else it has become difficult to say, to say or believe, but I do believe it. The surgeon began her examination just below my ribs, pressing very hard, first with the palm of her hand and then shifting the pressure to her fingers. She repeated this, moving slowly, asking each time if it hurt. It didn't at first, not really, but I stiffened anyway; she wasn't causing pain but she was seeking it, that was her goal, and she continued until finally I gasped. She lifted her hands just slightly, reducing the pressure; There it is, she said, I'm sorry. I need to go a little farther, she went on, I know it hurts but is it all right if I keep going, and I gave a quick nod.

Even before Ferrier begins to sing, in the introduction, when the clarinet enters against the English horn, there's a moment that's like a key slipping into a lock, and there's a line, almost at the end, that for me is where the key turns, at least as Ferrier sings it. I didn't know any German when I first heard it, I didn't know any languages, but I learned the words, *Ich bin gestorben dem Weltgetümmel, Und ruh' in einem stillen Gebiet*, they were printed in the little CD booklet alongside a translation, I am dead to the world's tumult, And rest in a quiet realm. At the start of the second line, Und ruh', the voice rises a minor third, F to A-flat, in the comfortable middle of the voice, nothing virtuosic or spectacular, but it creates a dissonance against the C-minor chord in the orchestra. At the same moment the double basses slide down to a C, the cellos join them, the fifth is in the second violins and the voice keens a half step above them (except that it isn't keening, not quite or not only), the violin's G is an octave below the voice, and they're holding the note from the previous bar, they don't reassert it. I'll be quick, the surgeon promised, and she was, though she wasn't any more gentle, maybe she couldn't be. Around my navel the pain was intense, I squeezed my eyes shut, and then it faded a little lower down; where she dug her fingers into the top of my pelvis there was hardly any pain. Ferrier leans into the word Ruh, rest, not dramatically but her voice becomes electric with longing and resignation; there's such intensity and restraint that the note asserts itself, so that as Mahler extends the dissonance your sense of harmony is unsettled, or mine is, anyway: the A-flat creates an alternative harmony, just for a moment one can hear a major chord against the minor. I didn't understand this when I first heard the song, I would study the score later, in music school, and really it didn't help me understand what I had felt when I first heard it. How can I say what it did to me, it unmade me, unmade and remade me around itself somehow. I could never capture that feeling when I sang the song myself, which was one of the things that made me hate my voice eventually, that I could never sing this song in a way that felt adequate to what she made me feel, what I still feel when I listen to her sing the song, no other recording comes close.

The other woman, the nurse at the foot of the bed, placed her hand on my ankle where it stuck out from under the sheet. It was a shock, her touch, as she softly stroked or rubbed my ankle; it surprised me and also it made me feel something else, I felt tears spring to my eyes. She was the first person here who had touched me in a way that had no medical purpose, no measurable end but comfort; and also I realized it was the first touch of that kind I had had in months from anyone except L. Since the pandemic began there had been no hugs, no shaking of hands, none of the daily unremarkable corporeality that I found I missed, even though I spent so much time alone. It was an animal need, maybe, some fundamental craving for the sociality the virus had thwarted; in any case I responded out of all proportion, I felt I loved her for that touch. The nurse with the IV was still holding my arm, I had felt her swipe a spot with alcohol, but she waited until the doctor stepped away to say A little poke now, okay, and I closed my eyes again as she pushed the needle into the vein. When I opened them Dr. Ferrier was rubbing her hands together, I smelled the sting of antiseptic. The other thing on the scan, she said, in addition to the dissection there is a lot of inflammation in the aorta, what we call aortitis, that worries us as much as the tear itself. We need to figure out what's causing it, an infection or something else. Our hope is to get you stabilized tonight in the ICU, I don't want to operate on you before we're sure we know what's going on. An operation, I said, the ICU, I don't understand. Sometimes we can treat this medically, she said, and if we operate sometimes we can just put a stent in. But worst case we have to replace the artery, which is a big deal, she said, I hope we won't have to do that. The nurse had gathered the various wrappers and swabs into a neat ball, which she tossed into the trash as she left, ignored by the two surgeons though she exchanged a nod with the vascular nurse. Renee, her tag read, the woman who had been so kind to me, I wanted to remember her. I'm afraid we're going to starve you for the next day or two while we figure this out, Dr. Ferrier said, no food or drink until we know if we're going to operate. It's not very pleasant but you'll be getting everything you need from these, she gestured to the IV bags, your mouth will be dry but we'll keep you hydrated. How long will I have to stay here, I asked her, when can I go home? She took a breath. I don't want to think about number of days yet, she said, we have to get you stabilized first. Our plan is to keep your blood pressure down, which isn't going to feel great either, you'll be lightheaded and tired, but it will keep the artery from tearing further. And it should help with your pain, the other surgeon said, as the pressure goes down the pain in your stomach should fade. You're going to be seeing a lot of doctors, Dr. Ferrier said, people are going to be in and out of your room at all hours, there will come a point when you'll hate us, and that's okay. But I'll be coordinating your care, and here she held up her badge, which she wore in a little plastic pouch that hung on a lanyard from her neck, and said her name again. If you forget it and need me to tell you again, that's fine, I know how disorienting this is, it's not your job to worry about remembering our names. It's not your job to worry about anything, she said, your job is to relax and let us do the worrying. There was movement at the door, a young woman with another cart, and Dr. Ferrier took a step away from the bed. Okay, she said, you'll see us again tomorrow, I'll come by with my whole team. But we'll be monitoring you all night, don't worry, even if you don't see us for a while we haven't forgotten you. And don't suffer in silence, the man said, we have lots of medication for pain here, if you need it just ask. And then they filed out, Dr. Ferrier leading and Renee last, she squeezed my ankle again before she left.

The woman at the door said hello, her voice cheery, she asked if she could come in. I said something in response but I wasn't listening to her, I was thinking about the doctors who had just left; already I couldn't remember exactly what they had said, or what they had said seemed impossible now. Had they really said something about surgery, about an operation to replace the artery—but that couldn't be right, I thought, replacing the aorta, I must have misunderstood. And before that, about a tear in the artery, surely that wasn't right either, I would have died if that had happened. I knew nothing about medicine, or about the body, really, my own body, it was a machine I took for granted, a complete mystery; but even I knew the aorta was the main artery, in movies and TV shows I watched as a child there was always someone whose aorta was nicked by a bullet or a knife and always that person died. It pelted out blood, I thought, thinking again of the poem I had remembered, or not remembered, the line that had flashed into my brain, the blown aorta pelting out blood; not even an aura of the poem remained, just the single line. Everything the doctors had said was bewildering, I knew I should be reacting to it but I couldn't quite, I couldn't think about it; it was like a movie or a dream, not my own life exactly but something with a different reality status, this cannot be my life, I thought. The woman had pulled the cart up next to the bed, she asked me for my birth date and scanned the barcode on my wrist. As she leaned over I saw how her hair fell down her back in many long tight braids, one of which she had used to bind the others. She asked if I had had an EKG before and I said I hadn't. It's just to get a picture of your heart, she said, she used that word, picture, it will be over in a second, you won't feel it at all. From a drawer on her cart she pulled a very long strip of stickers, smaller than the ones already on my chest but with the same button-like nub for attaching electrodes. She placed two on my ankles, apologizing that they were cold as she began putting them on my torso. I could feel her counting my ribs as she placed the stickers, reaching down the neck of my gown. She was quick, skilled; I lost track of how many there were before she began connecting the leads, a fistful she sorted and attached with the same speed. It seems like a big production, she said, but it just takes a long time to get everything in place, someday they'll come up with a better technology. She pressed a few keys on the keyboard, then started unclipping and gathering the leads as the machine produced a printed page, actual paper, it really was an old technology. Did she tell you it wouldn't hurt, Frank said, coming back into the room with more bags of IV fluid, she always lies about that, and the woman sucked her teeth. I wish it weren't so, she said, ignoring him, but these guys don't like to come off sometimes. She meant the stickers, which she had begun to pull off, starting with the ankles, which was fine, but then moving to my chest, where it did hurt, they pulled off hair and tore at my skin, which she held in place with the finger of one hand while she yanked the strip off. She moved quickly, collecting each tab and sticking it on the back of her gloved hand—though she missed one, low on my left side, I would find it the next day still holding firm. She tore the page from the printer and said I hope you feel better real soon, before she pushed her cart from the room, telling Frank I was all his.

Tired of doctors yet, Frank asked me. You've got them all excited, he said, you're an ER doctor's dream, you come in thinking you have something simple but it turns out to be much more interesting. Infectious disease called down, he said, they'll come to see you in the morning but they want to start you on antibiotics now. He set the two bags by the computer, then used the wand to scan my wrist, which I raised, obedient. He hung the bags from their hooks and plugged a tube from one into the other, which he attached to the new IV. I looked up at the IV stand, where there were now four bags. That's a lot of medicine, I said, and he shrugged. It's not so bad, sometimes we really have to fill it up. He turned back to the machine. Is it your first time in the hospital, he asked, and I said it was, or the first time since I was a kid. I've never had any problems, I said, nothing like this, and I realized that I had now said this several times, to several people, that I was repeating it like a defense or a justification. Frank responded with a platitude of some kind, you're in good hands, something like that, they'll get you out of here as quick as they can. He was still punching buttons on the machine when there was a knock at the open door, another woman with another cart, though this one was bigger, holding a computer, not just a monitor. Okay if I come in, she asked, and Frank said Oh sure, a perfect exchange of Midwestern politeness, he was on his way out anyway. The woman was there to get me registered, she said; she asked me to confirm my address, my phone and insurance, my primary care physician. I didn't have one, I said, a little shamefaced, after seven years in town I still hadn't established care, as they said; other than a trip or two to the university clinic I hadn't had any care at all. I hesitated when she asked me for an emergency contact. L was my first thought but sometimes English was hard for him, especially over the phone, and anyway he was no good at practicalities, and he was beside himself with worry already; my phone had been buzzing steadily while the doctors came in and out, I was sure with texts from him. I gave my sister G's name instead, she was a lawyer now, living in a different state, but I knew she would come if I needed her, probably she was the only person in my family that was true of, she and my mother, whom I would never ask to come; she had health issues that put her at high risk of the virus, for months I had been urging her to stay in her house. And then the woman asked if I had a power of attorney on file, or an advance directive, and at my blank look she explained she meant in case I wasn't able to make decisions about my own care. It's fine if you don't have them, she said, you can always add them later, and again I felt ashamed, they were things I ought to have thought of but hadn't. I didn't even have a will, or life insurance, and I thought of L, of how he wouldn't be able to afford our house alone. I realized suddenly how irresponsible I had been, I've always been bad at these things, administrative, adult things, I had never imagined I might be responsible to someone in the way I was to L; I had never imagined anything but a solitary life, maybe I still couldn't imagine it. It was my temperament, maybe, to think of everything as temporary, but that felt like a betrayal now, unfaithful to the life we had made. I would send an email to my sister later, the lawyer, I would tell her that if I died I wanted L to have everything, my part of the house, my savings, there wasn't much to claim or anyone else to claim it but it would be her job to make sure it went to him. The woman asked me then if I had a religious affiliation, if I would like a pastoral visit, and I was surprised to feel myself hesitate again. I hadn't been to a church in years, decades, I didn't have religious beliefs, but there was a time in my early twenties when every week I went to see a soft-spoken diminutive man in a small room in Boston, a priest; for a few difficult months I had found comfort there. The memory flashed with a kind of longing before I told her no. But I asked her about other visitors, whether they were allowed, and she said yes, once I was admitted, for all but Covid patients. But only one per day, and only between one and three. It was much later than that now, I wouldn't be able to see L until the next day, and I felt crushed by this, frantic almost. I hadn't realized until then how much I wanted to see him, among all these strangers how much I needed to be with someone I knew, how much I needed to feel loved is what I mean, I guess, to feel my life tethered to someone by whom I was loved. That feeling, the feeling of being loved, the surprise of it, had faded over the years, with domesticity and its constant minor frictions, its impediments to freedom; but it was still there, and it flooded me now. The woman asked if I had any other questions for her, not medical questions, she was no doctor, she laughed, but questions about the hospital, administrative questions, and I told her I didn't. I guess I'm through with you, she said, her voice bright with cheer, I hope you feel better soon.

For a few moments no one came in or out, I was alone. The titration machine chittered beside me, little clicks that came without any pattern I could discern, sometimes fast, sometimes with long pauses between, at times as the days passed it would be maddening but not yet. The bed was uncomfortable, they had raised the head to an inconvenient angle, my neck was sore from lifting it to speak to people; and the gown I had been given was uncomfortable, too, I had thought the material was cotton but maybe it wasn't, it seemed to be irritating my skin, I had been scratching my chest absently and told myself to stop. My phone buzzed in my hand. I was still holding it but I hadn't been looking at it, though usually in any unoccupied moment I scrolled mindlessly. That was another thing that had changed over the past decade, the quality of mindlessness, which now was populated by the endless feeds of social media, which didn't eradicate boredom but changed the texture of it, made it less restorative, less accommodating of creative possibility, I feared; I tried to set aside my phone but mostly I scrolled like everybody else. But I hadn't done that in the hospital room, something had broken the reflex, I had been blank for a minute or two before L's text brought me back. He had sent many texts over the past hour or so, they had accumulated while the room had been busy and I read them now in reverse order and decreasing urgency, Please, the most recent one read, I need to know that you're okay. I'm here, I wrote back, I apologized for being silent, so many people have been here, I said, it has been nonstop. He must have been holding his phone, too; the minute I pressed send he began writing a reply, three dots appeared on the screen, a pulsing ellipsis. Lovisao, he wrote, part of our private language, the code of affection we had constructed over the years, English words with endings from Spanish or Portuguese. How are you, he wrote, I've been so worried. I told him they were putting me in the ICU, I would have to stay there for a while, they couldn't say how long. While he answered I scratched my chest and my scalp; it wasn't the gown, I was itchy all over, it was hard to stop scratching long enough to type.

But what has happened, L wrote, I don't understand, and I said what I could: my aorta had torn and they thought maybe it was infected, I might need surgery, it wasn't very clear. I typed out the words I had asked Dr. Ferrier to repeat, the diagnosis; L's brother was a doctor in England, he would ask him to explain. When can I see you, L asked, can I come now, and I said that he couldn't, I repeated what the woman had told me about visiting hours. But the next day was his heavy teaching day, he would only be able to come for part of the time. Only weeks later would it seem strange to me that neither of us suggested canceling his classes, it didn't occur to us, it would have seemed a dereliction of duty. I'll stay as long as I can, he typed, and I had begun to respond when Frank came back into the room. He was carrying more IV bags, he turned his back to me as he let them spill onto the counter by the computer. We're just waiting for a bed to open up in the ICU, he said. Your pressure isn't coming down as fast as they'd like, we're going to add some other medications. I had put down my phone and was scratching my scalp with both hands now, unable to stop. Frank, I said, I think something is wrong. He had been typing but turned abruptly and stepped to the bed. Itchy, huh, he said, and pulled at the neck of my gown to look at my chest. He drew in his breath, alarmed, and I looked down and saw that I was covered in hives, and also that there were long red lines where I had raked the skin. It didn't alarm me, strangely, even though Frank was clearly dismayed; his whole bearing had changed, become alert, eager for action, no longer laconic and wry. I was fascinated, the reaction had been so dramatic and so swift; I almost admired it, as if it weren't my own body that had shown such a gift for transformation, for gro-tesquerie, even as I struggled to keep my hands at my side. I'll be right back, Frank promised, and after a minute or two he re-turned with a syringe he scanned and screwed into one of the ports on my IV. He paused before pressing the plunger. This is just Benadryl, he said, nothing fancy, but he asked if I had ever had problems taking it before he pushed it through. I had used it before, as a pill or a cream, but this was something different, I could feel it entering my veins, a kind of tingling or numbness,

I had an eerie awareness of the circuitry of my arm. This should start working pretty fast, Frank said, it's probably one of the antibiotics you're reacting to.

I closed my eyes for a minute as wooziness washed over me, not unpleasant, a kind of dullness and heaviness. It can hit hard at first, I heard Frank say, you might drop off for a minute. But I didn't drop off, I opened my eyes again to tell him that I felt better already, the itchiness was fading. He nodded. I'll hang out here a bit, he said, just to be sure you're okay. Anytime there's a reaction like that we like to be careful, he said, you're going to be fine but sometimes they can be bad. He went over to the computer again, making a note in my chart, then scanned the bags he had brought in earlier and hung them with the others. When he had finished he leaned back against the sink, folding his arms across his stomach, the first time I had seen him without some task at hand. So tell me what you do, he said. I told him I was a teacher, which was easier than saying I was a writer. I got tired of saying what kinds of books I write, of hearing people's surprise that poets still existed, I got tired of the questions about success, whether I had had any, which always made me think of an interview with James Baldwin, a clip that made the rounds on Twitter every few months or so, in which he says It is not *possible* for an *artist* to be *successful*, tilting his head to emphasize the words, languorous, faggy, both earnest and bored, wonderful. Here at the university, Frank asked, and I said no, I was teaching that semester at a college about an hour away, or would be if I was well enough, classes started in a week. I know that place, Frank said, meaning not the school but the town, there's a restaurant that has live music on the weekends, I've played a few gigs out there with my band. I asked him what he played, and he said clarinet, that he played jazz with his band but had studied classical performance as a student. That was what I studied here, actually, he said; after playing in his school band in the little town he grew up in he had come to the university on a music scholarship. It seemed like a great thing at the time, he said, and it was, it got me out of my hometown, but when I graduated I realized there isn't anything to do with a performance degree. He stopped himself. Maybe that's not true, I could have tried going someplace else, my teacher wanted me to go for a grad program at a big school, Juilliard or Curtis, he thought I had a shot, but I didn't want to go so far away from my family. Or maybe I'm just a chickenshit, he said. But you still play, I said, and he replied that he did, every few weeks with his band, but now his primary music making was as part of a choir. He had always loved to sing—in a different life, he said, I would have been a singer, but I didn't realize I had a voice until I started college, and my scholarship was for my clarinet playing, it wasn't easy to switch. So I never developed my voice, he said, and after college I went to nursing school and started all this. It wasn't clear what he meant, the little room, the hospital, the trudging back and forth for medicines, he conjured it and dismissed it all at once.

I had been a voice major, I told him then, before I studied literature, I had had a start as a musician and had given it up, too. Really, he said, interested, and he asked me what part I sang, what repertoire. I told him a bit of the story, how I had come to music late, too late probably, that I was never happy with what I could hear, that I could never *think* in music, that it was always a foreign language; and also that I was a student in a conservative department, that my teacher wanted me to focus on standard rep while my interests drew me elsewhere, to new music and early music; that my best experiences were with an early music ensemble the school was famous for, led by a brilliant lutenist, at whose name Frank lit up. I know him, he said, I've listened to him for years. He loved early music too, he said, early choral music, he loved singing it. His entire demeanor had changed now, he was buzzing with excitement as he told me he had gotten obsessed recently with John Taverner, a Renaissance composer I had sung in school. We had studied him in music history, too, when we learned about the use of popular songs in religious music, a mixture of the secular and the sacred, whole masses built on L'homme armé or Westron Wynde, which was what Frank played me now. You've got to hear this, he said, he had pulled his phone from the pocket of his scrubs and was scrolling through his music, it was an old recording of Taverner's mass but he had just discovered it. I miss the real thing, he said, owning records and CDs, but it's amazing to have everything in your phone, absolutely everything; here it is, he said, holding his phone up to listen. There was a moment of silence then, a pause while the song loaded, and then a solo tenor voice filled the room, tinny on the phone's speakers but still beautiful, an English tenor, I don't mean the singer's nationality but the type of voice. It's a peculiar sound, bright and unforced, lyric, pure somehow, nothing like Italian or German voices; maybe it's that you can hear the boys choir in it, in the shape of the vowels. And this tenor was very good, his voice rang out, not operatic but in an early style, mostly straight tone but vibrating just slightly on the sustained notes. It was a warm voice, full of light. Frank had come close to the bed, aiming his phone at me, and he leaned toward me, too, bending his head so we could listen together. I was surprised by how well I remembered the tune; it had been so long ago that I had sung it, and I had come to think of the words free of music. It was one of my favorite poems, authorless, mysterious, the first two lines unparsable: Westron wynde, when wyll thow blow, The smalle rayne downe can Rayne, a sentence with a broken back. I had taught it for years to high schoolers, I had encouraged them to imagine the speaker, somebody in trouble, a soldier maybe, alone, exposed to the elements, and not just to the elements. Think of the significance of the west, the direction the sun sets, the region of death; could he be longing for death, I would ask them, is he at that pitch of extremity; and what is the small rain, isn't it beautiful, the weird adjective, how can rain be small; and does he want it, the speaker of the poem, does he long for the rain, is that how we should understand the cracked syntax; and isn't the poem more beautiful for it, for the difficulty, for the way we can't quite make sense of it, settled sense, I mean, for how it won't stay still; isn't the non-sense what makes it bottomless, what lets us pour and pour our attention into it, what makes it not just a message—though it *is* a message, I would say to them, all art is a message, we want to communicate something but maybe not an entirely graspable something, maybe there's a kind of sense only non-sense can convey; so that the poem becomes not just a message but an object of contemplation, of devotion even, inexhaustible. It had been my whole life, puzzling over phrases, trying to account for the unaccountable in what art makes us feel; it had been my whole life, sometimes it had seemed a full life and sometimes a wasted one, it had felt full and wasted at once. The poem goes on, the second half makes an easier kind of sense: Cryst yf my love were in my Armys And I yn my bed Agayne. An easier kind of sense but I heard it in a new way, listening to it with Frank, I felt my eyes fill with tears. After the tenor solo the mass proper begins, the tune in the sopranos first, with the words not of the poem but of the Gloria, Et in terra pax. Frank let it play for a moment, the Renaissance polyphony that always sounds to me like petals opening, a rose blooming in time-lapse photography; I'm embarrassed by the image, it was something I felt as a teenager and I still feel it now.

Well, Frank said, when he finally stopped the music, not abruptly, he lowered the volume first, well. He put the phone in his pocket and moved to the other side of the bed, where he pressed a few buttons on the titration machine. He was back to his earlier nonchalance, shutting the door the music had opened between us. I guess I should get to my other patients, he said, I think you're doing okay now. You know, he went on, there's no telling when the ICU will open up, they might come to move you in the middle of the night, you should sleep if you can. He must have seen that I was tired, whether it was the Benadryl or my blood pressure going down or just the stress of the hospital, fatigue fell over me like a shadow, I could feel my eyes wanting to close. We'll keep you safe, Frank said, I'll be here all night, you don't have to worry about a thing. And this too brought tears to my eyes. Thank you, Frank, I said; I meant for everything, for what he had said and for the music, thank you. Oh sure, he said quickly, accepting the thanks but dismissing it, too, a Midwestern reflex, and then he pumped the sanitizer dispenser at the door and was gone. I wasn't sure I would be able to sleep; the fluorescent lights were bright and there was no way to cover my eyes, not even with my arms, one of which had the IVs and the other the blood pressure cuff, which began inflating again, as it had every fifteen minutes, pinioning my arm, squeezing it to the point of pain. I would just close my eyes, I thought, but first I would send a message to L. So tired, I wrote, and I fell asleep almost as I typed, I didn't remember pressing send but later I would see it in the chat, nearly a nonsense line, poor L must have puzzled over it, So tired try to sleep I love you I—

2

woke suddenly, jerking up in bed. I had been awake often in the night, first when a woman came—it was late, it must have been after ten, I had slept for a couple of hours—to push me from the emergency room, which had no respect for the night, which was busy as daytime, to the relative twilight of the ICU. Two nurses met us there, a man and a woman, both young; after aligning my stretcher with the bed of the new ward, they prepared to lift me from one to the other. They did things like that every day, there was no reason for me to feel ashamed, but I hate being trouble, I stopped them before they could try. I can do it myself, I said. Are you sure, the woman asked, the new nurse, and she looked to the woman who had brought me, who shrugged. She was an orderly, maybe it was her whole job to push patients from one ward to another, a kind of ferrywoman; she didn't know anything about my case. I'm sure, I said, and started to rise, but the nurse put her hand on my chest, there were wires to detach and IV bags to move; they had their own monitors in the ICU, newer and more elaborate. She and the man helped me, though it seemed like playacting as they placed their hands on my back, cupping my elbows as I took the single step from one bed to the other, the woman who had brought me holding the IVs out of the way. It felt like playacting until it didn't: when I stood up, even though I stood slowly, there was a wave of dizziness, of blankness or darkness; I stumbled and would have fallen if they hadn't been there. Easy, the man said, we've got you, and it was a relief to sit down, to have them lower my torso to the bed, then lift and settle my legs. I was out of breath, my skin pricked with sweat. That was weird, I said, I feel so strange, I wasn't really talking to anyone but the nurse answered. You're on a lot of medications, she said, just relax now, I'll get you settled and then leave you alone as much as I can, hopefully you'll get some sleep. I was in her care, it seemed, she thanked the man and he went back to his own patients, following the woman from the ER, who spun the empty stretcher almost carelessly out of the room. I did relax. There was something reassuring about the new nurse, her competence as she connected and calibrated her machines. But I didn't sleep, not really, though I was exhausted, I dozed and woke so many times that dozing and waking blurred into a gray half-consciousness. The pressure cuff dragged me into awareness, or an alarm sounded and I sensed the presence of the nurse, quiet as she silenced it. At some point she drew blood, an order had come in, the lab needed it right away; she opened and capped the vials with one hand and adjusted the needle just slightly with the other, keeping the blood flowing. Tomorrow you'll get an A-line, she said, there won't be as many needles then, and only after she had gone, as I closed my eyes again, did it occur to me to ask what an A-line was.

I had only just fallen into a deeper sleep, accustomed to the cuff and the coming and going, or maybe exhausted past any awareness of them, when a hand was grabbing my shoulder, jostling me awake. I opened my eyes to find a group of people around the foot of my bed. Oh, I said, pushing myself up a little, the back of the bed was raised but not enough to make it comfortable to speak; I wiped my mouth and passed my hand through my hair, careful with the wires and tubing. These were reflexes of presentability, I wondered how long they had watched me sleeping. There you are, the woman who woke me said, you were really out, I'm sorry to have to wake you up. She introduced herself as Dr. ——, I didn't catch her name at first, and as they hadn't turned on the overhead light in the room I couldn't read her badge; she was the vascular resident, making rounds with students, was it all right if she examined me. I looked from her to the others, all of them young, with clipboards they held at their chests to take notes. This was a class for them, I realized, I was on exhibit, a problem for them to study but not necessarily to solve. I hadn't responded to her question, and she paused, having begun to lift the thin blanket from my torso; Is that all right, she repeated, a little severely, and I said Yes, sorry. She lifted my gown above my stomach, then let the blanket fall back over my crotch. Do you have any pain this morning, she asked, and I said no, or nothing like the pain from the day before; the surgeon had been right, as my blood pressure went down the pain diminished, and also they had been giving me oxycodone, a light dose—but when she dug her fingers into my abdomen I cried out. She lessened the pressure but didn't apologize, continuing to palpate down to the groin, digging into my pelvis at the top of the right leg, feeling for the artery, I guessed. Do you understand what's happened to you, she asked, as she moved down to my feet, pulling off the thick socks they had given me when I arrived, with little nubs of rubber on the sole—the floors around here are slippery, the nurse had said, we don't want you falling when you get up to pee. The doctor pressed her fingers on the tops of my feet, pressing hard right at the joint with the ankle, feeling for my pulse. I don't, I said, they explained it to me yesterday but there was so much happening, I didn't really understand. Okay, she said, pulling the blanket back over my bare feet. The students stepped backward, making room for her as she moved to the other side of the bed, where there was a window, the shade drawn; on the wall beside it was a whiteboard I hadn't really noticed, partitioned by black tape, with spaces on the right-hand side for the date, the physician in charge, the nurse on duty, the treatment plan (BP Reg, it said, and beneath this, Pain). There was a marker clipped at the top, which she pried loose and uncapped. So the aorta starts at the heart, she said, drawing a line that ascended and curved to the right before coming down, then another, parallel to it, forming a candy cane shape; it connects with the arteries that go up to your brain and into your arms, she indicated the direction with the marker but didn't draw these, and then it comes down the torso, which she drew with swift vertical lines, it feeds the lungs, the liver, the kidneys; and here she drew a fork, the artery splitting to the right and the left as it traveled down the legs. Now, the artery has three layers, she said, and here she made a new diagram, three short vertical lines, very close together, and what has happened to you is a tear in the inner layer, here a line arced to the left, it creates something like a flap that then blood flows around, making what is called a false lumen—false lumen, I thought, such a beautiful phrase—the blood going where it shouldn't go. And this can weaken the wall of the artery, she said, and it can start to balloon out, here another curved line, this one arcing to the right, which is what an aneurysm is. She turned to me. Is that clear, she asked, and I said it was, more or less, and she turned back to her drawing. So the big dangers are that one, the aneurysm can rupture, which is catastrophic, she said, we need to be sure that doesn't happen; and two, that this flap can restrict blood flow and keep parts of the body from getting the oxygen they need. Now, we got lucky, she said, because your tear starts below the kidneys, so none of those organ systems above it have been damaged. Lucky, I thought, but I didn't say anything, I had become receptive, passive again, ideally patient. She drew a circle on her primary diagram, starting just above the fork and extending into the right leg. Your tear is here, she said, which is why we keep checking the pulses in your feet, we want to be sure the right leg is still getting the blood it needs; so far it seems it is, which is more good news. Good news, I thought. She had turned to face me. Any questions, she asked, I was her student now, and I had many questions: how bad is it, I wanted to ask, how long until I get better, when can I leave, is it still possible that I could die, but I said nothing. I was scared, I suppose, I only wanted answers I could bear. It's a dangerous condition, she said then, a serious condition, but we've got you stable now. We're going to keep you fasting today, she said, I'm sorry, but until we know whether you'll have surgery we can't let you eat or drink anything. And how will you decide, I asked finally, a question that wasn't just a plea to be comforted, I hoped, a reasonable question. The big mystery is why this happened to you, she said, and you're going to be talking to a bunch of people today to try to figure that out. Once we have an answer we'll know how to proceed. In the meantime, she said, capping the marker, I could sense she was eager to leave, I had taken up too much of her time, in the meantime you should rest as much as you can. Dr. Ferrier—do you remember her, she admitted you yesterday—will be in to see you later, she said, and I'll be back tomorrow. Before you go, I said, I'm sorry, can you tell me your name again. Akeyu, she said, Dr. Akeyu, enunciating it slowly, a little stiffly. She was used to repeating it, I could tell, it was exhausting to have an uncommon name, uncommon here, I mean, in the middle of the country; I wanted to apologize for asking her to repeat it. She stepped to the bed and leaned toward me slightly, holding out her badge; she uncapped the marker again and wrote it on the board. All set now, she asked, and I nodded, and then she stepped through the group of students, who thanked me as they followed her out.

It was an oddly shaped room, with a long exterior wall to my left, where the window was, and another long wall at my back, then three shorter angled walls, a kind of uneven pentagon. To the left of the door there were cabinets and drawers, a counter and a large sink. Mounted on the wall above the sink were the usual bins for sharps and biohazards, for boxes of gloves, for soap and sanitizer. A television hung just to the left of the cabinets, more or less where my bed pointed; I could operate it with a control that hung from a cord attached to the bed. The nurse had shown me how this worked the night before; the same device moved my bed in various ways and let me turn the overhead lights on and off, and there was a large button at the bottom that would call her if I needed anything. By the window was a clock that read quarter to five, still nighttime almost, but I knew I wouldn't sleep again, not right away. It was a nice room, not large but ample, with a little armchair by the window and a private bathroom. Beside me the machines beeped and whirred, and if I bent my head back I could see the large monitor behind me, with its pulsing lines and readings for pressure and oxygen. I was a part of the machinery, I realized, wired with the IV tubes and the pressure cuff and a clip on my finger, I was wired in as much as the machines themselves. At least I could still shit and piss on my own; the nurse had asked me the night before if I wanted a bedpan and I said no, the idea of it horrified me, the old stupid shame you never quite get over. To go to the bathroom I had to call the nurse, she had to unplug and rearrange the wires; there was a portable monitor she disconnected from the large screen and hung from the IV stand. It was a lot of trouble, I had to bite my tongue to keep from apologizing. I was apologizing too much, to everyone, she had finally told me to stop, she was just doing her job; and then she would help me up, telling me to be careful, it was only one step to the bathroom but she kept a hand on my elbow as she pushed the IV stand with the other, we pushed it together, though I was less pushing it than using it for support. I had to piss into a kind of plastic jug she gave me. It took a long time, it was awkward to hike up the gown while keeping the wires and tubes out of the way, then to hold the jug in one hand and my dick in the other, it was a little comedy, a miniature slapstick, and all while I had to keep closing my eyes against dizziness, it took most of my attention just to stay up-right. Doing okay, she asked finally, and when I said I was, she told me not to flush if I was taking a shit; but she didn't say that exactly, she said if I was having a bowel movement, what my mother had said when I was a child, we had made fun of her for it, it was so prim. She would want to check it, she said, the nurse I mean, she would want to make sure there wasn't blood in it, and that filled me with shame, too, the idea of her examining my shit. I was full of squeamishness, which whatever else it is is a way of clinging to life, I could still care about unessential things. I thought of L's father, how the whole family had come together, all L's siblings and cousins, the whole huge family, they had all surrounded his father as he died. After the funeral, L and I went to a bar and he said It was so beautiful, how there was no shame at the end, when we fed him or gave him a bath, there wasn't any shame at all. It was a kind of intimacy I had never known before with him, he said. And then I remembered a different death, when I was very young, my mother's best friend, probably the first person I had loved who died, a terrible quick cancer; and later I had listened as my mother described her last hours, how in the hospital room with her children and my mother she had covered her face, she had said no, no, she hadn't wanted to be seen, don't look, don't look, in a delirium of pain and fear she had never let go of her shame. It was the saddest thing, my mother said, we all loved her, we wanted to be there with her, but to me it had made perfect sense, her longing for privacy, and I remembered how I had pushed L away, when the pain first came, how intensely I had needed to be alone. They should have let her be, I thought of my mother and her friend, they had denied her the final thing she wanted. I would want to be alone too, I thought, when it came I wanted to be alone with death too.

The nurse came in then, right at 5:00 a.m. She wished me good morning as she set some things at her computer station, a syringe, little paper cups with pills, bags of IV fluid; she asked if I had slept well. I laughed. Yeah, she said, I guess it's a little much to hope for, I tried to be quiet but there are so many things we have to do. She was at the sink, opening drawers, collecting more syringes and swabs, then a plastic cup that she unwrapped and filled with water. And then vascular comes by so early, they're always here before five for rounds, they have to see pretty much everybody in the unit. She stepped to the bed and set the cup of water on the tray table at its side, where I had put my phone and a notebook, the novel I had carried to the ER. The good news is you get to drink a little this morning, she said. The bad news is I have to put this in it, and she emptied a packet of powder into the water. It was a laxative, she told me, mild, pretty much everybody spending more than a day in the hospital took it, so much time in bed means things can get backed up. She set pills on the table as well, an oxycodone and two Tylenol, every four hours I would get more, the regimen for pain. She busied herself with IV bags then, blood pressure meds and anti-biotics, she told me their names but I forgot them immediately. They didn't know what the infection was, or if I had an infection at all, so without anything to target they were trying to blanket my system, she said, which was such a strange phrase, a strange image, it brought me up short; if there is something they want to be sure they knock it out. I swallowed the pills as she said this, washing them down with the water, which I savored, my mouth and throat were dry; the powder didn't have a taste really but it was grainy, the density of the liquid was wrong, it pooled uneasily in my stomach. And now, she said, stepping back to the computer, scanning a syringe and then my wristband—I lifted my left arm across my body to spare her leaning over, like a countess expecting a kiss—now comes the bad part. This is heparin, she said, it's a blood thinner, we'll give it to you every eight hours. The problem is it goes right in your stomach, I'm sorry, and it stings. She was already pulling up my gown, and then she gathered some flesh to the right of my navel, pinching hard (This helps, she said) before she pushed the needle in. It did hurt, not the jab itself but the moment after she withdrew, there was a waspish pain that radiated out. I pressed my palm to it. Yikes, I said, every eight hours? She laughed. What a way to wake up, she said, as she placed the syringe in the sharps box and threw everything else in the trash.

And here comes another morning visitor, the nurse said then, sometimes she gets here even before vascular. At the door was a woman on a motorized vehicle, squat and square, both the woman and the machine. Chest X-ray, she said, stepping from her platform and swinging a device over me, a long metal arm with a circular lens at the end, which she aimed at my torso before asking me to lean forward so that she could place a hard board beneath me. Lean back and hold still, she said, then walked to the doorway and pressed a little remote in her hand, at which there was no sound or light, nothing perceptible at all, and then she returned and withdrew the board and stepped back onto the machine, and with a thank you left my room for the next. She would return every morning, though it couldn't have been the same woman every time, I was always sleeping and woke too bleary-eyed to tell the difference. No one ever explained what the X-rays were for, it was just something done each morning for everyone in the ICU, part of the rhythm of the day.

No one else came then for a while. I had asked the nurse to raise the shade on the window, and I watched as the sky turned pink and slowly the world became discernible, though there wasn't much to see; my window looked out over the hospital complex, from my bed I could see another tower like the one I was in, and nothing else, just sky and the other building, which was some distance away. I knew there were other, shorter buildings between, all of them connected by corridors and bridges; it was a huge complex. The one time I had come before, not as a patient but to visit a colleague of L's, it had been impossible to find our way; every hallway was identical, each section of the hospital named after a donor, the X pavilion, the Y pavilion, banks of elevators identified by letters of the alphabet. We had been told to find the K elevators, I remember, but we kept getting lost, we had to ask at every turn for directions. I lay for a long time watching the sky, feeling the oxycodone start to work, distributing unconcern. I had only been on opiates once before, after a minor surgery, nothing really, now they would never give me a prescription but this was before everyone knew how devastating they could be. There was a crisis in Iowa but you didn't really see it in my city, it was out of sight, though in the urgent care clinic I had seen a notice on the wall about naloxone, encouraging people to carry it, to learn how to use it; you could save a life, it said. The crisis was more visible in my hometown, in Kentucky, where quickly you learned the nodding look of it in people, the sunken eyes. I had friends who carried naloxone in their purses, their cars, and one who had used it, when she saw a man passed out at a gas station; he had pulled up to a pump and was still in the driver's seat of his car. She took it in stride, my friend, she was in recovery herself; she had used heroin for years, but now she had been clean for as long as she had used. She was healthy, she spent hours at the gym each day, lifting weights, she had made her body hard; I'm the hottest forty-year-old white girl in Kentucky, she would say, making us laugh. Laughter and weights, that was how she got by, by portioning each day out in laughter and weights. She made us laugh as she told us the story of the man at the fuel pump too, miming how she fumbled through her purse and sprayed the drug up his nose, and we felt her terror through her laugh. She could have been that man, I knew, she had told me how bad things had gotten, how she knew they could get that bad again; you're always on the edge of a cliff, she had told me, it's exhausting, I love my life now and also I am fucking exhausted.

It was the only drug I had enjoyed, the Vicodin they gave me years ago, before there was a crisis or before we knew there was a crisis; I didn't need it for the pain and so I saved it until the pain was gone, the pain was a distraction from the pills, which I rationed over a couple of months. On the weekends I would take one and sit in my armchair; I had just started teaching, I was tired from the week with teenagers, utterly overwhelmed. I would sit in my ridiculous secondhand armchair with a novel and feel what I imagined cats must feel when they purr, a feeling like being petted on the inside, immensely private, undemonstrative. For a couple of hours I sat free from anxiety and care, and as the weeks passed and the pills dwindled I found myself not planning exactly but wondering, in a kind of idle way, whether a friend or a friend of a friend might know a way to get more, until suddenly I realized what I was thinking and made myself stop. I savored the last few pills and when they were gone that was the end. In the hospital the oxy limited my fear, it didn't make it disappear but it set a kind of boundary; the panic I had felt in the first hours after I was admitted, the breathless runaway fear was reined in. And it did something strange to time, too, made it frictionless, buoyant, so that it moved without the usual properties; staring out the window I was unoccupied but not anxious or bored, I had lost my sense of time as a thing that could be wasted. I watched as the sky brightened, there was nothing else to watch until a single bird fluttered down, a sparrow, I thought, though I only saw it for an instant. I tried to lift myself up to see where it might have gone. It was just a sparrow, but I wanted to look at it; even in the years I had lived here, seven years somehow, longer than I had ever intended to stay, the number of birds had decreased, of all flying things, birds and butterflies and bees. It was part of the terrible slow catastrophe happening everywhere, the fires in the west and floods in the east, the storms that devastated the middle of the country, that had devastated Iowa just a couple of weeks before; the planet was becoming less accommodating of life, and I had begun scanning the skies for the flocks I could remember from my childhood and no longer found, it was impossible that so much could have changed so quickly but it had. Sparrows were one of the lucky species, still common, they thrived in cities but I sought them out anyway, each time I passed a bush loud with them I stopped to listen to them squabble. I had always loved them, their intrepid brave boisterousness, the beautiful patterns of their wings; outside at a café downtown I loved how they came up on the table, how they cocked their heads as if begging, how they pranced forward and back, how if you were very still they would snatch a crumb from an outstretched finger. They were wonderful, really, commonness didn't cancel wonder, or I didn't see why it should, not all the time. I was anxious to see it again, the bird at my window, but from the bed I couldn't see where it might have perched, and then that was all right, too, my eagerness melted into the oxy hum.

Gradually I became aware of activity outside my room, of voices and movement, chairs being rolled over the tiled floor, bags set on counters. It was shift change, a new group of nurses had come in. I heard them greeting one another, asking about the nights they had had, their plans for the weekend, the banal conversation of any workplace; though people were dying or possibly dying in the rooms that surrounded them it was a workplace like any other. The door to my room was open but there was a curtain drawn across the entry, I could hear but not see as they paired off to discuss their cases, the departing nurses conveying to the new arrivals what had happened in the night. I could hear my nurse giving my history, and another voice, a woman's, making sounds of agreement or understanding. I tried to listen for any new information, anything they hadn't told me, but I couldn't hear clearly, other conversations intruded. They were rehearsing the histories of everyone on the ward, cases that seemed much worse than mine, strokes and bypass surgeries, heart attacks, a man who was having a respirator removed, which was one of the big events of the day. I was lucky, I thought, remembering what Dr. Akeyu had said: I could walk and talk, I was conscious, I was still on the near side of real catastrophe. The conversations wound down, there was more transitory noise, keys dropped on a table, bags picked up, and then a sense of the space clearing out; nurses from the whole ward must have gathered there, there had been too many voices for just a few rooms.

I had lain passive through all of this, I had finally turned my head from the window but not to look at anything else, exactly. I glanced at my phone on the table beside the bed; I would text L soon, probably he was awake already but I hoped he might be sleeping still. I knew the phone would be beside the bed. Usually he hated to have screens in bed, if I looked at my phone or iPad he would scold me, so enganchado, put it down, he said; but now he would keep it near in case there was news. I could see it face down on the little round table on his side of the bed, on top of a book probably, Lorca or Machado, whatever he was teaching, beside the little digital clock he kept facing away so the light didn't trouble our sleep. I pictured him on his side, I imagined his hand in the open space where I usually slept; whenever I woke in the night his hand was on me some-where, my shoulder or my back, my stomach, just his hand; if he had his way we would have slept curled up together, but I couldn't sleep like that, I had never been able to, with anyone. I could see him in our room, a white room under the gables, the slanting roof embedded with south-facing windows that looked out into green; our house was set close to our neighbors but in the summer green was all we saw, maple and oak and pine. Through windows on the east-facing wall we could see a ra-vine that ran through the neighborhood, busy with badgers and deer, on winter mornings we would watch them brown against the snow, clusters of deer. The floor in the bedroom had been badly damaged, the beautiful old wooden floors we had salvaged everywhere else in the house; here they were stained beyond sav-ing, sanded too often to sand again. L decided to paint them white, a matte white that would always look dirty, the contrac-tors warned, that would show every speck of dust; but we loved it, our white floor and white walls and the green of old trees outside, I thought of L sleeping there and felt something in me clench with longing, I sucked in a breath even as I heard some-one approach my room, giving the curtain a little shake as she said good morning and came in.

Her name was Alivia, with an A, she said, as she wrote it on the whiteboard; Alivia, alleviate, allegory, alive, I thought. She held a Starbucks cup in one hand, a venti iced something; she was carrying it though she couldn't drink in the room, she would have to take off her mask and shield. It had been a full day since I had had coffee, and even through the oxycodone I could feel the withdrawal, a pressure gathering to a point in my head, I imagined snatching the cup from her hand. She leaned against the counters at the far side of the room, unhurried, relaxed; the night nurse had been all motion and activity but Alivia seemed settled in for a chat. She was tall, younger than I was but not by all that much, in her midthirties maybe, neither fat nor thin, her hair in a long ponytail. So, she said, folding her arms across her chest, the coffee still in her hand, you're really going through it. She asked me to tell her what had happened, my understanding of it, in my own words. She nodded when I finished. Yeah, she said, that's pretty much what I got from the other nurse. Have you ever been in the hospital before, she asked me, and I said no, and then yes, as a child, very young. I had had a hernia operation, and then a few years later my tonsils out, normal kid stuff, nothing since then, this is the first time I've spent the night. I thought of L's father again, how he had gone his whole life without spending a night in the hospital, until the very end, as he was dying. He had had a lucky life. I had only spent time with him one summer, the first summer I spent with L; L had kept his apartment in Madrid but we went to Granada every couple of weeks to see his family. His father was healthy then, in his seventies and active, vital, a short kind man who welcomed me though I couldn't understand a word he said, he and L's mother both spoke with an Andalusian accent I couldn't penetrate; every time they spoke to me L had to repeat it in a Spanish I could understand, and quickly we lapsed into smiles and waves. A good life, I thought, remembering how he laughed at the table with L and his siblings, the family at ease in a way my own had never been; if there was such a thing as a good life he had had it, a good life and a good death.

It's a weird place, Alivia said then, let's hope you aren't here long enough to get used to it. She uncrossed her arms and let them fall, shaking her cup a little so the ice rattled. That looks so good, I said, and she lifted the cup. You like coffee, she said, and then, it's my weakness, I only get to have one if I walk to work, and only one per day, I have to make it last. She said what it was then, a flavored latte, I know it's so bad for me but I love it so much. She laughed. What's your drink, she asked, but it wasn't fancy, just coffee, I said, a little half-and-half, and I drank it all day. I had never touched it until I started teaching, I needed help to get through the long days of six or seven classes, even the terrible burnt sludge in the teachers' lounge would do. A teacher, she said, is that what you do? Used to do, I answered, seven years of high school; I teach college kids sometimes now but it's not the same, not as hard and not as good, either, not as satisfying, not as fun. But that's when I got hooked, I said, four cups a day is my minimum. Caffeine and sugar, I went on, I put my hands on my stomach, that's when I got fat, too, though I should have said fat again; I had always been fat, except for a few years in my twenties when I ran three miles every day and lifted weights. I hadn't been able to keep it up once I started teaching, I had let myself go, as they say, though that wasn't what it had felt like; I had felt like I was holding on with all my strength, like I was just barely holding on. Alivia scoffed, she pushed herself upright. Listen, she said, there are worse things, if caffeine and sugar are what get you through you're doing all right. But I wondered: maybe if I had kept up the hours at the gym, if I had kept myself healthy, maybe I wouldn't be facing what I was facing now, it seemed likely to me but who could say. Well, Alivia said then, I just wanted to introduce myself, let me get myself situated, and she shook her cup again. In a few minutes we're going to get you set up with an A-line, do you know what that is; but she went on without waiting for me to answer: it's just a fancy IV, nothing to worry about. Sit tight, she said, ducking back through the curtain, which she drew shut behind her.

She returned a few minutes later, her hands full of the plastic packaging all of the medical supplies came in, endless boxes and envelopes and bags; so much plastic, I thought, as she sorted them on the counter and began tearing them open, so much waste. It's a little bit of work to get these in, Alivia said, I'm going to have our head nurse do that, she'll be here in a minute, but I'll get you started. We need to numb you a bit, hopefully this will be the worst part. She scanned my wrist and then a small bottle she had carried over, along with a syringe that she used to draw the liquid up. She lifted my right arm and palpated my forearm just below the elbow. The blood pressure cuff started inflating on my other arm. What a relief to get that off, she said, the A-line will give us a continuous reading, they need that while they try to figure out your meds. She was pressing into the flesh hard with her thumb, moving it slightly side to side and then inching down, tracking an artery; when she was satisfied she took the syringe and popped the cap, letting it drop onto the bed, and then I closed my eyes as she said A little sting, now, and I felt the prick of the needle just below my wrist. You okay, she asked, and I said I was. I should have asked how you do with needles, she said, but then you're already such a pincushion, and she made an amused sound as she pressed a square of gauze where she had stuck me, not quite a laugh. How are these doing, she asked then, pressing on either side of the two IV lines in the same arm, any pain, she asked, and I said no, though that wasn't quite true; the first one they had placed was beginning to sting, but it was tolerable, I didn't want to say anything about it. Well, she said, you let us know, they don't last forever. That's another good thing about A-lines, they don't give out like these little guys can.

An older woman entered then, sliding the curtain all the way to one side, decisively, as if declaring the room open. Hello, she said, good morning, and even in my dazed state something snapped to attention at her accent, which I recognized; it wasn't from Bulgaria, where I had lived, but from a neighboring country, Serbia, maybe, Romania. I wanted to ask her where she was from but that had become a difficult question in America, an offensive question, and I understood the reasons for that and also it seemed a little ridiculous, to have ruled out-of-bounds such a fundamental curiosity, it seemed corrosive to me of sociality itself. She introduced herself but the name didn't help me place her, it was Lara or Laura, she said she was the head nurse on the ward, did I understand what they were doing. Everything looks ready, she said, surveying the counter where Alivia had spread out the little packages, and I could feel the current of authority between them, the way Alivia perked up just slightly at the approval, her desire to please. The new nurse, Lara or Laura, made a production of scrubbing up, soaping her hands and forearms, drying them and coating them with sanitizer before she put on gloves. The package was a kind of kit; she pulled it open and withdrew a long coil of thin plastic tubing, complicated with attachments and ports, and a separate, shorter, stiffer tube, with a long needle, safe in its plastic cap, at one end, which she set on the little wheeled table Alivia had brought over. Then she unfolded a large drape, an absorbent paper covering, which she placed across my torso, lifting my arm and laying it on top. She tied a tourniquet just below my elbow, and then palpated my arm as Alivia had, making a little humming noise; Sometimes we use an ultrasound, she said, but I don't think we'll need it for you. I turned my head when she picked up the tube with the needle, I closed my eyes as she counted to three and there was a dull intense pressure on my wrist, not exactly pain but not exactly not. She kept my arm pinned down, she shifted the needle slightly to the right and the left. I opened my eyes when I heard her inhale sharply, not quite a gasp; I glanced quickly at my arm and saw a pool of blood, very dark, which filled the indentation where she was pressing the needle and spilled over either side onto the drape. Surely it was too much blood, I thought, something was wrong, I shut my eyes again. You okay, I heard Alivia ask, and I nodded; just a couple more minutes, she said, she's almost done. Then there was a different sensation, a different kind of pressure, and I opened my eyes to see that the head nurse was pressing what looked like a metal bolt to my skin, some connector between the catheter in the artery and the tubing outside. I never understood how any of it worked but on subsequent days when my blood pressure readings seemed inaccurate they would come and press on that piece painfully hard, until they were satisfied with whatever they saw on the monitor. It was a mystery, everything around me was a mystery—which is always true, I don't know how anything works: my computer or a light switch or an airplane or a car, how toilets flush, how electricity is generated or moves from one place to another, it might as well all be magic; and now my life depended on it, this brute metal the nurse secured to my wrist with three clumsy stitches, rough Xs binding it in place. My whole arm was covered in blood, it soaked the drape in dark wet patches. My ignorance was an indictment of something, me, my education, the public schools where I was raised, that I could be so helpless when it came to anything useful, that the only technologies I knew anything about were antiquated, unnecessary technologies: iambic pentameter, functional harmony, the ablative absolute. They were the embellishments of life, accoutrements of civilization, never the necessary core—though they were necessary to me, I thought, no matter how sick I might be they were still necessary to me. But I wished I understood something about the machines chirring beside me, the wires the two nurses were connecting, the new pattern of lines on the monitor that they agreed was a good waveform.

The head nurse lifted my arm and asked me to hold it aloft while she carefully transferred the sodden drape to the table, where she folded it around all the trash from the procedure and put it in a biohazard bin. You're all set, she said, and then she thanked me, as if I had just purchased something from her at a store. Alivia and I were alone then, she was getting the new wires and tubes in order, she unstrapped the blood pressure cuff and unhooked it from the monitor. I hate to say it, she said, but now that this cuff is off we'll be putting IVs in over here too, enjoy having it free while you can. I lifted it in the air, a celebratory flourish. She helped me to the bathroom then, where I pissed into the plastic jug, the IV stand beeping loudly in some kind of alarm beside me; Ignore it, Alivia called from outside, I'll take care of it when you're done. When I emerged she had changed the bedding, there was a new sheet crisp on the mattress and on top of it a new gown, and beside that two long green plastic packets, hospital-grade wet wipes. I thought you might want to go ahead and get cleaned up, Alivia said. She told me that I would be bathed every day, there was a shower in the bathroom but I couldn't use it with my IVs and A-line, not to mention the dizziness I felt when upright; instead I would use these antibacterial cloths. Let me just unclip the electrodes, she said, we'll put new stickers on, I can help you get the old ones off or you can do it for yourself. I can help wipe you down, too, if you want, she said, but hurry up while these are warm; she meant the cloths, which she had heated up in a microwave. I didn't have a change of underwear, L would bring some later, but anyway she said I shouldn't use the cloths on my face or my privates, that was her word, privates; the chemicals were too strong for the sensitive bits but they were safe to use everywhere else. I would do it myself, I said, and once she left I untied the gown and pulled it off, then pulled off the five stickers on my torso, which left black circles of adhesive the cloths wouldn't scrub away. There were instructions on the packet, a diagram of a body divided into zones, one cloth for the arms and legs, another for the torso and back. The cloths smelled sharply of chemicals, of hospital disinfectant, I hated to use them but I did my best, sitting on the edge of the bed, I drew them along my arms and legs, reaching everywhere I could. Soon I was shivering, the cloths were warm but the liquid became cold almost immediately on my skin, I felt like I was freezing. I tried to put on the gown but fumbled it, somehow I couldn't make sense of where to place my arms, and I was relieved when I heard Alivia call from the other side of the curtain, which she had closed again when she left. Need any help, she asked, and I said Maybe, yes, a little, and she came in. I held the gown against my stomach and lap, covering what I could. She had a damp washcloth in her hand, which she gave to me. For your face, she said. It was warm too, and I unfolded it and lowered my face into it, breathing in a wet smell of detergent, less offensive than the wipes, comforting almost; I held it to my face a moment before I wiped my forehead and eyes, the back of my neck. Want me to get your back, she asked while I was doing this, and I said Oh, it hadn't occurred to me to ask her but why not, and she made quick thorough unselfconscious work of it, with three or four big swipes it was done. She had already carried over a new strip of electrodes, which she placed quickly on my chest and stomach; I moved the gown aside so she could work, I was entirely exposed. But I didn't mind it as much as I might have, she had a way of working that took my self-consciousness away; her own lack of embarrassment helped cancel what might have been shame. You want to learn how to put these on, she asked, holding the bundle of wires. I guess so, I said, sure. They teach us a trick in nursing school, she said. Each of the cords had a colored clip on the end, she held them out one by one. White goes on the right, she said, snapping it on to the sticker on the right side of my chest. Smoke, she said, placing the black wire across from it, over fire, which was the red wire, which she attached beneath, on my left ribs. Snow she said, tapping the white wire, over grass, snapping the green wire across from the red. And that leaves brown, which doesn't have a mnemonic, really, it's just the last one left, and it goes right here, on your stomach. And that's it, she said, easy peasy.

She took the gown from me then and shook it loose, I had balled it up in my hand, and helped me guide my arms through before she tied it at the back.

I was tired out by this, it was a relief to lie back on the mattress, to have Alivia unfold the new thin blanket and place it on top of me. She went into the bathroom and held the jug I had pissed in up to eye level, reading the measurement marked on the side before she uncapped and flushed it. At the computer she made a note, they kept track of intake and outtake, and it struck me how much there was to know about my body, how much about it could be measured: heart rate and blood pressure and oxygen level, consumption and waste, all the information it was constantly producing; I knew there were apps and websites that claimed to put that information to use, to optimize one's body, lifehacking or biohacking, which had always seemed futile to me, a little sinister, fascist, a surveillance state of one. Or not just one, who knew how the data was stored and who had access to it, how it was monetized, turned into ads; you saw headlines about insurance companies adjusting premiums based on how much one exercised, how many steps you took on an average day. Everything we said or did fed into some terrifying voracious maw that made it at once utterly meaningless and indelible, no thanks, I thought, not that there was any opting out of it, not really; but I vowed to myself I would never measure my urine as a program of self-improvement. Alivia had other notes to enter, she asked about bowel movements, whether I had had one since entering the hospital, which I hadn't, and when the last one had been. I wasn't sure, I said, it had been a couple of days, but then I hadn't really been eating, they weren't letting me eat in the hospital but even before then I had eaten so little because of the pain, I had no appetite. She turned from the screen. Well, she said, that's not great. She would give it another few hours, she said, she'd give the laxative some time to work, but before the end of her shift we'd have to do something about it, a suppository or, if that didn't work, an enema. Had I had an enema before, she asked, and I said I had. They're not my favorite thing, I said, and she laughed. We'll cross that bridge when we come to it, she said, turning to the screen.

She worked for a bit in silence. I closed my eyes, then turned my head to look out the window, its snatch of sky and cloud. It looks like a beautiful day, I said, and Alivia hummed, the morning was nice but it would be a scorcher, she said, she didn't mind being inside, she hated the heat. Are you from Iowa, then, I asked her, and she said she was, just outside of Iowa City, she had spent her whole life here. What about you, she asked, where are you from, and I gave her an abbreviated account, how I had come here for graduate school, in my midthirties; I had thought I would leave after my program but I met someone, I said, my partner, I fell in love and stayed. I even have a house here now, I said, who could have imagined. She turned her head toward me slightly, still typing. Well that's romantic, she said, that sounds like a happy story, how did you all meet? It was a story I loved to tell, but she wasn't really listening, so I just said a friend introduced us, which wasn't exactly true; it hadn't been a friend but a professor, a young Portuguese professor I met in my first semester as a student. It was only her second semester, she had arrived halfway through the previous year, which probably explains why she was so friendly when I went to her office the first week of classes, I had missed the first session and needed to collect the syllabus. The space was small and dim, with a single square window staring at the brick wall of the neighboring building. It was a dreary room made drearier by its own blankness, she hadn't done anything yet to make it her own, the metal bookcases were empty, the off-white walls bare. The only personal touch was a lamp she had placed on her desk, a shawl draped across it to filter the light; she couldn't stand the overhead fluorescents, she told me, the buzzing gave her a headache, it made her feel like she was teaching in a prison. The building was a 1970s monstrosity, less a palace of learning than a fortress, a kind of architecture that proliferated on campuses after the chaos of the sixties but seemed tailored to the current moment, too, the age of school shootings, buildings ready-made for lockdown. She was surprised when she saw me, I was so much older than the other students in her introductory Portuguese class, almost all of them undergraduates; she and I were the same age, more or less, and both of us felt dislocated, a little bewildered to find ourselves in the monoglot Midwest, or what I thought of then as the monoglot Midwest. Bewildered and disdainful, maybe, we had the usual prejudices about Iowa; it would take me a long time to see the place as it is, or as it seems to me now. She had been in the States for several years, but in the Northeast, at one of the Ivies, and it was clear she had hoped for better from her career than undergraduate language classes; what she really wanted to teach was literature, and soon we were talking about Pessoa and Saramago and Antunes, writers I had only read in translation, which was why I was taking the class, I told her, I wanted access to their own voices. I had spent time in Lisbon and loved the sound of the language, I wanted to know what it felt like for thinking in. We liked each other, and soon half an hour had passed. Before I left, she invited me to join her the next evening for a drink with some of the other professors from the department, who went out after the faculty meeting they had twice a month; only the cool professors, she said, I would have a good time. I was a little taken aback; an American would never have made the invitation, there was a taboo about singling students out, inviting them for cocktails, only a European would have thought it appropriate. But I was pleased, too, she was being friendly and I was desperate for friends. And so late the next afternoon I found myself on the second floor of one of the old buildings that line the main street of town, facing the Pentacrest, the old state capitol complex now used by the university, in one of the city's few bars that had been mostly claimed by adults, where the servers wore ties and the walls were wood-paneled, a holdout against the sports bars and fast food the undergraduates preferred. My professor and her friends were seated at a table by the single large window that lit the space; the September day was just tilting toward evening, the table was folded in the room's sole pocket of light. My professor waved when she saw me, she introduced me as I sat in one of the two empty chairs at the end of the table nearest her. They were already deep in conversation, she and her friends, riding a wave of consternation from the meeting they had just left: the older, tenured faculty who wouldn't let them teach what they wanted, who were caught in the past, who foisted the lower-level classes on my professor and her friends. The classes where you have to really teach, my professor turned to me to explain, where it isn't just about stroking your big ego. These old guys who have been here forever, she said. But their biggest grievance was against a woman, an old Brazilian professor who refused to retire, who resisted, as my professor and her friends saw it, all innovation, any change to the curriculum, even though her classes were terminally undersubscribed. She didn't care if the department died, my professor said earnestly, as I hummed in non-commitment and sipped at the cocktail I had ordered, something bright and sweet and named after a pollinator, I think, the Bee's Knees maybe, or the Stinger; it was served in a shallow wide glass on a long stem that I lifted often in my boredom. I didn't know anyone they were talking about, and the whole conversation depressed me, the pattern of office politics; it was why I had left graduate school years before, such high passions over such low stakes, real ambitions, worthy ambitions set aside for the dumb game of university prestige. As soon as I felt I politely could I started to gather my things to leave. But you can't, my professor said, there's someone I want you to meet, the poet in our department, he's wonderful, where can he be. He's a visiting professor so he wasn't at the meeting but he said he'd join us after.

She had pulled out her phone and was checking her texts when a woman's laugh, raucous, braying, a wonderful sound, came from the bar. Everyone at the table turned. But that's M, my professor said, and someone got up to fetch a very tall blond woman who cried out on seeing us, a cocktail in one hand and a large multicolored purse dangling from the other. There you are, she said, have you been here this whole time—and there was much confusion and delight on all sides, a complete change of weather, so that I found myself smiling as M explained that she hadn't seen us, she couldn't believe it, for a whole hour she and L had been sitting at the bar talking, they figured we must have gone somewhere else. Only then did I notice the man who was with her, as short as she was tall, compact and fashionably dressed, with a shaved head and large, wide-set eyes. He had gone to the far end of the table, and M had come to the empty seat next to me, I drew my glass a little closer to make room. But just as she was sitting down she seemed to change her mind, But wait, she said, I need to talk to—, and she laid her hand briefly on my shoulder to excuse herself, though we hadn't been introduced, a gesture she repeated when she reached L, who had already sat down and had to gather his things to join our end. It was a little strange, a little awkward, but I didn't think much of it; weeks later, at another dinner, my professor would laugh in exasperation, wagging her finger at M: I had everything planned so carefully and you almost ruined it, she said. Her idea all along had been for us to meet; two gay poets in Iowa, she said, both single, it had to happen. Everyone at the table knew she wanted to set us up, everyone but us, and so there was a kind of conspiracy; they involved themselves in their own conversations, leaving us to each other—which was what L would have preferred anyway, he told me later, he hated their boring rancor. So depressing, he said, so small, which was the opposite of the impression his own conversation gave, of expansiveness and scope. My professor had told him that I was brand new in Iowa, I had just moved back from Bulgaria, she said, can you imagine, I was basically an immigrant—at which I demurred, America was my country, never more so than when I was abroad. But it was true that I felt like a foreigner, after so many years away; everything was too large or too small, even the language, it felt strange to be surrounded by it again, I had lost my sense of nativeness in it. It was a relief that L spoke English so badly, he hardly spoke it at all; and somehow this wasn't an impediment, anything but. I didn't have any Spanish, but I had French and some Portuguese, which helped, and the Latin I had studied in school; and he was so interesting, I was so eager to speak with him, the eagerness was like a bridge, eagerness and good humor, our laughter when we didn't understand. There was a poet from the city where I had lived in Bulgaria, a poet he liked, did I know him, L asked, and I told him I did; he was the country's most famous poet, almost the only one known anywhere else, and wonderful, I said. I loved his poems, meticulously metered and rhymed; and there was one I loved in particular, in which the poet, an old man, leans out his window and hears a child in the street below call to another by name, which was the poet's name—a common name, it wasn't much of a coincidence, but spoken in the exact tone of one of the poet's childhood friends, so that it was like a door opening onto the past. He had lived through a lot, I told L, he had suffered under the communists but not enough to escape the suspicion of those who followed, he had had a life of some trouble; and here was a door out of it, the door in the air his name had opened, to a time before all that. It was a beautiful poem, just four ballad stanzas, one of the only poems I had memorized in that language, the language I missed as much as anything else from that life I had left behind; it was like sugar on the tongue to recite a few lines to L, the lines where the poet's name appeared, the sound of childhood, and though of course L didn't understand any of it, or nothing but the name, his face lit up. I know that poem, he said, delighted. He had heard the poet recite it, at a reading in Madrid, at the cultural foundation where L had worked for many years; part of his job had been to host visiting writers, to organize dinners and excursions, and he had spent an afternoon with this poet, already old then though this was decades before, a short stooped figure with a cane and a cap, a tweed jacket, like a man from an old photograph, L said, very formal and very kind. They spoke in English—the poet had translated all of Shakespeare, when I taught the sonnets to my students I had taught his translations alongside. I liked him very much, L said, and at the reading he read the original and then his translator read in Spanish—not very good, L said, wrinkling his nose, it was a shame—and L remembered this poem, because of the name coming twice at the beginning.

I tried to ask L about his own poems, but he didn't want to talk about them, I could read them if I wanted, there were some versions in English; he wanted to talk about my favorite American poets, about the Spanish-language poets I had read. Only a few, I admitted, Lorca and Neruda, some Machado, though I loved Pessoa and Botto, not Spanish but Iberian, I laughed, maybe they could count. Botto, he repeated, happy that I knew him, I don't think many people here have read him. That was true, the only English translations were by Pessoa and they weren't very good, Pessoa is a great poet of course but those translations were not good. But surely I had read Cernuda, L continued, Luis Cernuda, and at my blank look he went on, a great poet, very great, and very English in a way, he loved Yeats and Wordsworth; English poetry was as important for him as Spanish, almost, I think you would like him very much. He was right; over the next weeks I would read everything of Cernuda's I could find, and this is what I mean when I say my impression of L was one of scope, of amplitude; I had a sense, vertiginous, exhilarating, of the world suddenly gaining in dimension, becoming larger and deeper. I'm not sure it's true to say I fell in love in that first conversation but I'm not sure it's not true, either; for two hours we talked, until finally the table broke up, and in all that time we didn't say a word to anyone else. It was deplorable behavior but really I was surprised they were still there, when my professor interrupted us to say goodbye, when M was at L's side suddenly, they had plans elsewhere, dinner and a movie; I was surprised they existed at all. I had been focused on L to the exclusion of everything else, on L and what he was saying, the poets he loved, his impressions of America, the pleasure he took in living here, which was good for his poetry, he thought: the new impressions, the new sound, the way Spanish retreated to a kind of privacy for him, not the language of the streets but a private language, at which I nodded and said I understood. I had felt the same thing, living abroad, it was a feeling I missed. I'm not sure I fell in love exactly but as soon as I got home I looked up the university's policies about relationships between professors and students. L wasn't my teacher, but I knew some schools had blanket policies, maybe it wouldn't be possible for us to see each other, to see if we wanted to see each other, and I felt a disproportionate relief when I discovered that the policy was narrow, so long as L wasn't supervising me it would be fine. He had given me his number, and the next afternoon I called him, and that evening we had a proper date, a wine bar and then a long walk through the quiet streets and then his apartment. It was the least dramatic, the least anxious beginning to any relationship I had ever had: no anguished uncertainty, no sleepless nights, just a new fact in the world.

All this was what I didn't say as Alivia typed her notes, though she would hear some of it in the days to come, as we grew to like each other, I think—or I liked her, anyway; I liked her already that first morning. She asked me if L would visit that afternoon, and when I said yes she opened a window on her screen to type in his name. Security's tight these days, she said, it was a good thing she had asked. He was just coming for an hour, I told her, he would have to leave then to teach, and she reminded me that I could only have one visitor a day, that even if L left early nobody else could come. But I didn't have anybody else, I thought, nobody I would want to see me like this. Seven years in Iowa but I hadn't really put down roots, not fully, I left whenever I could and spent months out of town, with L or on my own. And the worst thing about the city was that it was so transient, that hardly anybody stayed, all my friends from graduate school had fled as soon as they got their degrees; and faculty left too, almost everybody from that first dinner with L had moved away, all the young faculty, they all had ambitions that carried them to bigger cities, to the coasts, abroad. I would have left too if not for L, who loved teaching in his program, which existed almost nowhere else; even though he missed his family there was no work for him in Spain, nothing he would enjoy as much. Just L, I told Alivia, nobody else would try to come.

She turned from her computer then, she put her hands together, not quite a clap, and announced that it was time to try getting out of bed if I felt up to it; every day they wanted me to spend some time in the chair, what did I think. She began the careful choreography of moving the IV stand around the foot of the bed, asking me to lift my arm to keep the cords from tangling. Easy now, she said, as I swung my legs over the side, and slowly, with her hand at my back, I sat up, and then I stood and the world swam and I stumbled to the large armchair where I collapsed. Everything okay, Alivia asked, when I had closed my eyes for a moment, feeling dizzy? Yes, I said, very much, I just need a minute. She turned to the bed for the blanket, which she placed around my legs before showing me the wooden lever on the side of the chair; Be careful, she said, it's kind of sensitive, and it was, I had barely tugged it when the footrest sprang up, almost throwing my feet in the air. Later, Alivia said, if you're able to, we'll take a little walk around the floor. That's something else we'd like for you to do every day, to keep you mobile. Some of the older patients can start to have trouble walking, she said, they lose so much strength in their legs, and at that age once it's gone it's hard to get it back. Use it or lose it, she said. That's not going to happen to you, she went on, you're young and strong, but it's still a good idea. Young-ish, I said, strong-ish, and she laughed. But she wasn't really joking when she said Well, you should see some of the other people in these rooms, you'd be grateful you're in such good shape, and I felt chastened a little. I don't mean you're not sick, she said, it's serious, what you've got going on, we've got to take care of you; but it makes all the difference, being mobile like you are, it could be a whole lot worse. She tucked the blanket under my feet, a weirdly maternal gesture. She would leave me for a little bit, she said then, she would spend some time with her other patient. They only had two patients in the ICU, she had told me; on the main floors they had a lot more, there you could wait for an hour after pressing your buzzer, but here she would come right away if I needed anything, don't be shy.

The chair was closer to the window, I could see more of the world. But what caught my attention first was nearest, on the little ledge immediately outside, where a small brown mound sat huddled in shadow. It was midmorning, the sun had passed already; surely it wasn't the same sparrow I had seen earlier. The hospital must be a congenial spot for them, with so many people coming and going, the coffee shop, the outdoor tables I remembered from when L and I had visited his colleague—and of course with the pandemic everyone would be eating outside, scattering their crumbs. There were spots for foraging across the complex, areas outdoors where staff would gather in their scrubs, to smoke a cigarette or for lunch, I had seen them when I drove past. The bird gave a little shudder, as if coming awake, he fluffed his wings—I don't know why I thought of it as a he, I didn't know how to tell the difference—and gave a little hop. I thought of my mother, who hated sparrows, kicking her legs if they came too close; I remembered as a child how she scolded me for tossing crumbs to them from a park bench, though I can't quite place the memory, we weren't a family that visited parks, we didn't have picnics. But it remains anyway, the image of my mother putting her hand over mine, telling me they were dirty birds, we didn't want them near. My mother—I would have to call her soon. Even as a child I thought they were beautiful, as this fellow outside my window was beautiful, with a little bandit stripe across his eyes and the patterns on the wings folded across his back, like shadows left by waves, the feathers very dark at their tips but lighter, sandier where they broadened. I called him brown before but he wasn't, really, his breast and stomach were a light gray, nearly white in spots. What a handsome bird, I thought, as if I were speaking to a pet (it was the oxycodone, I knew, the weird drift of my thought), what a handsome, handsome bird.

At the little sigh of the sanitizer pump I turned my head to find a solitary woman in the doorway. The door was open, she hadn't needed to knock; maybe it was a sense of intrusion that made her apologize for disturbing me. You looked so peaceful there, she said. She was an older woman, a doctor in infectious disease, part of a team working on my case. Must be a busy time for you guys, I said, and she looked blank for a moment before Oh, she said, because of Covid? Yes, a lot of the department is handling that—a pandemic was something to handle, I thought, we have such strange ways of talking—but our team, we're handling everything else. So yes, a busy time. She had good news and bad news, she said, that dumb formula, an inauspicious start, though really the good news and the bad were the same. They had run all the usual tests, searched for the most plausible culprits, and then for rarer viruses and bacterial infections that show up in Iowa from time to time, farm diseases, things found in livestock or the soil. All of the results were negative, which was good, she said, they're nasty bugs, hard to treat; but also this meant they were at square one still, they still had no idea what had caused my artery to tear. You have some signs of infection, she said, the fever, the inflammation, but your blood work looks fine, your white blood cell count isn't high, so we're working in the dark a little bit. Hopefully these antibiotics will do the trick, they're broad-spectrum, but it would be good to find something specific to target, we wouldn't have to take this carpet bomb approach. Christ, I thought, carpet bomb approach; and I must have looked dismayed, she seemed flustered as she glanced down at my arm. How are these doing, she asked, meaning the IVs, and she pressed just above the one placed higher on my arm, the one with the double line; she didn't press hard but I sucked in a breath. Does it hurt, she asked. We'll have to place a new one, these drugs are hard on the veins, it's pretty common for them to burn out. Burn out, I thought, who taught these people, who gave them their vocabulary, their stock of images; I didn't want anything to be bombed or burned out, I wanted them to worry as much as I did about collateral damage. Since they had exhausted the usual suspects, she wondered if I would mind answering some questions, to help them think of other avenues. I saw in your file that you lived abroad, she began; she wanted to know whether I traveled often, and where. Only in the past few years, I told her, since coming back to the US; L and I spent time in Spain each year, or that was the idea, the pandemic had kept us home this summer; and we had been to Morocco, to Tangiers (this interested her), where L had shown me the places he had loved in his youth, when he had gone often, catching the twilight of the gay cosmopolis it had been. He had known Paul Bowles, he had seen when there was still a little life in them the bars and cafés and bookstores Williams and Genet had visited, that incredible culture almost vanished now, or so it seemed to me, though the bed-and-breakfast where we stayed had bookshelves lined with novels by gay writers, Baldwin and White and Vidal; so it wasn't entirely gone, I guess. And I've been to some far-flung places for work, I told the doctor, festivals in Finland and South Africa and Colombia and Chile. It was so strange to lay it out like that, that my life had taken me to those places; I hadn't even had a passport until my thirties, when one summer I helped chaperone a group of high school students to France. In the noise of everyday life it was easy not to take stock, but laid out like that I marveled a little. I had been asked a question once, in one of those places, about what I would like to tell my younger self, since most of the poems in my first book had been about the misery of childhood (childhood is *not* health, I said again and again, there's no bigger lie in literature). I had thought for a moment and said that I would tell him one day he would write a book that would carry him here, which was an exemplary answer, and cheap, flattering of everyone present, so that I cringed even as I said it; but also it was true, or not entirely untrue. The doctor was excited by these places, too, I realized that anywhere outside of Western Europe must open up new worlds of bacteria and viruses, things for them to test, and I worried she was getting the wrong idea. I'm not an adventurous person, I said, I stayed in big cities, I wasn't seeking out wildlife or traversing jungles, I was giving readings and talking about poems. Still, she said, these were good things to know, it would help them expand their search.

And I wanted to ask you, she went on, lowering her voice, I understand from your chart that in Eastern Europe you contracted syphilis. She asked me what treatment I had received and I told her that there hadn't been any penicillin in Bulgaria at the time, the distributor had cut them off, so I took the second-line antibiotic. Right, she said, that's what I understood from the notes. She asked me what the course of treatment had been, what dosage and for how long, and I told her as best I could remember. One possibility we've been thinking about, she said, though we're not sure how likely it is, is late-stage syphilis, which sometimes manifests in the arteries, with aneurysms or strokes. It's possible that the treatment you received didn't knock it out, or, depending on how long you had been infected, that the damage had already been done. Oh, I said, skeptical, but all the tests I've had since have suggested it did work, and I wasn't infected very long at all, I never had symptoms, I got tested because a partner told me he got a positive result. She nodded. It's such a strange disease, she said, there's really no pattern to it, it can hide for a long time and then manifest in a million ways. Probably it's a long shot, but we've sent an email to a tertiary syphilis expert in Seattle, one of the best; we'll see what he thinks. All in all a fascinating case, a real puzzle. She would keep me updated, she said, she'd be back the next day, and in the meantime her residents would check in on me. And then she was gone, and I was remembering those weeks of illness years before, my sense of luck at having escaped real consequence—since it was luck, dumb luck, not to suffer as Schubert or Flaubert or Keats had suffered, so many of the artists I loved (it was the disease of artists), not to have suffered at all, really; or only to have suffered the doctors, the bureaucracy of hospitals, the huge pills that made me sick for weeks. I had thought I had been lucky but maybe I was wrong.

I couldn't manage the chair for very long, even nearly reclined as I was; a heavy fatigue folded over me, and I asked Alivia to help me back to bed. So I was dozing when L arrived, in the midafternoon, and he woke me the way he woke me at home, by kissing my face. It was the feel of his mask against my skin that drew me out of sleep, that made me open my eyes to see him there above me. I started to lift my arms to him but the tubes had gotten tangled in the bedclothes, he had to help me free them before I could put my arms around his neck. My love, I said, as I often said to him, mi amor, mi vida, our usual names, but I felt them differently, felt them fully, in a way that maybe I hadn't for some time. Domesticity still felt new for me, cohabitation had come late. We had dated for three years before we moved in together, and another two before we bought our house, which was a kind of commitment I had never imagined and that wasn't entirely congenial, not always, I worried sometimes I had little talent for it. I had been single my whole life almost; I had always thought marriage or anything like it would be hell, a way of engineering hell, the hell of my parents, of many of my friends. I had only half committed to my life with L, I knew, always on alert for it to become intolerable, a prison or a trap. As I signed the papers for our house, alone, signing for myself and for L, who was in Spain, he had given me power of attorney—at every step we were out of our depth, my sister G, the lawyer, had to counsel us through it—even as I signed the papers I had wondered if I was building a prison for myself, the way I had seen my friends and siblings do; I wondered if it was just a way to cast off a freedom I didn't know what to do with, after a life in which I had felt so seldom free. I had finished my program, I had received a fellowship, I could have gone anywhere, why should I stay in a town I didn't love, in a part of the world that was for me, as I felt then, the opposite of poetry—it's always a kind of blindness to feel that, about any place, but I felt it.

But it hadn't become a prison, or not often, not yet, not a prison but not exactly bliss either. There were conflicts that I didn't know how to manage, little things, a stray word, an interruption; there were times when I got angry in a way I didn't understand, that I couldn't trace back to a source on the proper scale. I resembled my father at these moments, I feared, though L and I never shouted at each other, there was no threat of violence, the threat that had filled the house I grew up in, where I had seen my father knock my mother to the ground, where I had seen him strike my brother with his fist, full in the face, saying You son of a bitch, you filthy son of a bitch; my brother who would then terrorize me in the terrible basement we lived in, he was powerless against my father but powerful in relation to me, who never fought back, who cringed and pleaded, utterly without dignity in that house that violence filled, from bottom to top, from root to branch. There was nothing in that house but violence, no love, only violence, or if there was love there was only baffled love, curdled love, my love for my father and my brother, my brother's love, his desperate love. It was love I saw on his face when my father struck it but love there was nothing to do with, love only good for the garbage, love for the trash. Maybe my father felt it too, that baffled love, felt it for us, I mean, I doubt it but maybe it was so. The house L and I had made was nothing like that, it was full of love we had use for, full of love and still there were times I felt a kind of rage I didn't know what to do with, not against L, exactly, mostly not against anything I could name. Once in the car I had spoken sharply to him and he had begun to cry, silently in the seat beside me, he had turned his face to the window as fat tears slid down, and I had felt a kind of vileness I'm not sure I had known before, as I pulled off to the side of the road and unhooked my seat belt and put my arms around him and said again and again that I was sorry. There were things one couldn't apologize for, I knew, irreparable things, and if I hadn't quite committed one I felt the potential for it. I remembered a line from a novel I loved, I have the germs of every human infirmity in me; everything my father was I could become, which would be hell, I thought, actual hell, I promised myself I would never make L cry again. But they're inevitable, the little cruelties of intimate life. L had been guilty too, maybe not of cruelty but of thoughtlessness, dismissiveness, he could be exasperating, he had hurt me too; so that the key to a long life with another, the key that kept it from being a prison, wasn't devotion, which I had a talent for, but forgiveness, which was something I had to learn. And I had learned it, more or less, I was learning it day by day, even as I had begun to take our life together for granted, which was the real danger of domesticity. I felt that as I saw him now, as I put my face to his neck and breathed in the scent of him, his lotion and aftershave; I felt the way it had become easy to forget him a little, to forget the force of my feeling for him, which was impossible maybe to stay conscious of all the time but which I felt now, his preciousness to me, my thankfulness for him. Maybe it could teach me to cherish my life, I thought, if I got better, if I got to leave the hospital and return to the life we had made together, maybe I could undull myself to the luck we had had, that I had had, the luck of the love I felt embracing him, already I could feel my skepticism but I pushed it for the moment aside.

My life, I said again as L pulled away, but staying within reach, I kept my hand curled around his cheek as he tilted his head toward it, then turned his face to kiss my palm, holding it with both his hands. How are you feeling, he asked, and I shrugged, I'm so tired, I said, I wasn't in pain but I was tired in a deep way, an ultimate way; it was like a different species of tiredness, I knew it was the drugs but it was so strange, I said, I hated it. L looked at the bags hanging from the IV stand, at the tubes snaking into my arms. Technobello, he said, which made me smile. He touched my face then, still keeping my hand in his other hand, he traced the ridge of bone above my eye and then my cheek, and then he ran his thumb across my lips, which were chapped and dry. Your mouth, he said, pobre, and he turned to the chair behind him, where he had put his things. He rooted in a pocket of his backpack and turned back with a little blue canister of lip balm, which he unscrewed and then, with his index finger, applied to my lips, or tried to, I kissed his finger instead,

I kept my lips pursed as he said Hey, and then tonto, laughing until finally I relaxed and let him trace the circuit of my lips. When I rubbed them together there was the taste of kissing him, the taste of his mouth on my mouth. He twisted the canister shut and put it on the tray beside me, for me to keep. I asked him how he was, if he had been able to work that morning, and at first he said Fine, más o menos. But then he sighed and said it had been terrible, he couldn't concentrate, all I could think about was you, he said, I wanted to be here with you. He took my hand again. He had spoken with his brother, the doctor, and he had said that the operation to fix the tear was not complicated, that most of the time it could be endo—, he had to pause for the word, which was the same in Spanish and English, endovascular; they could put in a kind of mesh to strengthen the artery. A stent, I said, neither of us knew the word in Spanish. L's brother was sure that I would be fine, he was looking for articles, studies about best treatment: The whole family is thinking about you, L said, everybody sends you their love. I didn't tell him that the surgery would be more complicated, or could be, there wasn't any point in making him worry more. We have to see the good, L said, we have to see it as a chance, it's a chance to think about what is important. When you come home we have to make changes, he said, we have to change how we are living.

I had been thinking something similar; I had wasted so much time, traveling and teaching, I had wrapped myself in obligations that kept me from writing. It always seemed like there was plenty of time but there wasn't plenty, ever, there was never enough. And the past years had been hard, I had lost so much time. Buying the house had been a disaster, really, though we

had tried to be careful: we had set a budget when we were looking and stayed within it, we had followed the advice for first-
time buyers, we had gone through all the inspections. Now I felt
like we had no business being homeowners, neither of us knew
anything about houses, we couldn't fix the simplest things, even
routine maintenance was beyond us. The desire for a house had
come on me suddenly, I couldn't explain it; I had always thought
I would live in rented apartments forever, that I would be transient, untethered, I imagined a life of dignified bohemianism. L
was part of the change, I suppose, and also having, for the first
time, a little bit of money; I had published a book of poems,
finally, at forty almost, and it had been noticed in the minor way
that results not in sales but in invitations, to give readings, to
teach, to write reviews; and that income, along with L's salary,
which wasn't anything extravagant but was solid, dependable,
meant that we could make a down payment. L was game but
I was the driving force, suddenly I felt a need for something
stable. Maybe it was a sense of the world coming undone that
provoked the need, a sense of the country coming apart, tilting
toward violence; in which case settling down was exactly the
wrong impulse, we should have made ourselves lighter instead,
ready to flee. It wasn't rational but it was strong, the impulse
that had me combing ads on the internet, dragging L to weekend showings. He rejected most of the houses at a glance, citing
the layout or the light; at first he rejected the house we ended
up buying, too. It was hard to see past the worn green carpet
covering the floors, the decades-old wallpaper, the accumulated
furniture of the generations that had lived in it, the same family
for decades, their eccentricities, like the huge stuffed leopard
perched in the bank of windows that lined the west side of the

ground floor. The windows were one of the things I loved about
the house, from the first moment they had seemed beautiful to
me. It was a Dutch colonial from early in the last century, and I
had loved that, too, the shape of the house like the barns I had
grown up with. Most of all I had loved the studio they had made
out of the garage; the owner's mother had been a painter, and she
had converted it, installing windows on three sides and a sky-
light in the roof, but keeping the old brick floor, the bricks each
stamped with the name of the factory where they were made. It
could be a room to write in, I thought, I could imagine it right
away, a refuge. Over the next weeks I visited it almost every day,
walking over in the mornings or evenings. It was just across the
river, up a steep hill that marked the boundary of university
life, where the fraternity houses ended and family homes began.
Even L loved the yard, which was large and flat and a little wild,
a corner lot anchored by three huge oak trees, the largest to the
west of the house, where those windows looked out, and two
others standing sentry on either side of the short straight driveway. I tried to see it in all kinds of light, and with each visit I
felt I could imagine more vividly our life in it: the mornings
we would spend working, the walks we would take by the river
or through the neighborhood, with its lovely old houses, its canopy of trees; finally I made L see it too. It would need work, we
knew, but most of it could wait—the bathrooms, the roof, a new
kitchen. We would paint the walls and polish the floors—there
was old wood under the carpets, the listing said, we were bet-
ting it would be salvageable. The inspector found no problems,
or nothing unexpected, it was a good house, he said, it had good
bones.

What a piece of shit, I say now, every time I tell the story, what an absolute piece of shit. When we took possession I noticed a bulge in the floor, which had been hidden by all the furnishings but in the bare house was impossible to overlook. The first contractor I brought in to look at the floors, to pull up the carpet so we could see what was underneath, took me into the basement. L was in Spain for the summer, but I had stayed in Iowa, hoping to have the house ready when he returned. The basement was unfinished, and when I flipped the switch to light the bare bulbs hanging down, the man sucked his breath in through his teeth and exhaled with a long, drawn-out Holy shit. What, I asked, what is it, what do you see, and he pointed to the ceiling, where an old beam, green with mold, stretched from one side of the house to the other. You see that piece of wood, he said, that single piece of wood is holding up your whole house. I looked from the beam to his face, which was incredulous. How bad is it, I asked him, and he gave a half-hearted laugh. Well, your house hasn't fallen down yet, I guess. Didn't you get an inspection, he asked, and I said we had, yes, he said everything was fine. The man whistled. What should we do about it, I asked, and he looked away from the beam to me, then scanned the room, looking where the walls met the ceiling. I'm just a floor and carpet guy, he said, this is way beyond me, but it looks to me like the whole house needs to be reframed. I bet these floors have been sinking for a hundred years, he went on, looking up again at the beam. There followed months of something like panic; it took weeks even to find someone to take the project on, the first five or six contractors I brought in just shook their heads; and once work began they found more problems, until it seemed as though they were dismantling the house altogether. They put big metal jacks in the basement to lift the whole house up, which caused cracks to run through all the walls; and another primary support, the masonry wall between the kitchen and what would be my studio was failing, they told us, fatally failing, a terrifying phrase. The kitchen floor was taken up, parts of the house stripped to their bones, a disaster, I kept thinking, as the cost of it all ballooned from one impossible sum to another, as we went again and again to the bank to ask for credit, until there was no credit left. It was a full year before we could move in, and so we were paying both rent and mortgage, and I felt the dread I remembered from graduate school, when I had tried to live on a tiny stipend that was never enough; each month I wondered if we could pay our mortgage, our credit cards, our rent, begging the landlord for patience while I hustled for every gig, putting my real work on hold while I wrote stupid ephemeral pieces, fluff, anything that would pay. Probably I lost two years of writing, all told, two years of real writing, so that what I had thought would be the condition of work, possession of a haven, became the opposite, meant the suspension of work. It was time I would never get back, I thought in the thick of it, just when I was becoming conscious in a new way of finitude, aware, even before this latest disaster, that the tally of years lived was likely longer than years remaining. Two years I would never get back.

During the months of repairs I was mostly away, I took a visiting gig at a university in the South, which meant that L was the one who had to supervise and report back; he went to the house nearly every evening and sent me photos and videos, and then I would talk with the contractors about timelines and money, timelines that were always being pushed back and money that was always short. L made all of the decisions about design, anything affecting the look of the house; he's sensitive to so much that I'm dull to, things I don't even notice: the texture of paint on the walls, the shade of finish on a floor. He spent hours struggling to make himself understood, no one spoke Spanish, there were misunderstandings and frustrations, it was stressful for us both. Whole weeks I barely slept, lying awake doing sums, trying to find money where there wasn't any. I worried we would lose the house, I worried too that it might be the end of my relationship with L, that we would founder where so many couples founder, on money, the stupidity of money, because of my own stupidity, this one dumb choice. That was the only time we had really shouted at each other, over a video call when some repair had gone wrong, I don't remember what, and it meant more money to make it right. Something had snapped in each of us and we had shouted, and there was a quality in L's voice I had never heard before, a sharpness or desperation. It's just a house, I had ended by saying, it's just an object in the world, it can't be worth this. And then finally it was done, the school year ended, the contractors left; we were still, if only barely, solvent; and L and I found ourselves in something we had made together, a house more beautiful than anywhere I had lived, full of little graces that were L's graces: flowers in vases, a yellow teapot, plates with deep blue designs he carried wrapped in his suitcase from Granada; the graces of living he had a gift for I lacked. I was grateful for them, as I was grateful when he set a folding table under the oldest oak and we ate in our yard, a little plastic battery-powered lamp in a Bauhaus design the centerpiece as the sun went down; or watching the deer from our bedroom; or, once or twice, very early in the morning, just at dawn, standing at the bank of windows breathless as a fox investigated the yard. La casa de amor, L called it, I called it too, despite the effort it had cost, the surprises—effort and surprises both unfolding still, we would never be done with them, that was a condition of living in old houses, I knew now. I was proud of what we had done, though I wouldn't do it again, we had cared for something together and made something; it seemed worth it, some of the time, and the further we got from those hard early days the easier that would be to feel, I hoped. But maybe the cost was higher than we knew. They had asked me in the ER, in the long series of questions, whether there had been a period of particular stress and I had thought of the house, those months of sleeplessness, the desperate work; maybe they were part of what landed me here, in this bed with tubes running from my arms, maybe there was no telling.

Alivia came in then, with new bags for the IV. You found him, she said to L, whom she had directed to my room once he made his way up from the main entrance. He had had to wait in a long line, he said, you had to show ID and have your temperature taken, and since all the wards had the same visiting hours there was a rush; tomorrow he would come earlier. You don't really have anywhere to sit, do you, Alivia said—the armchair wasn't convenient for a visitor, too far away to hold hands, too bulky to easily move—and she set her bags down and brought us a plastic chair. Let me get these hung up, she said, gathering the IV bags, and I'll leave you two alone, I know you want to talk. But in fact I didn't know what to talk about. I wanted L there, I wanted to keep his hand in mine, but what was there to say. The pleasure was in not talking, in how he quieted the anxious monologue running through my head, nonstop, except maybe for an hour when the pain pill hit and I floated free of voices. It must be something similar, the chemical burst of his presence, the sight of him triggering the same reward center in the brain. He was better than oxy, I thought, looking at him, and it made me smile, so that he said What, and when I said nothing he said what again, tell me, and I told him that I was so happy to see him, that I loved him with my whole heart. He sat down while Alivia hung up the new bags, then started rifling through the canvas sack he had brought. I hope I remembered everything, he said, but there wasn't much to remember, just my laptop, a pair of underwear, earplugs, a sleep mask I kept for traveling, and a single book, a collection of poems I had made him search my studio for, the bookshelves and then the tall piles that had accumulated in the early months of the pandemic. The bookstore had closed in lockdown but kept making deliveries, and since it seemed possible it might not survive, might close permanently as stores all over the country were closing, ordering books became not just a pleasure but felt ludicrously almost philanthropic, a moral good. Each week the delivery man would pull into the driveway, behind the car that sat almost entirely unused, we barely drove anyway and now there was nowhere to go, he would carry a bag stuffed full of books to the door. It was the loveliest feeling, to buy books and feel like it was an act of virtue, books I would almost certainly never read, some of them, most of them maybe, but that gave me pleasure just sitting in their piles. They gave a sense of abundance in those months when so much seemed bare.

Alivia had finished by then, she was dropping the deflated bags, husks with little puddles in the bottom, into the trash, and then rubbing her hands with sanitizer. Okay, you guys, she said, I think I can give you five minutes without anybody bothering you, I'll try to keep everybody out for that long, so you all do whatever you want to do. She slipped out, pulling the curtain across and closing the door behind her. I looked at L, a little bewildered. What were we going to do in five minutes? I had an image of him climbing into the bed, overwhelmed by passion, a little snatch of copulation, something from a bad comedy; which was so far from anything I felt like doing, so far from anything we might conceivably do, that it made me laugh. L laughed too, he must have had a similar thought. Only later would it occur to me that she must have meant that L could remove his mask, that I could see his face, that maybe we could kiss; but we wouldn't do that, either. The whole time I was in the hospital, all those days, we followed the rules, as if it were some bargain we had struck, as if following them meant I would get well. I like her, L said, and I told him I did too, and that the nurse the night before had also been good. We were lucky, I said, that the hospital was so good, that I had his insurance; however awful it was we should remember how much luck we had had. L leaned forward and took my hand in his again. Everything will be okay, he said, I know it, everything will be good, we just have to take care. He had been thinking of the changes he wanted to make, he said again, how we would eat at home, no more going out to restaurants or, as we had been doing since the pandemic, ordering in, no more going to the Co-op for sandwiches and treats at lunchtime; from now on L would cook, he said, and when I started to protest he stopped me. I hated cooking, I always had, everything about it, from the shopping to the measuring, the waiting and vigilance; but L loved it, he had a gift for it, a comfort with approximation. The few times I had cooked for him he had laughed at my cups and spoons, the way I worked like a chemist, while he felt his way by instinct and pleasure. He could glance in the cupboard or the fridge and improvise something, the way his grandmother and mother had cooked, simple, delicious meals of vegetables and eggs and rice; give him tomatoes and olive oil and half an hour later there would be something on the table, on the white dishes painted with birds and flowers, beneath them the tablecloth he kept ironed and folded away, all the arts of living I had no gift for, so that I felt at once immensely lucky and ashamed. Left to my own devices I ate standing up, from cartons, I was such an American—not even American, such a Southerner, a Kentucky boy, such a hick. I loved it when he cooked but I felt guilty, too, since I couldn't reciprocate, I could only wash the dishes afterward. When we first started living together we had tried to alternate nights, but I grew frustrated, annoyed, I would take him to his favorite restaurant instead; te invito, I would tell him, he couldn't resist. No, he said now, I've been thinking, I will cook for us, I'll make dinner and in exchange every day we'll have an English lesson. His English was much better than it had been when we met, it was fine, but he was still self-conscious; when he had to speak at meetings or send emails, whenever he met someone, he would apologize, my English, he would say, it's so terrible, I'm sorry. He hadn't wanted to learn English his first year in the country, when he wasn't planning to stay, he told me that first time we met, in the hours we talked cut off from the others, struggling in our lack of a common language though it didn't feel like struggling, it felt like play; but America wasn't a place he was visiting anymore, it was his home, and though he taught in Spanish he had to use English with administrators, with most of his colleagues, he wanted to make an effort, he said. But I don't know how to teach English, I said to him now,

I've never taught anybody that. It's not like teaching literature, I told him, which was what I had done in the years I lived in Europe, where my students were already fluent; teaching language was hard, I said, a specialized skill, it wouldn't be fair to him. But he scoffed at this. Every day we will walk, he said, my brother says it's the best exercise for you; we'll walk and we'll have a lesson, and in exchange I'll make us dinner. Okay, guapo, I said, though I wondered how long it would last, most of our plans for better living faltered after a few weeks. You'll see, he said, it will be a good thing in the end, we'll make it a good thing; and as he said it he rubbed my hand between his, almost kneading it, so that I realized it was a kind of prayer, not an argument or a proposition but a prayer, and I brought his hand to my lips. He stood up and leaned over me, putting his arms around me as best he could, and I felt again the chemical change it wrought, the sense of happiness, of bienestar, I closed my eyes for a moment to feel it more. And then he pulled away and made a little sound, not a laugh exactly but a delighted sound. When I hug you the pressure goes down, he said, looking at the monitor, and it was true; my pressure was already low, they had lowered it with drugs but it lowered more when L hugged me. The best medicine, he said then, when you're home again we will eat very well, we'll walk and I'll hug you all the time. That sounds good to me, I said, I'm ready to go home now.

There was a tap at the door, and then Alivia's voice as it opened, asking if she could come in. She peered around the curtain. Everybody decent, she said as she slid it back, and we laughed. She left the door open, and the room felt public again, the noise and bustle of the ward broke the privacy of L's touch; though he stood beside me with my hand in his it wasn't intimate anymore, it wasn't a gesture made only for me. I meant to ask you before how your IVs were doing, Alivia said, and when she pressed on my arm just below the first one they had placed a burning pain shot up my arm, making me gasp. Not good, huh, she said, we'll have to get that out. You're going to lose that free arm, she said, gesturing to the hand L was holding, that's precious real estate. L stepped back to let her work, after she had grabbed a kit from one of the drawers in the corner. Sorry to do this while you're here, she said to L, but once they go bad we need to get them out right away. She placed the new one first, tying the tourniquet around my bicep and palpating my wrist, after which I felt the quick smooth slide of the needle. I looked at L while she did this, and saw that he had turned to the window, as squeamish as I was. You're good at that, I said to Alivia, it didn't hurt at all. Well, she said, this is the hardest part, and she uncoiled the tubing and draped it across me, crossing to the other side of the bed to connect it to the bag, then placing it along the top of the mattress, above my head. We have to make sure it doesn't catch on anything when you move this up and down, she said, meaning the bed frame, it's always more awkward when you've got them in both arms. But we'll manage, she said, no big deal. And here comes the best part, she said, peeling the tape off the old IV, disconnected now, and then opening a fresh little packet of gauze, which she pressed down near the needle, making me wince as she pulled it quickly out. Wow, I said, surprised at how good it felt to get it out, the sudden absence of pain. Nice, right? Alivia asked, and I said it was.

A noise at the door made us both turn our heads, Dr. Ferrier was pumping hand sanitizer and rubbing her hands, then putting on gloves. She was followed by three students who hovered behind her, silent, clipboards pressed to their chests. A visitor, Dr. Ferrier said, I always love to see my patients with a visitor. Alivia quickly put tape over the gauze and stepped away from the bed, ceding the field as Dr. Ferrier stepped forward; she discarded the failed IV before slipping out. I introduced Dr. Ferrier to L, and she smiled—even in her mask you could see it, the narrowing of her eyes, the fanning out of creases at their corners. How is he doing today, she asked L, genial, treating him like a peer, casting a kind of bonhomie over the room, which I appreciated and also chafed against. It was all make-believe, a game of pretend, and what I wanted was reality, facts, I wanted to face squarely whatever was ahead. I wanted it and also I didn't want it; faced with truly bad news I knew I would flinch. Still, I steeled myself, and even as L was struggling to reply—he never knew quite how to respond to Midwestern cheer, it was a tone he couldn't catch—I asked her whether they had decided anything about surgery. It changed the mood of things, I could see her recalibrate, shifting from preliminaries to business. Is it all right if I examine you as we talk, she asked, already pulling up the blanket from around my feet, reaching under the sock to press the tips of her fingers around the ankle, feeling for a pulse. We can't know yet, she said, we still haven't been able to identify a cause. I know infectious disease has been in to see you today, they're very excited about all the travel you've done—the pleasantness returned here, she couldn't help it—it gives them all sorts of tests they can run, so maybe we'll get lucky there and something will turn up. And rheumatology should be in, too, and we'll see if genetics can come by, they're a little hard to get ahold of but I'll ask them for a consult. So you see we're working hard, she said, I know it's frustrating to have to wait. Can you say how long I'll have to stay here, I asked her, do you know when I'll be able to go home? She had moved from the foot of the bed to the side opposite L, next to the IV stand, and she asked for my permission again before pulling up the gown and pressing into my stomach. L was still holding my hand and he tightened his grip as she did this. It cost him something to hold my hand, I knew. Early in our relationship it had caused me pain, the way he would pull away from me in public, if I tried to take his hand or link arms with him; it made him uncomfortable, it was still a foreign place to him, he didn't know the codes, in Madrid I know what's okay, he said, but not here. But really I wondered if it was something else, our difference in age, the fact that he had grown up in a conservative country, under the dictatorship. In private, among friends, he was affectionate, his hand always on my knee or the back of my neck, but it must have been hard for him there, in the hospital, in front of strangers, and yet the whole time he never let go of my hand. No, Dr. Ferrier said, it's too early to say how long we'll have to keep you. They're still working on getting your blood pressure stable, that's always a matter of trial and error, and before we can move you to the main floor you need to be on oral meds. I'm not ready to give you a timeline, she said, I'm sorry. And I'm not ready to let you eat again, either, I want to keep you at least another twenty-four hours without food. That doesn't matter, I said, I wasn't hungry at all, I didn't want to eat. She was moving down to my groin, which was still tender, I tensed up against the pain. Your anti-bodies test came back negative, she said, so we know you haven't had Covid, which was something we were considering, we think it can mess with arteries and veins. Good to know, I guess, I said, as she finished her exam; she rearranged the blanket and stepped back from the bed.

You're a professor, is that right, she said to L—I must have told her the day before, though I didn't remember it—and he nodded. And are you guys teaching in person this semester, she went on, and again he said yes, classes had started the previous week. There had been a lot of dismay in the department, everywhere in the university, when the announcement was made that they would teach in person despite the virus, despite the fact that there wasn't a vaccine, though we kept hearing that one was imminent, that it was a matter of months—and not only that, but there wouldn't be a mask mandate, teachers wouldn't be allowed to require masks in classes. It was absurd, another sign of American madness, but politicians in Des Moines called mandates an infringement of personal liberty, government overreach, the onset of fascism; the internet was full of videos of people chanting in Target and Walmart, telling others to take off their masks, to assert their agency, I guess, to be free men and not sheep. My crazy country, I thought, my coming-apart country. Would you be willing to ask for an exception, Dr. Ferrier asked L, I think it's important, we can get you the form. Professors could ask to teach remotely if they or someone in their family was high risk, as Dr. Ferrier made clear I was. Look, she said, as though we needed convincing, you're going to have to be careful, with your condition Covid could be catastrophic, a word she said with a weird emphasis, *catastrophic*, as though she were afraid we wouldn't understand, or wouldn't take seriously what she was saying. Of course, L said, yes, of course I can teach online, it's what I prefer. Good, Dr. Ferrier said, and she asked him if he would be back the next day, they could get the form signed then. And what about me, I asked, I was supposed to start the following week, my classes would be online but did she think I'd be able to teach at all. I'm sure somebody can cover my classes for the first week or so, I told her, and she furrowed her eyebrows. Oh, she said, I think it will be longer than that. Even when you're out of here I need you to take care of yourself, it's going to be a full-time job, you're going to have to keep coming to see us several times a week. If there's any way you can swing it I'd say six to eight weeks at least I'd like you to be resting. I glanced at L. I wasn't sure what would be possible, I was just a visitor and didn't have benefits or long-term leave, and I wasn't sure we could manage if I lost the job. Don't worry, L said, don't think about it, nothing matters but you getting better. Okay, I said, I would write the chair later that evening, I would ask for the first quarter off, which would give me almost two months, I wouldn't teach until the end of October. It would mean a scramble for them, I knew, probably the professor I was replacing would have to delay his sabbatical, I felt guilty already. Good, Dr. Ferrier said again, as she stepped farther back, rejoining the three students who had remained silent and attentive through her examination. I'll let you enjoy your time together, she said, I know it's short. We're taking good care of him, she said to L, and then turned to me. I know there's so much to worry about but please, let me do the worrying, the most important thing you can do is relax, as best you can. Try not to think about how long you'll be here or what happens when you leave, let all of that go. That would be nice, I thought. But I said okay again, I would do my best.

She left then, trailed by her duckling students, who nodded their heads at me as they filed out. Alivia came back in, asking if I wanted my pain meds, which I did, the examination had hurt and, worse than that, my head was terrible, with the low blood pressure and lack of caffeine; and then L had to leave, too, he had to teach his class. It was in person but it was a small group, his graduate seminar, and they all wore masks. None of them was American, it would never occur to them to protest; it was only the undergraduates who walked past the box of surgical masks L put by the door and took their seats barefaced. He put his arms around me again before he left, while Alivia busied herself at the computer, giving us what privacy she could, and again I breathed him in, a last lungful. It seemed suddenly like a very long time before he would be back. I am thinking of you every minute, he said, and then he was gone. I felt a desolation that surprised me with its force, that didn't lighten until the oxy deadened it, making it something I didn't feel exactly but sensed hovering, not inside me but an object in the world.

It was late afternoon already, almost evening, soon Alivia had left and a new nurse came in, I would only see her that single night. The ward was quiet, preparing for nighttime though there was still light outside, late August light, the long summer evening. The doctors' rounds were done and I was left mostly in peace, except for a woman who came to empty the trash, another to restock the cupboards, always asking permission before they entered. I opened my computer, I wrote the emails I needed to write, I thought about calling my mother, I put it off another day. I didn't want to talk to anyone, or not to anyone but L, who called when he got home from class, his image appearing on the little screen of my phone, unmasked, his whole face. There wasn't anything to say really but we kept the call open for a long time, I wanted to look at him. We said good night finally when the nurse came with my heparin shot; when she removed the needle I grabbed my stomach and kept my hand there as the burning radiated out. I tried to read but found myself scanning the same sentence again and again, comprehending nothing. I turned on the television for the first time, clicking through the few channels, pausing for a moment when I saw images of demonstrations, cars on fire and broken glass; a line of police, their plastic shields locked in front of them, moving forward as a single body; clouds of gas and milk-stained faces; armored men with batons striking figures huddled on the ground. For months these images had filled the news and still they made me hot with rage, with grief and rage.

That was something else L and I had fought about, months before, when a woman had been shot in her home, a sleeping woman the police had murdered in her bed, and the streets of my hometown erupted. Thousands of people faced off with the police, demonstrating through the night, Louisville was at the center of the news and I felt an impossible dismay. I spoke to my sister G every day, she was working pro bono with a group of protesters, representing them when they were arrested; before a demonstration they wrote her number with Sharpies on their arms. It's amazing what they think they can get away with, she said to me about the police; just saying the name of her firm made a difference for her clients, she said, all the difference, the police know we'll fight them, we'll take it to court, they have to be careful. It reminded me of how she had been in college, idealistic, fired up, eager to change the world, before the realities of student loans led her to take a corporate job; just another suit, she had said to me once, disillusioned, surprised to find herself in a life so different from what she had imagined. It made me proud to see her doing what she could, it made me ashamed of myself. I should be there, I said to L, I want to be there, and I told him I would join the protests, I wanted to be part of what was happening. What do you mean, L had said, what are you saying, he had seen the images too, how can you even think about it. People are being shot in the streets, he said, why would you go there, it's not your home anymore, what would you do. Why would you seek trouble, he said, and en plena pandemia, bello, he said, no, please, don't go. I didn't know what I would do, I told him, I would be a body in the streets, maybe that was enough. It's my country, I told him, my hometown, how can I not be part of what's happening. We spent hours saying the same things to each other, L increasingly frustrated, bewildered; If it was where you lived I would understand, he said, if it were here, but to travel, no, he said, please, it doesn't make sense. And I had given in, finally, I had agreed not to go, I kept watching the news with hopelessness and horror. I went to a march downtown, though in our college town it just felt like theater, the city government fell over itself to show solidarity, the mayor led the march. What was it for, I wondered. I watched the news, I sent money to bail funds, I brooded on my uselessness.

I slept without meaning to sometime after darkness fell. I hadn't used any of the things L had brought, the mask or earplugs, which was why I woke when the man spoke my name from the door of my room, from the very threshold, as though hesitating to come in. The ward had shifted to its muted nighttime lighting, but the hallway was still brighter than my room, so that what I saw first was just a dark outline, a barely human shape. And then he spoke again, and I pushed myself up a little, and the second time he said it I processed his name, though it was only when he reminded me, seeing I hadn't placed him, that I realized we had met before. Only once, at a dinner party where he was also a guest, he and his partner, who was an artist in town. It was a well-intentioned gesture, a group of gay men, it was meant to spark new friendships but it hadn't gelled; it was pleasant, fine, but L and I hadn't followed up with any of them, we had let it drop. But he had remembered me, he had seen my name among the new patients. I remembered that he was a doctor, a surgeon, probably he had told me his specialty was vascular but it hadn't meant anything to me at the time. Now I seized on it, it was such a relief that he had known me as something other than a patient. I'm sorry, I said to him, I hadn't remembered, I would have asked for you. But my relief was short-lived. He came closer. How much do you understand about what's happening to you, he asked, and I said I wasn't sure, they had explained to me what it was but it wasn't clear what would happen next, it wasn't clear how bad it was. He cut me off. It's bad, he said, I'm sorry, it's a big tear, it's really bad, and I felt my breath catch, I had a peculiar sense of what light there was in my darkened room turning liquid and draining away. There was a kind of relief in the draining away, I had known Dr. Ferrier was protecting me, not giving it to me straight, it was a relief to have the unvarnished truth. Okay, I thought, so let's see all of it. Tell me what you mean, I said. I was looking at your chart, he began, and I saw that you waited five days to seek care. Look, he said, you got lucky, at five days post-incident untreated most people die of this, the mortality rate is something like seventy-five percent. What, I said again, not really a question but an expression of shock. You're lucky you got here in time, he said. Hopefully they've got it stable now, at some point they'll scan you again and we'll know more. But I was still processing what he had said. Seventy-five percent, I repeated. I hadn't really believed what the surgeon had said in the ER, just the day before, time had become so strange, so deranged; when he had said that I might die it had seemed impossible. Of course I knew it wasn't impossible, that it was the only inevitable thing, the one big certainty; but I had been sheltered, so few untimely deaths had struck near. My grandparents had died, my mother's siblings, but all late in life, one couldn't think of it as unjust, and the shocking deaths had all come at a remove: acquaintances who had overdosed, a beautiful poet I had known who died of leukemia, a student who, years after I taught him, lost control of his car; they had all been tragic, desperately sad, but they weren't intimate friends, they hadn't struck at the center of my life. I had been luckier than I had any right to be, luckier than anyone could reasonably expect. You're stable for now, the doctor repeated, but it's still a dynamic situation, the next few days are going to be crucial. I know they're still trying to figure out what's happening, and the goal is to keep you stable until they know how to proceed, what kind of surgery or whether we can treat it medically. The thing that worries me most is the possibility of tertiary syphilis, he went on, that could compromise the whole artery, and it's hard to test for. I saw that Infectious wants a tissue sample, but Dr. Ferrier thinks that's a bad idea, and I agree. A tissue sample, I thought, no one had said anything to me about that; I wondered what it would mean, how they would get it. It's a lot of waiting, I know, and I know it's scary. But I think it's best for patients to know the truth. It's what I would want, anyway. Yes, I said, it is what I want, thank you. Listen, he went on, Dr. Ferrier is a good surgeon, and the whole team discusses all our patients. I'll keep watching your case, but I want you to have my number if you have any questions, if anything's unclear, you can call me. He reached out to give me his card. Thank you, I said, and I meant it, it had been a kindness for him to come. I'll let you get back to sleep, he said, I'm sorry I woke you, I'm on call tonight and was down in the ER. I thanked him again, I said I was glad he had woken me up, that he had told me the truth, and I was.

I didn't sleep again, not for a long time. I took my computer from the table by the bed and opened it. I hadn't searched for information before, maybe because I hadn't wanted to know, and also anytime I looked for medical information online I was bewildered, and then with the little I could understand became a catastrophist; better to have someone who understood filter things for me, explain them. But now I searched, scrolling through the first pages of results. Most of what I saw was familiar, a diagram like the one Dr. Akeyu had drawn, it was still on the whiteboard, I could see it in the dim light: the three layers of the artery, true lumen and false, the most common interventions. I typed into the search bar again, aortic dissection and aneurysm, and in the terms that appeared in the predictive search I saw mortality rates. Different sites came up now, many of them papers in medical journals, almost unintelligible. I tried to get through the abstracts but couldn't make sense of them, and more than that I couldn't make myself focus, the text skittered under my eyes. I kept scanning ahead, scrolling down, I didn't care about methodologies or literature review. Finally I found what seemed like the numbers my friend—not friend, my acquaintance—had quoted: that in almost half the cases the event itself is fatal, that after that mortality increases one to three percent an hour, that at a week untreated it rises to eighty percent. And then there were statistics for the longer term, for patients under treatment: sixty percent survival rate at five years, forty percent at a decade.

I closed the computer, I didn't want to read more. Five years, I thought, even at five years the odds weren't great, and the deaths in the study were from sudden rupture of the artery, quick and without particular warning, the kind of death I had brushed against when I was gripped suddenly by pain out of the blue, standing in the kitchen one moment—it was morning, the start of the day—and then bent double, blind with pain. It had brushed past, the great banality, not grand and literary but a brute crushing fact, a hammer pounding meat. It frightened me, the thought of only a few years, of how little I could do, the things I had imagined making after my long preparation, I had only just begun. When had I started to believe that I had time, that I would get to be an old man, I hadn't believed it always. As a teenager I had assumed life would be short, too short to prepare for anything, in those years when I failed my classes and made my mother despair, when life was only long enough for appetite; it seemed to me that any life worth living could only be short. That was the bargain I saw in the men who were dying around me, and it was a terrible bargain but one I took without hesitating; what other option did I have, what could I do with all that time, what was the life my life was preparing me for. And then the dumb luck of not getting sick, though I had been so reckless, though I had taken no precautions, had done everything that anyone who did get sick had done, that the friends I had just begun to make had done, the dumbest luck; and then too the luck of music, of having a talent that could carry me to another world, the opening up of a future that I came to care about, the future I still cared about. I wanted to be old, I wanted to work until I was old, I wanted to see what I could do, I mean the poems I could write, and also the life I could make with L. I thought of the Gospel of Thomas, the line everyone quotes about being saved by what is inside you, by bringing it forth, but then there's its corollary, that darker promise Jesus makes that what you do not bring forth will destroy you. They were terms I could understand, being lost or saved by what one made or failed to make; and I had brought forth so little, I had laid up all my treasures for that future time I wouldn't have now, maybe, the time that had been cut short.

I was being stupid, I thought, or really I had been stupid before, stupid to have let myself be lulled, I had been wiser as a child. There were no guarantees, it was ridiculous to imagine life at sixty or seventy, to think of the future as a broad passage, an avenue, when really it was a narrow corridor of slamming doors. But that isn't true either: planning for the future or living for the moment, nobody knows how to live, there's no way to know, anything anyone says is bullshit, entirely arbitrary, true or false by chance. There are no arts of living, I thought. I looked to the window, though the shade was drawn. Beyond it was the tower where I knew children's oncology was housed, Alivia had told me when I asked her earlier in the day. Why should I feel aggrieved, I thought, if you want injustice look there, dying at forty-five or fifty isn't unjust. So you haven't seized every moment of your life, who has; people die young every day, I said to myself, younger than you, why act like it's such a tragedy. But none of it helped, I was aggrieved, more than aggrieved, I felt enraged, not just at some abstraction, at fate or death or chance, but at actual concrete beings: at the doctors for whom I was not an infinitely cherishable bundle of pathos and need but an interesting case; at the nurses I heard chattering through the day at their desk outside my room; at absolutely everyone not facing what I faced, what I felt I was facing, even at L. The closeness I had felt with him earlier was gone, now there was a great gulf and I was on one side of it alone. If I died what would I be for him but a story, not even my own story but a segment of his, larger or smaller, I would be something he lived past, something he got over, an elegy's inspiration, maybe. Where did it come from, that rage, and where did it go, after a moment, as suddenly as it came, I watched it as it went, merely afraid again. The great banality, I repeated to myself, commoner than dirt, inspiring a scale of feeling that was ridiculous the moment it passed—as was true of all the immensities, of love and oceans and the night sky filled with stars. Everyone is ridiculous encountering them for the first time, when feeling swells to match them and is laughable for trying, grotesque with bigness, why should death be any different. Where is your philosophy now, I asked myself. But human beings aren't ever philosophical, I don't think, not really, at least I was the opposite of philosophical, a minuscule crouching thing, a bit of matter terribly afraid, utterly insignificant, the entire world.

3

---

n the morning of the fifth day the pain came back. It was still early, though the first rounds were done, the routine of X-ray and morning meds, the heparin shot and pills and powders, all of which I received mechanically, docilely; Dr. Akeyu had come round and had nothing to report, we were in a holding pattern, she said; infectious disease was still searching, twice a day the A-line spurted blood into vials for ever-obscurer maladies and everything came back negative, I was an enigma, they said, a conundrum, they were running out of ideas. The day before a kind woman from rheumatology had come, young and squat, who felt along my fingers and limbs, flexing all my joints, having me spread my arms as best I could so she could check for Marfan syndrome, for Ehlers-Danlos syndrome, for Loeys-Dietz syndrome, connective tissue disorders that all can make someone prone to dissections and aneurysms. Really they would like me to get a PET scan but it was always a fight with the insurance, she said; she would rest easier knowing that there weren't other points of inflammation, hot spots, she called them, that the problem wasn't systemic, but they'd have to see, sometimes they approve it and sometimes they don't, we'll make the best case we can. Her white coat was covered with little badges and buttons, a rainbow pin, a decal that read LGBTIowa, another for what must be a group of queer employees of the hospital. It made me relax a little with her, everyone else had seemed so relentlessly heterosexual, which must have been why, as she asked me again the questions I had been asked so many times already, about my medical history, about recent traumas, illegal drugs, I paused after saying no; I said Well, yes, maybe, amyl nitrate. Sometimes I did use poppers recreationally, I said, it hadn't occurred to me to mention it before, I hardly thought of them as drugs. This wasn't really true; I had withheld it from the other doctors, because I didn't think it was relevant, and also I had never thought of them as dangerous. I knew there were warnings, that they could interact with certain medications; but they were so common, ubiquitous really, and no one I knew had suffered any ill effects. Thank you for telling me that, the woman had said, which struck me as odd, and then as she resumed checking my joints—she was moving from my head to my toes, at every point bending and palpating—she asked me how long I had been using them, and how often. Just in the past few years, I said, which was true. In my teens and twenties men had offered them to me, and there was a video store I used to go to in Manhattan, on Eighth Ave, where the whole upstairs reeked of them, the warren of little cubicles and the open space with the large screen where men sat and raised the brown bottles to their noses, sometimes with another man on his knees between their legs and sometimes alone, jerking themselves off. I loved those places, I still do, sometimes I was there less to have sex myself than just to bask in the atmosphere they made, other men fucking and watching porn together, the camaraderie of filth. I had tried poppers there and other places, too, when a man reached down with the bottle, holding it to one nostril while he pressed the other one shut, always a gentle act, even tender; sometimes it was a way to make someone more compliant, to turn them on and make them more eager, but also it was a concern for pleasure, a desire to draw each other into an altered space. But it never did that for me, I would inhale and feel nothing, or only a high bright tone somewhere deep in my brain that would sharpen eventually to an ache. Only a few years before had I finally felt for myself what I had seen others feel, when a man insisted I use them, it was a scene he liked, a kind of domination, not so tender with him: he held the bottle to my nose and counted down, slowly from ten; he made me hold my breath until he told me to exhale; he repeated it on the other side and I felt a warmth climb up from my chest, rise into my cheeks and to my scalp, and with it a rush of lightness and buoyancy, not ecstatic exactly but a kind of euphoria. And this was followed by a desire that had nothing to do with my dick; they made me go soft, actually, that doesn't happen to everybody but it does to me, it was a different kind of intensity I felt, it was like I wanted to dissolve into that atmosphere of filth I loved, and the agent of dissolution was sex, sucking and being fucked. It was a lovely feeling, and the man laughed a little as he saw me feel it, he capped the bottle and ruffled my hair before he slid his cock back into my mouth.

But you don't think, I started to say to the doctor, surely it couldn't be poppers that caused this. She had my left foot in her hand, she was rolling it in a circle as she felt the ball of my ankle in her other palm. She set it down. Well, she said, it's good information to have. She picked up my right foot. It seems unlikely to me, she said, poppers are vasodilators (a beautiful word, I thought), which means they soften the walls of your veins and arteries, and that causes a drop in blood pressure. I need to do some research, but I don't see why that would cause this kind of tearing. The drugs we'd usually think of for this would be cocaine or methamphetamines. She paused again. Has meth ever been something you've used, and I said no. I had never tried it, though it had also been ubiquitous in the places I went; through the closed doors you could hear the click and hiss of the little torches they used to heat it up. I had been in those cubicles sometimes, though mostly I avoided it, I hated the smell, like burnt plastic; and once a man on his knees in front of me took a hit and I got a mouthful of smoke as it drifted up. It was pure poison, I had thought, coughing, there was nothing innocuous about it. Those would be very dangerous for you now, the rheumatologist said, they could be fatal, it's very important that you know that. Her tone wasn't censorious but concerned, compassionate, as it had been her entire visit. I wondered if the tone was sincere, the manner she had of making me feel that what happened to me mattered to her, my outcome; I wondered if it was real or merely an act, a way of navigating or enduring the day. I was nothing to her, really, I was her job, she would clock out and enter her real life, which had nothing to do with me, and in a week or a month there would be no memory of me, I wouldn't have left any impression at all, whether I lived or died I would be entirely erased; or if anything remained it would be some unindividuated fact, divorced from my person. Of course it wasn't real, I thought, it didn't have any reality at all. It didn't matter that we were family, as I used to say when I was a kid, when I really did feel solidarity with anyone who was queer, when it seemed to mark us out as members of some tribe; I didn't feel that now, or not as much. But I was grateful to her anyway, whether it was real or not, I was grateful for her kindness even if it was a performance.

And that was why, when, having finished her examination, she asked if I had any questions, I asked her if she could tell me how this was going to change my life. My voice was thick. Oh, she said, and though she had taken a step away from the bed she came close again and put her hand on my leg, below the knee, and I felt gratitude well up afresh. They weren't the right categories, I knew, sincere or performed, they didn't pertain exactly, they weren't proper to her office. I thought about my own feelings as a high school teacher, how important it had been to let go of a certain understanding of sincerity, that all-consuming concern that had made my first years so difficult, so utterly, so unsustainably exhausting; how important it had been to learn to leave my feeling for my students in the classroom, to mark some separation from the rest of my life; and how that didn't invalidate what I felt but demarcated it, it set a boundary that made it finite but didn't make it unreal. All I want is infinite love, I thought now, from everybody, all the time. Like everybody else, my thought went on, that part of my thought that could stand to one side, that might let me laugh at myself at some point down the road; but not now, now I was all earnestness, waiting for her to speak. She waited a moment longer. I don't think anyone can really answer that yet, she said finally, I don't think we can know. But you're right that your life will change. You'll be on medication, for one thing, she said, probably for the rest of your life, and as somebody who has basically always been healthy that will be a big change. It's going to take you a while to recover, she said, depending on what kind of surgery they do that may be longer or shorter, but even in the best case you're not going to be able to do the things you used to do, for months at least. And you may never be able to do them, she said, this may mean that you have to rethink things in a permanent way, things like travel and how much work you can do and what kind of activity you can take on, all those things may be permanently changed. But look, she said, I know it might be hard to hear but all of that can be a blessing, it can clarify what you care about, how you want to spend your time; and I remembered what L had said on his first visit, that it could remind us how we wanted to live. I know those aren't the answers you want, she said, stepping back again, I wish I could be more concrete. But that's all anybody can tell you for now. She promised to be back, to work on a PET scan, to follow my case. You can always ask to talk to me, she said, and then she was gone.

For five days I was in a holding pattern and then the pattern broke. It happened while I was in the bathroom, standing to piss, aiming at the plastic jug while I held the tubing out of the way. I had IVs in both arms, and my veins kept giving out, so that now they had a special team come in with an ultrasound to find deeper veins that might hold up a little longer, though the first man who came glanced at the bags hanging from my IV and shook his head. Man, he said, they've got you on the heavy stuff, those just burn through veins; that was the phrase he used, burn through. I was standing, holding the tubes out of the way, my gown tucked beneath my chin, I had just begun to piss when the pain began, as suddenly but not as sharply as before, deep in my groin, less a tear than a kind of shifting, tectonic, something strange that made me stop pissing, not because I willed it but because something cut it off, something was in the way; and then there was the twisting low pain that had come before, bad enough that I made a noise and doubled over, clutching my stomach. Immediately there was a knock at the door, Alivia's voice asking if I was all right. She had been gone all weekend, I was relieved to see her that morning with the changing of the shift; she smiled when I told her this, Aren't you a sweet one, she said. She had been changing the bedding while I was in the bathroom, that was how she had heard me. I reached over and turned the handle, popping the latch, and she came in, she helped me back to bed, pushing the IV stand with one hand while keeping the other on my lower back. Can you tell me what's happening, she asked, and I tried, I said the pain had come back, the same pain as before, it was happening again; and once I was settled she took out her phone. That was how they communicated within the hospital, she had told me, there was a special app they all used and she said now that she was writing to the vascular team, that way she could let them all know at once, not just Dr. Ferrier but everyone on duty. And then she sent another message to her own team, to the ICU doctors, one of whom arrived just a minute or two later, while Alivia was at the computer. He came to the bed, still rubbing his hands with sanitizer, and as he pulled on gloves, he asked me to describe what I was feeling, then asked my permission to examine me. I cried out again when he pressed into my stomach, which caused a spike of pain. Please, I said when I could speak, please stop. He lifted his hands immediately, I'm sorry, he said to me, and then to Alivia he said Let's get him something for the pain, and they conferred about what medications I had taken already that morning. It had only been a couple of hours since I had received my morning oxy but he ordered another dose, and he upped my blood pressure meds, too. You're going to feel woozy, he said, I'm sorry, but we want to keep you safe. Alivia's phone pinged then, she drew it out of her pocket and told the doctor vascular wanted a CT scan, they were putting in the order now. Alivia came near the bed to program the titration machine; she glanced down at me, and seeing something on my face, spoke to me in a tone I hadn't heard from her before, a tone I didn't like, telling me it would be all right, I should just relax. Trust us, she said, at which I felt a little flare of rage, not at Alivia but at the hospital, the ward; they had promised me before that I would be safe and yet here we were. And not by accident; it was their fault, it was the incompetence of the nurse I had had the day before, her gross disregard, I thought. I was doing the opposite of relaxing or calming down, I was flaring up the way I had the afternoon before, the slow Sunday afternoon that had become such a trial, I was falling again into grandiloquence, the accusations I had made; it was outrageous, I thought, gross negligence, and then Alivia spoke to me again. Honey, she said, I need you to take a breath for me, I know you're scared but if you relax these numbers will come down a lot faster. I tried to do what she asked. I'm going to go get you that pain pill, she said, that will help relax you, too, and then we'll take a trip downstairs for the CT.

Every shift had brought a new nurse over the weekend—they were fine, I had no complaints, but it was disorienting; it was true that I had missed Alivia, even before Sunday morning, when the final new nurse had arrived at 7:00 a.m. for the start of her shift. The night nurse brought her in to introduce her, as they did at every shift change when there was a nurse I hadn't met. I would have taken her for a student, an undergrad, she might have been eighteen or nineteen, short and extremely thin, with long blond hair in a ponytail that reached halfway down her back. We made the usual chitchat when she came in for my morning medicine, her arms full of bags of IV fluids and vials. Just from the way she dumped them on the counter by the sink, letting them fall uncontrolled in a heap, thrusting her hips forward to keep them from falling to the floor—just from that I could tell she hadn't been on the job long; but I was still surprised when she said she had only been in the ICU since May, when she had graduated from a little college in Cedar Rapids. This was her first job. That alarmed me; her first job and it was in the cardiovascular ICU. I thought of the patients Alivia had told me about, the ones sicker than I was, the full-on catastrophes. I wondered if she had been assigned to me because I was verbal and ambulatory, still on the near side of real debility; the only nursing I needed was medication and monitoring. Though if either of those faltered I could quickly shift from one category to the other, I knew, I could become one of those patients unable to act in the simplest ways for themselves. Replacement of the artery, I thought, Dr. Akeyu had said just that morning it was still a possibility. She was the only familiar face over the weekend, appearing even on Sunday morning, faithful at 5:00 a.m.; it must be hell to be a resident, I thought. I was stable, which was a promising sign, but they hadn't removed surgery as an option. Each morning she told me that I would need to keep fasting, she was sorry, and each morning I had said I didn't care, I still had no appetite; I would murder for a cup of coffee but I didn't care if I never ate again. This new nurse's greenness alarmed me, but it endeared her to me, too, as she fumbled to open her envelopes and vials, things I watched Alivia do unthinkingly, with a single hand. It was a hard job, I thought, and everyone begins as a beginner; the competence I admired in the other nurses was only earned over years, all of them had started out like this. Even when she gave me the heparin shot, jabbing it in my stomach without pinching the flesh first or even counting down, just bluntly shoving the needle in; even then I thought, gritting my teeth, well, finesse, what does it matter, the little graces that Alivia and the others had, they weren't so important, they would come with time. She was nervous, I thought; she held herself rigid like a dancer or a cadet, though she also chewed a massive wad of gum, it must have been two or three sticks, her mouth in constant motion.

There was nothing alarming for the first few hours, until 11:00 or so, when I glanced at the numbers on the monitor above my bed and saw that they were higher than they should be, my pulse around 80, my systolic pressure above 110, outside the ranges of what the doctors had said they wanted. They crept up further while I waited for the nurse, who came less frequently than the others; it seemed like I waited a long time before I could point to the monitor and ask her if the numbers weren't high, if maybe she should adjust my meds. She was standing at the foot of the bed, stiff as a rod, I thought, standing at attention, except that her mouth kept moving around her gum like a sloppy machine. She flicked her eyes quickly up and gave her head a brisk shake. Nope, she said, that's right where we like to see them, nothing to worry about. Well, I said, but shouldn't my pressure be lower, aren't they keeping it under 110? The protocols in the ward, she said, her voice a little harder, not quite affronted but firm, a little ersatz, I thought, so that it seemed to me she was pretending at confidence; the protocols in the ward are 140 over 80. Now I did feel a flare of alarm. Oh no, I said, that's not right, I'm on a different protocol, and I told her what Dr. Ferrier had said. And now it seemed to me that she stiffened further, it was her response to having made a mistake, I thought; she was decidedly hostile as she said Well, I'll have to check on that, nobody told me anything about that. Which was a real cause for alarm, I thought, that such a basic thing hadn't been communicated in the morning shuffle of voices, when the outgoing shift debriefed the incoming; how could it have fallen through the cracks, I wondered, when Dr. Ferrier had said it was the most important thing, the only thing they could do short of surgery, to keep my pressure and pulse down and give my body a chance to heal. They were hoping for the artery to stabilize itself, she had said, that was the best-case scenario. It was so easy for things to go wrong, I thought, you read about horrific mistakes in hospitals, the wrong limb sawn off or a body sewn up with something left inside, a surgical instrument, a piece of gauze; but all it took was something misheard or left unsaid, the simplest breakdown in what was really I thought a very fragile system, one person passing along the news to another.

I remembered something from my childhood then, a case my father had had, representing a family whose boy had been in a terrible car accident, I hadn't thought of it in years. He had been out driving with friends in a rural county. I could imagine the roads, the sharp turns on two lanes, death traps, I remembered my mother saying as we drove each weekend to my grandparents' farm, at each sharp turn she would say it, this is a real death trap. It was part of her constant narration as she drove, as constant as the cassette tapes she pulled out to flip from one side to the other, Juice Newton and Kenny Rogers; still those songs can place me in that car, in the backseat beside my brother, strapped in: I can conjure the smell of my mother's cigarettes, the cheap upholstery, the foam of the headrest my sister, in the front, leaned back against, exasperated as my mother narrated the dangers of the road, filling the little car with the anxiety that whitened her knuckles on the wheel. Pray that we get there, she'd say, pray we arrive safe, and later, are you praying, she'd ask, and my brother and sister would groan, Come on, they'd say, are you kidding. But I was still young enough to take her seriously, I did pray, the whole long trip from Louisville to Sonora, watching the trees stream past. They had run off the road, this boy and his friends, he had been sitting in the back but hadn't been strapped in, the car had rolled I think and he had been thrown out of it. I'm not sure of the details anymore but my father had said it was a miracle he survived, I remember that. His friends had survived, too, he was the only one who had been badly hurt. The EMTs had come, they had done everything right, they were faultless, my father always said, let's give credit where credit is due; as he told us about it he was rehearsing too, trying out lines for trial. I loved it when he did this, I felt the value of my response for him, so that it became a performance for me, too. They had assessed the boy on site, they had strapped him to a board, they had transported him to the closest hospital, a little podunk country hospital, my father had said, they couldn't handle him properly, they should have stabilized him and gotten him out as quick as they could, to Louisville or Cincinnati; but they didn't, they thought they could handle it there. He shook his head at this, sad and scornful. When they evaluated him in the ER they didn't even follow their own protocols, they didn't check him properly; they didn't check his spine, he said, even though by their own standards—he underscored this, tapping his finger on the table—by their own standards he was high risk, more than high risk. Vehicular trauma, he said, major trauma, any hospital in the world would know you check the spine. But they just had him wiggle his toes—scorn again—and assumed he was fine, even though by their own protocols he was showing signs. He counted them off, these signs, I don't remember all of them but one was that he couldn't pee, he was conscious and kept saying he needed badly to pee but he couldn't, any competent staff would have recognized that as a sign of a problem with the spine. I remembered it because it made me sympathize with him, it made me think of long drives with my father, of his exasperation when I asked him to stop, so that I didn't ask, I waited until the last possible moment, until I was in agony, only then would I tell him we had to stop so I could pee. That poor boy, I had thought. They rushed him to surgery, they operated on him for internal injuries, and maybe that was right, I don't fault them there, there's no question that they saved his life; but why didn't they check once he was stable, he asked, as if I might answer, why didn't they follow their own damn protocols and keep his spine stable until they could check it properly? It's so needless what happened to him, a sixteen-year-old boy, an athlete, a baseball player, the star of his team, paralyzed for the rest of his life because nobody thought to check his spine.

His spine had fractured, though the cord was intact, that was why he could move his toes; the cord was intact until later, maybe a day had passed, everyone thought the worst was over. His surgery had gone well and he was stable, they thought, and since he wanted to be more comfortable his father raised the bed and suddenly the boy was screaming. Can you imagine, my father said, his own father, trying to help his boy, and instead he snaps his spine, because nobody thought to check it he severs the boy's spinal cord. Paralyzed for life, he said again, a tragedy. It was months before trial but already my father was rehearsing cadences and repetitions; a trial is a performance, he would say, a great lawyer is a great actor, it's about selling a story. How many times did I hear him say that, when I was still young enough for us to talk with each other, before that terrible silence came down in adolescence, when I admired my father and he loved that I admired him. I may never get a dime on this case, he would say, I might make nothing at all, they had gone to other attorneys who turned them down because they couldn't pay, this poor family from the country, they had gone to four or five lawyers before they found me. But you don't do it for the money, he would say, you do it because it's right—though that wasn't true, I would realize later, and even then I knew he represented tobacco companies and railroads; he was a defense attorney mostly, he helped companies dodge consequences. He only took on plaintiffs for medical malpractice suits because there was a chance of a big payout; he took them on contingency and only because he thought he could win. But I believed that he was selfless when I was a child, fighting for this boy because he had been wronged, it made him a hero to me. I remembered his triumph, weeks later, after a deposition where he got an ER nurse to admit that she had made a mistake. You have to be a psychologist, too, he would say, not just an actor but a psychologist; when you work a witness you have to find their weak spot, you have to circle and circle until you see the chink in the armor. He had played on her sense of guilt, on her grief for the boy; he had gotten her to admit that she had seen the signs of injury, that she had meant to flag them, to tell the surgeon. But you have to understand, she had said, it was chaos, we had four boys there, they had all come in by ambulance, we were trying to process them, to triage. And my father was all understanding now, having brought her this far, anyone would understand, of course; but did she agree now that it was a mistake, would it be fair to say that she should have done something differently, that everything might have been otherwise, and she said yes. On the record, my father said to me, under oath; his cheeks were flushed, triumph had lifted him up and up. She said yes and my father retreated with his prize, I want to thank you for your candor, he told her.

All because of a break in the chain of communication, he would say in his summation, which was what made me remember it now; all because a nurse didn't pass along essential information, all because of human error. It was a repeated point, a theme of his argument: it would have been so easy to avoid a tragedy if they had just followed their own rules. He won that case—he always won his cases, or almost always. He got a big judgment, more money than that family had ever seen, he said, which meant the boy could get the best care, all the accommodations he needed, including the specially equipped car he was driving years later, when he got drunk and went out on those little winding roads and wrecked the car and died. He was twenty-five. I learned this from my youngest sister, G, I wasn't speaking to my father by that point, he had cut me off, disowned me. But I remembered the photograph he had put in his office after the trial, in which he knelt next to a skinny blond boy in a wheelchair, beaming, the father and mother standing behind. They were all smiling but my father wore his face of fresh triumph, they had just learned the judgment; the boy and his parents must have felt triumph, too, thinking of how their lives would change.

Everything had a cause, I thought. That boy might have recovered from the accident, might have been frightened or chastened by it, might have lived a whole life in his whole body, except that someone made a mistake, not even necessarily a catastrophic mistake. He could move his legs, she must have thought; in nine cases out of ten it would have made no difference that she had noticed something and failed to share it, that the chain of communication had snapped. When I arrived at the hospital I had felt the relief of being a patient, of having handed myself over to others; I remembered the faith I had placed in them, the sense that the last thing in the world I had to be was vigilant. I was vigilant now, watching the numbers creep higher, my pulse well above 80 now, my systolic pressure 118. She was taking her time, I thought, surely ten or fifteen minutes had passed. I needed to relax, I could feel my anxiety rising, which would only make my pressure rise too. I took a deep breath, then another; I tried to count to four as I inhaled, something I did sometimes when I couldn't sleep, I had read that it helped you relax. But it had never worked for me, and it didn't work now. I watched the numbers climb over the next ten minutes, until the systolic pressure, the number on top, reached 130 and the monitor started emitting a high chime every fifteen seconds, some kind of alarm, surely the nurse would come soon. But she didn't come. It had been at least half an hour now, longer than any of the other nurses had gone without checking in. Though I had to twist my head up awkwardly to see it I couldn't take my eyes off the screen. I imagined the blood in the artery where the tear was still fresh, pressing against the wall where it was weak, where it was bulging already; I remembered what I had seen online somewhere, that if the artery ruptured there was no hope, you died within a minute, even if you were already in the hospital there was no chance of survival (the blown aorta pelting out blood), no hope at all. I was panicked now, I searched by the side of the bed where the wand with the call button had fallen. I had barely used it; I shifted the bed in the morning and at night but otherwise I hadn't needed it, so that once I had pulled it up by its cord it took me a moment to find the right button, on the bottom left, the one marked with a red cross. Even as I watched my pressure climb past 135 I hesitated before pressing it, feeling the old dread of being trouble, but finally I did; I closed my eyes and held it a full second before I let go. And still she didn't come.

Five minutes passed, then ten. I texted L, who would arrive soon, probably he had arrived already, he came early each day to be near the front of the line. There's a bad nurse today, I wrote, my pressure is very high, I told him that I was scared. I regretted sending it almost at once, it would make him panic too, and without anything he could do about it. I wrote my sister G, who was good in a crisis, with any problem really, confronting it head on; I could almost see her square her shoulders as I sent the text, she would start strategizing right away, thinking of options, possibilities. This annoyed me sometimes: my approach to a problem was often to wallow in it, I didn't want to solve it all at once, I wanted to think about it, to formulate it in various ways, sometimes all I wanted was to talk about it; I thought leaping at a solution just created more problems, often enough, which drove her nuts, we drove each other nuts. But now I wanted her to solve the problem, I wished she were there with me, she would have taken charge of things. Can someone advocate for you, she wrote back, but no one could, there was just L, as lost as I was, maybe if I could have more visitors there would be someone; and I thought again of the solitude of the place, the way the pandemic locked us up in our rooms alone. You have to tell

someone, L wrote back, you have to report it, which wasn't helpful either; and then he wrote be calm, the most important thing
is you have to be calm. I put my phone down. My pulse was 90
now, my systolic pressure 140, I pressed the button again and
then again. Finally she came in, arms loaded again with medications, which she dumped on the counter before stepping to the
monitor to silence the alarm. I don't understand, I said, why did
it take so long, my pressure is too high, I know it's not what my
doctors want. She was tense, churning her gum in her mouth;
she crammed it to one side to speak. We do have other patients,
she said, openly hostile now, there are other people we have to
take care of, and a lot of them are sicker than you. Patients, I
thought, plural, when I knew she only had one besides me, that
was what Alivia had told me; the point of the ICU was that each
nurse only had two patients. But maybe they were short-staffed,
I thought, maybe she was telling the truth and they were spread
thin. The news was full of that, nurses and doctors and technicians who were leaving their jobs, burned out by the pandemic,
by the sheer number of patients and the horror of the deaths.
Just a few months before there were more bodies than could be
processed, so that Twitter was full of terrible images, black bags
loaded into cold trucks outside hospitals; it was terrible to see, it
punctured all one's pieties to see people treated like blunt matter, like trash. They were exhausted by their jobs and exhausted
too by attacks, by people who argued that the whole thing was
a hoax, the virus, the deaths, the images, all of it engineered to
pave the way for fascism, they said, for the authoritarian state.
Twitter was full of that too, everyone calling everyone a fascist,
so that the word meant nothing—which was the real danger, I
thought, words that meant nothing, the way any word could

be made to mean nothing; it was a way of erasing reality, or of placing reality beyond our grasp, real facts, real values, it was a tyranny of meaninglessness. Nurses and doctors, hospitals, were drawn into it; there was a vast conspiracy to falsify infection rates and deaths, the story went, and they were part of it, so that not only did they face a wave of illness and death the likes of which they had never seen, but half the country insisted it didn't exist, that they were lying or exaggerating, inventing numbers or mischaracterizing deaths.

Of course they were quitting in droves. Surely that was why she was here, fresh out of college, the ink hardly dry on her diploma, in the cardiovascular ICU without any supervision, or any I could see, letting my pressure mount higher and higher. Anyway, she went on, they want us to switch out your meds, and pharmacy had to approve the change, and that takes time. The monitor started chirping again and she came near to silence it, standing beside the bed where I could see her ID badge, her name and the photo that showed her face without mask or visor. Her blond hair hung loose around her shoulders and on her face there was a tremendous smile, full voltage, an American smile, a smile of triumph, I thought, a smile of that Midwestern confidence and cheer I found so odious, a pernicious smile, privileged and coddled, a smile that had never known hardship or fear, a smile of utter complacent harmony with its world, a smile I had always hated. It was the smile of the enemy, I thought, of course there was animosity between us, instinctive on either side, unearned; that smile was the flag of the enemy's army, the army of those at peace with the world. Or it was the smile of a girl excited for her first day of work, I told myself, for Christ's sake. She was at the titration machine now, opening the front panel to pull out the half-deflated bags, then replacing them with new ones. She struggled with the envelopes of new tubing, she had trouble getting them open, and then the front panel wouldn't close. She tried shutting it several times, resituating the bags, she tried forcing it, making little noises of frustration. For fuck's sake, I thought. She left without saying anything more, leaving the hatch unlatched, the tubing disconnected from the ports on my arms, so that I was getting no medication at all; she had disconnected everything, the antibiotics as well as the pressure meds, and who knew how long she would be gone. There was no point to pressing the call button again, there was nothing at all I could do, nothing except be frightened; as my pressure reached 145 I felt a total helplessness. G texted me again, she had tried to call but they wouldn't speak to her, I had to authorize them to share my medical information, apparently it wasn't enough that she was my emergency contact.

L arrived then, as the machine began sounding its alarm again; he looked at the monitor and I could see his eyes widen. But before he could say anything the nurse came back, accompanied by a man I recognized, the male nurse who had been at the transfer the night I arrived, ready to help lift me into the bed. He greeted me, calm, at ease, as he reached up to silence the alarm and as L positioned himself beside me, taking my hand and speaking softly in Spanish, urging me to calm down, to breathe. I'm here, he said, I love you. The new nurse was brisk and confident, he and my nurse were murmuring to each other. Oh, he said, taking out the bags and resituating them, you just, and then he clicked the compartment shut. It must have been humiliating for her, having to bring in help; I felt sorry for her again and also enraged at her incompetence. The male nurse looked at me then, while my nurse was connecting the tubes to my ports, he looked at me and at L holding my hand, and then at the monitor. Those are going to come down, he said, meaning the numbers on the screen, don't worry, we'll get them back where they need to be. I nodded but didn't say anything, I didn't trust myself to speak, I squeezed L's hand. He left then, the male nurse, and my nurse stepped back and asked, tight-lipped, if I needed anything else. I shook my head. Once she left I put L's hand to my mouth. I'm so scared, I said to him, she's terrible and there's nothing I can do. Be calm, he said, speaking English now, be calm, be tranquil, I'm here. Tranquilo, he repeated, and he bent to put his arms around me; la medicina, he said, and I could feel myself relax as I took deep breaths, my lips at his neck. He straightened and looked at the monitor again. It's working, he said, it's coming down, and as my pressure lowered I felt my anger deflate, too, at least for a moment, my anger but not really my fear. I had never realized how important they were, nurses, I mean, how really they made the difference between life and death; just six hours had been enough for my pressure to spike, and there were six hours left on her shift, who knew what else could go wrong. Don't worry, L said, stay calm, but also he said again that I had to report it, that they had to know there was a problem, and I agreed with him but didn't know who to talk to or how to go about it. L didn't sit down, he stood by the bed with my hand in his as he told me that his department chair had granted his request to teach remotely, as he passed along greetings from his family, from his colleagues, the few that I knew, they are all thinking about you, he said.

I want to speak to someone, I said to the nurse when she came back, twenty or thirty minutes later. I want to talk to your supervisor, I want to talk to the head nurse. L had sat down in the armchair, leaning forward to talk to me; I didn't want to ask for the plastic chair we had used on his earlier visits. He stood up now to take my hand again. The nurse had laid supplies out on the counter but now she turned, still again, drawing herself up. And what do you want to talk to her about, she asked. I took a breath. About the quality of the care I'm receiving, I said, hearing my voice brittle in the room, I hated the way it sounded. She hesitated a moment, as if she were going to ask something more and thought better of it. Okay, she said finally, and turned again and left, the packages she had placed on the counter unopened. I feel like my stepmother, I said to L, and I told him about visiting the hospital after she had had G, a difficult labor and finally an emergency cesarean, after which she was imperious in her hospital room; I cringed as she spoke to her nurses, hectoring them, making demands. I had thought she was horrible, ridiculous. But I was conditioned to think that by then, from the start really; I thought of her as the woman who split up my parents and who then was terrible to us, the children from my father's first marriage. She couldn't wait to have children of her own, whom she christened my father's new family, his own children as opposed to the children he shared with my mother. Of course I hated her by then, and so it didn't occur to me that she might be frightened, that she was bewildered or in pain; the cesarean was unexpected, and it must have been terrifying, as terrible as the scar that she would show to me later, livid on her abdomen, a thick vertical line. I didn't think of any of that then, when my father took me to her room and drew me into a conspiracy by pointing to a handwritten sign taped on the door that read BITCH in capital letters, a memory I question now, it seems implausible but there it is; I can see the heavy black lines as clearly as I can hear the noise of amusement my father made before knocking lightly and opening the door. I still don't know how to hear it, whether he was pleased with my stepmother's self-assertion, her strength of spirit, or whether by then he agreed with whichever nurse had put it there. It was a word I had heard him use often enough in the fights they had so frequently, had had from the very beginning, so that one household was indistinguishable from the other and I wondered why he had left the first for the second. I hated feeling like her, I said to L, I didn't want to be like her.

We only waited a few minutes before the head nurse arrived, alone, without the nurse who was attending me. It wasn't the woman I had met before, Lara or Laura; this woman was younger, maybe my age, tall and thin and as blond as the nurse I was complaining about. She introduced herself, I hear you're having a hard day, she said, what's going on? And I told her, the rising pressure, the slow response; I didn't understand, I said, how could there be such long delays. Well, she said, cutting me off, I want you to know that the rising pressure didn't have anything to do with her. That was an order from the doctors, they swapped out one of your IV pressure meds for a pill, and it's a tricky thing, blood pressure always is, there's always trial and error. Nobody said anything about that to me, I said, why wasn't I told? She looked a little flustered. Well, she said, I'm not sure, usually the nurse would go over your meds—which was true of Alivia and the others, but the nurse that morning had just handed me the little paper cups of pills. And who made the decision, I asked her, was it Dr. Ferrier, and she said no, it was the ICU doctors who ordered the change. Did Dr. Ferrier approve it, I asked, and she said no again, stiffening a little, I thought. The ICU team handles your pressure, she said, that's the responsibility of our doctors, they make those decisions. I need you to have faith in us, she said, I know you're concerned but these hiccups are normal, it's important not to overreact.

I bristled at her tone, which was paternalistic, condescending, a tone I recognized. It was the tone my sister had used—not G but my older sister, my parents' first child, my full sister, though I hated that term since of all my siblings I was closest with G. It was the tone she had used with me early in the pandemic, that terrifying spring when it was becoming clear how serious the virus was, how catastrophic in Italy and Spain; the CDC had just that morning recommended that senior citizens should isolate in their homes. I had called my mother to make sure she had seen the news, and she told me that she was going out to dinner that evening with my sister and her family, to celebrate my niece's birthday at a restaurant they loved, a popular restaurant, always packed with people. My sister had insisted it wasn't dangerous, urging my mother to go; and I want to be there, my mother said when I protested, it's your niece's sixteenth birthday, I would hate to miss it. You'd hate to miss it, I said, exasperated, and I reminded her of all the risks: she had asthma, high blood pressure, she was in her seventies; this isn't a joke, I said, please, you have to be careful. Well, she said, I guess she would know, meaning my sister, who was a nurse though she hadn't tended patients for years, she worked for an insurance company now, at least I think that's what she does; I'm sure she wouldn't have invited me if it wasn't safe, my mother said. I called my sister then, for the first time in months, we've never been close and were all but estranged as adults; maybe once a year I called or texted, on Christmas or her birthday, I kept my distance from most of my family and certainly from her. I could hear her surprise when she answered. Hello stranger, she said, but I cut her off before she could say more. Please tell her not to go, I said, what are you thinking, it's so dangerous, how can you invite her out to a restaurant. You need to calm down, she said, putting on a tone of authority, condescending, cloying; I understand that you're frightened but you're overreacting, she said, and then she launched into a litany of talking points from conversative media. I knew her politics had drifted rightward but I was amazed to hear her echo so exactly the arguments from Fox News, that the virus wasn't so dangerous, that it was exaggerated by the media; and when I told her that was bullshit, that L's friends and family were seeing it firsthand, she scoffed. Don't you understand that they have a different lifestyle in Europe, she said, that the population density is greater, even if what they say is happening there is true it won't be like that here. Are you out of your mind, I said. I know you don't have medical training, she went on, I know all this is hard to understand, I need you to trust that I understand it better than you do. If you do this, I said to her, and if our mother gets sick, I will never forgive you, at which her composure broke; How dare you, she started to say. I hung up before she could say more, I hadn't spoken to her since. I called my mother again and pleaded until finally she agreed not to go, and the next day the governor announced he was closing all the restaurants in the state.

Fuck you, I thought, as the head nurse made her promises, aiming it too at the younger nurse, wherever she was in the ward, fuck you, fuck you. We want to get you out of here, she went on in a lighter tone, we need to get you on oral meds so you can move out of the ICU; you want to get home and we need the space for sicker patients. Sicker patients, I said. I don't mean you're not sick, she hurried to say, but I cut her off. So you're rushing to get me out of the ICU—I didn't mean, she tried to cut in, but I kept speaking; you're rushing to get me out, but the only thing keeping me from being a sicker patient is the quality of the care I receive. And this is when I felt myself become lawyerly, I drew myself up, not so much physically as in my speech, I gathered all the force I could. Something went wrong this morning, I said, your nurse didn't know the most basic information about my care; and I ask myself now, I said, oracular, not for nothing was I my father's son (though I wasn't his son, he had renounced me as his son), I ask myself whether your lack of urgency was communicated to her, whether that's why my care today has been so poor, so grossly incompetent, I said, though I knew I would be ashamed later. I was already ashamed of the words I was using, the bullying words, I'm sure that's why you assigned me someone with so little experience, three months out of college, and here the nurse drew in a breath but again I didn't let her speak, I squeezed L's hand more tightly and went on. I shouldn't have to be so vigilant, I said, I shouldn't have to watch those numbers, I pointed at the screen with my free hand. But if I receive such bad care I will become one of your sicker patients, I said, I could die—and here my voice caught, I was humiliated to find myself in tears. I'm scared, I said, I feel so scared, I don't feel safe, and L let go of my hand to put his hand on my shoulder. Be calm, he said, as I used both my hands to wipe my face. I'm sorry, I said. No, the nurse said; she had been ready to argue with me, she had girded herself for battle but now there was no need, I had defeated myself. I want you to know that I've heard everything you said, I want you to know that you *are* safe, we'll keep you that way. But I didn't believe her, I waved my hand dismissively. Well, she said, you don't need to worry about anything, your numbers are looking good. I'll keep an eye on them, too, I'll check back a little later. But that was a lie, I didn't see her again, not even when, shortly after L left, I told the younger nurse I felt strange, and then I began to feel very cold, I began to tremble. My teeth were chattering so much I could barely speak, I was trembling violently but she just looked at me coldly and said That can happen when you let yourself get anxious, you need to calm down. I don't think this is anxiety, I said, but she offered nothing more, and when I asked her for a blanket—I'm so cold, I kept saying—she told me I had to wait, she had other things to do first, I had to be patient. It would have taken a second to snatch a blanket from the heated cabinet where they kept them; instead I lay shivering for twenty minutes before finally she brought me one. She refused to take my temperature, insisting it wasn't the right time, protocol only required it every four hours; when finally the night nurse took over it was 103. I flared in anger, why hadn't the nurse taken it earlier, I asked the night nurse, who was kind, she had been my nurse the night before and I liked her. She hesitated before saying that she didn't know.

I told Alivia all of this on the way down to the CT. I'm sure that's why this is happening, I said, because she let my pressure get so high. Alivia clicked her tongue. That sounds really scary, she said, I'm so sorry that happened. But the best thing you can do right now is relax, try to think of happy things. Think of L, she said, it won't be too long before he comes in, or just enjoy the view, it's been a while since you've gotten out of the ward. We had left almost immediately; Alivia had barely returned with the pain pill when her phone pinged and she started getting me ready to go. She removed the little module from the monitor and set it beside me on the bed; she pulled up the guardrails; she handed me a surgical mask to wear outside my room. That was fast, I said, remembering how long I had waited in the ER. You get priority this morning, she said, it's your lucky day. She had some trouble wheeling me out of the room; the bed turned more easily than she expected, she knocked me against the doorframe. Sorry, she said, I promise I'm a good driver, don't worry, and I laughed. The pain was receding already; it had only ever been an echo of the original pain, the crippling pain, and now both it and my worry ebbed, as the extra oxy crept over me. You ready, she asked me as she pressed the button to open the doors from the ward, and then, as she pushed me through, the big wide world, she said. We emerged into a kind of atrium, a bright and noisy space, a square tower with a walkway along each side. The noise came from below, the ground level, where people must have been milling about; we were on the fourth or fifth floor, not quite at the top.

The walkway was empty, we didn't pass anyone as Alivia pushed me along the sides of the tower. It was only when we were directly across from where we had started that I saw a small man emerge from the same door we had used, walking quickly but in a contained way, holding one of his arms bent at his chest. He was a priest, I realized when I saw his white collar, he must have been making rounds in the ICU, visiting parishioners, his Bible tucked under his arm—or maybe not parishioners, maybe strangers who had requested the pastoral visit I had turned down in the ER. I was surprised by the yearning I felt when I saw him now, yearning I wasn't sure for what. He was older, sixty or so, with an expression that wasn't kind exactly but seemed capable of kindness; he seemed grave, worried maybe, concerned. Maybe he had just visited a serious case, somebody who wouldn't get to go home, as I still hoped to, whatever setback I had suffered that morning. Maybe it was his gravity I wanted, maybe I wanted to talk with someone whose job wasn't to fix what had gone wrong in my body, to deflect my worry, to assure me I would get well; maybe I wanted someone who would sit with me and let me contemplate the possibility that I wouldn't, the possibility of long debility, the possibility of death; someone for whom that wouldn't indicate failure, of their own abilities, of technology or science, someone whose job it was to contemplate death. Which is one thing priests do, I guess, the main benefit of religion: that it faces death and finitude, that it doesn't imagine death as something we can defeat or eternally delay, not in our human lives; that it doesn't urge us to fantasize some endless material futurity, that American dream. Of course the priest would want to talk about heaven and judgment, that other horizonlessness I couldn't believe in, even when I was young and had made an effort to believe, talking to that priest I had liked in Boston, sitting in his little room. I didn't believe the promises he made, or that his system made, though often enough I thought that if I could just slightly alter the terms, if instead of God I could think beauty, or art, it might make sense; not God that guaranteed some source or ground of meaning but art; not God that offered a primal knot of revelation to worry at through human time but art; the source of plentitude art; the loaves and fishes, the beatitudinal promise—for months it seemed to me that could work. I could even imagine that I was mistaken, maybe, that at some point I would realize behind art stood God, the gates would swing open, the angel step aside; as a hypothetical for a long time I thought I could stomach it. And then I couldn't.

The priest turned into the first ward after ours, through a door we had passed, he *was* making rounds, I thought; and then Alivia pushed through the door directly opposite the ICU. It's so annoying, she said as she steered me down a short white corridor to the elevator. The CT is directly below the ICU, it's usually a quick trip, but they've closed off that elevator for construction. So now we have to go all the way across to this elevator, and then cross again all the way back. The doors opened and she pushed me inside. And the worst part, she went on, is that this elevator doesn't go all the way to the lower level, so we have to cross over on the ground floor, through all those people. Are you covered up, she asked me, and I tucked the edges of the sheet under my thighs. I guess that's as good as it gets, I said, and she made a sympathetic sound. We passed through the open space, the center of the atrium, where groups of hospital personnel and people in street clothes, visitors and outpatients, milled about. Take a breath, Alivia said, the worst part is coming up. After another short corridor we passed through the café, a little alcove jammed with people, a glass case of pastries and behind it two baristas making drinks. People were waiting in line, or waiting for their orders, or pulling their masks down beneath their chins to sip their drinks. They made way for us, staring at me and then looking away; I was a spectacle, a little mobile disaster, of course their eyes were drawn to me, I resented it but also I understood. I held my breath until we had passed through.

The walls in the ICU were bare, everything on them was functional, charts and protocols; or everything except a glass case I had noticed on our daily walks around the ward, three shelves of photos in cheap drugstore frames, a gallery of Nurses of the Month. I had scanned them and seen Alivia wasn't there and felt affronted on her behalf. But in the public areas there was art on the walls, bright geometric abstractions or gauzy photos of Iowa scenes: an old barn, the sun setting behind it, fields of corn. One showed a stretch of prairie in bloom, though there wasn't a prairie anymore, not really. It was the most devastated ecosystem in the world, I had read somewhere early in my time here, replaced by fields of soybean and corn, by pasture for cattle, the checkered landscape that was so beautiful as the plane descended coming home, that made my heart lift with its beauty, as the sight of farmland always had, even in childhood. That landscape was actually devastation, I knew, my heart lifted at devastation, saw beauty in devastation, even now, when I knew it for what it was; and I thought of Walter Benjamin, what he says somewhere about our taking aesthetic pleasure in our own destruction. He was talking about fascism, I think, or maybe the First World War, I should look it up; I think he says something about that kind of pleasure being a degradation of the spirit, the final degradation, maybe, though I'm not sure that's true. It seems to me maybe it's not degradation so much as fulfillment, the end of some design flaw, some faulty wiring drawing a straight line from the first human who found beauty in fire to the images that popped up online every few months or so, tourists holding shopping bags aloft as they ford waist-high waters in Venice, laughing, men playing golf as behind them forests burn. The line of our rapacity, I thought, which when I was a kid I had imagined reparable, an accident of ideology, capitalism, colonialism, etc.; but now I feared we would never fix it, that it was ingrained, not the consequence of ideologies but their cause. The moment

Homo sapiens appears in the fossil record the great fauna die out, I had read, from the moment we came into being we were bent on extinction. And that was another benefit of religion, I thought, the recognition of primal fault, that death isn't just something that happens to us but something we carry within us, our own deaths and the deaths of others, of worlds, the marvel is we have lasted so long. I thought all that was true and also I mistrusted it, it was despairful but there was a kind of comfort in it, everything inevitable, out of our hands, a question of wiring; it made us responsible and also blameless, both at once.

Would you look at those, Alivia said then, they must have just put them up. We had reached the elevator that would take us down for the scan, she had pressed the call button and then angled the bed to face a dozen or so drawings mounted to the wall, children's drawings, some barely more than crayon scribbles, others with recognizable shapes: a nurse next to a bed, a house, a solitary cat with a snaking tail. They put them up every month or so, Alivia said, all around the hospital, drawings by child patients, I love to see them. I did too, I thought as the elevator doors opened and she pushed me through, they were better than the other art we had passed. At least now they were letting both parents stay with their kids again, Alivia said, at the start of the pandemic only one could visit each day. It broke my heart to think of that, she said. It's hard for everybody, all these restrictions, it's hard for you too. But those poor kids, can you imagine.

She placed her hand on my chest when I tried to get up a moment later, after she had parked the bed in the small room, hardly bigger than the CT scanner at its center. Hold on, she said, you just sit tight. There were two people in the room with us, a woman wiping the scanner's long slab with disinfectant and a man fiddling with something around the side of the machine; another woman sat behind the glass pane of the control booth. Until we know what's going on we're not taking any chances, Alivia said, I don't want you to get up. The man had finished whatever he was doing, he signaled to the woman in the booth, and then, once Alivia had lowered the rails and locked the wheels of my bed, they took position on all four sides of the bed, one of the women reaching over the slab to my left, the man at my head. Wait, I started to say as they prepared to lift me, I can—but Alivia cut me off. Just relax, she said, we've got it, just relax, and each of them grabbed the sheet with both hands. Alivia counted to three while I closed my eyes, mortified, too much weight. But they didn't have any problem, I was lifted very slightly up, shifted very slightly to the side. See, Alivia said, easy peasy, and then one of the women placed a blanket over my legs—the room was cold, colder than the ICU—and the man, who was young and thin, in his twenties, a short beard visible around his surgical mask, took my arm to examine my IVs. Great, he said, one of these will work fine. We're giving you a higher dose of the contrast this time, he explained, because of where the tear is, we want to get the clearest image we can, and he told me I would feel warm; sometimes people even feel like they're wetting themselves, he said, don't worry, it's normal. He asked me to lift my arms above my head. Is that comfortable for you, he asked, and I said it was. While he was connecting the tubing—there was a titration machine on the side of the scanner, that's what he had been adjusting when we came in— the woman put a cushion under my knees, and Alivia arranged the other tubes and wires, checking that nothing would catch as I was drawn in and out of the machine. I closed my eyes again, feeling them industrious around me, I tried to be as passive as I could. You okay, the woman asked, concerned, and I opened my eyes and said I was. It only took them a minute or two to get everything situated, they were efficient, a team, and then they retreated into the booth.

There was a moment of silence, in which I heard my phone buzz with a text, it was on the bed, out of reach, and then again before there was a click and a voice—one of the women in the booth—told me to breathe deeply and hold. It was L probably, I thought, I hadn't texted him anything about the morning's drama but he checked in often; or my mother, whom I had finally called over the weekend and who had texted constantly since. The machine drew me in, clicking and buzzing, and then ejected me again, splayed with my hands above my head, like Saint Sebastian, I thought, which might have made me laugh if I hadn't been holding my breath, trying to be as still as possible. The voice told me to relax, to breathe normally. She had reacted as I expected her to, my mother, even though I began by saying that I was stable, that I wasn't in immediate danger; I couldn't even say that much before she was interrupting me to ask questions, which weren't questions at first but expressions of shock. What, she said, and then What do you mean, and then But I don't understand, but how, and then she was in tears, through which brokenly she said But all my children, all my children have *always* been healthy, emphasizing the always, as though defending herself, or as though protesting; I've always been so lucky with my children, she went on, at which I bristled, I didn't want to think of my life as an element of her good fortune. But why did you wait so long to tell me, she asked. I didn't want to worry her, I said, I wanted to wait until things were clearer, until there was something to say, some concrete news. Though there wasn't, I realized as she started to ask real questions, making me repeat myself so she could write everything down, which was what she always did, whenever I had news, and I knew that over the next days she would tell everyone, all her family and friends. I remembered hearing her do this as a child, the hours she spent on the phone after work, telling the same stories, in the same words almost, checking her notes, until she had a script she would rehearse, a little drama, it drove me crazy to hear it again and again.

I'm coming up there, she said suddenly, changing tack, and she called to her husband, a man I barely knew, though I liked him, after decades of loneliness he had made my mother happy in a way I had never seen; all I needed to know about him was that, that he made her happy and treated her well. Like a queen, she would say, he treats me like a queen, and she would laugh in a girlish way that was new to her, too. He was God's gift to her, she always said, it had been God's plan, after so much hardship, after my father abandoned her, which she also always said, in those words; after years of working multiple jobs to raise three children, as a single mother, she would say, I know I wasn't perfect but I did the best I could; after so many years of no money and no man—there were men but they were terrible, mostly, she made a face whenever she mentioned them, I dodged a bullet, she would say, thank God; after years in which I worried about her solitude and sadness, years when my brother and I would confer about what we should do, all of it was redeemed when she met the man that she would marry. It was all worth it to get here, she said, it all turned out just how it was supposed to. She called to him now, telling him to get the car ready, they were driving to

Iowa City that minute, she said, my baby—and she started crying again, my baby is in the ICU, my youngest boy. You will not,
I said, you absolutely will not come here. They hadn't traveled
anywhere for months. They drove once a week to the grocery, in
the early morning, masked and gloved, at an hour that was reserved for senior citizens; my mother did the shopping while her
husband stayed in the car; she wiped down every container with
bleach; she wore gloves to open their mail; she took every precaution. I don't care, she said now, I want to see you, I want to
be with my son. But she couldn't be with me, I told her, I could
only have one visitor a day, if she came it would mean not seeing
L. This made her relent, the thought of L, whom she loved. He
loved her too, es estupenda, he would say, she's wonderful, and
I would agree that she was, especially when you couldn't understand what she was saying, I would laugh, when thanks to her
accent every second word was lost, that would make her easier to
take. Poor L, my mother said now, he must be worried out of
his mind. He's the son I was meant to have, she said then, as she
did every time she mentioned L. You are the best thing that's
ever happened to my son, she said the first time she visited our
house, after the months of renovations; standing in our home she
had repeated it, holding both his hands in hers, you are the best
thing that has ever happened to my son, and then she hugged
him, swaying back and forth, and L was charmed and moved and
a little dazed, I think. Her love for L was genuine, and also it
was her way of showing how far she had come, from the woman
who had told me decades before how much she hoped it wasn't
true that I was gay, because it was a sin, because it would mean
a lifetime of loneliness, it would cut me off from the joys of life.
But even as she said this she also said, always, that she loved me,

that I was her son, which was the difference between her and my father, when she took me in after he severed all contact with me: that she said she loved me and that I believed it. It allowed her slowly over the years to change her mind, to unlearn what she had believed, and allowed me to forgive her, and allowed us in turn to arrive here, with L in her arms, her happiness, melodramatic and overwrought, a blessing that filled our house.

Have you told your siblings, she had asked when I called her from the ICU, it was the phrase she always used, your siblings, she meant my older sister and brother, her children, and I said I hadn't. I hadn't spoken to my older sister since our fight, months before, and my brother and I were hardly in touch, we had been close at times but not now, not for years. You have to call them, she said, they'll want to know. And your sister a nurse, she went on, your sister can talk to the doctors, she can make sure they're doing everything they should, I know she would want to help. My mother would call them as soon as she hung up, I knew, they would be the first to hear the news that would become a story, a performance; she would call all our relatives, all her friends, so that I imagined it rippling out through little capillaries in the air. I would get emails and Facebook messages; the privacy of what had happened would be broken, which was another reason I had waited to call my mother, the most important reason.

A door opened then and the young man was beside me, asking if I was okay. Oh sure, I said, no worries. The pain had faded to a dull ache around my groin, I could mostly ignore it, thanks to the oxy, I was basking in bienestar. I'll start the contrast then, he said, and reminded me what I would feel as he pressed a button on the machine and then retreated to the booth. The scanner came back to life, shuddering a little, and then the voice told me again to take a deep breath and hold, and the tray slid forward. I felt the contrast, a wave of liquid warmth that flooded my chest and then my groin, where it pooled, building to an intensity that was almost scalding, that wasn't pain exactly but was almost too intense to bear. It reminded me of poppers, the warmth and rush hitting my body instead of my brain; there was the same sense of something inflating, of a membrane growing taut. But there wasn't anything sexual about it; nothing had been sexual, not since the pain had started. Usually I couldn't go an hour without thinking of sex, without something turning me on, ever since I was a kid; I had never really grown out of the rampant horniness of adolescence, which sometimes I thought of as an affliction and sometimes as a point of pride. When they moved me into the ICU, when it became clear how complete the surveillance would be, my first thought was that it would be impossible to jerk off. In thirty years I had hardly gone a day without it, even if I was sick or depressed or exhausted or whatever else, probably I could count on the fingers of one hand the days in all those years; and now I would have to, for some unspecified time it would be impossible. But in fact I was completely free of desire, it was like a switch had been flipped; even if I thought of things that never failed to turn me on, memories or fantasies, it was like some circuitry had been snipped, so that the whole elaborate imperious vital mechanism, sometimes it had seemed like the seat of my consciousness, was a dead machine. I didn't know whether it was a consequence of what had happened, the tear or the infection, if there was an infection, or the antibiotics that were carpet-bombing my system, or the medicine to bring down my blood pressure, beta-blockers they had already told me I would be taking for the rest of my life; so that maybe for the rest of my life I would be cut off from desire, maybe I would never get hard again. It was impossible to imagine, a contradiction of some necessary aspect of my being; I would be a different person entirely, a prospect I considered with a mixture of panic and relief, would I even be recognizable to myself, who would I be.

Back in my room, when Alivia had swung the bed into place and locked the wheels, before she reconnected me to the monitor, I told her I needed to use the bathroom. Okay, she said, one sec, and she crossed the room to the cabinets, retrieving from a lower drawer a shallow blue plastic basin wrapped in plastic. Have you used one of these before, she asked. Alivia, I said, I am not going to use a bedpan. She laughed. It's no big deal, she said, it'll feel a little weird at first but you'll get used to it. But the thought filled me with horror. Really, I said, I can't, the bathroom is right there, I gestured to it, it's two steps away. Look, she said, we take bed rest pretty seriously, you don't need to be so squeamish about it. But I was squeamish, and again I felt like squeamishness was all I had, my connection to the world I knew; Alivia handling basins of my shit would mean entering a different world altogether. You were like this about the suppository, too, she said, and that wasn't a big deal, remember? Which was true, in the evening of the first day with her, when the laxative and stool softeners still hadn't worked as shift change approached, she gave me an ultimatum: either a suppository before she left, or the night nurse would give me an enema. So I gritted my teeth and did as she asked, lowering my underwear and turning on my side, closing my eyes at the shame of it. But there wasn't any shame, really, she lifted one buttock and I felt her gloved hand insert the capsule, which must have been lubricated, it slid in easily, and almost before I could register it her other hand was tugging on my raised hip to turn me back. Those things work pretty fast, she had said, call me when you need to go and I'll come right back. She was right, it was only ten or fifteen minutes before I pressed the button on the little wand beside the bed, the only time I had used it until the terrible day with the incompetent nurse, I pressed it twice in quick succession as I felt the first cramps. Alivia rushed in, I told you, she said, it comes on fast, and she helped me out of the bed and into the bathroom. Be a little careful, she said, it's important you don't strain, and then I had barely lifted the gown and gathered it around my waist like a skirt, before everything rushed out, scalding and liquid, and the intensity of the relief I felt made me realize how much I had been suffering. I hadn't been able to shit since the tear happened, even though I felt bloated and full and like shitting would have helped; for several days it had been impossible, and as I emptied myself finally—that was what it felt like, like opening a corked vessel and emptying it out—I realized how crucial to humanness that was, too, being able to shit. The whole metaphysical edifice, love and artmaking and thought, poetry and painting, the possibility of God, all of it rested on brute mechanism, on the body taking things in and processing them and voiding what it couldn't use. That was what I was protecting, that edifice, when I said to Alivia that I was sorry, I wouldn't do it. I knew I was being ridiculous, but there it is, I said, I'm ridiculous, I would walk two steps to the bathroom, I wouldn't shit in a pan. You need to get over yourself, she said, not quite sternly, you need to let me do my job. But she put the bedpan back, still in its plastic bag. At least let me bring the urinal to the bed, she said, you don't need to walk to the bathroom for that, you can use it here and just hang it by the bed for me to empty. That I could do, I said.

L was there when Dr. Ferrier arrived. I didn't tell him what had happened until he was at my bedside; I didn't want him to worry when there was nothing to be done, while we were still waiting for real information. Maybe the pain meant nothing, maybe everything was fine. He was carrying a plastic shopping bag, a pair of underwear inside; each day he brought a fresh pair, it gave him something to do, washing them and folding them, taking away each day the one I had worn. I had told him that he didn't need to, he could bring several at a time and leave them, there was a drawer where Alivia could store them. Maybe you will come home tomorrow, he said each time, as if bringing multiple pairs would be a betrayal of hope. And he liked doing it, I realized, it was a way to take care of me when he couldn't take care of me; and I liked it too, each morning when Alivia handed them to me I liked knowing he had washed and folded them for me just the day before, they were a kind of contact between us. I was surprised by how much I missed him, more than missed, how much I longed for him. A phrase swam up in Bulgarian, though I hardly ever spoke the language anymore, for years I had spoken it every day but now it lay dormant: *ispulnen sum s kopnezh po tebe*, I'm full of longing for you. It's strange the things that stick, I had never said it to anyone but somehow the phrase came to me now, cutting through the haze of drugs. It surprised me, I was used to spending time away from L, weeks and months, and sometimes when I had been in Iowa too long I ached to get away, to be in a new place, to touch again the pleasures of singleness. Though it was also true that when I was home I resented how little I saw him sometimes, the long hours he spent in his studio upstairs, whole days if he was wrestling with a poem. After a string of these days I could become cruel, especially if they coincided with stretches when Iowa felt small to me, sterile, unbearable, as it did sometimes. You're the only reason I'm here, I would say to him, and I don't even see you, we don't do anything together, I might as well be in New York or Lisbon, places I could be happy living. I let myself go in those moments, I said too much, I became dramatic, and L would silence me by saying what he always said, in English or in Spanish: For me it is the greatest happiness, he said, to work in our house knowing you are here, the greatest inspiration, my dream is the two of us working together, it helps me to work knowing you are here. And he was right, I thought now, that *was* happiness, to sit in my studio filled with light, which fell from the French doors, from the windows on three sides onto the rugs L had chosen, bright, crazily patterned, to lay over the brick floor that I loved. It was my studio but L's eye was everywhere, his gift for design, for making beautiful spaces, so that he was right, even when I was alone working I was surrounded by him, writing in a space he had made, that we had made together, as we had made the whole house together. It was happiness to live there with him, even our quarrels were happiness, I longed for all of it.

He set the plastic bag in the chair and leaned over the bed to kiss me, as he always did, my lips against his mask. I told him what had happened, that the pain had come back, that I was waiting to see what the CT scan would show, and I watched him struggle with himself, I saw him compose his face. In our relationship I was the catastrophist, of all possibilities I always imagined the worst, which made L laugh sometimes, Bello, he would say, why do you always think the worst, what does it help; and he was the optimist, putting the worst out of mind until there was no denying it, until it was staring us in the face. L'Allegro and Il Penseroso, I thought sometimes, except that was unfair to us both, and to our life together, which was marked more than anything by laughter, by lovers' games and teasing, by cracking each other up, as when I strung together all the insults and bad words I knew in Spanish, joder gilipollas sinvergüenza caradura, when he tried to pronounce the difference between sheet and shit, impossible for him to hear, or between beach and bitch, it's a question not just of vowel sound but of quantity, the weight of the syllable. There were words he had to avoid in English, except at home with me, when he used them to make me laugh. His sunniness annoyed me sometimes, it could feel as though the burden of reality, of looking at things squarely, fell on me in a way I resented; except that L was so often right, mostly the worst thing didn't happen, mostly all my worrying was wasted energy and time. But now, in the moment it took for him to compose his face, I could see him imagine the worst thing, just for a moment there was an aperture to an unbearable world, I saw him confront it and then turn away. He took my hand in his and said It will be okay, bello, don't worry. Everything will be okay.

For the next half hour he didn't move, not even to sit down in the chair Alivia brought in; he stood, holding my hand, as we waited for Dr. Ferrier to come with news. She wasn't alone when she came, there was another surgeon, the man who had said, that first day in the ER, that I might die, I hadn't seen him since then; and also one of the vascular RNs, not Renee, the woman who had been kind to me in the ER, but a young guy, heavyset and bearded, he had come before and we had struck up that quick camaraderie gay men sometimes forge amid straight people, a little playful and coded, a little flirty, he was the faggiest person I had met in the hospital and I liked him for that. Oh good, Dr. Ferrier said to L while the three of them took up stations at the end of the bed, I'm glad you're here, and then she turned to me. So there's bad news and good news, she said. The bad news is that the artery has torn more, not a huge amount, but it's significant. L squeezed my hand. Why, I said, interrupting her, why would that have happened? She looked at the other surgeon. It's hard to say, she said, but what's important is that we stop it from getting any worse. I remembered the previous day, how my blood pressure had spiked, how I had waited for the younger nurse to come and she hadn't come, even as the alarms chirped. Could it have been what happened yesterday, I asked, could it have been—and I paused, I knew there was a balance to strike but I didn't know how to strike it, between being assertive and being adversarial. I didn't want to be difficult or imperious, I wanted them to take good care of me, which was their job I knew, and still it felt like something I had to deserve. Could it have been what happened with my care, I continued finally, hoping it was neutral enough, and I saw her glance at her colleague again. They were protecting each other, I thought, or the hospital, they were worried I might be litigious, they wanted to manage me. I wondered if her colleague outranked her, if he was here to supervise, or if they always gave difficult news in pairs, so that if there was a dispute about something they could support each other, there would be two of them against me. They could say that my recollection was faulty, I was on pain medication, my blood pressure was low, and L wasn't a native speaker, it would be easy for him to misunderstand. They could forge a little conspiracy to deny they had done anything wrong, the hospital, I mean, and I wished I had my phone in my hand, I wished I had thought to set it to record. That's legal in Iowa, it's a single-party state, and I had gotten in the habit of doing it with one of the contractors who worked on our house, who I think was embarrassed by mistakes he made, and who tried to cover his embarrassment by lying to us, by saying one thing and then claiming he said another.

The house had been built in stages, before there were standards or codes, with whatever materials were at hand. When he stripped the aluminum siding from the back of the house, the contractor found roof tiles that had been used as insulation, and beneath those what he called a poor man's stucco, a cement mixture that he had never seen before, he said, in thirty years of working on houses he had never heard of such a thing. They had to knock it off before installing new siding, and for the next week the noise and dust were unbearable, as they pounded with hammers, making the whole house shake. L and I knew we had made a mistake, we had gone with this man because his quote was so much cheaper than the man we wanted, who did a lot of work in the neighborhood, who knew the houses and how they were built and wouldn't have batted an eye, probably; our neighborhood was known for its weird houses, for the anarchic way they were built. But already we were spending money we didn't have, and so we hired the man from out of town, whose quote was thousands less but who primarily worked on newer houses, who ended up flummoxed by ours. And now we were stuck, he had had to special order the new siding, and so we had put down a big deposit, twenty thousand dollars, we couldn't walk away. We have a problem, he told me over the phone, while the pounding was still going on; when they removed the stucco they had discovered damage to the columns on the front porch, which were structural, not decorative, they held up L's studio, that whole side of the house. He sent a photo the crew had sent him, the exposed brick of the column crumbling away. That happens sometimes, he said, the material decays over time, sometimes when you open an old house up you find things like this. He was in Des Moines, two hours away, he would drive in so that we could talk about options, he said, which I knew would mean more expense. Both L and I were home, I had come up for a long weekend, relieved to get away from the town where I was teaching, and both of us went out to see for ourselves, and to talk to the crew, six or seven guys, all Guatemalan. With me they were polite, professional, but L they treated as a friend, they smiled and shook his hand. I was exhausted, by then, of talking to contractors, which L insisted I do because he was self-conscious of his English; it is so delicate, he said, to get the tone right, you have to be firm but not rude. He couldn't hear that in English, which meant all the communication went through me, double communication, from the contractor to L and then from L back to the contractor, since L was very demanding; we must be exigent, he would say, exigentes, and he noticed problems I didn't. This meant I had to field the annoyance of the contractors, their demands for more money; it was months of conflict, I started to feel like a character in a nineteenth-century novel, ruined by living above his means. But now L could be the one to speak, which changed everything for the crew; they became friendly, chatty, they called him paisano, though he wasn't their paisano, the language was all they shared. We'll do top work for you, they told him, since you're our paisano. They saw us come out, and the head of the team, a man L liked and respected, came over, and we looked together at what we had seen in the photo. It looked like the bricks of the column had just fallen in on one side, it was clearly a safety issue, something that had to be fixed. I'm sorry, the foreman said, my guys were careful, but it's hard to get this stuff off, the stucco, he meant, the pseudo-stucco; I'm not sure there was any way to avoid this happening. So you all did this, L said, and the man said Yes, ruefully; but really, he said, my guys were as careful as they could be. Which may have been true, what did we know, maybe there wasn't any way to remove the stucco without doing damage, we didn't know anything. And that made owning a house a mistake, I sometimes said to L, these guys could say anything to us and we wouldn't know the difference; we didn't even know what we didn't know, we couldn't even ask the right questions.

But now we knew that the owner of the company was lying; he had said it was time that had damaged the column, a natural process of decay. He pulled up later in his pickup truck, a huge American flag painted on each side, the name of the company emblazoned in its folds. He was in his midfifties, maybe around L's age, a white guy, wiry, with a buzz cut under the red ballcap he always wore (a flag on that, too), his sunglasses perched atop the bill. I never saw him put the sunglasses on; when he took off the cap, as he always did when he shook my hand, he held them in his left fist, he squinted into the sun. He had always been affable with me, warm and eager to chat, full of promises—it will be perfect, he said, you're going to love it, you have my word, a salesman even after he had our money, the huge deposit we had put down. Everything about him said Trump voter: his cap, the gun rack (empty, always, when he came to our house), the huge romantic flags, the stories he told me about hunting, the casual pitch he once made for the home invasion workshops he led. You think it'll never happen, he had said, but it's a crazy world, and it only has to happen once, better safe than sorry. Maybe we shouldn't have worked with him; I had wondered early on about the ethics of it, giving our money to someone who so clearly didn't share our politics, our values. Many of my friends felt that way, every dollar is a vote, they said, you had to be mindful, otherwise you were part of the problem, you were giving money to the enemy, funding evil, you don't do business with fascists. I could see the argument but I hated that whole way of thinking; I couldn't help wanting some part of life to be exempt from politics, which was a middle-class value, maybe, complacent, conservative. But I still believed in civility, in neighborliness, I still wanted to shake hands and say hello and talk about the weather, which seems more important to me sometimes than we think, or it does now. When I was younger I felt differently, I wanted to be confrontational, provocative, to get in people's faces; when I went home to Kentucky I covered my backpack with buttons: We're queer, we're here, Silence = Death, another that just read FAGGOT, in capital letters, pink against a black ground. That seemed meaningful to me then, if somebody was a homophobe I wanted them to declare it, I wanted to have it out with them, to rub their face in their wrongness; and maybe I was right, maybe that's how we should live. But the little gestures I was so disdainful of, the little graces of civility, seem precious to me now, even if they're a façade or a veneer, even if they're a lie and everything really is always just the struggle for power, violence root and branch. I can see that too, maybe it's naïve to think anything else; but then for that very reason I think too how really miraculous it is, every moment we don't have our hands at one another's throats, every spot of ground that isn't, at this instant, being drenched with blood, how precious any form of life that lets us extend another instant the suspension of violence. That's more important to me now than the purity of my life, than living with absolute integrity. I wanted to live in a world where I could shake this man's hand, who was polite with us, who greeted L warmly, Qué pasa, he said, as he always did, though he didn't speak Spanish, and L smiled as he always did in response.

He had brought another man with him, a younger man I had met before but whose name I had forgotten, though I thought I remembered that he was a son-in-law, maybe, that he had married the man's daughter and now worked for the family business. So you guys, we've got a problem, the older man said, sometimes this happens, a house seems to be fine but when you open it up you find problems like this, it's hard to say what causes it, just time, but once you've found it you have to fix it. And this here, he said, circling around us to put his hand on one of the columns, where the damage was, he kept three fingers circled around his sunglasses but used his index finger to stroke the stone, this here is a safety issue, and now we've got to fix it. I had glanced at L several times, but neither of us had spoken—it would have meant accusing him to his face of lying, though he *was* lying, shamelessly, bald-facedly; and worse it would have meant selling out the foreman, pitting him against his boss. Anyway he didn't give us time to speak, And you guys, he went on, that isn't even the half of it. This job is going to cost me double what I quoted you, triple. If I had known this crap was under here, well, to be honest, I wouldn't have taken the job at all, nobody would have, it's just not worth the trouble, I would have just walked away. But don't worry, he said, I'm not going to leave you in the lurch, high and dry, we're going to figure this out. We just need to be reasonable, he said, I need to do right by my guys, we need to come to some agreement. He paused here, and I glanced at L again. Well, I began, I remember that first time you came out here, you asked me what was under the aluminum and I said I didn't know, and you said you'd come back with your team and take a look. Why didn't that happen, I asked, and he spread his hands to either side of his body, as if placating or supplicating. Look, he said, I've been doing this for thirty years, I know houses, and I've never seen a house where aluminum siding was put on over stucco. And this isn't even stucco, stucco we could deal with, stucco would come off. This is something I've never seen before, nobody's seen this, nobody could've imagined something like this. He looked at the other man, who nodded along, giving his support. But you didn't check, I said, feeling a little fed up with his bullshit, knowing he was trying to play us; you said you'd check and you didn't. I could see him getting agitated but I didn't stop. You took a risk, I said, you ordered all this siding without checking what the house was made of. I know houses, he said, cutting me off, repeating himself but in a different tone, a harder tone, the salesman falling away; this is my work, he said, it's what I do, my livelihood, I don't need you questioning how I do my job. But look, he said, softening his tone again, that's something I wanted to ask you, this new wood siding is nice, but it's real heavy, I'm not sure we'll ever get it on here. What we could do instead, he said, is put aluminum back on. Now wait, he rushed on, he had heard the noise L made, he

hated the aluminum, it made the house look like a tin can, he
thought, cheap, temporary, he had insisted on wood. Now wait,
I'm talking about nice aluminum, he said, it's not going to look
like that crap you had on before. This will be nice and textured,
you know really it's hard to tell apart from wood, I promise you,
it's good product. I wouldn't use the cheap stuff, he went on, I'm
proud of my work, this is my reputation, my company's reputation, you're going to be happy when we're done, I promise.

I don't think so, I said, squaring my shoulders, I'm pretty
sure we want the product we ordered, we want what we paid
twenty thousand dollars for already. That was enough, I should
have stopped there, but I went on. I'm sorry if you've run into
a problem, I said, I wish you had done what you said you were
going to do, I wish you had kept your word. But the fact that
you didn't do your due diligence, I went on, that was the phrase
I landed on, due diligence, as if we were in court, a lawyerly
phrase—well, I don't think that should be our problem, and
I turned to L, taking him in, I don't see why we should pay
for your mistakes. We need you to fix this, I said, and I drew a
breath to say more but he cut me off. You stop right there, he
said. His whole body was tense, his cap crushed in one hand,
his fist clenched around the sunglasses in the other. You stop,
he said, you shut up. I saw the younger man's face go pale, he
started to step toward us but then stopped. You're trying to
make me feel small, the man said, you're trying to use your in-
tellect to make me feel small, and it's not going to happen. He
was nearly shouting now, he had stepped nearer me and I had
angled my body toward him, instinctively, turning my back to L
as if guarding him, which was what I was doing, I guess, I wasn't
conscious of it but that's what it was. Not today, he said, raising

the fist with his glasses, his right fist, and pointing his index finger at me. Not today, you are not making me feel small today.

I wasn't angry, the way I usually became when confronted, usually there was some unwilled chemical change that made me embarrassed later, ashamed of myself, that clouded my judgment. I felt none of that toward this man, even though he was threatening me, that was what his raised fist meant, his pointed finger, and in my own house, in front of my own door. I could feel how my father would bristle, how dare you, he would say, one of his favorite phrases, how dare you in my house; he had said that to my brother before he struck him full in the face. It was a sacred thing to him, homeownership, the idea that his home was his kingdom, the basis of his tyranny. But all of that felt far away, because though this man was threatening me I could see how overcome he was, how tormented, his face twisted in rage but also in pain, I thought, in humiliation. I had triggered something in him, something I had said or my tone, my way of drawing myself up in language, of taking on my father's voice, officious, authoritative; whenever we do that it's to make the other person feel small, the man was right, but I hadn't wanted to make him feel as small as this. I felt I could see straight through to his childhood, it must be something he had felt many times, a particular flavor of humiliation, any anger I might have felt melted away. I'm sorry, I told him, I didn't mean to make you feel like that. He must have heard that I was sincere, I saw his anger melt away too, he lowered his hand, his face unclenched; and then I saw a look of something like shock as he glanced at the younger man and realized what he had done. I had been recording, my phone was in the breast pocket of my shirt, positioned so the end with the microphone faced up. We have the whole thing on tape, though I've never listened to it, it would shame me if I did. But I kept recording every conversation we had with him or his workers, I still have them stored on a folder on my hard drive, just in case. After that day both of us were more restrained, he didn't ask for more money, though his workers were there for two weeks, erecting a kind of wooden frame to hang the heavier siding from; and we let a little shoddy work pass, even L wanted more for them to be gone than for everything to be perfect.

It hadn't occurred to me until now to record the doctors in the hospital, I wish it had, not for legal reasons but because it was so hard to remember what they said, to remember and understand. But they had arrived without warning; my phone was in reach but I couldn't set it recording surreptitiously. Usually, Dr. Ferrier began, we associate tears with sustained high pressure, not the instability you had yesterday, so, and she paused, glancing at her colleague again, so I wouldn't be comfortable making a causal link. We've got your pressure a little lower now, we'll keep it there about twenty-four hours, and I'm keeping you on bed rest, too. I'm sorry, I know that's not pleasant, but I think it's best. If the artery tears any more we'll have to put a stent in, and I really don't want to do that. I almost asked why, since I knew it was a simple procedure, endovascular, why wouldn't she do it if it might help, but she was eager to go on. So that's the bad news, she said, but there's good news, too, and the good news is more important. The inflammation we saw on the first scan, the aortitis, is almost entirely gone, she said. Whether it's the antibiotics or just the artery healing it's terrific to see, it makes us much less worried about a rupture. And so I think we can take emergency surgery off the table for now, she said.

L squeezed my hand again, I could feel him relax beside me. And that means we can stop starving you, she went on, we're going to let you eat and drink again. Don't get too excited, the RN said, though I was less excited than I might have expected, I still had no appetite; the food here is—and he paused, as if considering his words—not the best. But we'll get you the menu so you can order something. He checked his watch. It's too late for lunch already, he said, you'll have to wait till they start serving dinner. I'll get you some crackers, Alivia offered, she had entered the room and was doing something by the sink, we keep a supply. Good, Dr. Ferrier said, that's a good way to start. Any questions for us, she asked, and I only had one, whether she could say yet when I could go home. This is a big step closer, she said. It will be a few days still, I don't think we're ready to say how many, but the end is in sight now, and that wasn't true before. She looked at L. We'll get him home to you soon, she told him, I know you want him back. They filed out then, the three of them, and Alivia followed, and L and I were alone. L still gripped my hand. You see, he said, I told you it would be fine, I was right. Tonto, he said, squeezing my hand harder, tontito. Joder, I said, but I was smiling, too, I hadn't realized how braced I was for bad news. L bent over me, he pressed his forehead to mine. Hey, he said, you're coming home soon, and I kissed him through his mask. Sinvergüenza, I said, caradura, and he put his forehead to mine again, moving it just slightly side to side, calla anda, he whispered, gilipollón.

4

―――――――

still couldn't read. But I could stare at a poem, a short poem, letting my eyes focus and relax, my attention come and go; and there was one poem in particular I stared at hour after hour, in the book I had asked L to bring to the hospital. It wasn't a special poem, or not to anyone I knew of but me. I had thought of it because it was about a sparrow, it had come to mind every time I saw the sparrow outside my window, or the several sparrows; there was never more than one, but it couldn't have been the same bird every day. The poem was by George Oppen, a poet I had come to love in graduate school, though I found him hard, even when I wasn't in a hospital bed, drugged and groggy; I seldom felt I understood him, not in a way that I could package or paraphrase, reduce to propositions. They were hard poems to teach, though I kept trying to teach them; they were gnomic, almost impenetrable sometimes, abstract. He liked to play with the little function words of English, participles and prepositions; words were like gravel for him, little stones he sifted through his fingers. I liked that about him, I liked that his poems were less psychological than the poems I was usually drawn to, less shifting moods than blocks of light or sound, tonalities; I liked how different they were from the poems I wrote. And I loved how, among the abstraction, his images became luminous, shards of the real, non-abstract world, occasions for wonder. He had a poem about deer that was one of my favorite things; I had read and taught it so often it felt internal to me, like a bit of my consciousness that had somehow stumbled into the world, a prosthetic consciousness—which is something poems can be, they can create new spaces in our interiors sometimes, not just giving language to something that was mute before but generating something new. Poetry is the accoutrement of the self, one of my professors liked to say. That they are there! the poem exclaims, the one about deer, a line that came to me every time L wore his pijama de ciervos; when he came to bed and I put my arms around him it was just the expression I wanted of wonder, making no claims, demanding nothing, postulating no predicate, a wonder at sheer being.

I taught the sparrow poem less often, and it never went well, as it hadn't gone well when I tried to write about it in graduate school; I found I didn't have anything to say, or nothing that captured why it was wonderful. A fragment would come, surprising me, each time I saw the bird at the window, a line like a nursery rhyme, Little sparrow round and sweet, and I remembered the next two words, Chaucer's bird, but nothing else, which was why I made L search the house for Oppen's Collected, because I wanted the whole poem. For long stretches I held the book open on my lap, though maybe I wasn't reading it, exactly, maybe mostly I was just looking at the shape the words made on the page.

STRANGER'S CHILD

Sparrow in the cobbled street,
Little sparrow round and sweet,
Chaucer's bird—

        or if a leaf
Sparkle among leaves, among the season's
Leaves—

        The sparrow's feet,
Feet of the sparrow's child touch
Naked rock.

Why do I love it so much? Three movements, three gestures, I had said to my students, baffled high school seniors in Ann Arbor; it might have been my first year teaching, I can't remember, there were so many things I tried that year that didn't work. I love it because it exists, I wanted to tell them, this record of a mind's noticing, a moment of particularizing attention. From a flock of sparrows *this* sparrow, in a forest of shimmering leaves this particular leaf. Maybe it helps to know more about Oppen, not that I knew very much: the career-long worrying over the relationship between the one and the many, the communal claims of politics—he was a communist, he and his wife, Mary, they were hounded out of the country after the war and spent years in Mexico—the communal claims of politics and the individualizing claims of poems. He couldn't reconcile them, or not for a long time, and so for more than twenty years he wrote no poems, while he and Mary were in the party; he wouldn't write the poems the party would have demanded, responsible poems, poems for the struggle, propaganda poems, and so he wrote nothing, I loved him for that. Everyone loved him, or respected him at least, every poet I knew, every teacher I had had; whatever little aesthetic fiefdom you claimed you could claim he was yours, that he shared your values. I hated all that, the little fiefdoms, the battle lines drawn around what poetry was, what it could or should do, the battles that were so loud in the tiny world of poetry, which no one outside cared about, even knew about; and it was because no one else knew or cared that they were so fierce, the smaller the stakes the more vicious the fighting, as if *poetry* cared, as if the fighting had anything to do with art, which is always so much bigger than anything we could say about it, as if—

Little sparrow round and sweet. The simplest words, the simplest response to reality, a child's response. And then Chaucer: there was a specific reference I never remembered, a note in the back of the book would have reminded me, but I didn't look for it. I didn't need to, the salute was enough, the hailing, turning from the modern street to the inaugural poet, opening up the abyss of history and seeing a light shimmering there, a voice one recognizes; that's something else art does for us, finally, it makes the abyssal less abyssal. Or that's how it seemed to me now, riding out the morning's oxy, sitting with the poem on my lap. It was a play on an old idea, the mortal poet meditating on immortal nature, what we take for immortal nature; it's what Keats does in Nightingale, when he says, The voice I hear this passing night was heard In ancient days by emperor and clown. Oppen is doing the same thing, mentioning Chaucer; he's making this particular sparrow all sparrows. It's a way of turning over again the one and the many, I guess, that problem that always plays out in poetry, in all art probably, of wanting to be faithful to the concrete, particular thing, which is where the love in art comes from, I think, what I care about most, devotion to the actual; and wanting too to pull away from the concrete, to make it representative. One wants to cherish an object in time and also nail it outside time (that was a poem too, an image from a poem, I couldn't remember which), nail it to eternity; it was a tension you could never resolve, you had to make the tension resonate too. That was also in the second stanza, not just the one and the many but the question of time, the *season's* leaves, this *passing* night. But what to do with sparkle, which is the strangest word in the poem, I think, naïve but in a different way from round and sweet. It was a word less consecrated by poetry, maybe, I couldn't think of another poem that used it, a great poem, a poem from the canon, though I'm sure they exist. That's a hard thing about teaching poetry, the fact that so much of a poem's meaning comes from the way a tradition echoes in it, the way words chime across poems and poets, so that *sweet* shimmers with Sidney, Wyatt, Spenser, all the Petrarchan sonneteers who made sweet and bitter one of the polarities defining love, in Shakespeare's sonnets the word repeats obsessively, sweet self, sweet love, sweet silent thought, sweets and beauties, sweets with sweets; not to mention Keats, who anyway is soaked through with Shakespeare, it's like he downloaded the sonnets into his brain; so that when Oppen uses the word he activates a whole tradition, which makes up much of the resonance of a poem and also much of its pleasure, the palming off of words from poet to poet, little touches across time. But it's a pleasure that only comes late as a reader, after years; you can describe it to students but you can't make them feel it; and so for them it's just a word, simple, nothing special, inert on the page. Maybe that's my case with sparkle, maybe in ten more years, or twenty, if I can read enough poems, the word will come alive for me, will become consecrated, will take on that shimmer that is all the other uses chiming with it. If I have ten or twenty years, I suddenly thought.

I love the music of the poem, the way though there are so few words on the page so many of them are repetitions, sparrow, leaves, among, feet, the way a single rhyme chimes through the whole thing, a repeated tone: the full rhymes, street, sweet, feet, a child's rhymes; but also leaf, leaves, season. It makes the poem a lullaby almost, all this repetition, the feeling it gives of lilting, especially at the beginning of the third stanza, with its two repetitions, interlocked, sparrow's, feet, feet, sparrow's. It's a crossing repetition, a chiasmus, one of the five or six figures I made my students learn, which was something they liked, concrete and findable, a label they could place, making a poem a puzzle they could solve, a treasure hunt. But it doesn't really feel like a chiasmus here, which usually has a sense of finality or enclosure, imprisonment, it's the figure of a cage (lust in action, and till action, lust); but here after the two interlocked terms there's a third term, immediate, bound by a genitive, so that looked at another way it's a figure of transformation: if the first term is sparrow's feet the second is sparrow's child. And that's the turn of the poem, as I experience it, the real shock. It transforms the sparrow, or that's what I felt in the hospital, over those days when I stared at the page in my lap; already the poem has been about the one and the many, the individual and so also about the mind that can distinguish the individual (His eye is on the sparrow, the song went, the song I sang as a child among children, in a happy group of children), it made the bird *more* individual—and this is the curious thing, it seems close to a paradox—more individual because related to another. Maybe that's why I wanted the poem, because it understood that, it explained to me why the particularizing attention of the doctors and nurses, all the precise data they collected from my specific body, had nothing to do with me, really, left the crucial me unseen, untouched (only the first day, only Renee's hand on my ankle, that had been the only actual touch), why when L was there I felt so much more a person, so much more real. It's another meditation on time, it makes the sparrow's access to eternity, Chaucer's bird, biological, generative, not like Keats's Nightingale, which was not born for death, etc. It's anthropomorphizing, which makes it a strange poem for Oppen, who usually doesn't go in for that sort of thing, the appeal to pathos; but child is a human word, a human relation. And of course it's repeated too, from the title, which creates another relation, or non-relation, possible relation: to the stranger to whom any other is particular and dear, the stranger we have to imagine, if it's true what I just said, if to recognize another means to imagine them in relation, to conjure for every stranger the stranger to whom they are dear. I don't know if that's true in the world but it's true in the poem, I think, which is something else art can do, it can be a laboratory for thinking, for trying out ideas, not just abstractly but feelingly, so that we can live with them and see them through.

And not just ideas, faculties, too, ways of being. If it's true, what Kant says about the kingdom of ends, I used to say to my students, if it's true that standing in an ethical relation to another means recognizing that their life has exactly the same value as my life, as the life as those I love, which is to say immeasurable value, boundless value: if each life, even if we say *human* life, bracketing off that whole set of questions, problems, about the exceptionality of human life vis-à-vis other sentient life, in turn bracketing off the problem of sentience, of how we measure or judge it, how we know it's there; if every human life makes a claim upon the world, for resources, possibility, regard, love, that is infinite in its legitimacy, if each of the billions of human lives has that much value, then of course we can't bear to live in that kingdom, in the full awareness of all that value. In the same way our bodies filter out the innumerable bits of data our senses take in, that endless stream, filter them so we can function, so we can perceive any particular thing, so maybe our moral senses, if we can speak of moral senses, have to filter out data too, have to blind us to value. Just imagine, I would say to my students, just imagine what it would be like to try to see each person you pass in a day, to recognize them, their value, to cherish them as any adequate relation would demand they be cherished; imagine granting to each of their sufferings the priority you grant your own suffering. Even if we limited this to the people we see, to our actual encounters, leaving out of it the billions of lives that can only ever be abstractions to us, the faces we will never see; even then it would be utterly debilitating, it would make life impossible, even the thought of it is unbearable, as unbearable as the thought of all we betray in failing it. Maybe we need the idea of saints because we need to believe there is some category of person adequate to the demands of others, whose eye can be on the sparrow, I don't know; if so it's a category that excludes me. But that's the power of a frame, I would tell them, to take a bit of the world, a person or a sparrow, to make a boundary within which we can establish that relation that is the only acceptable relation, in which we can see all that there is to see and feel all that there is to feel, which is what makes me think that the disciplined attention of art is a moral discipline, even when the content of that morality isn't obvious, in the way Cézanne paints an apple, say, or the bowl that gathers the apples, the hundreds of strokes he makes, each an act of seeing, a judgment, each an attempt to activate in us that awareness we nearly always shut down. And even within the frame this awareness is fragile, which is something else I love in Oppen's poem, its truth telling, though also it's something I only saw after years of reading it, after decades. And if a leaf sparkle: it's the poem's first verb, conjugated not in the indicative but the subjunctive, not sparkles but sparkle; it isn't stating a fact but suggesting a possibility. It's an acknowledgment of the contingency of the act of attention the poem commemorates, the contingency of our faculty of caring, I mean, of attending to the world, of tending to it. Why does one leaf sparkle—it *is* the perfect word, I realize, the precise word, an intermittent light, it conveys contingency, too—why does one leaf sparkle and not another, one sparrow claim our attention. Why do we love what we love, why does so much fail to move us, why does so much pass by us unloved.

Little sparrow round and sweet. Oppen sent the poem to his daughter, I remembered, I had read it in a collection of his letters, when I was writing my paper for graduate school. He sent her an earlier draft, a much longer version, he hadn't condensed it fully. All I remember of the letter is a single line, where he tells his daughter he has always felt lucky, because, he says, and these are the exact words, We have the right child. Twenty-five years later and I still remember reading those words, being pierced by them, by their lack of the usual piety about family and blood, their acknowledgment of contingency there too, that it was all just luck, whether one's life was blessed or blighted, or the beginning of one's life, whether one was the wrong child or the right. There's another turn in Oppen's last stanza, maybe subtler but also maybe more key for the experience of the poem, at least if you're doing what one of my teachers called the work of the poem, the work the poem asks you to do. An exercise I give every time I teach poetry, whether it's a workshop or a reading class, is to track the sensorium of a poem, the data it gives our senses to process. I make them do this with Keats, usually, he's so drunk on his senses, just a few lines can be revelatory. There's that moment in Grecian Urn, where the priest is leading the cow to sacrifice, and first we see her, and then hear her, lowing to the skies, and then there's the line that stops me cold; it's so familiar, that poem, so often people treat it as pure affirmation, sweetness, beauty, but it's a poem of horrors, really, a poem about the violence that lies behind art, behind all of civilization, a chilling poem. I feel that with many lines but maybe especially with what comes here: And all her silken flanks with garlands drest. It's a perfect line: gorgeous, untroubled, smooth iambics, the commonest, most comfortable rhythm in English. Or almost smooth iambics, in fact there's a little tension in the line, a little trouble, the two two-syllable words are each divided between metrical feet, *silk-en*, *gar-lands*, the first falls across the second and third iambs, the second across the fourth and fifth. It's easy not to notice but you feel it if you're paying attention, it gives the line a feeling of imbalance, of an oddly weighted wheel, something just slightly out of joint. But what's really important is the adjective silken, which engages a new sense, if you're paying attention, if you try to process the information of the poem, to activate it, a whole new aspect of existence lights up, and also an entirely new strategy in the poem's approach to the image. Remember that he's looking at an urn, I would tell my students, he's in a museum, looking at the scenes painted on an urn. One can imagine that to this point he has been describing what he sees, the painted figures, the priest and the cow; even the word lowing, which we do hear, I think it's important that we hear it, but you can imagine seeing it, too, the cow's head outstretched and lifted up, you can imagine it's something he extrapolates from what he sees. But you can't do that with silken, which puts us in the scene, and not just in the scene but right next to the cow, because touch is more intimate than sight or sound, it puts us in closer proximity (only taste is more intimate), we have our hand on her flank. It's a shift of point of view, but more than that, the whole world of the scene springs up around us. And that's the horror of it, to feel the animal flesh, terrified, being led to slaughter, covered in flowers and moaning in distress. It's a whole theory of civilization, that image, the flowers and the slaughter, the flowers covering the slaughter. And all her silken flanks with garlands drest.

What Oppen does isn't so radical maybe, it doesn't require such an extreme displacement. But it opens a door. Everything has been visual to this point, the round sparrow, the sparkling leaf; only sweet implies something else, maybe sound though I think most likely it's affective, part of the naïve emotion the poem starts with. I guess it's possible to read the final stanza as purely visual as well, as an observation of touch rather than touch itself, but I can't read it that way, maybe because the contact between the bird and the rock is so emphasized, with the repetition of feet, maybe because the idea of the sparrow as a child already knocks us into a different order of sympathy. It feels like it does what the Keats poem does, brings us further into the scene, into a more intimate relation with it—and here it *is* as radical as Keats, more radical—it cracks open a door into the experience of the bird, almost as though we become the bird, our feet touching naked rock. The tone shifts, too, the lilting nursery rhyme tone; the last line breaks it, more than breaks it, refutes it, I think, makes continuing it impossible. Rock is an entirely new sound, it doesn't chime with anything, it shuts down the poem—which also isn't typical of Oppen, often his poems seem to flow past their endings, to resonate into the white space; often, mostly even, they end without any punctuation at all. But here there's the heaviest punctuation, a full stop, and before that another kind of stop, the consonants snapping off the vowel that anyway has wrenched us out of the world we were in, the nursery world of street and sweet and leaves and feet, it's like an opposite frequency. It feels like a violent ending, really, though only if you're reading in a certain way, which is something else that makes teaching poetry difficult, though it's also why we need poems, I think: they exist in a different relationship to attention and to time; it's impossible for harried students worrying about exams, for harried readers checking their phones, to see and feel what's happening in them. Whole strata of reality are lost to us at the speed at which we live, our ability to perceive them is lost, and maybe that's the value of poetry, there are aspects of the world that are only visible at the frequency of certain poems.

Read it again, I would tell my students, read it more slowly, when they looked up baffled by a poem, a poem by Elizabeth Bishop, maybe, whom I loved, baffled not because anything was difficult or unclear, but because nothing seemed to happen, because, they almost always thought and sometimes said, what was the point. Read it again, read it more slowly, that was the whole of my pedagogy when I taught my students, who were pressured everywhere else to be more efficient, to take in information more quickly, to make each moment count, to instrumentalize time, which is a terrible way to live, dehumanizing, it disfigures existence. But it was difficult to defend the alternative, to justify it in terms of outcomes and deliverables, costs and benefits; it was indefensible by that logic, its value lay in demonstrating the possibility of other logics, other relationships to value, I mean other ways to live. The point was to perceive reality, I wanted to tell them, to see things that are only visible at a different speed, a different pitch of attention, the value of poems is tuning us to a different frequency of existence. But that knowledge is experiential, you can't explain it or demonstrate it or guarantee it, you can only try to tempt students toward it, entice them, and that had become harder and harder over the years when I taught high school, which were the years when everyone got smartphones; when I started they were novelties, prestige items, and when I finished they were ubiquitous. It had become more difficult for me, too, to find my way back to poems, to the mindspace of poems; I'm on my phone as much as anybody else, scrolling and liking, atomizing my attention. Probably I wouldn't have seen Oppen's poem in this way anywhere other than that bed, staring at the poem as I might stare at a painting, which if you do long enough you make discoveries, the painting opens up, you tune yourself to its frequency. I had never experienced the end of Oppen's poem so powerfully, had never felt so starkly the finality of it, the way the world is stripped bare, how the cobbled street—which is a made thing, shaped, familiar, welcoming of human life, human comfort—becomes naked rock. It's a different scale of time, too: everything else in the poem is transient, the sparrow, the leaves, even a cobbled street is transient, of the order of created things, a style; but naked rock is uncreated, uncreated by us, I mean, I'm not being theological, it invokes a scale of time that, so far as we're concerned, might as well be eternity. The naked rock, the sparrow's foot. It made me think of one of L's poems, one of my favorites. The speaker is in the mountains, watching sunlight on cliffs, and he makes a kind of account, considering how much time what he sees will last in relation to him. Las rocas, mucho más, he says, los castaños, bastante. Los juncos, las avispas, mucho menos. That's how the poem ends, no plea to sentiment, just dispassionate observation, mucho más, mucho menos, what more is there is to say. Oppen doesn't plead for sentiment either, it isn't pathos exactly or obviously, but there's something irremediable there, in that naked rock the child has to stand on, in this poem he sent to the daughter he loved; and there was something weirdly that comforted me, that time in the bed, when I was unable to get up, to walk around the ward or even move to the chair. The irremediability of it was a comfort, that he had seen it and faced up to it, and in facing up to it made this poem.

Little sparrow round and sweet. Things changed in the days after the second CT scan, not the routine of the days but their tone. Even before they let me off bed rest, which only lasted thirty-six hours or so, I felt a change in the doctors, who seemed to have decided I was more likely to live than to die, and it was only then that I realized how tense the first days had been. There was still no clarity as to cause. Infectious disease had finally thrown up their hands: all the blood tests had come back negative, even for the most exotic possibilities, which still didn't rule out infection; the world is large and our knowledge of it small, they said, we can only find something we know how to see, and so I would stay on the antibiotics that were carpet-bombing my system. The doctor in Seattle, the expert on tertiary syphilis, had responded to their inquiry noncommittally; possible but unlikely, he had said, an interesting case. The infectious disease doctor passed this on to me, the expert's interest, as if it were information I might want; he recommended a tissue biopsy, and infectious disease agreed, they told me, but Dr. Ferrier still refused. And with that they checked out, as they said, we've done all we can do, we won't bother you anymore, and their twice-daily visits stopped. Rheumatology had stopped their rounds, too, though they were waiting for the PET scan, which my insurance had only approved after a fight, the doctors told me, apparently they had made their appeal multiple times. I was supposed to get the scan the day before, we had spent all day waiting for them to call that they were ready for me, until, at six, Alivia said they had closed up shop, I wouldn't get the scan that day. People wait weeks to get these, she said, they're booked way in advance, they've got to sneak you onto the schedule. It would have been easier to be patient if I hadn't been starved all day; the scan had to be done on an empty stomach, so just a day after Dr. Ferrier cleared me to eat I was fasting again.

It had been a little carnival, at first, after Dr. Ferrier announced she would let me eat and drink; Alivia had brought in the menu with a ta-da of pomp, but the vascular nurse had been right, it was nothing to get excited about. Once Alivia had left and we had the room to ourselves L was indignant, How is it possible, he said. The menu was full of processed food, canned soups, macaroni and cheese, hamburgers and French fries, toaster-oven pizzas, everything full of salt and fat; there was nothing fresh, even the fruit was canned. How can this be the food in a hospital, L said, this is food to make you more sick. We settled finally on wheat toast, a hard-boiled egg, sugar-free fruit-flavored yogurt that came watery and sickly sweet in its plastic cup, L carping all the while, until finally I asked him to stop. Okay, bello, he said, putting his hand on my forehead to push back my hair, I'm sorry. I had thought maybe my appetite would return at the taste of food, but it didn't, even though I wasn't as disgusted by the food as L was; it was the food I had grown up on, processed food with its chemicals, if you taste it as a child you crave it your whole life. But none of it tasted good to me now, the bread like cardboard (L had snatched the foil-wrapped pat of butter from the tray, Absolutely not, he said, no way, and dropped it in the trash), the egg vinegary and dry, it had been sitting since the morning. I took a bite or two of each thing before pushing it aside. Bello, L said, you have to eat, but I told him it was enough, I should start slow. I had no appetite the next day, either, I ate mechanically, as an obligation, without any pleasure. But there was pleasure that day: at morning rounds I had asked Dr. Akeyu if I could have a cup of coffee, if one small cup would be all right, and she had smiled; it may have been the first time I had seen her smile, to the extent one can see someone smile in a mask. I think one cup will be all right, she said. I was ready to order it as soon as food service started, at seven, the same time Alivia arrived, but she stopped me. Trust me, she said, you don't want that. If you only get one cup a day, make it the good stuff, wait a few hours and have L bring up something from the café. L tried to argue when I texted him a few hours later, immediately my screen was filled with a video call from him. No, bello, he said, it's not a good idea, but I cut him off, I told him the doctors said it was fine. Don't argue, guapo, I said, please, and he must have heard in my voice that I meant it, because he relented. Crazy bello, he said, so enganchado. But he enjoyed it, too, my pleasure when he brought it to me in my bed, first holding it out of reach when I lifted my hand up to take it, asking me if I was sure. Don't play with me, I said to him, laughing a little but meaning it too, I felt desperate for it now it was so close. He handed it over then, and sat on the chair Alivia had brought in—it was always waiting for him, she made sure it was there for visiting hours—while I held it in my hands, able to take my time now that I knew it was there. I closed my eyes, relishing the warmth of it, the heat almost burning my palms. There was no better feeling, I thought, even in high summer, on the hottest days, I wanted my coffee hot so I could have this feeling. I pried off the plastic lid and brought the cup to my face, not sipping yet but breathing in the smell, at which I moaned in pleasure, which made L laugh. The moan was genuine, the smell of the coffee was pure pleasure, it must have been a jolt of dopamine, the addict's reward; and then I brought the waxed rim of the cup to my lips and took the smallest sip I could, drawing it in with my breath; if I only got one cup a day I wanted to make it last. The deprivation was almost worth it for the intensity of those first few sips, the way immediately they eased the low buzz of discontent that radiated even through the oxy. The headache didn't go away exactly, but it loosened its claws as my mind sharpened, my thoughts cleared; I felt the pleasure in my whole body, a slow spark along my arms and legs, my spine, traveling down and then back up again. How can this be legal, I said to L. To have let me have it that once and then cut me off seemed cruel; now I was craving it again, I had told Alivia when she came in. How was your coffee this morning, I asked her, though she was empty-handed; when she asked me how I knew she had gotten one I told her I could hear the ice in the cup at the nurses' station. She laughed. I guess you're feeling it bad today, she said. They promised they'd get you in for the PET scan as early as possible, I'll stay on top of them, I'll call them every hour to make sure they don't forget us. Maybe if we get in early you can still have your coffee.

Alivia had her back to me, sorting and arranging at the counter; each day they changed my meds, every few hours, trying to wean me from the intravenous blood pressure medications to pills. But when I asked her how she was, how her night had been, she turned to face me and leaned back. Well, she said, it's a stressful time. Have I told you about my fiancé, she asked, and I said she hadn't; I knew she was engaged but nothing more. She hadn't said much of anything about her life outside the hospital. I knew she lived near enough to walk to work, I knew she had a dog, a little white Pomeranian she had shown me pictures of on her phone; but for all her friendliness and eagerness to talk she hadn't told me anything more. You know that bar downtown, she went on, and she named one of the sports bars near the university; I had never been inside but it was always packed at night, with students pouring onto a patio that was separated from the street by a padlocked gate, drunken undergrads lounging on lawn chairs and picnic tables visible through the bars. Her fiancé's family owned it, she told me now; they had opened it forty years before, it had passed from his grandfather to his father, and the expectation was it would be his, eventually. Which made them something like Iowa City royalty, fixtures in the transient town. Wow, I said, and then, what has that been like during lockdown, it must have been hard. That's the thing, she said, everybody's been under so much stress. They were closed for three months, she told me, totally shut down. And they're good people, it's a family business, I mean there are students who work there but they've had a lot of their staff for years and years. But what could they do? It's not like a restaurant that can do takeout or delivery—nobody goes there for the food. So they had to let everybody go, she said, which was awful, really awful, they were torn up about it, but it's not like they have piles of cash to burn, they live pretty close to the bone. But how were things now, I asked her, it seemed like the town was more or less back to normal: the bars were open and packed again, soon football season would start and thousands, tens of thousands of people would flood in and pack them more; surely they had gotten through the worst. Well, she said, it's not that clear-cut, it would take them a long time to recover from the months they had lost, and even now they had to close at 10:00 p.m., all the bars did, it was a concession the governor made to outrage at the early reopening, they couldn't stay open to 2:00 a.m. like before. And the numbers aren't the same as before anyway, enrollment at the university was down, she said, had I heard? That was another disaster of the pandemic, people didn't want to come back to school, though they were mad about being sent home the semester before. There were a bunch of lawsuits, she said, because people had come for one kind of experience and got another, and the university didn't want to refund anybody, which wasn't cool at all, obviously, though also the state had slashed funding so deeply what else could they do; and some students had gone home to get jobs and then decided to keep working, to get on with life. It isn't easy for everybody to come to college, she said, a lot of these kids, they're the first ones in their families to go, it was a huge effort to get here in the first place. It breaks my heart to think about it, she said, all that hope lost. Maybe that's how we should measure the cost of all this, she said. I saw the other day they're saying however many trillions lost but really it's all that hope, people's plans for the future, their lives, all of it down the drain. Thank God they passed the stimulus, she said, thank God people got some money to put in their pockets, to feed their kids. But what can you do about all those other losses, you can't give people back a year of their lives. And let's hope it's just a year, she went on, who knows how long all this will last. Even if they've come back lots of kids are staying in their rooms, they don't want to go out like they did before. And who can blame them, she said, that's the real problem, the real source of stress, I don't know what to think. People need to work, businesses need to survive, kids need to go to school, I see all that, and I see how bad it's been for my fiancé and his family. If things don't get back to normal they could lose the bar, which would mean losing everything, forty years of their family's history, of course I don't want that to happen. But this is a terrible disease, she said, you work in a place like this and you see how terrible it is. You can't imagine what it was like, back in April and May, how scary it was. She was quiet for a minute. Anyway, last night we were having dinner—am I boring you, she interrupted herself to ask, and I said she wasn't, not at all, and it was true, I loved that she was talking to me like a real person, please keep going. Well, so we were having dinner with his family, and it was fine, I like them all a lot, we get along great. But last night his uncle was there, who's kind of an asshole, she lowered her voice to a whisper at the word, I'm sorry but it's true, I've only met him a couple of times but he's always needling somebody, he's one of those guys who always wants a reaction. And last night it was my turn. He starts mouthing off about Covid, how the shutdown is so much worse than the disease, how it's setting the economy back a decade, how the government is using it to take away our rights, making us wear masks. They're going to make us carry vaccination cards next, he said, you wait, they'll be putting us in camps. And my fiancé's mom, poor lady, he's her brother, she's trying to make him stop, telling him to calm down. But he's gotten all worked up, he starts talking about how the virus is overblown anyway, it's not so dangerous, it hasn't killed as many people as they say, maybe it hasn't killed anybody, anytime anybody dies of anything they say it's the virus, they want it to seem worse than it is. I think he really thinks that, she said, he really believes it's all a hoax, a government plot. How he thinks it's a government plot when the guy he loves is president I don't know. Well, I couldn't take it, I started arguing with him, I told him he didn't know what he was talking about, that I had seen it firsthand and knew it wasn't a hoax. And what did he say to that, I asked. I couldn't even tell you, she said, because I started crying, like an idiot, that happens to me when I get upset like that, I start crying. But also I remembered what it was like, when we were so scared, when we didn't know what to expect. And it wasn't even that bad here, I mean it was bad, but it wasn't like New York, we didn't have to put bodies in freezer trucks, she said, it wasn't like what you saw on the news about Europe. But we didn't know it wouldn't get that bad, we didn't know what was coming or not. They were awful weeks, just terrible, and then this guy tells me it didn't really happen? It's all made up? I'm sorry, I couldn't listen to that, I don't regret saying something, but then I start crying and make a big fool of myself. She laughed. Did your fiancé say anything, I asked, and she laughed again. Oh yeah, she said, he told him to shut up, but that just made it worse. He should know better, he means to be sweet but I like to fight my own battles, you know. Anyway everybody was already making a fuss over me, the guy felt bad already, but I didn't change anybody's mind, I can tell you that. She paused, and I thought of the helicopters flying above my studio, the sickest patients from across the state ferried here through the air. I just wish I knew what to think, she said after a moment. I want things to go back to normal, for everything to open up and go back to how it was, I know how much people are suffering. But things aren't normal, and part of me wishes we would lock everything back down and keep people safe. There's no right answer, I guess, I'm glad it's not my job to tell people what to do. We can all be glad of that, she said, pushing herself up off the counter where she had been leaning. But look at me, talking your ear off, like I don't have any work to do. Let's get you these meds, she said, bringing over several little cups of pills, a larger cup of water grimy with laxative.

It was still morning, only a couple of hours had passed, when she came in to say that the PET scan was ready, we had to rush down, chop-chop. Did I need anything before we went, she asked, and I almost said I needed the bathroom, but she was already preparing to leave: the rails on the bed were up, she was arranging the tubes and wires, the module from the monitor that would let her keep an eye on my heart rate and blood pressure; and anyway I had just been up to piss maybe thirty minutes before. It was one of the medications, I thought, I had to piss every hour, sometimes more often; I would be fine, I could wait until after the scan. But then the woman in the little room where Alivia delivered me, not the room with the scanner but a room where we would wait, said that I would need to stay there an hour, without moving, while I absorbed the radioactive tracer she carried in a small metal case she set beside me on the stretcher, and my heart sank. How long will the scan itself take, I asked, and she said Well, it can depend, but about forty-five minutes to an hour. And then, as she undid the clasps on her case, I processed the other thing she had said. Sorry, I said, did you say radioactive, and she laughed. I know, it's a scary word, but it's perfectly safe, it's barely radioactive at all. And it doesn't stay in your body long, you'll want to drink as much water as you can this afternoon to help flush it out. I saw that the lid of the case, raised toward me, had a symbol on it, the black trefoil on a yellow ground, and I had a quick flash of the Cold War disaster films I had seen in the 1980s. But I didn't feel anything when she injected it into one of the IV ports that they kept changing out, the lines were failing more frequently now; I had looked away when she began to press the plunger and was surprised when she said And that's it, now we just wait. She would stay a little bit just in case there was a reaction, but there won't be, she said, it's very rare, I've been doing this for years and have never had a problem. Alivia had claimed the only seat in the room, she had her phone in her hand; the woman leaned back against the wall. So where do you live, she asked me, and I told her, just a few minutes from the hospital, on the same side of the river. And what about you, I asked, and she made a curious sound in her throat, somewhere between a laugh and a groan, I'm a little farther away than that, she said, I come in every day from Cedar Rapids. This was a city maybe thirty minutes away, where I had only ever been for the airport. It had been in the news recently, not just local but national news, after it was hit by devastating storms earlier in the month, storms that had hit Iowa City, too. I had seen shocking figures in the paper, hundreds of thousands of trees downed, a third of all the trees in the city, how could that be possible, I had asked myself; roofs were torn off buildings, electricity was out for people across the county, in the terrible August heat; the damage to agriculture was in the billions. It was a disaster, and I asked her whether she had been hit hard. Oh, she said, it's awful in the city, you drive around and it's just devastation, they're still trying to clear out all the trees it took down, it's hard to imagine them ever being done. But we got lucky, we live on a couple of acres and we only lost two trees, far from the house, thank God. We were so much luckier than a lot of folks, my heart goes out to people who've lost their homes, and you know it just tore through the fields, there are farmers who lost their whole season, just torn up by the wind, God bless. You just hope they'll get some of it back from insurance, I don't know, it doesn't look like the government is doing much to help. But it hit Iowa City hard too, she said, she asked how we had come out, and I told her we hadn't been so lucky, that it had sent one of our oak trees, one of the huge, hundred-year-old oaks that I loved, crashing down on our house. My goodness, she said, and then, you poor thing.

I had never even heard of a derecho until suddenly it was on everyone's lips a day or two before it hit, a storm of straight-line winds, not twisting like a tornado, a land hurricane it was also called; decades before one had done damage here, longtime Iowans knew to worry. But I wasn't worried. I had grown up in tornado country and loved when the huge black clouds rolled in, when the sky turned sickly green, I loved the lightning and thunder and the big winds driving the rain, I had always loved it. When I was a child on my grandparents' farm my cousins and I would run in the rain, our arms outstretched, in the wind and the rain, ignoring our grandmother as she yelled from the porch for us to stop playing the fool and come in out of the weather. Finally we obeyed, breathless and laughing and dripping all over her kitchen, it would serve us right to get zapped by lightning, she said. I thought I knew storms and so I wasn't worried; that morning I was even disappointed that the skies were clear, that it looked to be a false alarm. I spent the morning reading, luxuriating in the peacefulness of the house, which still felt new to me; we had only moved in a year before, after the year of renovations, and I had spent several months of that year away, teaching and traveling, I had only just returned from a summer festival. I was alone in the house. L hadn't returned yet from Europe, he was stretching out his summer; ever since his father's death he wanted to be with his family as much as possible. He needed it, he said, and especially to be with his mother, who was healthy thank God and in good spirits but she wouldn't live forever, and L was so seldom home with her. I missed him but also he would be back soon, in a week, and so it was a pleasure to miss him, or almost a pleasure, I could imagine how happy I would be for him to be home.

It wasn't until the afternoon that the sky began to change, freakishly quickly; all at once it was night, the dark that means a real storm, so that even before the sirens started you wanted to take cover, you felt an animal impulse to burrow or hide. That was what I liked, to defy that impulse, the thrill of risk, I stepped out onto the humid porch as the rain began. Even before the wind came the power flickered, then went out for good, leaving the house behind me dark and weirdly silent, the air-conditioning off, the humming of the fridge, that electric cicada buzz of a living house suddenly mute. I went back inside. The sirens went off then, wailing in the still air. My phone dinged with an alert from the city, they had been coming in all morning, first a watch and then a warning, and now in all caps an order to take shelter. I wasn't very sheltered where I was, on our sofa, with the three large windows to my left, through which I could see our trees beginning to move. We had lots of trees, the huge 150-year-old oak, the patriarch, but younger trees too. The previous owner had been a little tree crazy, there were young oaks, two young birches that had shot up skinny and fast, I loved their chalk yearning but the arborist we had brought in said they didn't make sense, they were competing with the oak, the big guy she called him, rushing up toward his canopy, I just don't see what future they have. She was a young woman, rail thin, her body all muscle; when she arrived to inspect our trees I half expected her to scurry up like a squirrel into the branches. I liked her from the start, the way she talked about trees, the way she looked at the little one nearest our windows, which I loved though I always forgot the name of it, it had the most elegant leaves I had ever seen. These don't usually do well in Iowa, she said, but it was placed right where all the rain ran, the yard had a slope and he could drink his fill. He's a happy guy there, she said. And she thought our dogwood was happy too, also young, in the front of the house; for the week or so it was in bloom I had stood at our bathroom window every morning to gaze at it, the little pink flowers flaming our yard, our gay harbinger. The first time I saw it in bloom I thought of Shakespeare's first sonnet, Thou that art now the world's fresh ornament And only herald to the gaudy spring. The lines had flashed suddenly in my brain, as they had twenty years before, beneath a different flowering tree, when I lay with my head in the lap of a boy I loved and spoke them to him without thinking, stupid with happiness and then mortified; it was too extravagant, quoting Shakespeare. But it worked, he was charmed, he leaned down and kissed me, it was one of the few perfect moments in my life. Our tree reminded me of it even when the petals had all fallen, jewels in the grass. The arborist blessed our two burr oaks, too, younger but still huge, century trees, sentinels at either side of the driveway. You can never redo this, she said, tapping the concrete of the drive, already old and discolored, cracked, you might hurt these trees.

The only thing that worried her was the sugar maple out back. Its trunk, scarred by lightning, was just a foot or so from my studio windows, a highway for squirrels. People love them because they grow so fast but their branches tend to be weak, she said, I don't like the look of some of those hanging over the house. I thought of that tree now. She had removed the troubling branches, but even from the couch I could hear things falling onto the roof above my studio, which was flat, always covered with leaves and seeds, L had to go out every couple of weeks with a broom. There was a door in the upstairs hallway that opened onto it, and we dreamed of making it a deck, it was on our list of improvements in case of a windfall, once we had recovered from the big repairs. The flat roof was always loud, I heard the noise of small branches falling, every acorn, every squirrel running overhead; that didn't bother me while I was working, I liked them, a little buzz of life on our quiet street. But now there were louder sounds, heavier things falling, and I thought of the branches the woman had considered removing but hadn't in the end. There was one in particular that reached elephantine over my studio; it made her nervous, she said, she wouldn't want it hanging over her house. But they would need a crane to take it away, and it might kill the tree altogether, it would be a radical operation; we should let it be for now, she said, we can reevaluate in five or ten years. I thought of that as the trees I could see from the couch started moving more violently, as I realized I should probably go to the basement. I could feel that huge branch hanging above me as I walked through my office to the stairs leading down to the basement, which was pitch-black, there were only two small windows high on the walls and in the dark of the storm there was almost no light passing through them; the air was wet and clammy, the walls damp. It wasn't worth trying to make the basement a livable space, the contractors had told us, it would be almost impossible to keep the damp out, prohibitively expensive, better just to think of it as storage, they said. So there wasn't anywhere to sit, except on top of the washing machine, and it was creepy, I never liked being in the basement, even with lights; and I didn't have service there, my calls always dropped if I went down to put laundry in the dryer. It occurred to me that if the big branch did fall, God forbid, if it crashed through the ceiling of my studio and brought the walls down around it, my only exit from the basement would be blocked; I would be stuck, who knew for how long, in the dark and the damp, and at that thought I went back upstairs, I'd take my chances aboveground.

I sat again on the sofa, uneasy, watching the trees thrash, debris falling into the yard. Twenty minutes had passed, maybe, the wind all the time increasing. For all it was called a derecho the wind whipped, I felt like it swirled, so that the canopies of the trees thrashed like dancers' skirts, like a flamenco dancer's skirt when she gathers the fabric up and throws it down, violently, like that, as though something were grabbing the limbs of the trees, were grabbing the house too. It felt like a fist had grabbed the house and was shaking it, trying to snap it off the foundation, maybe the same hand that two weeks later reached into my gut, devastating, overpowering, Jesus, I said, as a huge branch from our old oak slammed to the ground. It was as large as a young tree; even in the tumult of the wind I heard the sound it made on the sodden earth, I thought I could feel the impact. The end where it had snapped was splintered and raw, a wound. I felt a kind of terror now, I knew it was stupid to be on the couch but I was pinned there, I couldn't make myself get up to go back to the basement, even as the wind became, impossibly, fiercer; terror for my own safety but also for the house, which seemed fragile now and for which I was responsible. What would I do if something happened, if a tree fell or the wind ripped off the roof, what does one do when something like that happens, how do you know what to do. The noise was overwhelming; there was nothing organic about it, it was like a jetliner maybe, or innumerable cars driving impossibly fast. And then through that general huge noise there came a more specific sound, a grinding or groaning, a terrible noise I responded to with panic, with a sharp animal fear that froze me where I sat though also I wanted to run, in whatever direction—I was petrified, I think it's the first time I've really understood the word, or almost the first— and then the house jolted with an impact, a concussion, there was a great crack and debris, plaster, wood chips, leaves, came skittering down the stairs. I did move then, though the wind still raged, I pushed myself off the couch and rushed to the stairs. I climbed the first few steps, careful of the debris, among which there were nails, old and twisted, savage looking, just the few steps leading from the kitchen to a little landing where they turned and continued to the second floor. There, at the turning, high where the wall met the sloped ceiling, the roof was torn open, the façade of the house punched through. An oak's long arm reached in, its leaves dripping and green. The hole the tree itself had made wasn't very large, but one of the beams in the wall had snapped and fallen forward, tearing the interior wall open; it blocked the way upstairs, with more nails jutting where it hung suspended, so that it looked like a medieval weapon, a mace or a flail. I stared unmoving at the damage to the house, with my hands raised to the sides of my head, my fingers digging into my scalp, a cartoonish image, I think now, I would have laughed at the sight of me. Even as I stood there the wind was dying down, it was the very end of the storm; another two or three minutes and we might have gotten through it unscathed.

I was still standing there when someone knocked at the door, quickly and loudly, at the same time shouting Hello, hello. The wind had passed, the light was returning, it wasn't even raining when I opened the door. It was a neighbor, I had seen him walking his dog but we had never spoken. Is everybody okay, he asked me now, are you okay, was anybody in the car. The car, I asked, and stepped onto the porch. The yard was unrecognizable, the tree had fallen in three huge pieces, and as it fell it had struck the other burr oak, on the other side of the driveway, and had torn what seemed like half or a third of that tree away; the rest still stood but precariously, it seemed to me. The yard, the driveway, all were underneath the huge weight of the trees, which had crushed my car, I saw now; though it was barely visible I could see that it had taken the brunt of the impact, the passenger side was pancaked, flat, not a car anymore but a crushed tin can, I couldn't imagine the force it must have taken, how hard the trees came down. Jesus Christ, I said, and then, remembering the man's question, no, I said, no one was in the car, it's just me here, I'm alone in the house, I'm fine. Okay, he said, there are trees down all over the neighborhood, I'll keep checking on people, and I thanked him as he took off at a jog down the street. I stayed on the porch for a moment, staring at the mass of tree limbs and trunk, the explosion of tree across my lawn, the branch—not a very large branch, we had been lucky—that had struck through the roof. It could have been so much worse, I could see where the smallest branches were bent against the French doors of my studio, just a few feet from the pancaked car; it could have taken out that whole half of the house. But the trees, I thought, our beautiful trees. They were my companions as I wrote, I loved looking out at them from my desk, the huge creatures that lay now across our lawn. The other one, too, though it was still standing I knew it would have to come down, it was a hazard. We would lose them both, and the thought of it made a fist in my chest. The house could be fixed, I knew, the car replaced, but the trees were irreparable, irreplaceable, and I thought of the decades they had stood, as long as the house. It was time that lay strewn across our yard, not just wood and leaves but the decades and decades they had lived, and I felt grief for them, real grief, it knocked the air out of my lungs.

Already the neighborhood was coming alive, a chain saw started up on another street. The yards were full of branches and debris but I didn't see any other trees that had fallen, the houses around us had been spared. A car came up the hill, slowing as it passed the house; a woman's face stared at the wreckage, her mouth hanging open. That was one of the worst things, the way people gawked; there were other houses damaged in the neighborhood but ours was the worst, with the house and the car, the carnage of the two oaks, and over the next days there was an endless stream of cars, people with their phones taking photos and videos, opening their doors to walk around the shattered trunk. I hated them, ogling my misfortune, which was a way of relishing their own better luck; it was all I could do not to open the door and shout at them to get off my property. That was what I had felt in the hospital, too, as doctors and students streamed in those first few days, wanting to see the interesting case, the conundrum; it was the same exposure I felt, the same resentment, being made the object of others' attention, even when they meant well. I'm so sorry, people said, when they caught me outside, you poor thing, and our neighbors were kind: the second morning after the storm I saw that the other half of the yard, the half not covered by the two oaks, had been raked clean, all the sticks and branches, all the leaves dragged to the curb. That was an unadulterated kindness, as were the casseroles and pies, the plates of cookies, sometimes the people who brought them rang the bell and sometimes I found the dishes on the porch; it isn't just a myth, neighborliness, not all the time. And yet the photos were a kind of neighborliness, too, the families that got out of their cars, that walked up the driveway to get a better angle on the metal twisted underneath the tree, staring at someone else's trouble, staring and being pleased, I imagined, staring from the pleasure of their own luckier lives. And so I hated them, even though I knew it was human, not malicious, and knew too that I wasn't any better, I had the same urges. I might have driven around the neighborhood myself, my jaw hanging open, feeling the thrill of disasters I wasn't touched by, the way I watched videos on YouTube or Twitter of hurricanes and floods. It was a terrible tendency to indulge, though really who knew why we were drawn to such things, whether it was pity or empathy, a desire to share in others' suffering, or some darker exaltation we take in catastrophe. There was no telling them apart, our better impulses and our worse, that was the terrible thing, that our interest contained all of our impulses at once.

The only person I could think of to call was the contractor we had used after buying the house, not the siding guy but the general contractor who had done the bulk of the work, everything inside, jacking up our floors and knocking down walls; I had sworn we would never work with him again but there was no one else to call. It wasn't that his work had been bad—the contrary, actually, he had done good work, there had been some mistakes but finally it was careful, excellent even—but things had grown rancorous toward the end. Everything cost more than he had said it would, as we ran out of money our conversations grew more difficult; we raised our voices, he spoke down to us, I felt, he took advantage of our ignorance, though maybe that's not fair. It had been a year since we had spoken, I didn't expect him to pick up, but I left a message and he called back right away. He was calling from the road, on his way to a job. Were you all hit by this, he asked, and I said Yes, for the first time I found it difficult to speak, yes, I said, one of our big trees fell onto the house. Shit, he said, I'm sorry, I know you all have really been through it with that house. Listen, we're getting slammed with calls but I'm going to take care of you, he said, I'll get my guys out there tomorrow to take a look and get a tarp up at least, we'll see if we can go ahead and waterproof it. And then we'll just have to take it bit by bit, as we can, it's going to be a process. I've never seen damage like this, he said, not even the tornados we had a few years back, it's just pure devastation. He was true to his word, the next day they came with tarps and plywood, the same men who had worked on the house before, the foreman I remembered, an older guy, grizzled, laconic, in a T-shirt and jeans, a ball cap pulled almost over his eyes. Sorry about your car, he said when I walked out to greet him, a cigarette as always at his lips, and I shrugged. That's the easy part, I said, I don't care about the car—and it was easy, I was right, the insurance covered it, a week later we had a replacement. But this, I said, gesturing to the house, leaving the thought unfinished. He couldn't see much from the outside, the tree blocked too much from view, so I took him in to have a look. Well, he said, looking at the snapped beam, the torn wall, that's no fun. He studied it a minute. But I've seen worse. He asked me when the appraiser was coming, and I told him they couldn't say, the guy I had spoken with on the phone had said they were swamped with claims, they were calling in teams from all over the country. But they had already approved waterproofing, I told the foreman, and he grunted. Hard to work around that tree, he said, and I told him that I had called the tree service, they were slammed too, every tree service in Iowa and Illinois was slammed. The arborist I had met before had been by early that morning, I hadn't even seen her, she had driven around town doing triage. They were clearing trees off houses first, she told me later on the phone, trees on the ground were going to have to wait a while. You're third or fourth on the list, I hope we'll be able to get to you soon. The problem was that all the cranes were booked, the heavy cranes they needed for trees like mine; they didn't have one of their own, they rented one when they needed it, and every crane was booked, everywhere, Iowa, Illinois, they had even tried Missouri. They were on every waiting list, it was a day by day thing, they might get a call in the morning that a crane was available and we'll snap it up, she said. Stay by your phone, she told me, if you don't answer you'll miss your chance. I repeated all this to the foreman and he grunted. The forecast didn't look too bad, he said, maybe we'd get lucky and they'd get the tree out before there was more rain. And if not, well, he shrugged, what can you do.

We did get lucky; the third morning after the storm the arborist called, very early, before seven. I was up already, with coffee and a book in the armchair in my studio, the first time since the storm that I had been able to concentrate; the anxiety had lightened, everything was out of my hands. I could sit and read and enjoy the weird sensation of being in the trees, with their canopy pressed against the French doors, the uncanny quality of the dawn light filtered through the leaves. I watched the squirrels and chipmunks scurry past, I laughed as they peered in at me, it was a festival for them. I loved my studio in the trees, it was like a child's dream. But a few hours later I watched as they took it away. They were a team of five, the woman I knew and four men, two of whom operated small vehicles, something like forklifts, little green cars with a complicated grappling mechanism on the front, an extendable metal limb with a pincer on the end that they used to carry branches to the big chipper parked around the curb. This fed into the back of a dump truck they would drive off and empty three times over the course of the day. They had a variety of chain saws, small ones that hung at their waists and then several of increasing size, the largest requiring a special harness to distribute the weight. Only one man used this, the boss, though it wasn't clear to me if he owned the company or was just in charge of the crew. They all wore helmets with face masks, which they pushed up when they weren't operating their chain saws; the helmets had ear protection, too, and inside there was a little microphone so they could communicate with each other. They got to work quickly, not waiting for the crane; they pruned the small branches with their smaller chain saws, gathering them in piles for the little carts to gather. I stood across the street after saying hello to them all. I hadn't seen the damage from that vantage, I had hardly stepped outside, I had a better view now of the scene as a whole. The trunk had snapped ten or twelve feet from the ground, leaving a huge shard of wood, nasty-looking and sharp, like it was on the watch for something to impale, and then the bulk of the tree must have twisted as it fell, falling at an angle across the yard and driveway. It could have fallen right on top of me, I had been so stupid not to take shelter in the basement despite the damp and the dark.

These brilliant creatures, I thought as the workers clambered around the trees; these brilliant creatures, they stand up for so long and then they lie down. The oak that fell was dying already, it turned out, it was rotten inside, straight through the trunk. The woman had apologized to me for not flagging it in her inspection; sometimes it takes a long time before they show signs, she said, a tree can be dying for years, decades, and you'd never know. It was beautiful how they died, in the wild, in forests; as they rotted and the wood softened more animals took shelter in them, more insects feasted on them, even after they fell they served a purpose, enriching the soil, they had long lives and long deaths. And there was so much we didn't understand, the way they communicated through intertwined roots and fungal networks, their huge lungs moving oceans. It wasn't hard for me to imagine them sentient, ensouled, the only religion that has ever really made sense to me is the worship of trees. After an hour or so the woman walked over with a wooden ring in her hand, a segment of one of the larger branches she had cut. I thought you might like this, she said, a souvenir. It was maybe twelve inches in diameter, a thin disk but heavy; I thanked her, it was thoughtful of her, a kindness. She waved this away. I know you loved that tree, she said. I looked down at the wood, which was a light tan color, untouched by rot. I studied the rings, which I remembered learning about in grade school, a ring for each year, thicker rings in wet seasons and thinner in dry. Even on this segment there were dozens, I would remember them when Dr. Akeyu showed me my CT scan, the second one, an image of cross segments, slices she called them; she moved up and down my torso, scrolling the little wheel on her mouse, the organs increasing and decreasing in size, circles growing and shrinking, the aorta expanding suddenly and splitting into two circles (almost circles, the true lumen and false), rings within rings.

The crane arrived then, an enormous machine driven by a small old man who never left his cockpit, even when the tree guys took their lunch break, spreading out food on the grass, lounging and laughing. He was part of the rental, his only job to work the controls that lifted and extended the huge arm, ferrying branches, some of them the size of trees themselves; it was surreal to watch them float up and over the power lines to be lowered into the street. The tree service had cordoned off my block when they arrived, putting orange cones at the nearest side streets, which they moved so that the driver could park the crane in the yard, somehow finding a way between the fallen tree on the east side and the standing trees on the west. The crane made deep gouges with its wheels and left deeper marks from the two metal buttresses the man lowered from either side, buttresses with large square feet the impressions of which we'll never get out of the yard, probably, they're part of the topography now. The work really began then, once the crane was parked and anchored. As I watched from the other side of the street I marveled at how well they worked together, everyone always in the right place, securing a part of the tree to be lifted or receiving it when it was lowered back down, the little green vehicles moving constantly, the buzz of chain saws. I took pictures with my phone, wanting to document everything, to have a record; I sent the most spectacular photos to L, who responded with exclamation marks, or with two zeros for wondering eyes, finally with Wow, bello. He was having lunch with his family, a long late lunch that might last for hours; he was distracted and I resented him for it a little, that he could dip in and out of the drama and strain of the day. I told him how sad I was that the trees were gone, how stressful the thought of repairs was, which elicited his longest response: that it would pass, it would become a story, it would be part of the history of the house; be tranquil, he wrote, be calm. Just the day before I had almost been in tears, telling him that I hated the house, that it was a nightmare, a huge mistake, the biggest mistake of my life; I hate this house, I said to him, I want to sell it, we'll do the very minimum to fix the damage and then let's sell this fucking house. Are you crazy, L said, after all this work. But he hadn't been there, when the house rattled like dice in the wind's fist, he hadn't felt the whole structure jolt with the weight of the tree, he hadn't spent the past nights in a perforated house, the air hot and humid, the limbs of the tree still reaching into the stairwell. I hadn't touched them, I had left everything as it was, except for sweeping up the nails and plaster, the bits of bark and leaf from the stairs. I was surprised by how much it bothered me, to sleep in the perforated house; there wasn't anything rational about it, it wasn't a big hole, nothing could get in but a bird or a squirrel, and yet there was the queasy feeling of a boundary having been breached. Even when I closed the door to my studio, sealing it off, I felt vulnerable, exposed. Calm down, L had said to me, you're still in shock, you don't really want to sell the house. He was right, I thought as I watched the team working, I realized I felt something new for the house, something protective, a new affection; I felt attached to it, I guess I want to say, bound. Something had happened to us both, to me and to the house, the same misfortune, so that now I was part of its story in a way I hadn't felt before, we were in a story together. There were happy surprises as the day went on, as they cleared the tree from the front of the house and I saw how it had punched through shingles but had mostly left the new siding untouched, only a few short pieces by my studio doors had been damaged; and when the crane lifted the huge mass of branches and leaves from the dogwood it seemed mostly unharmed, too. It was a little ragged maybe, not quite as happy as before; but the arborist gave it a quick once-over and said she thought it would pull through just fine. What good news, she said, what a lucky break.

Shortly after the crane arrived neighbors started to gather in front of the house, I spoke to more of them that afternoon than I had in all the months since moving. I didn't mind their watching now, since I was watching with them. One man, young, a

professor, almost as new to the neighborhood as we were, came
out with his kid, who was three or four, a little towheaded boy
who pointed and shouted Crane! at the machine, then again,
as the father smiled at me apologetically. He's a little obsessed,
he said, trucks, fire engines, cranes. The boy was riding on his
shoulders, his father was holding his ankles to his chest, but he
wanted down, he said, still pointing. In his hand I saw he had
a toy crane, a little Matchbox car, his fingers clenched around
it. Okay, his dad said, but you have to stay by me, you have to
hold my hand, we can't get too close. The father and I exchanged
names, and he tried to introduce me to the boy, who had no
time for me, or for anything other than the amazing machine
lifting the tree into the air. His father narrated, See how one
guy wraps the ropes around the piece they're lifting, he said,
see how careful he is to make sure they're good and tight, see
how he waves to the man in the crane to lift it up, there it goes,
he said, though it wasn't clear to me that the boy heard any of
this, he was bouncing on the balls of his feet with excitement.
But I guess he was listening, since he echoed his father's words
when the tree went up, There it goes, he said, almost singing it,
so that his father said it again with the boy's intonation, There
it goes, they repeated it back and forth the whole time the tree
was in the air. Other children came too, younger kids with their
parents and older kids alone. There was a group of boys, maybe
eleven or twelve years old, who had ridden around the neighborhood all summer on their bikes; two or three of them came
by too, though they didn't say anything to me, they kept their
distance. Even so I could see that they loved watching it; they
hid it but they felt what the boy felt, I thought, the boy and his
father. It cheered me, all the kids who came, the little carnival

they tried to make in the street, though the arborist kept chasing them back; stay on the sidewalk, she said, don't get too near, it's dangerous, and the parents apologized and pulled the smallest kids close, catching their hands again.

They came and went, kids and adults and dogs, no one stayed very long; even the little blond boy left after half an hour or so, not protesting too much when his father pulled him away. Only I stayed the whole time, watching them work, I went inside while they ate their lunch but otherwise I watched until they stopped, finally, very late; it was almost seven when they finished sweeping up the sidewalk and the street. They had worked so hard, I thought, they must be so tired, and with days and weeks ahead that would be just as hard, all those downed trees. They had been kind, they had cleared most of the yard, doing more than the woman had said they would; only two big segments of the trunk remained, logs laid out on the lawn. The woman promised to take care of them sometime in the fall, she couldn't say when. Over the couple of weeks since the storm I had come to like these logs, they had almost become part of the terrain; I liked how busy they were with bugs and birds, the squirrels and chipmunks scavenging. But L hated the mess, when he returned from Spain, he couldn't wait for them to clear it away, as he couldn't wait for them to repair the house, which they had done soon after, at least the interior repairs. The roof would take longer, his usual roofer was overwhelmed, the contractor said, roofs had blown off all over the state. It turned out we had good insurance, thank God, we hadn't even looked at the policy the bank sold us with our mortgage. We had lived in such ignorance, I thought now, such expectation that we would be spared, such complacency; it had never seemed necessary to wade through the impenetrable language of house insurance or health insurance, language that made my head hurt, that made me feel stupid, I had always just pushed it aside. But we would get the replacement cost for the repairs, not the cash value. I hadn't even known the difference before, they were terms of art; we would still pay thousands of dollars I knew but it wouldn't be like before, with the repairs to the house, it wouldn't mean more years lost to scrambling.

The house was still scarred, with blue tarp over the roof and deep gouges in the yard. That all felt far away as I lay in the room waiting for the PET scan, letting the radioactive dye saturate my system, if that's what it was doing. The woman had left after a few minutes, once it was clear I didn't have an immediate reaction to the tracer, but she was nearby, we could hear her voice through the curtain she had drawn across the entrance to the little cubicle or cell where Alivia and I were waiting. I needed badly to piss now, but the woman had said I had to remain as still as possible for the hour, she didn't explain why, it was something to do with how the dye moved through my body. Try to just lay flat, she had said, try not to move at all. I closed my eyes, willing myself to drift, to ride the tail end of the morning's oxy, though I couldn't feel it really, the weird stroking pleasure, I tried to find it behind my closed lids but it wasn't there. When I opened my eyes only fifteen minutes had passed. Have a little nap, Alivia asked, you looked very peaceful. I wish, I said, and then, Alivia, I'm sorry, I need to pee, I don't think I can wait until after the scan. Okay, she said, putting down her phone. How bad is it, she asked, can you get through the hour, you're not supposed to move until then. I don't think so, I said, it's pretty bad, and I apologized again, which drew a sound of impatience from her, she sucked her teeth behind her mask. Don't be sorry, she said, it's just your body, you can't help it, and she stood and drew the curtain partway open, leaning out to speak to the other woman. I heard Alivia tell her what I had said, answering that no, I didn't think I could wait the full hour, and then the other woman's voice, concerned, annoyed maybe, saying it was important I stay still as long as possible, and she drew the curtain further aside to speak to me directly. Can you make it to the half hour mark at least, she asked, just another ten minutes or so? I said I thought I could. I'll go get a urinal then, she told Alivia, better if he can use it here instead of going to the bathroom down the hall.

I watched the clock until a half hour had passed, then Alivia stepped in the hall and drew the curtain shut behind her, and I stood with the plastic jug in one hand and my dick in the other, gown and tubing tucked under my chin, and knew right away that despite the pressure in my bladder I wouldn't be able to piss. That had been happening since the tear, though the doctors couldn't figure out why; the tear was below my kidneys and shouldn't have affected urination, they said, there was nothing on any of the scans to suggest any problem, and yet several times in the hospital I had struggled, getting up two or three times before finally something released and I could fill the little jug. The first night in the ICU, after I had been up twice without success, the nurse had worried I might need a catheter; she used an ultrasound device to scan my bladder, which was only about half full, she said, full enough I felt the urge to pee but not so full they would need to intervene. It was an annoyance but nothing too serious, an annoyance for the nurses mostly, since I had to call them in multiple times to rearrange the machinery and wires so I could walk the few steps to the toilet. I stood there a little longer, I took a couple of deep breaths, trying to relax, and then, after a minute or two, I called Alivia back in. No luck, she asked, seeing the empty jug in my hand, and I responded with an echo as she took it from me and I lay back down on the stretcher, No luck. We can try again before the scan, she said, but I didn't have any luck then, either, when Alivia wheeled the bed out of the little cubicle where we had waited and past the room for the scanner, where the other woman was ready for us—she called out that we should be quick, that other people were waiting, they had a full schedule—and down the long hallway to the bathroom just inside the doors we had entered through. Well, that doesn't help, Alivia said as she lowered the arm rails so I could swing my legs over the side of the bed and stand up; she meant what the other woman had called out to us, her admonishment, you take all the time you need. But time didn't help, as I stood in the stall, the IV stand Alivia had borrowed from the radiology ward like a second person beside me; again I knew the moment I tried to relax that it wouldn't work, something was wrong, as if some tubing was twisted and pinched, there wasn't anything I could do. Alivia thought it was anxiety, especially after the second tear in the hospital, which had happened while I was pissing, when I felt something shift and then the pain; I was trying to hold myself together, she thought, I was trying to keep that from happening again.

Dr. Ferrier had talked about anxiety more generally, she had asked if I had a therapist; it might take some time for me to process what I had been through, she said. In the hospital everything is so busy we don't give you time to think, but once you're home you might want somebody to talk to. It's a big deal, what's happened to you, and it came out of the blue, it wasn't something you were prepared for; trouble sleeping, feeling unsettled, panic attacks, all that's totally normal, those are all things patients deal with when they go home. Just think about it, she said, maybe sensing my skepticism though I was trying to hide it, I knew it was knee-jerk and dumb, cultural baggage; I wasn't proud of how dismissive I was at the idea of paying somebody to listen to my troubles, as if they could tell me something I hadn't already thought. I had turned over the pieces of myself endlessly, I didn't think there was anything new to say. Medication was something different, I didn't doubt it could work, or could have an effect, anyway. For a brief period in grad school, after a crisis that had frightened me, I took an SSRI and it did change things, which frightened me more; the texture of my interiority changed, became foreign and strange, I didn't like it at all. You're attached to your suffering, a friend said to me, a friend who did believe in therapy, she thought everyone should have a therapist, not as a response to crisis but just as general maintenance, part of the project of being a human being. That seemed a grand way of putting it, melodramatic; I didn't think I suffered any more acutely than anyone else, though I had gone to the emergency room several weeks earlier, when I had thought I might do myself harm, not in the minor controlled ways I was accustomed to but in large, irreparable ways. That *had* been melodramatic, it had offended my sense of aesthetics, of good taste. But still it had seemed ordinary to me, something everyone must go through or might go through, a stutter in one's commitment to life; I would rather risk that than become someone unrecognizable to myself. And so despite all the warnings I stopped swallowing the pills each day, without returning to the doctor or tapering them off, as I knew you were supposed to. I just quit, cold turkey, and over the next week or so observed strange phenomena, anomalies in the weather of my brain, sudden flashes like electric sparks, or patches of dullness, lost moments, as when I realized in the grocery store that I had been standing immobile in the aisle, a box of cereal in my hand, for I didn't know how long. A few days passed like that, more interesting than alarming, and then I settled into myself again.

I felt anxious now, feeling the pressure in my bladder, already sharp, imagining it becoming sharper and more painful over the hour I would spend immobile in the scanner; but there was nothing doing, finally I resigned myself to it, tucking myself back in my underwear, letting my gown fall. No luck, I said to Alivia before she could ask. I'm sorry, she said, detaching the bags from the stand, all the inconvenience I had put her to for nothing, I thought, though I knew better by now than to say it. Will you be okay, she asked as she put up the rails of the bed, even though it was just a few feet to the door where the woman was waiting, radiating impatience. I'll get through it, I said, there isn't another choice. She started the bed moving with a little shove, then swung it wide to turn into the room with the scanner. This was larger than the room for the CT, and the machine was larger too, with a much longer tube; it wasn't just a ring you passed through but an actual chamber you were enclosed in. They let me move myself to the long slab, where they put a pillow under my knees, like they did for the CT, but they told me to put my arms by my sides, not stretched above my head. Alivia worried with the tubes and wires, making sure they wouldn't snag or get tangled, and then the woman who had injected me with the dye, who had been impatient about the bathroom, stood over me with a sheet outstretched in her hands. We're just going to use this to tuck your arms in place, she said, it will help you keep still, and then she was swaddling me with it, pushing the sheet beneath me until it pulled tight, binding me in place. Is that okay, she asked when it was done, though she wasn't really interested in the answer; when I said something half-hearted, I guess so, or I'm not sure, she just repeated that I needed to stay still, if I didn't they would have to start the scan over. Okay, I said. I was positioned to enter head first, and Alivia was at my feet, the little console from the monitor in her hands. I'll be right outside, she said, I'll be keeping an eye on your numbers, don't worry about anything. Then she stepped out, and the woman entered the booth where she joined another woman at the controls. There was a click and then a voice close to me, from a speaker on the machine, said One sec, we're just making sure everything's set here, we'll get started soon; and then, a moment later, it told me to relax. I was anything but relaxed, my bladder had become a sharp pain, but I closed my eyes, I took a deep breath. Or I tried to, with the mask on it was hard to take a deep breath, you had to regulate your breathing when you were wearing them, the fabric stuck to your nose and lips if you inhaled with too much force. In the first weeks of the pandemic, when I kept my mask on outside, putting it on at the first sight of another person, even on the other side of the street, even blocks away—it seems ridiculous now but it was my response to how frightened I was, and also it was a kind of politeness, a sign of caring for other people, an acknowledgment that we were all going through the same thing. In those first weeks if I walked too quickly, or up the steep hill from the river to our house, I would pinch the fabric and hold it away from my mouth so I could catch my breath. Of course that wasn't an option now, with my arms pinned as they were to my sides, I could only breathe in more gently, more slowly, I tried to breathe through my nose. I kept my eyes closed as with a little jolt the slab I was lying on began to move. It wasn't like the CT scanner, which sucked you in quickly and spat you back out, all in the span of the breath you had to hold, expanding the abdomen so the image would be clear; this was slow, almost imperceptible, after the initial shudder I hardly felt I was moving at all. It wasn't so bad for the first five or ten minutes, I lay with my eyes shut and tried not to think of time passing, tried to be blank, tried not to feel the pain of needing to piss, tried not to move, not to imagine the machine finding inflammation throughout my system; hot spots, the rheumatologist had said, and I imagined them as little red Xs on the map of my arteries and veins, mines about to blow.

And then I opened my eyes. She had asked me if I was claustrophobic, the woman with the radioactive dye, she had said they could offer me a sedative if I was, to keep me calm, to help me through it. But I had never thought of myself as claustrophobic before, I had never had an issue with elevators or enclosed spaces. Once, when I was a child, on a field trip to a cave—they were rituals in elementary school, each year we went to one, Kentucky was proud of its caves—a girl had to be carried out hyperventilating from the chamber where we were crouching but I felt fine, I wasn't bothered at all. But when I opened my eyes now and found the wall of the tube just inches from my face, from my arms bound at my sides, I felt something entirely irrational; it made me inhale sharply, which I couldn't do, the fabric of my mask stuck to my mouth so I could hardly breathe at all. Stay still, I said to myself, though movement was the only thing I wanted, to free my arms and crawl out of the tube that felt intolerable to me now, like a straitjacket or a grave; it took all my will to hold myself still, the stillness of an animal about to bolt. Be calm, I said to myself, to the part of myself I could feel with its hands on the bars, ready to rattle its cage. I thought of how hard Dr. Akeyu had said they had to fight to get the scan approved, how expensive it was, how long the wait; if I moved they would have to start again from scratch, it would mean pushing the schedule back, someone else who needed one, someone with a greater need than mine, maybe, would be pushed off until tomorrow. Or maybe they would push me off until tomorrow, delaying my discharge from the hospital, which though not yet definitely set had seemed more and more possible by the day, as they slowly transitioned me to pills for the blood pressure, as I went one day and then another without fever; and I was desperate to leave by now, I was desperate to be home. I placed that desperation against my desperation to escape, to move my arms and rip off my mask, to breathe; I had to stay still, I would stay still.

I felt a weird pressure clawing its way up my throat, and realized it was a scream, an actual scream, a sound I hadn't made since I was a child; to scream now would mean a reversion to childhood, a breakdown of the personhood I had built, I would not scream, it was impossible to scream, I was on the brink of screaming. I opened my eyes, just for a moment, and saw again the tube inches away, bathed in a dull blue light. I must have moved since the last time I had looked but it was impossible to gauge how far. I closed my eyes again, quickly, screwing them shut. I tried to think of poems, the poems I had memorized; for years I had been memorizing poems and then reciting them at night, as I tried to sleep, as a way of calming my mind, Th'expense of spirit, I thought, When I do count the clock that tells the time. They were sonnets I had had my high school students memorize and recite, for years I had listened to them, some of them perfect and poised, some suffering, their voices trembling; for some of them it was an ordeal, I would coach them privately and still they would crash and burn, as I remember one saying to me after, I crashed and burned. Mostly they got better but sometimes they didn't, and I wondered now if there was any point to it, not to making them memorize the poems but to the performance, I wondered if it did more harm than good. It did no good for me now, a line would come and then slip away, taking with it the poem, Busy old fool, I work all day, I wake and feel, How vainly men; no sooner did I catch a phrase than it was gone. It was like spinning the dial on an old radio, though that wasn't quite right; they scattered of their own accord, they were creaturely somehow, skittering spined things slipping through my fingers, they were of no use at all. I tried to inhale, deeply, through my nose. Surely Alivia would stop it, I thought, my numbers must be so high, my heart rate and blood pressure, surely she would tell them to let me out; it wouldn't be shameful if she was the one to stop it, it wouldn't be my fault. But she didn't do anything, and after the scan she would say to my disbelief how well I did, how stable my numbers were, she would say it with a kind of pride. I could feel my heart pounding in my chest, which is the kind of phrase I hate, it's never precise except when it is, my heart was hydraulically pounding, a piston. Love set you going like a fat gold watch, I thought, that too was a line that went nowhere. I tried to think of my studio, I tried to imagine myself in the armchair where I read, I tried to remember the days after the storm, the emerald light, my studio in the trees, the feeling I had loved, which did nothing to calm me now; and then our bedroom, the white floor and walls, the white ceiling, it's like sleeping in a cloud L had said one of our first nights there; I thought of our bed, which I longed for, to stretch out in our bed, unencumbered by wires and tubes; I thought of L, of his face, of touching his face, I thought of his hands on my body as we slept, his hand on my stomach; I thought of his face against mine in the hospital room, the smell he brought of home, and none of it helped, they were like images on water, scattering at my touch. My whole mind was like that, an image on the water, my self quicksilver, anywhere I tried to grasp myself I fled myself, there were no images or poems. And then suddenly I realized I had been repeating something, not a poem, not even a line, but two words I made into a kind of chant, the smallest possible patch of stable ground. I kept chanting them even when I opened my eyes a third time and found that I was emerging from the scanner, inch by inch, that I could see the ceiling tiles, that it was almost over, it was a way of gathering myself to chant it: naked rock, naked rock, naked rock, naked rock, naked rock.

5

They told me it was my last day, that finally they would let me go home. Assuming the schedule works out, Dr. Akeyu had said, very early that morning, with her students crowded into the smaller room I had been brought to the day before, after being discharged from the ICU. There was one procedure left, to insert a PICC line for antibiotics; for six weeks I would stay on intravenous drugs, I needed a special port put in. The regimen of pills had been set, I had gone a whole day with stable pressure, low enough still that I would have to be careful walking, Dr. Ferrier had told me the previous afternoon on her rounds; you might feel dizzy and weak, she said, I'm sorry, but we have to keep you safe. I'm so ready to go home, I told her, I need to get out of here, but I don't understand, what happens now? Everything was unresolved, why this had happened and what would happen next: they had never found an infection; the PET scan had turned up nothing, that whole ordeal had been meaningless—not meaningless, Alivia had said when the news came in, we needed to know and now we do. But we knew nothing, it seemed to me, everything was inconclusive, nebulous, nothing was clear. They hadn't done anything, I wanted to say, though that wasn't true, there had been all the pills and injections, the endless bags of fluids and drugs, the IVs that burned out now as quickly as they were placed, it seemed, even the A-line had given out, finally, now a new one ran into my other arm; they had bombed me with antibiotics and flooded me with radiation; but there had been nothing climactic, nothing decisive. Surgery had been discussed and put off but was surgery off the table forever, I asked. It's not off the table forever, she answered, I know it's frustrating that we can't tell you anything more certain. It's a waiting game really, we'll scan you at two weeks and four weeks, then at three months and six, and from then on every six months you'll have an ultrasound and every year a CT scan. If things become unstable we'll go in and fix it. But I don't understand, I said, if it can be fixed, why don't you fix it now. Nobody would want to do any of those things until we had to, she said, certainly not the big surgeries, and even a stent can cause complications, we're not going to do anything like that while there are other options. Probably we'll have to at some point, she went on, but every year we can push it back is a victory, that's how to think of it. How many years, I wanted to ask her, how many years are left, I meant, but the question caught in my throat. The real test now is whether you get sick again, Dr. Ferrier went on, when you go off antibiotics in six weeks, we'll see if the fever comes back or the pain, we'll know then whether we've managed to clear out any infection, if there was an infection. Well, I said, that is just really unsatisfactory, I don't like that at all, and she laughed. I like to see my patients get ornery, she said, that's how I know you're feeling better.

I was feeling better, that was true, there wasn't any pain. But I kept asking for oxy every four hours, it helped me bear the days; I didn't even know how many days it had been at that point, more than a week, it took an effort to tally them up. The new ward was a novelty, at least, an alteration, though it was less comfortable than the room in the ICU. Alivia had warned me, You've been in the lap of luxury, she said, the main ward won't be so nice, and I had been apprehensive all the previous day, waiting for a room to open up. It must be someone's job, I thought, or several someones, deciding who went where; with Covid filling up the beds it must have been a nightmare to find rooms. I remembered the cots lining the corridors of the ER, the patients lying in them, the publicity of it, the indignity, I remembered the fear I had felt. I still felt it though it was muted now, its edge had dulled. Maybe I would have to live with fear forever, that was what Dr. Ferrier had meant, buzzing or blazing it would be with me for life. You'll have a roommate probably, Alivia went on, there are a few singles but most of the rooms are doubles, it's the luck of the draw. I tried to brace myself, I hadn't had a roommate in decades and I had hated having a roommate then; in college I had gotten out of the dorms as quick as I could to live alone. I wasn't a sociable person; the thought of a stranger, a sick stranger, a stranger as sick and as scared as I was, filled me with dread.

But I got lucky—You won the lottery, Alivia said as she wheeled me into the single room. I came down in a wheelchair, not the bed I had traveled in before, which was a sign of health, I thought, of relative health. There was no one to greet us, just the tiny room, barely big enough for the bed, a sad rectangle with a TV mounted at one end and, at the other, a smaller version of the monitor from the ICU. Everything was dingy, old, the walls scuffed and discolored, the radiator flaking off paint beneath a window that stared blindly at a brick wall. It was like a roadside motel, I thought, a way station between nowheres. But Alivia made the best of it; not too bad, she said as she surveyed the little room, stepping around the bed to peer in the corners, opening the drawer of the bedside table. No Bible, she said, and laughed, sometimes you find them, I don't know who puts them there. She opened the door on the wall facing the bed and slipped into the bathroom, where she whistled. Wow, she said, you really did win the lottery, would you look at this bathroom, though I couldn't, bound to the chair by my wires and tubes. I would see later that it was nearly as big as the room itself, though all it contained was a sink and a toilet, and an industrial-seeming shower big enough for three or four people, with heavy bars mounted to the walls for support.

Not bad at all, Alivia said, stepping back into the room. She might have been inspecting a new apartment, and for a moment I felt almost like we were newlyweds, just arrived at our first home. I would never see her again, I thought. She had hung my things—my computer bag, the little sack of clothes—from the grips of the wheelchair, and now she took them off, putting the computer bag on the table by the bed and asking if I wanted her to put my underwear in the drawer. That's okay, I said, don't bother, and she set it on the broad windowsill. The room looked like it had just been vacated, it smelled of disinfectant, there was moisture in the air; the bed wasn't even made, a sheet lay at the foot, folded into a neat square. Let me get this ready, Alivia said, and she shook it out over the mattress, quickly tucking the corners under. I guess there's a blanket somewhere, she said, I'll ask, I need to find the nurse anyway to hand you off, she'll get you hooked up to their equipment. She returned maybe five minutes later, trailing a heavyset older woman, whose name Alivia announced though I forgot it right away. She moved slowly, shuffling, and her face sagged in a way that conveyed an absolute of exhaustion. Alivia told her my name, and the woman raised the thick sheaf of papers she held in her hand, the pages half-sized and bound together by a large binder clip. Hold on, she said, let me find him, they gave me his info already. She had a low voice, graveled, stripped raw by cigarettes, not a Midwestern voice at all but a city voice, a New York voice, I thought. I wanted to ask her where she was from but I never would; the two or three times she entered my room it was impossible to ask her anything about herself, her whole demeanor forbade it.

She opened the sheaf of papers, leaving the clip attached, and I realized that they were her patients, her rounds, which seemed impossible, it looked like dozens of pages; surely she couldn't care for so many. It took her a long time to find my information; Alivia waited until finally she said Okay, got it, go on, and then quickly went through my history and protocol, the woman grunting in acknowledgment. And then Alivia stepped back, into the doorway, and looked at me. Well, she said, I'll head on upstairs. It's been a pleasure, I hope you'll keep feeling better. Thank you, I said to her, which was inadequate, and I was struck again by the asymmetry between a patient and those who care for them; Alivia said goodbye to patients all the time, after shepherding them through whatever crisis, she was used to it. But for me she was singular, she had cared for me in a way no one ever had, I was attached to her, and what could I say now that she was passing me on. It's like teaching, I guess, a relationship that engendered intensity but had transience built in, so that the sign of its success was its ending. It didn't occur to me to ask for her email or social media: it wasn't a personal relationship though it had felt personal, it was a bond that existed only in the hospital, not even the hospital, only in the particular ward I had left; here in this other place she had already withdrawn, become formal. Thank you for everything, I said, and she was gone. I meant to write a letter about her, to the hospital, to say how diligent she had been, how kind, how she deserved a place in that gallery of honor we had passed, a nurse for each month. But I never did.

Let's get you into bed, the woman said, can you stand up on your own? I could, more or less, though I was glad for the arm she held out for me. She moved the bags of antibiotics and fluids from the wheelchair to the IV stand by the bed, then hooked me up to their machines. She showed me how this was done, just unclip here, she said, holding up the wires, when you need to go to the toilet. So I don't need to call you for that, I asked. Nope, she said, you can take care of that yourself. I was surprised at the flare of joy I felt, the sense of freedom; and she didn't say anything about using a urinal, I could regain a bit of privacy, own again some of the data they had made my body produce. I'll be back to check on you, the woman said, and she asked me if I needed anything before she left, though her tone made me feel that I better not. I liked her, I decided, for all her gruffness. She would do her job and nothing more, and this restored something to me too, some independence, some dignity; I felt almost like a human agent again, I began to believe I might really get to go home. She grunted in displeasure as she took the wheelchair grips in her hands, and I heard a rebuke of Alivia when she said Somebody will have to get this back upstairs. Then she was backing out of the small space, towing the wheelchair behind her. The night passed slowly and without incident, dinner arrived on its tray, a little dish of canned vegetables, a cup of yogurt, toast; I thought with relief that maybe this dinner would be the last. I called L, as I always did, and showed him the little space. Hopefully it's just for one night, he said, hopefully tomorrow you will be home, I miss you so much, and he made a gesture as if he were hugging me, wrapping his arm around the air.

The nurse that last morning was young, in her twenties, full of energy, as quick as the night nurse had been slow. She was nicer than the other nurse, too, or ingratiating, maybe, as if I might fill out a survey evaluating her when I left. Are you comfortable, she asked, after she had given me my morning meds; maybe it would be my last cup of grainy water, I thought, my last heparin shot. She asked if I would have any visitors—guests was the word she used—and I said yes, my sister G, could she add her name in the system. There was a computer in the room, an old monitor beneath the television, in the little corner by the door to the bathroom, and she stood there making notes, tapping loudly on the keyboard. Her brown hair hung around her face in ringlets, and she had a way of giving her head little shakes that set them trembling, increasing the darting sense there was about her, the constant motion. Does she live here in Iowa, the nurse asked, just making conversation, not really interested, and I said no, she was driving in from Kentucky, she was going to be staying in our house for a few days. That's a long drive, the nurse said, her back still to me, and I made a sound of agreement. G had wanted to come from the start, it had been her first impulse, but I had put her off; there was no point, I said, if I could only have one visitor a day I wanted it to be L. Maybe I should come for him, she said, it's got to be so hard on him, I can help out. It was true that he would love to have her there, L had loved my sister from the moment they met. She had visited us my first summer in Madrid; she was studying in London then, or maybe she had already finished her degree and her husband was the student, her ex-husband now, her then-fiancé. She had met him in London, where she was doing her master's and he a PhD. I felt dread about it from the beginning, not that he was a bad guy or would treat her badly, but there was a kind of heaviness in him, of spirit, I mean, a kind of ambient dullness, again I mean of spirit; he was brilliant actually, studying on a prestigious fellowship. But from the start I knew he wasn't the man for my sister, and their engagement was like watching an accident unfold, maybe not a catastrophe but something that might have been averted; at any moment they might have turned away, they might have only grazed each other or missed each other entirely, but they stayed locked on course. And what could I do, her brother, there wasn't any way to warn or advise her, any way even to raise a doubt, to make her take a breath in the exhilaration she felt in their first months together; there wasn't anything I could say against him, and anyway what man would I ever think was good enough for my sister. My beautiful sister. He didn't come with her to Madrid, she came alone, and L was delighted. Qué alegría, he said, her alegría he meant, a kind of lightness she had, a kind of light. I'm not sure that's true anymore, or not to the same degree. It wasn't a catastrophe but there was suffering, on both sides; the separation had been amicable, but she had emerged chastened, I thought. It had been her first big mistake in life. Not that it was the first terrible thing to happen to her—she had been raised in that house too, the house filled up with rage, she had seen her parents' marriage founder, which *had* been a catastrophe, utterly savage; they had done all they could to destroy each other, her mother and my father, with no thought for my sister, or with the thought only of the weapon they could make of her. It wasn't the first terrible thing but it was the first she had wrought herself, and it had sobered her a little, it had taken a little of her shine.

But she was radiant in Madrid that summer, when L showed her the city, showing me the city too; we were radiant ourselves, I guess, new in love, intoxicated with each other and with Madrid, its brilliant light and dry heat, its long lit evenings. It was evening when I took a photo of them I love, early evening, there was still plenty of light. We were sitting in a square somewhere, I don't remember which, at a table with a large umbrella above it, not yet folded from the afternoon. My sister wore a huge-brimmed hat, though she didn't need it under the umbrella; maybe she put it on just for the photo, because it was glamorous and silly. Her bright sundress left her bronzed shoulders bare, and she looked unbearably young, which was another thing I wanted to say to her, you are unbearably young, too young for marriage; but I couldn't say it, one never feels too young for love, even love that locks in a pattern for life. Maybe all love does that, I don't know, maybe all love demolishes one pattern and sets another. And anyway G had always been eager to cast off youth, to be serious, mature, she had the impatience of the youngest child. But she's silly in the photo, and L is silly too, they lean toward each other, gazing moonily, hamming up their adoration, a real feeling they performed for the camera—an actual camera in those days, I hadn't given it up yet for my phone. The table was strewn with tapas and bread, cocktails served in oversized glasses; you can see my sister's in the photo, filled with fruit and ice. That was part of our silliness too, those endless cocktails that left me stumbling home, leaning on L in the early morning hours, after we had walked G to her hotel; L's apartment was too small for all of us, though he had tried to insist we could make room.

L would have loved to have her there those days I was in the hospital but it made more sense to wait. And she had her job, I reminded her. The firm was working remotely but the pressure was still intense, I knew, she was a junior associate; and she had the extra pressure of her pro bono cases defending protesters, she had to file motions and appear on Zoom calls with judges. And besides that she had her dogs, two hounds, one she had had for years, she had gotten her with her ex-husband and kept custody after the divorce; and a new one I had never met, a pandemic rescue G had fostered and then couldn't let go. That's a job in itself, I said, taking care of those dogs. We had decided it would be best for her to come when I got out of the hospital, when she could help us settle into the new life, the new routine. I wouldn't be worth much, I had told her; she could drive me to my appointments and take L, who didn't drive, to the grocery store, she could help him around the house. She had checked in with me every day, calling and texting. I had urged her to wait until I was actually discharged; I'll believe it when it happens, I had said the night before, from my new room, they can't promise I'll get out tomorrow. But she wanted to be there when I got out, she insisted, she wanted to drive me home.

She was on the road now, I told the nurse, it was a seven- or eight-hour drive, she should arrive that afternoon in time for visiting hours. The nurse reminded me that the hours were short, the rules were the same down here, she said. I asked then if she thought I would really get to go home. Well, she said, I think all they're waiting on is the PICC line, I'll send them a message to see what their schedule is like. There's no telling, really, don't get your hopes up too high, but I'd say there's a chance. If there's anything you can do, I said, please, I've been here so long, I want to go home. She had been getting ready to go, gathering up the packages she had opened, patting the big pockets on her scrubs for the sheaf of pages she had consulted, the same sheaf from the night before, I thought, the previous nurse must have handed it off; but she stopped for a moment and looked at me. Have you been in for a long time, she asked, and I said yes, I wasn't sure how long, ten days or eleven, I had lost track. Neither she nor the nurse from the night before had asked me for my history, the story I had repeated so many times in the first days, which was a relief; it was another step toward normalcy, not to be seen as so interesting, as having gone through something so worthy of re-lating. It was a relief to feel I was fading back into the usual dis-interest people have for each other, just a patient moving through a machine. For the moment it was a relief, I mean, now that I wasn't caught in so acute a crisis, now that the machine was pro-cessing me out. Shit, she said, breaking into candor, making me like her, that's a long time. All I can promise is that I'll do my best, I'll stay on the PICC team so they don't forget about you, I can't do much but I promise I'll do that. And there's something I need you to do for me, she said. She ducked into the bathroom, where there was a series of cupboards, some of them locked, and returned with two long green packages of antibacterial wipes. I must have made a sound of dismay, because she laughed. I guess you know the procedure, she said. Even if I'm leaving today, I started to say, but she cut me off, Even if, she said, it's proto-col on the ward, a bath every morning, and I took them from her outstretched hand. She didn't even offer to warm them; that must have been a luxury of the ICU. There's a washcloth in the bathroom for your face and privates, she said, why don't you go ahead and take care of that now so you'll be ready for the PICC line, and with a last little shake of her head she was gone.

I sat up once she had left. Even that was complicated, I had to curl my hands into fists, not tightly, which put pressure somehow on the metal nub of the A-line, bound against my wrist with tape; I curled them into loose fists and then, as gently as I could, trying not to jostle the needles, slowly I pushed myself up. I leaned forward to untangle the blanket from my legs, setting it to one side, and then I swung my legs, though swung isn't the word for the gradual slow movement I made, over the bed's other side, pivoting my torso after them. Even moving as slowly as I could there was a threat of dizziness, a wave that only slowness, only stillness kept from cresting. I made a sound at this point, every time I sat up, a long sighed whoa, the sound my grandfather made to cattle when they rushed up steaming on winter mornings, wanting their feed, a calming sound, whoa. I uncovered it then, my animal body, I undid the snaps of the gown, which I wasn't sure I would be able to do up again without help, and let it fall. I couldn't reach the plastic bag with my underwear, the windowsill was just one or two steps away but it wasn't worth it, I decided; I would go home that day, I would change them there. Nor was it worth it to take off my socks, which anyway I wasn't sure I could manage, Alivia had always helped me with them; and I guessed I wouldn't change the stickers with the electrodes, either, since the nurse hadn't suggested it, though Alivia had replaced them every day, always clipping the wires back on with her little rhyme, grass is green, smoke above fire. I would clean around them, I would do the best I could. I pulled open the package and made a face at the foul smell. They were almost unbearably cold, I could hardly force myself to run them over my skin, which puckered with gooseflesh.

I had never thanked Alivia for warming them, I had taken it for granted, as I had taken for granted the way she wiped down my back and my feet. I had never thanked her, not even when she washed my whole body, which she only did the one time, when I was on absolute bed rest. She told me to lie back, to relax, to move as little as possible as she washed me. She started with my legs, beginning above the knee but not too far above, well below my underwear; she dragged the warm cloth down the front of my leg first, then cupped her palm around my ankle, my left ankle, and lifted it up. She chastised me for lifting it myself; that's just what we want you not to do, she said, let me lift it, we don't want those muscles working at all. She was thorough but quick, entirely professional, so I can't explain why it felt so intimate to release the weight of the limb into her hand as she ran the cloth down the back of my leg, except that I'm more sensitive there, especially on the back of my knee. I remembered suddenly how once, years before, fifteen years, more, how is it possible, a man I had been flirting with at a bar touched me there. I had been talking to someone else, one of his friends, whom we were facing together, side by side, when surreptitiously, without my noticing—but how did he manage it, I can't figure out the logistics now: we were at a little table, I think, maybe I was standing and he was perched on a stool, this was in Avignon, the first summer I had spent abroad. It was August or July and I was a little drunk, I think, on gin and on the summer, too, on this man beside me I liked, the pleasure of knowing we were each of us steering the night toward the same conclusion, the pleasure of French, which I had studied for years but never really used, not like this, surrounded by it, immersed; it was amazing to me that the language worked, it was like a magic trick to speak and be understood, like the suspension of gravity or breathing underwater, a violation of natural laws. He was my age, twenty-something, an actor performing in the Festival, not in any glamorous way; he was a local, an extra or maybe something a little more than an extra, I never saw him perform. He touched me surreptitiously, so lightly that at first I thought it was a breeze against my legs; I was in shorts that summer, a ridiculous American in shorts, though it was in that little window of time when I was fit, or almost fit, and young enough that maybe it was charming to be ridiculous. That was something he said to me, at some point—it only lasted a few days, our little affair, and on one of them he said to me *t'es charmant*, which was pure romance, a moment of pure romance. So slowly that it might have been the wind he touched the back of my knee, with a single finger, tracing featherlight and slow a little line, and then again and again, stroking just an inch or two of skin that lit up the whole surface of my body, and not just my body, his body too, I'm sure. It was our first private touch, it made a circuit between us, it must have lit up the air all around, so that though I'm sure I didn't visibly react his friend responded right away, feeling the change of weather, he left us to ourselves. I hadn't thought of that for years, I'm not sure I had ever thought of it again, after that summer, which had other, more substantial adventures, but my body had remembered it, that inch or two of my body; how lovely that it had remembered it, triggered by so different a touch, by Alivia smearing me with the foul hospital disinfectant. It bathed me in fondness for that boy—what was his name—and that moment, for the boy I was in that moment. All of this came in a flash, instantaneous, time taken out of time, compressed the way memories compress when they lodge in the body, in taste or smell, in touch, when they leapfrog language and therefore time; it was as present to me again as when it had happened. That boy with his long hair, I remembered the way in bed it fell around my face like a curtain or a veil, the taste of his mouth, the wind in the plane trees outside my room, that ocean sounding in their leaves, all of it came in the instant before Alivia set my left foot down and took up the right.

She wiped down one arm then and after that the other, lifting those, too. Only then did she take off my gown, she undid the snaps at the shoulders and put her hand under my back (I was sitting upright, they did allow that) so she could pull the gown free. Stay like that a minute, she said, removing her hand to open a second package of wipes, one of which she used to wash my back. Now for the fun part. There's no good way, she said, as she always did, unclipping the wires from the stickers on my chest, fast or slow, giving me the choice; and as always I said fast, get it over with. One of the stickers was always falling off, two or three times a day an alarm sounded and I found it dangling from its wire in my gown. She plucked that one first, and then for each of the others she pressed one finger to its edge, holding the skin in place, and then pulled quickly but gently, as if she were afraid the skin might tear. It stung each time, it pulled out hair and left behind outlines of adhesive, dark grimy circles of dirt and fabric from the gown, sticky to the touch. She used a different cleaner for these circles, little pads with some kind of specialized agent for adhesive, and even these never quite got it all. I had closed my eyes while she was pulling off the stickers; I didn't want her to see me flinch, I'm not sure why, maybe it was a kind of politeness to hide my discomfort. She saw it anyway, I know it hurts, she said, I'm sorry.

I opened my eyes as she cleaned off the adhesive, the pads cold on my skin. I think usually I would have shut my eyes again, I don't like looking at myself, at my torso especially; I try not to see myself in mirrors, even clothed, on the street, I avert my eyes from shop windows as I pass, whether the image is distorted or true I don't like the look of myself. But I looked at myself now. Poor body, I thought. My stomach was covered in bruises, each heparin shot, three times a day, had left a mark, dark brown where they were fresh and yellowish as they faded, like punches from tiny fists; poor body. I felt so much shame for what I saw, the pectorals (which had been muscle once, briefly, for a year or two) sagging, the nipples dark and large, puckered from the cold, and beneath them the rolls of my stomach, three rolls of flesh that I had had since I was a child. My sister had always laughed at them, my older sister, she would pinch them and call me fat and laugh, the cruelty of children. Three rolls of flesh that grew progressively larger, like the image of a wave receding, though the last, the lowest, broad where it curved, seemed lunar to me somehow as I lay back, upright, as Alivia took the final wipe from the package; she had done the best she could with the adhesive, which would linger for days, impossible to scrub away. The cloth was warm at first, pleasant, she was gentle as she started at my chest, wiping across and then moving down, lifting my arms again to wipe my armpits. The liquid left a kind of shine on my skin, which was pale, even at the end of summer, because I never uncovered myself, not since I was a child. For years even with lovers I refused to take off my shirt, and I'm not sure I can remember ever being shirtless outside; it's ridiculous how much the thought horrifies me, even now, when I do take off my shirt in front of others, when I've learned there are men turned on by it, in back rooms and bathrooms, when I let men press their faces into my stomach and chest, sucking on my nipples or burrowing under my arms. All through my twenties I couldn't bear it but now I strip down without hesitation and still I can't imagine taking off my shirt in public, even at the height of summer, even at the swimming pool or the beach, places I avoid anyway.

There's a poem I love by a man I heard read once, at the university in Ann Arbor, a famous poet, a great poet, I think. He was a huge man, and already old then (he's dead now several years) and it was difficult for him to move, he lumbered, so that I thought how hard it must have been for him to travel, it's hard for me and he was much larger than I was, even at my heaviest, he must have been four hundred pounds or more. He has a poem I've never forgotten about being shirtless at the beach, feeling himself looked at by the other bathers with pity or amazement or disgust, politely or with pointed fingers, how he waits for open derision and finally it comes. The pistol-shot laughter, he writes, which of course you can't respond to, however painfully it strikes; you have to act as though you haven't felt it, you have to seem insensible, imperturbable, whatever dignity you can salvage depends on that. Bared body is not equal ever, that's another line I remember from the poem, and I remember how moved I was by him at the podium: distinguished, honored, reading about a humiliation I had felt and had never seen described in a poem. I had spent so much time avoiding that laughter, trying to avoid it, I had given up so much, I had let it, the fact of it or its specter, determine so much of my life. I had never felt the sun on my chest or my stomach, not a single time I could remember, so that the skin was moonish and pale, with five or six small moles, I've always had them, lunares, they're called in Spanish, a beautiful word, moon-marks. L had taught me that, pressing his finger to them as we lay naked together, one of the first days I had spent in his bed, learning to be with him like that, hungry for each other, then satisfied, then hungry again, lunares. Where my stomach was broadest it was streaked with even paler vertical lines, stretch marks, I have them at my shoulders too but they're darker there, a pinkish color, almost blue in spots, on my stomach they're white. I've had them too as long as I can remember. My father saw them once, I was maybe twelve or thirteen and he came to a doctor's appointment with me, I don't know why, he didn't usually come; and I remember my mortification as the doctor examined me, making me take my shirt off while my father was in the room, and then when the doctor stepped out and I struggled into my clothes again, as quick as I could, I remember my father's disgust. Jesus, he said, did you fill out so fast you got stretch marks, that was how I learned what they were called.

Alivia was thorough, the broad swipes she made across my chest and stomach left the hair there matted and wet, not that I'm very hairy, not as hairy as I'd like; I wish I could qualify as a bear, it would help with my erotic life, so many guys fetishize it, as I do too, I guess. The hair I have is thickest in the middle of my chest and then again low on my stomach, where it grows toward the navel; and it was thinner now than usual because so much had been torn out by the stickers for the electrodes, a new strip of which Alivia was fetching from the cupboard, having thrown away the used wipes. What a strange thing a body is, I thought, how eerie to be filled with blood and covered with hair, to be a machine any part of which might fail; and how strange to have hated it so much, when it had always been so serviceable, when it had done more or less everything I had needed until now, when for more than forty years it had worked so well. Poor body, I thought again, looking down on it. I had hated it so much and been so ashamed and I might have loved it instead, I thought suddenly, it had been all that time available for love and it had never occurred to me to love it, it would have seemed impossible, as it seemed impossible now. I don't think L knew how much I hated it, I had learned to hide it by the time we met, to act unashamed, I had learned if not to enjoy being naked with him at least to bear it. But maybe he did know, maybe that was why he slept the way he did, with one hand on my stomach, why he loved to touch me there, and not just when we were sleeping; he would come up behind me at all hours of the day and reach under my shirt, and on the couch, too, reading or watching a movie, he always wanted to touch me there, if I pushed his hand away he would reach for me again. Maybe he had sensed what I felt and wanted to teach me a different feeling, I don't know. But there are feelings we don't get to have, I thought as I washed myself alone, with the cold wipes smelling foul, there are lessons we can't learn. Or maybe that's not true, maybe I just needed more time. Maybe I could still get over myself, I thought, maybe L would teach me yet.

Every hour or so the nurse popped her head into my room to say she had texted the PICC team and asked for their status, urged them to bump me up the list. I'm telling them you're a priority, she said. They arrived late in the morning, just before noon. I was becoming aware of time again, as I considered leaving the hospital, where everything had happened to me I felt and also nothing, where time was both regimented—my pain pills every four hours, the heparin shot every eight—and didn't exist at all, was glassy and motionless, an expanse of water on a day without wind. Soon I would reenter the world of schedules and classes and events, I was eager for it and also cowed. G had texted from the road, she would be at the hospital by one. The PICC team consisted of two older women, ladies, I want to call them, in their sixties, with an air of respectability I associated with a certain kind of country life—with my grandmother, who never left her house anything but tidy, her house and her person, with the pride of a certain kind of poverty. She had had her hair done every week, at a salon in the home of one of her friends; it was my grandmother's one social event, seeing the other ladies at the parlor, as she called it. That was what I thought when the women came in, it made their green scrubs and face shields incongruous, as did their voices, which I heard before I saw them, familiar with each other, squabbling like old friends. They were pushing a large wheeled cart with various drawers and a large monitor on top, and they had trouble getting it into the room. It was an awkward room to get into; you turned from the hallway into a little alcove with my door on the left and another room on the right, where an old man—he sounded old, I never saw him— coughed day and night, struggling at times to breathe. Now, not like that, I heard them say, and A little more my way, and then finally they were in the small space with me, the machine lodged at the foot of the bed. The taller woman had her hair tightly

curled, undyed, a dark gray—that put me in mind of my grandmother, too—and wore glasses behind her visor; the other's hair
hung dark and straight to her shoulders.

They introduced themselves and quipped cheerfully that
they heard I was going home soon, I must be so happy, they
loved their job because mostly they saw people on their way
home. They took positions on either side of the cart, the taller
woman shimmying her way behind it, a tight squeeze, she said,
and then stood facing me, like salesmen delivering a pitch, I
thought, or students giving a presentation. They asked me if I
understood what a PICC line was, and I said I wasn't sure, a kind
of IV, I thought, was that right? Kind of, said the taller woman,
who was taking point, you're in the ballpark, and she spelled out
the acronym, what it stood for, which I forgot so immediately
I'm not sure I heard it at all, which is my response to whole
realms of experience, I just glaze over, and then she explained
the procedure. We'll start here, she said, using her right hand
to clasp the crook of her left arm, though then she alternated,
clasping her right arm with her left hand, we can do either arm,
she said, whichever you prefer, it makes no difference. Are you
right-handed, she asked, and I said I was, probably it would be
best to use my left arm. Great, she said, and the other woman,
the shorter one, stepped close to the bed and asked if I minded
if she took a look. I held out my arm to her, obedient, and she
said Wait, but this already has an A-line, that might be a little
tricky to work around. Should we use the other arm, she asked,
I wasn't sure if the question was directed to me or to her colleague, I started to say that was fine, I didn't care, anything to
get me home in good time, but the other woman spoke over me.

I bet he can go ahead and get that out, she said, if they're letting him go home today, why don't you see if you can find his nurse and ask.

She went on with her presentation while the shorter woman stepped out. She clasped her left arm again and said We'll start here, we'll give you a little injection to numb you up—that should be the worst of it, a little pinch and you won't feel the rest. Then we make a small incision here, she hadn't changed posture but she patted her left arm again, and we'll insert the catheter in the vein and push it up. Here she used her index finger to trace a line slowly up her left arm and across her chest, it goes all the way to the other side of the heart, to the—; and she used several words I didn't understand, I glazed over again, though I did catch the final two, *vena cava*, because they were short and also beautiful, and even with my almost nonexistent Latin I could translate them: empty or hollow vein. This was the large vein that conveyed blood to the heart, she told me, the catheter would rest there, where it could deliver the medicine most efficiently, the heart would pump it right through my body. All along they would be using ultrasound, that's what the cart was, or the top of the cart, an ultrasound machine, to monitor the placement in real time, to be sure everything gets where it needs to go. The nurse came in then, my nurse from the morning, trailed by the other woman. I'm so sorry, she said, I should have taken this out before you guys got here. No big deal, the taller woman said, her lecture done, it won't be a minute. The nurse washed her hands in the little sink in the corner, then struggled to pull on gloves. She took from the pockets of her scrubs two plastic envelopes, from which she extracted a small pair of scissors and tweezers, which she used to lift and then snip and pull out the three sutures holding the metal nub of the A-line in place. And now, she said, pressing a piece of gauze just behind the nub, at the insertion site, the main event, and in a single motion she pulled the line free. I closed my eyes at this, the sensation not of pain but of contrary motion, of something being turned inside out, and then I felt the relief of having it free. All done, she said, and I opened my eyes to see her holding the long dangling tube away from her body, still pressing the gauze to my skin. Do me a favor, she said, hold this in place for me for a minute, and I dutifully put my finger over the cotton while she discarded the line in the sharps box. She secured the gauze with tape and stepped back. He's all yours, she said, I'm sorry again. Nope, the taller woman parried, dismissing the apology, that's just perfect, we're all ready to go.

Once they started it was clear how practiced they were. The shorter woman gave me the shot of anesthetic, then placed a board under my arm, with Velcro straps to hold it still, while the taller woman opened a large plastic package and extracted a paper drape, like the one they had used for the A-lines but large enough to cover my whole torso, down to my knees; and she lowered me in the bed, too, using the controller to lay me out flat. Is that okay, she asked, when the bed was already in motion, it makes it a little easier. I didn't see much after that, I would have had to crane my neck to watch, which I didn't want to do anyway, especially after I glimpsed another plastic packet she had pulled from a drawer, with a coil of tubing that seemed inconceivably long; at the thought of it snaking through my veins I felt a surge of nausea. Better to look at the ceiling, the tiles scuffed and water stained. What a place to die, it occurred to me. I wasn't going to die there, not today, but people had, surely, in this room; how many people, I wondered, and how was it possible they had left no trace. All the people dying in this hospital over years, they had just been wiped away, which was the point of places like these, they were places for containing death, places where death could come and then be scoured away. They were someone's last sight, the tiles I was looking at, it was monstrous to think of their being anyone's last sight. I felt the gel of the ultrasound on my arm, but nothing else, just pressure as they made the incision, though they were active, both of them, I heard packages opening and items passed between them, I could sense them both working on my arm.

You doing okay, the shorter woman asked, any pain, and I said I was fine, no pain at all, I might just take a little nap. She laughed. I hope we won't give you time for that, she said. You guys make a real team, I said then, inanely, you must have had a lot of practice. Oh sure, the taller woman said, day in and day out, it's all we do, and we've been working together for what, and she paused, tossing the question to the other woman, who had the wand of the ultrasound, if that's the word for it, at my chest now, she had undone the clasps and folded down my gown. Ten or twelve years now, she said, I guess we could do this in our sleep. Well, I said, I appreciate it, I could talk like a Midwesterner too, it's good to be in such good hands. Does that look about right, she asked the taller woman, who was standing now at the monitor and chirped a quick Yep, I think we've got it, and then my mouth flooded with the taste of saline, that ghost taste, and the shorter woman applied a large dressing to my arm. Already done, I asked, genuinely surprised; it had all only taken fifteen or twenty minutes. The taller woman took the controller for the bed and brought me upright again. The dressing was transparent, I could see the tube where it emerged from my arm, just above the elbow, and split into two tubes that hung outside the dressing, one of them short, the other long enough to reach my hand. The ports at the end, one red, one blue, were each sealed with a white cap. The shorter woman curled the long tube and attached it with tape to my arm, just to keep it out of the way, she said, a nurse will be by in a bit to show you how it works. While she did this, the other woman gathered up the drape and other trash, which she placed in a small white bag she took from her cart. That's it for us, she said, we've got you ready to go home, and I thanked them both. It's looking good, my nurse said, coming back in once they had left; I think we can get you out of here in another couple of hours, the only thing left is for the home aid nurse to come by. She's supposed to be on her way, she'll show you how to use the PICC line, and then you'll be good to go. She took a step farther into the room, almost to the foot of the bed. The only wrinkle, she said, is getting Dr. Ferrier here, if you want to see her before you go home. I guess it's her clinic today and she's tied up until late afternoon.

Do I need to see her, I asked, she was by yesterday, and I know I'll be going in for an appointment next week. She had told me the day before that it would be the first of many appointments—with her, and also with infectious disease, each week they would draw labs to be sure the antibiotics weren't damaging my kidneys or my liver, with genetics, with a primary care doctor; I needed one of those, Dr. Ferrier had said, it was time, I needed somebody to help keep me on track. On track for what, I had thought. I've already assigned you to somebody here at the hospital, she said, I've set up an appointment for you, if you don't like her it's no problem, you can see somebody else, but she's my doctor, I think she's great. She had stayed with me longer than usual the previous afternoon, while I was still in the ICU; and she had been alone, I think for the first time, without any students in tow. When I expected her to leave she had sat down in the armchair instead, taking a load off, it seemed to me, wanting a minute to breathe. Everything okay, I asked, since it was a different affect than I had seen from her before, it seemed to invite intimacy. Yeah, she said, sure. But then she seemed to think better of it. It's been a long day, she said, one of my patients, she's not doing well, it's never easy when you have a day like that. She pushed herself forward to perch on the edge of the chair, leaning toward me. But let's talk about you, she said, that's a cheerier subject, and she asked me more questions about how I was feeling, what my appetite was like. Fine, I said, I don't know that I'd say it's back to normal but I'm eating. With hospital food who can say, she said, I don't think anybody has much of an appetite in here, and I agreed. I've been dreaming about the food at home, I said then, deepening the intimacy, I don't cook but L does, he makes delicious food from Spain, and I found myself telling her how he had cooked for me in the first weeks we were dating. Iowa City isn't a foodie town, there aren't many places for a proper date, and so most of the time we ate at L's apartment, a tiny one bedroom at the top of an old yellow house, not far from campus; sometimes I drove past it just for the flare of joy I felt at the sight of it still, though it wasn't a very nice apartment and L hated to remember his time there. It was barely a one bedroom, with only one proper room, the roof slanting low over the bed; and then a simple kitchen, nothing special, a small table in one corner; and on the other side of the kitchen the tiny study L used, barely large enough for his table and chair, with drafts of poems taped up on the walls. He had to teach himself how to make vegetarian meals for me, I told Dr. Ferrier, he searched the internet for ideas—I remember arriving one night to find heavy tomes of Spanish poetry pressing slabs of tofu wrapped in towels. He made a delicious tortilla, to die for, I said, with eggs and potatoes, and he had a dish with leeks, that was what the tofu had been for, I loved it; and croquetas, I said, almost moaning at the memory of them, with spinach and mushrooms, just the best. Though actually the best, I said, making her laugh, are his cremas, purees with butternut squash and carrots and potatoes; he's promised to make one for me when I go home, I'll definitely be hungry for that.

Great, Dr. Ferrier said, rubbing her hands together, that's great to hear, I'm glad you're thinking about happy things, about what's waiting for you at home. But what worries you, she asked, is anything keeping you up at night—anything other than us poking and prodding, I mean. Well, yeah, I said. And maybe it was the new intimacy we had established, the intimacy of her posture and of my talk, the fact that she was alone, maybe it was all of that that let me ask her the question I had always until then held back. So I've been poking around online, I started, and she groaned theatrically, Oh no, she said, falling back in the chair again and covering her face with her hands, that never goes well. I know, I said, and I know I don't understand a lot of what I'm reading, but I can't help myself, and some things that I've found are pretty scary. Okay, she said, serious now, let's talk about them. So the studies I was looking at, I went on, the mortality rates are pretty bad; I've forgotten the exact numbers, but at five years, at ten years, the outcomes aren't good. So I wanted to ask you what you think that means, for me, in terms of life expectancy, in terms of how much this has shortened my life. Oh, she said, with a tone of skepticism or dismissal, a reassuring tone, and so I said quickly, I want the truth, please, your best judgment, it's important for me to know. I thought of L's father, how the family had hidden from him that he was dying, how wrong that had seemed to me, how horrifying, though of course it wasn't my place to judge; but I would want to know, I thought, if I only had five years left I wanted to live them with that knowledge. Though what would it change, I wonder, and would it change anything for the good, or would it ruin the time I had left, had L been right with his family to keep it from his father, to let him hope; what gives value to time, the knowledge of its scarcity or the illusion of everlastingness, what takes value away. I was frightened as I waited for Dr. Ferrier to answer, some deep cord in me had drawn tight. Okay, she said, I'll give it to you straight. The answer is that we don't know—and the cord slackened, not in relief but disappointment. The fact is there's not enough data, she said, there just haven't been enough guys in their forties in the literature for us to have a real idea about outcomes. But I can tell you, in my professional judgment, that there's every reason to think those numbers you found don't apply to you. Those are based on people in their sixties and seventies, most of them already sick with other things. Look, she said, leaning forward again in the chair, I can't see the future, nobody can, but there's every reason to hope you can move on from this, you should think of it as an accident, something that happened to you that you can get over and go on to have a full life. I think there's every possibility that's true, and whether it's true or not I think believing it will let you have the best life.

Look, she said again, you could get hit by a bus tomorrow, so could I, knock wood, she looked around for wood to touch but there wasn't any, so I rapped my knuckles against my skull and she echoed me, knock wood. Any of us could get hit by a bus, we could catch a virus, we could die in a million different ways, that's just the fact of it, and working in a hospital you see them all. I don't think you should worry about this, she gestured to me in the bed, more than you have to. And you're going to be compliant, she said, you're going to take your meds and keep your appointments, you and L are going to take walks around the neighborhood, you're going to take care of yourself. She heaved herself out of the chair and stood beside me, putting a hand on my shoulder, which was another new intimacy, she had never touched me like that before, a non-medical touch, a human touch. Okay, she asked, and I said okay.

I don't think I need to see her, I said now to the nurse, I think it's fine. Great, she said, with a little shake of her head, I'll communicate that to her and so long as she agrees, you should be ready to go. She had already turned out of the room but I called her back, reminding her about the home nurse. Right, she said, holding her index finger up and then cocking it forward, let me get them on the phone. And I'll see if I can get your prescriptions sent down to the pharmacy so they'll be ready. She turned again, calling over her shoulder Almost there as she stepped into the hallway. Almost there, I echoed, mimicking her enthusiasm, I was embarrassed by the sound of my voice in the empty room. The man in the next room coughed again, he was always coughing, wet, dredging coughs that left him struggling to breathe; he wasn't almost there, I thought, and I imagined how the cheer in my voice must have grated. We could hear everything between our rooms, every word the doctors said, there wasn't any privacy, the walls carried sound; even in the ICU, where it was better, the walls were thicker, if doors were left open voices carried. In the ER, in one of the lulls between doctors, I had heard a conversation in the next room, a woman introducing herself as the psychiatric triage nurse, another woman weeping, saying I didn't know what else to do, he may never forgive me but I didn't know what else to do. The first woman, the nurse, said calmly, Let's take one thing at a time, and then, to the third person in the room, So you've been having thoughts about harming yourself. There was a pause that seemed full of tension, full of drama, and then a low voice, quiet, flat, said Well, I guess I have. It was a man's voice, my age I would guess or a little younger, not a city voice, a farm voice; they must have come in from miles away, who knew how far, where else was there to go, I wondered. As always when I heard that kind of voice I thought of my grandparents, of my grandfather, who was always distant, withdrawn, who disapproved of us, I always felt; impossible to imagine him in a place like this, saying those words, responding, as the woman asked if he had thought about how he would hurt himself, if he had a plan, in the same flat tone, Well, I guess I do. It was a flat tone that was also a tone of pure misery, the same misery the woman felt as she sobbed, or not the same, that was the problem, two miseries locked away from each other; and I thought of the nurse, who must ask such questions again and again, and hear such responses again and again, I wondered if she was a third locked misery in the little room. She told them she wanted to admit the man overnight, so they could keep him safe, a doctor would evaluate him in the morning. You did the right thing, she said then to the woman, and to the man, I'm glad you're here.

My phone lit up with a text from G, who had just parked and was in line at check-in, and a few minutes later another text said she was in the elevator, and then she was in my room, escorted by the nurse, who said Look who I've brought. I was so happy to see her, even in a mask and face shield, which she must have brought herself, they didn't give them to visitors; she was a piece of the outside world. She made the room bigger with her presence, lean and long as she had always been though with a new elegance, a new sophistication, in a dark pantsuit over a lighter blouse, her makeup fresh; I imagined her doing it in the car before coming up, the picture of a young professional, a young lawyer. It had been almost two years since I had seen her. Hey, she said to me, after thanking the nurse, drawing the syllable out in a way that grated a little; it was enthusiastic, full of cheer, but also ginger somehow, careful, as if probing a wound, and this was both because I was sick and because we weren't sure how to be around each other now. It was artificial, that was what grated, and the artificiality seemed thicker somehow, more solid, each time we met. Even before the pandemic we seldom saw each other, though I thought of her as the family I was closest with, so that each time we met we found the other older, in another stage of life almost, almost a stranger; there was a kind of stiffness, it took longer each time to find the intimacy we had known in childhood. But she was here, I told myself, as she bent over me for a hug; she had taken the face shield off and pressed her cheek against mine. That was what mattered, that I had needed her and she had come. Hey, I said.

I drew up my legs to make room for her on the bed, since there wasn't really anywhere else to sit and visit, just a rolling stool in the corner the nurses could use if they wanted. You look so fancy, I said as she arranged herself, perching on the edge of the bed, both feet on the floor. She laughed. I thought I should come looking like a lawyer, she said, I wasn't sure what you might need. She had come to advocate, I realized, to do battle, though there hadn't been any problems since the one day with the bad nurse, I hadn't seen her since and everyone else had been exemplary; my outburst had worked, or maybe G's call, or maybe it had really been an anomaly, a bad day. I could even feel sorry for the woman now, so young and so new to her job, so obviously overwhelmed. I think everything's fine, I said to G, you can consider yourself off duty. She put her hand on my leg, where it curled under the sheet. I saw her look at me, in my gown, with my unshaven face; I saw her take in the IV, the tubes where they entered my arm, the bags of medication, which were fewer now, just fluids and the antibiotics, and the new PICC line with its more elaborate tubing curled and taped to my arm. Her smile froze on her face, then faltered. It's okay, I said to her, I'm okay. She took a breath, she squeezed my leg. I brought some things for you, she said brightly, bending forward to gather the large canvas bag she had set at her feet; she pulled it into her lap and started laying the contents out on the bed between us. I thought you might be sick of hospital food, she said, so I made a quick stop on the way over. She meant at the Co-op, the organic market in town; she had brought chips and pretzels, hummus, a sandwich with roasted vegetables, a cup of cut fruit, pineapple and melon, a bottled smoothie. G, I said, you brought so much. She shrugged, opening a bag of chips, a chichi brand made with avocado oil, which she held out to me. I hesitated; the doctors hadn't said anything about diet, the presumption seemed to be that medication would do the work of keeping my blood pressure down, but L and I had talked about eating healthy, avoiding sodium and fat, and I had done my best with the hospital menu, sticking to fruit and hardboiled eggs and steamed vegetables with rice, chips were exactly what I shouldn't eat.

But that would mean telling G she had brought the wrong things, I imagined her feeling hurt, and so I reached into the bag, taking just one chip. It was thin and almost weightless, an amazing object, really, if you think about it, a miracle of engineering, a kind of transubstantiation of a root vegetable, which is an absurd thing to think and also true. When I put the chip in my mouth the pleasure was extraordinary, the taste of it but also the feel as I crushed it with my tongue; closing my eyes I could almost see lights shooting off in the interior, fireworks, after so many days without anything like it it was almost an orgasm. And it was entirely engineered, nothing in nature was like this, so perfectly tuned to our pleasure, whole teams of chemists had designed it. I knew it was pernicious, one of the manipulations of capitalism, a deformation of our natural response designed for addiction, it was the reason I was fat, the reason the whole country was fat, really it symbolized in miniature the utter decadence of all genuine value, the fall of a culture, absolute bliss. Fucking hell, I said. I thought of a conversation I had listened to sometime back, a podcast, between a theologian and a political pundit, a liberals' conservative, who had made a brand for himself in recent years as that beleaguered thing, a genuine moderate, he said, party-less now that his party had been radicalized, isolated in his integrity. It was a kind of martyrdom schtick, since there was a whole ecosystem for his kind of thinking, he had a weekly newspaper column, millions of followers on Twitter. This was before the pandemic, they were talking in front of a live audience, and the subject was wonder, which they were both advocating for, cultivating wonder; the theologian had published a book about wonder in everyday life, a kind of devotional posture toward the world. The pundit, who often wrote about what he called religious values, liked this idea, he was a churchgoing man, though also he styled himself as practical, no-nonsense, a middle-of-the-road American; he was a kind of homegrown, aw-shucks philosopher, and as the theologian waxed rapturous on his subject, the pundit stopped him short. I hear what you're saying, he said, I agree with you, but the problem with all this wonder is that it can lead to feeling like everything's extraordinary, to blissing out over a Snickers bar, at which the audience laughed. That laughter was the pundit's point, he was playing to the audience, he wanted to puncture the theologian's earnestness; and maybe he was right that it needed puncturing, but I was disappointed at how quickly the theologian conceded, joining in with the laughter, laughing at his own earnestness, at the rapture he had let himself feel.

But maybe a Snickers bar *is* a wonderful thing, I had thought, I mean in a strong sense, a source of wonder, like G's chips; maybe it's unfathomably wonderful, both in itself, as a product of science and experiment, and also as the end point of a whole system of production and distribution, the ingredients sourced I'm sure from all over the world, which can only be abstract to me, I don't have the brain for complexity and systems. But even in my dumb cartoonish way I could imagine what it must take

to make the chip that had lit up my brain, my whole sensorium: the potatoes came from somewhere, they had been planted
and harvested and packed and shipped; the salt had been mined,
which is a process I don't know anything about, I'm entirely ig-
norant; whatever machines had been designed and built to slice
and fry, all of it at scale; and then there was the packaging, which
was its own miracle, really, an extraordinary invention, a bag
filled with air to cushion these impossibly fragile things, somebody had thought of that; and then the systems of distribution
to carry them all over the country, the world, so that you can
walk into a store in the middle of America, in a college town
in Iowa, and for a few dollars fire up those points in your brain
that mean pleasure. If all that wasn't a source of wonder what
was, and of deep wonder, there was nothing saccharine about it;
of awe, really, since of course it was at once amazing, proof of
ingenuity and genius, and also the product of unimaginable suffering, of exploitation and violence and labor, whole histories of
conquest and colonization, industrial agriculture and ecological
devastation; and along the whole chain the devastation of human
bodies, from laborers in the fields to fat Americans shopping
organic markets; and there was truth in that, too, the intrication
of wonder and depravity, pleasure and violence. It's something
that saturates the past, that soaks the very root of history, and
that permeates the future, too, the whole scale of human time,
no document of civilization which is not at the same time a
document of barbarism, no truer thing has ever been said, and
it's a truth we should acknowledge. Of course I see what the
pundit was saying, it would be ridiculous to try to live like that,
in the glare of all that wonder and horror, it would be absurd,
simply impossible. But acknowledge that it would also be true,

I thought as I listened to his laughter, the laughter of the audience, the conciliatory laughter of his interlocutor; acknowledge the inadequacy of any other response, acknowledge that it's a failure to shut our eyes to it, a failure in the face of reality, a failure of perception and also a moral failure; acknowledge that the only vision of life we can bear is a lie.

It's good, right, G said. She reached into the bag herself, first pulling her mask down under her chin, which for a moment made me uncomfortable, I remembered Dr. Ferrier's warning about Covid, her word, catastrophic. But we would be spending days together, the whole weekend, at least, and if I asked her to wear a mask I was afraid it would fix the unfamiliarity between us, that chill I was waiting to warm. I took the cup of fruit, I wasn't hungry but it would give me something to do with my hands, which otherwise would, as if independent of my will, keep dipping into the bag G held. I asked her how work had been, and she shrugged, It's fine, she said, whatever. She had been excited when she first got her job, it was a prestigious firm, but in the two years since her excitement had faded. That had been part of adulthood for her, the fading of enthusiasm, which had been a little sad to see, it happens to almost everybody but I wish it hadn't happened to her. She drew one of her legs up onto the bed and turned toward me, making us a little more brother and sister, letting some of the formality melt. If it wasn't for the pandemic I'm sure they would have fired me, she said, they keep telling me I need to be more productive, to earn more, but all I want to work on are my pro bono cases, the protesters. What's going on with those, I asked, and she leaned forward over the knee she had curled on the bed. Mostly they're dismissed, she said, the bullshit charges like stepping off the sidewalk, mostly the minute they see you're going to fight them they give up. But she had a couple of clients they wanted to make examples of, she said, especially one man who had been a leader of the protests, a young guy, twenty-two. They were trying to throw the book at him, he had blocked access to government buildings, they said, he had incited violence; which is bullshit, G exclaimed, making a gesture of exasperation, a chip in her hand, the violence is all on the other side. They shove people with their shields, they hit you with their batons, and anything you do to defend yourself is assault. I don't usually do these kinds of cases, she went on, this is the first time I'm really seeing how dirty the cops are, how bullshit the whole system is. She paused. Or it is sometimes, when it doesn't work right, when they manipulate it, it's an education for me. The big thing they're trying to pin on him, the scary thing, is that he was part of a group of guys who set a police car on fire, that's the charge we have to fight. Did he do it, I asked, and in the look she gave me I saw she expected the question and also that it disappointed her. He says he didn't, she said, and I wondered if she believed him. But come the fuck on, she said. They want to put people away for years for burning a car, and those cops, they shot a woman in her bed and what's going to happen to them. In her bed, she repeated, and nothing's going to happen. They shot another guy in his bar, in his place of business, and nothing will happen to them for that, either, that's what's got to stop, these cops think they can do anything and get away with it, the impunity they have is disgusting. What's a burned car next to those bodies, she said. Hopefully they'll let it drop, she went on, they don't have any hard evidence, just a statement from a cop who didn't have his body camera on, which he should have, that's embarrassing for them; and it was dark, and everybody was masked, I'm not sure they'll try to charge him just based on that. So long as something else doesn't pop up, another witness or a video on social media or something, if that happens I have to find somebody to take the case, somebody who really knows this kind of law, I couldn't give him the best defense. So I've been reaching out to people, trying to find a good lawyer to take him on pro bono, just in case, she said. It's good you're doing all that, I said, helping those guys. She shrugged. It's not enough, she said, it doesn't feel like enough. She put the chip in her mouth, finally. But it might be enough to get me fired, she said, changing the tone, and I laughed. I guess I don't care, if they fire me they fire me, I'll find another job.

And what about the dogs, I asked, who's taking care of them, and she gave me a half-guilty, half-mischievous look before she said Nobody, I brought them with. You brought them with, I said, surprised, where are they, and she told me she had found an Airbnb just out of town, a guesthouse on a farm where the dogs would have plenty of space to run. It was easier than trying to find somebody to watch them, especially Mary, she has so much anxiety, G said, prying the top off the little tub of hummus, new people are really hard for her. That's the new rescue, I asked, and she said Yeah, the poor thing, she was in a puppy mill that got raided, all these dogs that had been in cages their whole lives, permanently pregnant. When I first saw her I almost burst out in tears. A rescue agency had put a call out on Facebook, asking for foster homes; there were dozens of dogs, G said, all in bad shape, when she saw the photos on Facebook she reached out, then drove to West Virginia to see for herself. You wouldn't believe how skinny she was, G said. She had opened a bag of baby carrots for the hummus and held them out for me; I waved away the hummus but put a carrot in my mouth, enjoying the crunch, the bright freshness, it was something I had missed. She was just skin and bone, literally skin and bone, you could count her ribs—and her teats, the way they hang down, I've never seen anything like it. All she had done her whole life was give birth to puppies and feed them, the poor baby. She had lost almost all her teeth, from malnutrition or from gnawing on her metal cage, it makes me sick to think about. It had taken hours before G could touch her, hours of sitting in the grass in the yard at the rescue, speaking softly to her, offering treats. Finally she took one from my hand, G said, and then she let me pet her, she decided to trust me, I guess. Pretty soon she'd laid down next to me and claimed me as her person. I fell in love with her, G said, it's my first time and I'm going to be a foster failure, I'm pretty sure, I just can't imagine letting her go. And she had bonded with Leia, G went on, her other dog, the one I loved, they were inseparable now, sisters; and Mary had started putting on weight, she had learned to ask to go out when she needed to pee, she could almost sleep through the night. She's doing so good, G said. How was she on the drive, I asked, and she said That's still hard for her, I had to give her something for that, she and Leia both, they're sleeping it off now at the Airbnb. You know you could bring them to our house, I said, you don't have to stay at an Airbnb, we could make room. I know, she said, dismissing this, but I think it's better this way. The dogs will be calmer, and I'll be close enough to come by whenever. But I want you to meet Mary, she said, and Leia will want to see her uncle. I thought I might bring them by tomorrow morning, we could stop by the house and then go to a dog park not far away, if you're feeling up to it, I googled it, it's just a few minutes from your house. Will Mary be okay there, I asked, and G said she loved being around other dogs, it was just people who gave her trouble.

There was a knock at the door then, the nurse coming back, and G put her leg on the floor quickly, almost guiltily, as if we had been doing something illicit. You guys look like you've been having fun, the nurse said, ushering into the room a small, middle-aged woman, brown haired and tidy, who carried a large paper bag in front of her, holding it with both hands. The home aid nurse is here, my nurse said. G hopped up and put her mask back on. Let me get out of your way, she said, and gathered the food back in her plastic sack. The home aid nurse introduced herself, telling us her name and the company she worked for. She set her bag down on the left side of the bed, and I shifted a little to make room. She was here to show me how to use and care for the PICC line, she said, pulling items out of the bag: individually wrapped antiseptic pads, a large ziplock bag of syringes, and what looked like a sock, an elastic mesh tube open at both ends. It was a complicated procedure, giving myself the medications; she demonstrated first and then had me go through it several times, with G watching and asking questions. It's helpful to have a second person there, she said, but you can do it by yourself. The biggest danger with PICC lines is infection, she told us, and she emphasized how important it was to sterilize surfaces (she had a drape that she laid over the foot of the bed), that I should wash my hands and sterilize the ports for a full ten seconds, the syringes, too, whether the medication or the saline, I should rub the end for a full ten seconds with an alcohol wipe before screwing it into the port. If there was any redness at the injection site, if it started itching or if there was any pain, there was a number I should call; someone would be on duty and could assess whether I should go to the emergency room. It wasn't likely with all the antibiotics I was on, but it wasn't something to fool around with, if an infection set in it could be hard to knock out, she said, you need to be vigilant. Morning and night the procedure was the same: open the port, inject saline, then the first antibiotic, then more saline, then the second antibiotic, then finally a third syringe of saline. That's why there are so many of these, she said, holding up the big ziplock bag, this is a week's supply. It was important to do all of this slowly, especially the first injection of saline, I should set a timer for thirty seconds and make sure I took at least that long to depress the plunger; the second and third times it wasn't so important, I could inject it more quickly. And you want to go even more slowly with the antibiotics, she said, and here she pulled the last thing from her paper bag, a small styrofoam cooler, which she opened to show me the two bags with their smaller syringes, fourteen of each, also a week's supply. She held them up for me to see and then replaced them in the cooler. Put these in the fridge as soon as you get home, she said, they can only be at room temperature for a couple of hours before they have to be replaced. The cooler was just for transport and in case we should ever lose power, we give them to all our patients, with the storms we have rolling through you never know when you'll need it.

You've been getting those drugs through the IVs, so we won't use them now, you'll take them for the first time tonight. But they're powerful, she went on, taking them slowly will help you tolerate it, so you don't get sick to your stomach. This was true, I would find, later that night, even going slowly I had to clench my teeth against the nausea. Set your timer for two minutes, she said, go as slowly as you can and see how you do. Some people just can't tolerate it, and if that happens it's not the end of the world, we'll come set you up with an IV drip. But that would mean we have to come more often, so the insurance doesn't like it, and it's a lot more sitting still for you, if you can manage it most people prefer getting it done in a couple of minutes instead of an hour. There were other points of care, especially the need to keep it dry, which would mean having L wrap my arm in plastic wrap before I took a shower, and still I should do my best to keep out of the water; If the dressing gets wet I'll have to come out to change it, she said. Assuming there aren't any problems I'll be out to do that once a week, when I drop off fresh supplies, someone from our office will give you a call today or tomorrow to schedule that. I would look forward to these visits over the next weeks, the relief of her pulling off the bandage, the few minutes of exposure to air, and especially her wiping down my arm with the disinfectant cloth, the prickling cool on my skin was weirdly blissful. Last thing, she said, holding up the mesh sock, this keeps everything out of the way. She showed me how to put it on, coiling the long tube of the PICC line and then dragging the elastic mesh over it. All done, she said. She went over again the various complications that might arise, which to call the nurse on duty about and which to take to my doctor, and which should send me straight to the ER. She was packing up her things as she said this, throwing away the syringes we had used, placing the cooler in the large bag, which she left for me. Okay, she said, by way of farewell, you know where to reach me, and G and I both gave her our thanks.

G had been standing all this time, since there was nowhere to sit, or half standing perched in the little windowsill; now she sat back on the bed. My nurse came back in; she was still waiting for the final sign-off, she said, any minute vascular should let me go. How about we get you off all this equipment, she proposed, and I said yes, please, I couldn't wait. There was just one IV port now, on my right arm, and it came out easily, the worst part, as always, the tearing off of the tape. I stretched my wrist in circles after it was gone, then unclipped the electrodes from my chest so she could pull the wires free of my gown. Once this was done she pushed the monitor back so it was flush with the wall, and moved aside the IV stand, from which she had unhooked the last bags of fluids and medications. Freedom, I said, I can't believe it, and I asked her if I could go ahead and get dressed, I wanted to leave as soon as I could. Oh sure, she said, as she stepped out into the hall again, and I asked G to hand me the bag from the windowsill, I slowly moved my legs off the bed to sit upright. G looked away as I unclipped the gown, which I balled up and set beside the pillow; never again, I thought, goodbye gown. I pulled out my T-shirt from the plastic bag, a cotton white undershirt, I have to wear them in the summer, otherwise I sweat through my button-down. Alivia must have folded it, I thought, it was a neat square, another kindness, and I shook it out before sliding in one arm and then the other and pulling it over my torso. I did this gingerly, the PICC line didn't really impede my motion but I could feel it bulky on my arm, and *in* my arm; I kept waiting for a pain that didn't come. I put on my shirt next, leaving the buttons undone as, still sitting, I put first one leg and then the other into my jeans. These were the clothes I had worn into the ER, so many days before, they had the feel of life outside the hospital, the life I had chosen and made, of movement and action; they were the same clothes but so many things had changed. Even though I rose slowly my head swam, I fell back upon the bed and G stood quickly up. It's okay, I told her, just dizzy, and she supported me as I stood again, her hand on my shoulder as I pulled up the jeans and fastened them at my waist. I sat back down to slowly thread the belt through the loops. I was like a child again, having to think about motions that had long been automatic, what a little time it takes to part us from the life we knew. But I was in my own clothes again, buttoning up my own shirt. I was going home.

Everything was ready when the nurse returned and pronounced me free. I can't believe it, I said again, inanely, I can't believe they're letting me go. I tried to pick up my computer bag but G insisted on carrying everything, that and the plastic bag with the book L had brought me, and the third bag with the food from the Co-op, and the large bag the home aid nurse had left. She stood beside me as I rose again from the bed, keeping my hand on her shoulder as the world around me spun. Are you all right, she asked, and I took a deep breath, then another, and said I was. I'll show you guys the quickest way out, the nurse said, and we followed her, walking slowly, G at my side, down the narrow hall. I kept my eyes on the floor. I didn't want to look into any of the rooms we were passing, I had had enough of sickness. I wanted to be on the other side again of that gulf that separates the sick from the well—or what seems like a gulf, I had crossed it in a flash; I wanted as much distance as possible between myself and the narrow beds in those rooms, their cargo of misery and hope, I wanted to put it all behind me. At the end of the hallway there was a reception desk, a flurry of activity behind it, they paid us no mind. Probably someone was cleaning my room already, I thought, stripping the bed and scrubbing the

floors, making it a sterile space again, ready for another sickness
to come in, another desire to live. Construction has everything
messed up, the nurse said, the elevator on this side isn't working,
and she pushed through the double doors leading out of the ward,
then pointed toward another, single door on the left, a staircase. If
you can manage it, she said, this will take you right down to the
pharmacy, it's just two flights. G looked at me, uncertain, but I
said it was fine, I thought I could do it. The nurse took her leave
then, wishing us luck.

I was a long time getting down the stairs, I had to take them
one by one, like an old man, I thought, holding on to the railing
as I lowered one foot and then the other. G, too burdened to offer
me a hand, stood in front of me. I'll break your fall if you trip,
she said, which made me laugh, I was twice her size, more; If I go
down you'll be coming with me, I said, better just get out of the
way. The pharmacy was across the large open space the stairwell
opened into, a kind of lobby, a place for passing through. My prescriptions were ready, two different blood pressure medications, a
bottle of oxycodone, the laxative I had been on in the ICU, which
I should keep taking, they said, for at least a couple of weeks.
When the pharmacist asked me for ID I started to hold my wrist
up toward him, as if he needed to scan the bracelet still hanging
there, and then was flustered when I realized my mistake, and
flustered too that my wallet wasn't in my pocket, that I didn't
know where it was. G had to search through the bags, I felt a
pang of embarrassment as she rooted around before finding it.
The pharmacy was right by an exit, and I made a sound as we
passed through, a grunt of animal happiness; I stopped moving,
I closed my eyes to take it in. I had been in a cage, I thought,
an animal in a cage; there was joy in movement, in being out of

doors, detached from machines. Try to remember this, I admonished myself, since I knew it would fade. All happiness fades, or does for me; misery digs deep gouges in memory, sets the course of the self, I sometimes think, it lays down the tracks one is condemned to move along, whereas happiness leaves no trace. Remember this, I said to myself. Why should only suffering be a vale of soul-making, why shouldn't the soul be made of this moment, too, this unremarkable moment, remember this. You okay, G asked again, and I realized I was in the way, it was a busy entrance, people were coming and going for visiting hours. I stepped to the side. The afternoon was warm, not brutally hot as it had been when I arrived; it was September now, I thought suddenly, early September, soon it would be fall.

There was a large circular drive just in front of the sliding doors, to either side of which there was a bench. Why don't you sit down, G said, it's kind of a walk to the car, and she pointed to a parking structure to the right. It wasn't so far but the stairs had tired me, the stairs and standing, I was happy to sit with the little bag from the pharmacy perched in my lap. I had been sending L updates all morning, and I texted him now that we were on our way, we would be home soon. There were three or four cars in the circle, opening doors and discharging passengers before gliding out toward the parking garage, or turning the other way, the way back to town. There wasn't much else to see; beyond the cars and the road there was just another building, another segment of the hospital complex, a little city within the city. But I didn't need to look, I was happy just to feel the air; even mixed with car exhaust it was still uncanned, moving, it smelled of the world. I closed my eyes for a moment, and then G was beside me, I felt her hand on my shoulder and saw that she had pulled up to the curb, that the passenger door was open. She helped me up, and I needed help, there was nothing to hold on to but her; I had become someone who needed help to stand up. We waited a minute for the dizziness to pass, and then I took the few steps to the car, moving slowly, G's arm under mine; I had become someone who moved slowly, a shuffling old man.

It was a short drive to the house, just a few minutes. I gave G directions as we followed the road that twisted among the hospital buildings and then turned north along the river. G had never been here before. I wish you could have seen the house before the trees fell, I said, it's still pretty banged up. And the yard is a mess, I went on, not that it had ever been anything but a mess, it's pretty far down the list of priorities. But she didn't care about any of that, she countered, she was happy just to see it, she was here to help; if she could have she would have fixed the roof herself. Our street was just past the art library, a building I loved, the books housed in a segment that extended from the main building like a boxcar over a small pond, the walls lined with windows. It was the best place in town to study, quiet and mostly empty, with tables looking out over the water. L and I had spent hours there, in the first years when I was still a student; we would sit across from each other and work, or mostly work, our legs entwined. Just past that, up the hill, was the main art building, which I also liked, it was like a series of boxes piled helter-skelter, the façade covered by a kind of metal lattice or screen, a sort of sheet perforated by small circular holes. It was beautiful at night, with the windows lit up, and it was lovely inside, too, L and I walked through it every now and then, a huge bright open space bridged by walkways, warrens of classrooms and studios along the sides. Everything was white, which

L loved, he had wanted everything white in our house, the paint, I mean, flat white, white against white; and the floors as light as possible, the natural wood, with no stain, there was a cleanliness to it he liked, I think, a sense of openness and possibility, of freshness. Past the art buildings there were a couple of apartment complexes, newish and mostly dire, the threat of things to come; off to the right was a street lined with sororities. After the apartments the road curves to the left and you leave the university behind; it's as though there were a hard boundary, a border, between the world of students, of rentals and youth and transience, and the more settled world where we lived. An old house marked that border, older than ours, its three levels just slightly misstacked, like a storybook house; it was on a huge parcel of land, a triple lot maybe, no new house would get so much land in our neighborhood, I wondered how they had held on to it. Half of the property was given over to a garden, a serious garden, with corn and cabbages and rows of peas and several huge sunflowers that towered over the high fence meant to keep out deer. It was like my grandmother's garden, where I spent most of my time when I visited the farm as a kid, I was too little to go out into the fields but I could work with my grandmother, long mornings and afternoons doing whatever tasks she gave me. A picket fence, ragged now, the paint chipped off, separated their yard from the road, but they had planted there, too, it was an extension of the garden, both sides of the sidewalk riotous with wildflowers. Other houses in the neighborhood had followed their lead, there was a movement to replace lawns, which take up so many resources and offer so little in return, they're ecological nightmares, with native plants and flowers, with prairie grasses, hardy and beautiful and home to a million creatures, shelter and food. L and I wanted to do that to our yard eventually, when we could afford it—afford the money or the time, since we had either to pay someone thousands of dollars or become the kind of people who could do it ourselves. G was driving slowly, looking at the yards, too, and obeying the signs that warned of children at play; the street was empty now but often there were kids on bicycles or kicking a soccer ball in the streets, which was something else I liked, all the kids playing, another thing that made our street feel a little old-fashioned, a throwback.

The ravine was next, running through the neighborhood, deep and wooded, impossible to build on, home to foxes and deer, and then I was directing G to turn into our drive. Whoa, she said, seeing the huge stump of the fallen oak beside the drive, the logs the tree service had left, the blue tarp over the patched roof. She pulled up behind our car, the replacement car, which had been inert since one of L's colleagues had driven it back from the ER parking lot—I had to get a card to thank her, I thought—and beyond it I saw the French doors of my studio, opaque in the sunlight. This is it, I said, but G was still marveling at the trees, the logs from the one that had fallen, the gash in the one that still stood. Holy shit, she said. I had sent her photos but they didn't give a real sense of scale, and she opened her door now and stepped out to gape. I'm so sorry, she said, and then again, holy shit. We were lucky, I told her, cracking my own door, it could have been so much worse. She came to my side of the car, gave me her arm as I stood up. But look at your house, she said then, as we turned to walk toward it, it's so beautiful; and it was, I thought, even with all the work it needed, it was a beautiful house. The front door opened and L stepped out, calling my name. You're home, he said, bello, you're home. There was a tone to his voice I hadn't heard before, an edge or pressure of excitement, something almost frantic. My guapo, I said to him. He was wearing the apron he put on to cook, bright yellow, festive, it always made me laugh. He waited for us on the porch, the old beaten porch that needed replacing, it was springy, half rotted through; and when I reached him I threw my arms around him. My guapo, I said again, burying my face in his neck, then lifting my head and holding him in a way I liked, with my hand on his nape and my chin resting on the top of his head, his face against my chest, enfolding him, I felt; that was what I liked about it, the way he fit against me, though I was big and he was little, the way we made a perfect shape. Mi vida, I whispered to him, mi amor, and he turned his face from one side to the other, nuzzling me or burrowing into me, echoing my words. I pulled back after a moment, I hooked my fingers through the straps of his apron. Mi cocinero, I said, and laughed. He hugged G then, kissing her on both cheeks. I'm so happy to see you, he said, thank you for coming.

He pulled the storm door open, and I followed G over our threshold. There wasn't any entranceway, you stepped through the door into the living room, and G stopped just inside, pulling off her shoes. It's beautiful, she said, looking from the huge windows on the right to the kitchen, an almost open space now, there was just a half wall separating it from the room with our two couches, one blue, one red. That was the key, L had said, touches of color against the bare wood and the white walls, and the bay window in front of which we had placed the round table where we ate, beyond that the white counter with our stove built in, which L rushed to now, stirring the pan. He was making tofu and leeks, the house was rich with cumin and turmeric, It smells delicious, G said. Above the counter were three hanging globe lights L had ordered from England; they weren't expensive in themselves but the shipping had been outrageous. I had protested but they were the only lights L liked, he had spent hours searching, nothing else was as good. He had worked so hard, he had spent hours on every choice, I thought, as I watched G take it in, and they had all been right: the stove on the counter so he could talk while he made food, though at first the contractor had wanted to put it on the back wall, next to the oven, L had seen it would be better like this; he had insisted the window be widened over the sink; even the smallest things, like placing the handles on our cabinets horizontally instead of vertically, which the contractor had almost refused to do, he had never heard of such a thing, we were going to ruin our brand-new cabinets, he said. I had to have a long talk with him, saying it was our choice, that if it was a mistake it would be our mistake. Finally he had done it, and L had been right about that, too. He had made it all beautiful, the most beautiful place I had ever lived. It's incredible, G said. L only stayed at the stove for a minute, he came back to me and put his arms around me again. You're home, he said, the same weird tension in his voice. He returned to the stove but again just for a minute; it was like he couldn't stay still, he came back and put his arms around me once more. I feel so nervous, he said, it's so strange, I feel nervous that you are home. He pulled back and put his hands on my arms, making me flinch when he touched the PICC line. Oh, he said, snatching his hand back, bello, I'm sorry. But it was fine, it hadn't hurt, and he touched it again, more gently putting his hand over the mesh covering. Pobre bello, he said, and he bent down to kiss my arm, or almost kiss it, his lips hovering just above the fabric. He hugged me again. I'm so nervous, he repeated, and then he was back at the stove. I walked to him, leaving G in the living room, I stood behind him and wrapped my arms around his stomach. Is this better, I whispered to him, are you less nervous like this, and he put his head back, rubbing his face against mine. Much better, he said. I saw then how much food he was making: the blender was full of a crema, slices of potato were soaking in eggs for a tortilla, he had laid out lettuce and tomatoes for a salad. But guapo, I said, you're making a feast, it's so much food; G, I called to her, I hope you're hungry. She came into the kitchen, pulling a seat out from the table. I'm always hungry, she said, the more food the better. I wasn't sure what you would want, L said, he had made all of my favorite things. I put my arms around him again. And tonight we go for a walk, L went on, a slow walk around the neighborhood, the doctor said it is important. I told him we would try, I wasn't sure how far I would get. Day by day, he said, and I echoed him, Day by day.

The food was delicious, though L was tyrannical about what and how much I could eat: a tiny sliver of tortilla, a small portion of the tofu and leeks, which were cooked in oil, as much crema and salad as I wanted, but no salt. It was a sign of how scared he had been, how scared he still was; I knew his policing my meals would be a problem eventually but I let it go for now. Okay guapo, I said to him, okay. Mostly he and G talked, it had been years since they had seen each other. G told him the stories of the dogs, he said he loved the idea of the park the next morning. We talked all afternoon, the three of us, my sister and I finally intimate again, our old selves. Over L's food we talked about our family, which was so broken; the brother G hadn't seen since she was a kid, the sister I wasn't speaking with now, our different mothers and our father. G had seen him recently, after years of estrangement. He had been in failing health for a long time; a decade before, while I was abroad, he had seemed to be on the point of death and had seemed on the point of death again that spring. He had collapsed, his abdomen full of blood from a source it took them days to identify and stanch; finally G had gone to him, she had wanted to see him again, maybe for the last time, she had thought. We had talked about it over the phone, she had asked me what she should do. I can't tell you, I said. In the earlier crisis I had chosen not to go; my life is better without him in it, I told her, but that's my life, I can't tell you about yours. But aren't you afraid, she asked me, she was in tears now, on the phone, agonizing over our father who had hurt her and whom she loved; aren't you afraid that when he dies you will regret it forever. But that's true either way, I said, regret will come whatever you do, with any action or inaction; it's a false kind of reasoning, a kind of divination, you might as well read the stars. There's no proof against regret, was what I meant, and no way to assign it a weight among other possible consequences; I distrust how it can swamp our reasoning, it's always a motive to do anything, or a motive to leave anything undone. But maybe I distrust all reasoning, at least in some moods, when it seems to me all our actions are blind, that we act out of impulses we don't understand and reason backward from our acts, seeing wisdom or folly where there's just luck or misfortune, when I think there are no arts of living, just helplessness.

I hadn't gone and G had, and she made all three of us laugh with her stories of the trip. My father lived in Florida now, where he had dissolved into American insanity, his Facebook was full of posts about the president and rigged elections; if he were younger and well, if he had more courage, he would have been out marching with guns, another terrified old man desperate to feel strong. Sickness could be a blessing, I thought, at least it had saved him from that. He had recovered in the hospital; by the time G arrived he was on his way back home, weak but able to shuffle around the house he shared with his wife, not far from the beach. What a piece of work, G said about the wife, my father's third, who had been his mistress while he was married to G's mother, as G's mother had been his mistress when he was married to mine. They're miserable together, G said, all they do is bicker and swipe at each other—A form of love, I interrupted her, that can be a form of love, and L shot back Not in our house, malo, which was another name we had given each other, malo, malísimo. The whole meal he had kept his hand on me, on my arm, my knee, it was like he couldn't bear to break contact. Maybe, G said, but they seem to hate each other. And yet on the third day of her visit, the last day, while our father was napping, this woman, his third wife, accused G of being a bad daughter, accused all of us of being bad children. All of you are ungrateful, she said, none of you know what a wonderful man your father is, none of you love him enough. She didn't, I said. G had told me about the Florida visit but she hadn't told me about this. She did, G insisted, and I laughed. I stayed very calm, G said, I'm pretty proud of myself, actually, I told her I was sorry to hear that, but I wasn't sure she was the best person to judge my family. Bravo, L said.

But I'm glad I went, G went on, I think it was the right choice. For me, she added quickly, as if I might have heard a reproach. I held up my hands, a gesture of surrender, of not taking offense. Good for you, I said. I asked if she would go back, and she shrugged. We've stayed in touch a little, he texts me some-times. I don't know when I'll go back down, maybe seeing him once was enough. He's pretty sick, she said, his health has been bad for years, he could go any day. Her voice caught, and I looked up in surprise, the tone had been light until then. I just couldn't bear it, she said, the thought of my father dying, of never seeing him again. L reached across the table to put his hand on her arm. I know he's an asshole but he's my father, she said, and I said I knew, I understood. But you don't feel it, she countered, as the tears that had welled up spilled over. I'm sorry, she said; she put a napkin to her eyes to catch them, careful of her makeup, I'm so stupid. She was quiet for a moment. But why don't you feel it, she asked me. I don't know, I said, but I don't. Maybe some-thing had been broken in me, I had sometimes thought, broken early, so that always I felt a sense of detachment, always I felt on the verge of disappearing from my life, of slipping free and leaving no trace, no tie had ever really anchored me. Even now, even this beautiful house, this table, even L, I might slip free of all of it, maybe there was something in me that wanted to slip free. I looked at L, I put my hand to his face. I love you, I said, and that was true, too. Maybe everyone feels the way I do, that it takes an act of will to hang on to a life, maybe it's a myth to think anyone fits so seamlessly there's no chance of slipping free. L put his hand over mine, he turned his face to kiss my palm.

It was still light out when G left. She needed to check on the dogs and I was exhausted, tired in that deep way that was new, the medication I was on or the damage I had suffered, a fatigue that fell heavy and quick. I stood up to hug her but stayed at the table while she and L walked to the door, my hand on the wood to keep from falling over. And then we were alone,

L and I. He came back to me and we wrapped our arms around each other, for a long moment I breathed in the scent of his hair. The days were long still, there was another hour of light at least, but I was ready for bed already, I told L, no walk tonight, I just wanted a shower before sleep. A real shower, I said, I hadn't had one since the morning I went to urgent care, when I had stood under the water with my hand against the wall, braced against the pain, still in the grip of that fist that wanted to turn me inside out or rip me apart. I could have died, I thought suddenly, with L in my arms, I felt the shock of it again. Seventy-five percent, I thought, remembering what the doctor had said about the mortality rate, each day I had waited to go to the hospital, each hour, it had mounted, at any point the artery might have ruptured, the blown aorta pelting out blood, I might never have held L again. I held on to him more tightly now, and maybe in response he said to me I was so scared, bello, I have never been so scared, I'm so happy you are home. I put my hands on his shoulders and drew back, giving him a little shake, giving myself a little shake too. His eyes were wet. But we were laughing a minute later, when L was cocooning my arm in plastic wrap. There was no graceful way to do it, he passed the roll over and then under the arm I held out, again and again, until finally I stopped him. I think it's enough, I said, laughing, I'm a mummy already. He had covered a large area, just to be sure, he said, from just below my shoulder to below the elbow, so that I had to hold my arm out stiff beside me, I couldn't bend it at all. L thought this was hilarious, Mummy bello, he said, he held his own arms stiff and rocked back and forth, making a horror movie growl. Tonto, I said, estúpido, which only made his monster dance more exuberant. I had to keep my arm above my head in the tiny shower, the bathroom was small and we had run out of money, we had wanted tile but instead it was a plastic prefab, like a shower in a cheap hotel. That was something else on the list of future improvements, below the porch and the yard; we would never replace it, I knew, it was fine the way it was. The water on my skin was pure pleasure, I leaned back to feel it on my face and my torso, I watched it run over the bruises on my stomach, the marks from the IVs on my unwrapped arm, the traces of adhesive on my chest; I imagined it carrying away the residue of the terrible antiseptic wipes, the ultrasound gel, my sweat and fear and pain, I could feel my body relaxing beneath it, and then suddenly I was sobbing, I wasn't sure why, I was so happy under the water and I was crying in a way that shook my whole body. I tried to be quiet, I choked down the sounds, I didn't want L to hear me. He would have freaked out, I knew, he would have burst in to see what was wrong and what could I have told him. They were private tears, mine alone, I let the water wash them away too.

It was a struggle to get the plastic off. Finally L took the kitchen scissors and made cuts at the top and bottom, then we were able to unwrap it, there were layers and layers; Maybe I was a little exaggerated, L said. He went upstairs while I brushed my teeth and took my pills. I had a special box for pills now, like the one my grandmother had at the end of her life, a double row of little plastic chambers, a whole week's worth of pills. G had helped me fill them before she left, checking and rechecking the prescriptions with me. Morning and night I would take these pills, for the rest of my life the doctors had said, morning and night for the rest of my life. L called down when he heard me on the stairs, asking if I needed help, but I said I didn't, I was just being slow. The staircase was narrow and I kept a hand on each wall as I took the steps one by one, wondering if I would always climb stairs like this now, I knew I should be grateful to climb stairs at all. There were so many things to be grateful for, I should be grateful for everything, which is always true but in that moment I felt it, a little bit anyway, I felt a part of what we should all feel all the time. I was grateful for my body, that I could lift one foot then the other to each step, that I could grip the bannister with my right hand and trace the opposite wall with my left, that I was in my house, on my way to my bed, that L was waiting for me there. It's impossible to live counting the beads of one's luck like that, but for a day, an hour, I would feel it, I told myself, for the space between now and sleep. L was under the covers already when I reached the bedroom, but I didn't join him at first, I stopped on the threshold. I stood for a moment looking at the white room I had longed for, more than any other place in the world I had wanted to be here, and now I wanted to long for it a moment more, or I wanted to feel the moment of letting longing go, the moment of possession. It's a weirdly shaped room, not the master bedroom, which L had taken for his office; we made it by combining two other bed-rooms, children's rooms, each too small on its own but together they made a comfortable space, the roof slanting down on one side in the Dutch colonial shape I loved. The previous owner had shown me the two small rooms when she walked me around the house before we bought it, one of them her sister's room and the other her own, the room she had grown up in. I had wor-ried about her reaction to the changes, that she might feel we had erased her childhood, but when after all the renovations I invited her to see the house, she was wonderful. She seemed delighted about everything, exclaiming over the floors, which she had never seen, her parents had laid down the green carpet when she was young. If I had known I would have pulled it up years ago, she said. And she exclaimed at the bedroom, too, saying that it was perfect, what she had hoped for; the house had had its life with us, she said, and now it has a life with you, a new life.

Bello, L said, what are you thinking, come here, and he folded back the covers, inviting me under them. He wrapped himself around me once I had lain down on my side of the bed, the side nearest the door since I was always up in the night, to the bathroom at least but often just up, unable to sleep; I would creep downstairs and work if I could, falling asleep again on the couch at dawn. Over the next days I was up four or five times in the night, always for the bathroom, it was the medication, which would have other side effects, too: rashes on my arms, a tingling that made me kick my legs at night, like electric shocks, so that I couldn't sleep at all; finally they would change one of the drugs and mostly it went away. But that would come later, now I was sure I would sleep, breathing in L's smell, we were holding each other as tightly as possible, as we always did before sleeping, our way of saying good night to each other. For years the same embrace, with his right leg between mine and my left curled around him, twisted together in a way that had become one of the natural postures of my body, so that I realized it wasn't true, what I had thought before, happiness did leave a mark, the mark was this. Usually we only held each other for a moment before letting go, I would turn away, toward the edge of the bed, and L would put his arm around me, his hand on my stomach; but tonight we didn't let go, we stayed like that, pressed against each other, for a long time, not saying anything, unmoving. L lifted his head and we kissed, then kissed again. And then L felt me start to get hard against his leg, there was a sense of suspension and then I felt a door opening, and L's mouth opened too, I took his tongue in my mouth. It had been some time since we'd had sex, some time before I went into the hospital, I mean; what happened to most couples had happened to us, sex had become an event, something remarkable. In the first year or so we had been insatiable, I remember one winter night leaving L's apartment, his little one bedroom, a student's apartment, really, and at the foot of the stairs I looked back up at him. I was bundled against the cold, which was bitter, the deep Iowa cold, but L was in just a T-shirt, leaning over the threshold to see me off, and something kindled in the look, a struck match. We had just had sex, I thought we were sated, but I ran back up the stairs to him, I stripped off my things and we dove into bed together, back into the warmth of the bed. Maybe that kind of hunger never survives long, through years of familiarity, though it had seemed inextinguishable those first months, irrevocably new, impossible to imagine then how it would fade. But it had faded for us. I had been sad to see it go, there had been a time I had felt panicked almost, frantic, though I didn't feel that anymore, as our life had grown steady with some element more durable than heat, than that quick heat that had burned so brightly, there were compensations for its loss. But something awakened between us now, not the same early hunger but a hunger, and L felt it too as he started to move against me, as we moved against each other. He reached between my legs and gripped me through the sweatpants I slept in; I had been so happy to put them on but I was happier to take them off, to push them down so I was bare against him. I started to fumble with the buttons on his pajamas, he was wearing his pijama de ciervos again, there was a line of buttons I undid with one hand, slipping the plastic discs through the eyes. I was fully hard now as he stroked me; for the first time in two weeks, since the onset of the pain, I was hard. He was using both hands, reaching down to cup my balls while he stroked me, his hands warm, warmer than mine, my hand was cold as I slipped it under his shirt, my free hand; the other hand was on his back, his head still pillowed on my arm, as it always was when we hugged before sleep. An embrace before sleep, an embrace in the morning, in bed sometimes or if we woke separately then at the first noise the other made; we had never discussed it but it was a rule, inviolable, whatever we were doing in the morning at the first sound the other made we stopped—the page half read, the sentence half written—and went to him, L to me, me to L, and hugged each other, we gave each other a morning kiss. For seven years every day we had spent together had begun and ended the same way, with the same signs of love, which was a small thing and also profound, one of the lasting marks happiness had made.

It wasn't really sex, what we did, I was too exhausted, too weak, we mostly used our hands. I wanted to touch him everywhere, after so many days unable to touch him, only our hands had touched in the hospital but now I stroked his back and his chest, his face, I sucked on his tongue in my mouth, and even that was a kind of exertion; when I came, from his hands and my own, while he kissed my neck and face, while he whispered to me his love, my heart was pounding, I had to close my eyes against the spinning dizziness I felt. I didn't know if I could do that, I said to him then, the whole time in the hospital it was like that part of me had died, I thought maybe I would never do it again.

Have an orgasm, I meant, get hard, I thought maybe that whole part of me was a thing of the past, for some men it was, I knew, when they started the drugs I was on, I was so relieved. Thank you, I said to L, thank you, thank you. I turned toward him, I reached down to take him in my hand again, he hadn't come yet; but Don't worry, bello, he said, I don't need it. I tried to insist, I hate when my partner doesn't come, I always have, it's a point of pride, it makes me feel selfish to be the only one who comes. But he said Tomorrow, you need your rest, relax now, and finally I let him pull his pajamas back up. He curled his leg between mine and pulled me close again, I put both arms around him. Okay guapo, I said, but tomorrow, it's a promise, and he laughed. Be quiet, he said, go to sleep. And though we never slept like that I didn't pull away from him, I felt the curtain of fatigue falling again, it had lifted briefly but was coming down hard now; he would be so happy, I thought, L always wanted to sleep like this and tonight we would, and it made me happy to think of him happy. That was what we had built together, I thought, the real unprecedented thing, a happiness that was equally ours, his and mine, and falling asleep now meant falling into it, into the noise of contentment he made as he held me more tightly, his happiness that was my happiness too, my happiness that was his.

We got to the park a little before noon. I'm sorry, I'm sorry, G had said when she stepped out of her car in our driveway, not in her work clothes now but jeans and a T-shirt, her hair pulled back; they were clothes for getting dirty in, clothes for wrangling her dogs. She had been caught up in a work call that morning, then the owner of the Airbnb had stopped by—G was in a guesthouse on the property—to say that one of the dogs had gotten into something and made a mess in the barn and G had to help clean it up. I had spent the morning in my studio, not working, reading a little, sitting at my desk, basking in the sensation of being home. I saw G pull up and walked out on the front porch, where I could barely hear what she was saying over the racket Leia started making, her drawn-out sounds of longing, which began as a bark but became a kind of lowing or moaning, the sweet girl; and she started pawing at the hatch at the back of the car, which G opened now, swinging it up as she said Settle down, Jesus Christ. Leia came tumbling out, giving a quick sniff at the ground before lifting her head and bounding toward me. She was a big dog, her bark sometimes scared people, when they got too close to the car or walked by my sister's home, but she was gentle, sweet, I loved her, I called out her name. She was gentle but she was strong, I used my right arm half to pet her and half to hold her off as I held the PICC line behind me so she wouldn't snag it. She leapt up to put her paws on me, leapt up and then back and to the side, then up on me again, trying to lick my face while I laughed and said she was a good girl, I was so happy to see her. I wasn't sure she would remember me, she had been a young dog the last time I had seen her, not a puppy but young still, And now look at you, I said, you're a grown woman. Finally she calmed down enough to stand still, on her hind legs with her front paws on my chest, and I lowered my face to her kisses, which I half accepted and half dodged, laughing. When she had grown quieter, I got down on my knees and put both my arms around her, bringing my left arm from behind my back, and she shifted her paws to my shoulders, twisting her neck to press her face flat against my chest. I rested my chin on the top of her head, while she made short huffing whines, a sound that could as easily mean suffering as joy. Baby, I said to her, I love you, what a good girl. She shifted once, turning her head to the other side, along the way lifting her snout to lick my face, stealing kisses, I said to her, laughing; but otherwise we settled into a kind of quietness, both of us, the only movement her tail beating its pattern in the air. For two or three long minutes I held her like that, murmuring to her, my beautiful girl.

And then she shoved herself back and off the porch, giving a single loud bark as L opened the door behind me and stepped out. She came forward again when he said her name, she stretched her neck to sniff his outstretched fingers, and then like a flipped switch she was all joy again, pressing her lean body against his legs, looking up at him as he scratched the top of her head. I wondered whether she had recognized his smell, which must have been all over me, and his hand must have carried my scent, too, each of us must be signed all over with the scent of the other. L was happy too, though he was sometimes uncomfortable around dogs, there had been an incident in his childhood that scared him, and in general he had a European sense that animals belonged outside. He had been bemused, a little shocked, the first time we went to the house of a friend and I dropped to my knees to play with their dog, then lay full length on the ground so she could scamper all over me, a gorgeous little cattle dog rescued from an Iowa farm, I spent the whole evening playing with her. He had come a long way, I thought as he crouched down to talk to Leia, he wasn't ready for a dog yet but maybe someday we could have one. He stood up to say hello to G, who was standing in the yard. The other dog was behind her, pulling the leash taut, keeping as much distance from us as possible. Is that Mary, I asked. She was the same breed as Leia but smaller by a third, and even after weeks with G she was painfully skinny, her thin legs trembling, from infirmity or fear. It's okay, baby, G said, coaxing her forward, and I took one step off the porch. Hey, I said, reaching my hand out, fingers curled. She took a hesitant step forward, then another, but after a quick sniff she scrambled back. I laughed. Stranger danger, I said to her, you're not wrong.

Leia barked again when we reached the park, she stood up between the seats and strained forward, as if to climb through the windshield. Down, G said as she pulled into a space, and Leia dropped obediently back, but she barked again when we got out of the car, and when G opened the hatch she tried to rush out. G held her back until she got the leash fastened to her collar, then Leia strained at the leash; G had to pull with her whole weight to keep her in check. Mary was slower to come out, L and I had to step back before she half leapt, half stumbled to the tarmac of the parking lot. But then she was eager too, straining toward the other dogs. The parking lot was nearly full and there were at least a dozen dogs in the enclosure, some playing with their owners, fetching balls or sticks, but most socializing with other dogs, chasing after each other in groups of three or four, wrestling over toys. It was a big space, the size of a football field or larger, mostly grass but with patches of bare dirt, and there was water somewhere, though we couldn't see it from the front fence; at a station with a hose by the parking lot a man was spraying down a muddy dog, who leapt up joyfully, snapping at the water. We passed through a double gate to reach the grass, there were signs about closing one gate before opening the other, and G was careful about this. God help you if you don't follow the rules at the dog park, she said. To the right, after the first gate, there was an entrance to a smaller enclosure for the little dogs, where two small guys were chasing each other in circles. Mary sniffed at that gate but Leia was fixated on the entrance to the main park; G had to hold her tight as she opened it, waiting until L and I had latched it again before she unclipped the leash and Leia shot off. Mary followed her, and we watched them run from one knot of dogs to another, sniffing at each and being sniffed in turn, saying hello to everybody; it was a dream of sociality, I thought as a dog broke from its little pack and started chasing Leia, who first ran and then spun and leapt, delirious with play. We stood watching them. Es pura vida, L said, which was something he usually said about art, about poems or paintings, his highest praise. He leaned against me and I put an arm around his waist. Mary was maybe halfway down the field, sniffing at the fence, and G set off after her, holding up her roll of plastic bags in explanation.

L and I started walking in the opposite direction, on the

sidewalk that circled the field, two or three benches along each side. We'll take it slow, L said, hooking his arm around mine, but I felt okay as we set off. It was a warm day but the air was fresh, it had been cool that morning, with a trace of chill in the air, it would be autumn soon. Fall was my favorite season in Iowa City, the air crisp, the trees, for two or three weeks, a blaze of red and gold. We moved slowly, watching the dogs. One sporty middle-aged woman had a device for throwing balls, a flexible plastic stick with a cup at one end, like a little cata-pult, and we watched as a German shepherd ran back to her and dropped a tennis ball at her feet, a good boy. He kept his eyes on it, his body tense, as she loaded the device and cocked it over her shoulder, and when she let it fly he charged after it, his back legs pounding the grass, fearsomely strong and fast. At each bench L asked if I wanted to sit, but I was okay for a while, we kept shuffling along. Most of the dogs were muddy and wet, and eventually we could see why, there was a shallow puddle almost three quarters of the way to the back fence, right in the middle of the field. We watched as a golden retriever trotted up to it, then looked over his shoulder at his owner, who had been talking with another woman at the back fence and realized too late his intention. She called out, saying Don't you dare, and started after him, striding; he looked at the mud then back at her once, guiltily, I thought, calculating risk and reward. And then he leapt into the center of the puddle, lying down and roll-ing on his back in the black mud, wriggling, his tail thrashing back and forth. Oh my God, the woman said, bending over and planting her hands on her knees, a posture of dismay. She stood up and looked back at the woman she had left, who was laugh-ing, and then she laughed too, raising her arms in surrender.

Go on then, she said to the dog, eat your heart out. L was rapt watching the dog as he luxuriated, He's so happy, he said, I've never seen anyone so happy. He looked at me wide-eyed, It's amazing, bello, he said, and I took his hand.

The fatigue came on suddenly, I collapsed onto the next bench, my head spinning, suddenly out of breath. So strange, I said to L, I'm fine and then bam, I can't keep going, I've never felt anything like it. But are you okay, L asked, concerned, did something happen. He spoke with real fear, I heard the presence not far off of panic. I would hear this many times over the next months, L's flares of fear, each time realizing again how hard the days in the hospital had been for him, how much he had suffered; at any hint of weakness or pain he wanted me to call the number Dr. Ferrier had given us, to talk to the vascular resident on call and ask if I should go to the ER. I'm okay, I said, I just need to sit for a minute. When he asked me a short time later if I was better, I was. But let's keep sitting a little longer, I said, taking his hand and curling my fingers through his. Okay bello, he said, okay. It was nice to sit in the sun with him, watching the dogs play with each other, running to their owners to check in and then back to their friends, it filled me with happiness. L laid his head on my shoulder and I tilted my head toward him, he pressed my fingers again and again. A phrase came to me then, not quite language at first but a possibility of language, an idea of language, of ordered language, a line from a poem, I waited for it to coalesce. Earth was given to me in a dream, I thought, those were the words for what I felt, they weren't my words but they were the best words I had: Earth was given to me in a dream In a dream I possessed it. Maybe it wasn't true that there were no arts of living, with L's hand in mine it seemed that maybe there were, as we laughed watching the woman egg on her dog now, telling him to get it all out, to go whole hog; maybe they were just simpler than I had imagined. It was a sentimental thought, probably I don't believe it; but as the sun poured down it seemed possible that it was true, that it was one truth at least, as true as what I had thought sickness had shown me. Maybe there are only ever provisional truths, about the big questions I mean, the questions about how to live, maybe only competing truths, and maybe that isn't the same thing as no truths at all, maybe we have to take them as they come. But I don't think I believe that either, I don't know what I believe.

I closed my eyes for a while, with my head propped on L's. I don't think I slept but maybe I did for a minute or two, until L lifted his head, saying Hola in the voice he used for animals and children. I opened my eyes to see Leia in front of us, expectant, her tail beating, her stomach wet and dripping with mud. Have you been having a good time, I asked her, and her tail wagged more quickly, she went tense with excitement, with the pleasure of my attention, and I thought of the old idea—is it in Milton or Dante, maybe it's in both—that the pleasure of heaven is God's gaze upon us, the bliss of being seen by him. Maybe we got that idea from how dogs respond to us, the way they lift their ears and shiver with excitement, how you can work them up with the sound of your voice; it's intoxicating to be the object of such devotion, of course we love dogs. I didn't notice the ball in her mouth until she dropped it at my feet, soaked through and black with filth. What is that, I asked her, leaning forward, where did you get that, that's not yours. She looked at me, her head cocked. No way, I said to her, I am not throwing you that ball. L laughed. Leia bent down and pushed the ball toward me with her nose, then looked up again, pleading. No way, I repeated, laughing, absolutely not. She dropped down on her forelegs, like a puppy, she gave a short muffled bark and stood back up, trying to provoke me. She was irresistible, and when I bent forward to take the ball between my thumb and forefinger she started whimpering. Okay Leia, I said, get ready, and she pranced, giddy, lifting each of her feet in turn. I couldn't throw it like that, just using two fingers, I had to hold it properly, curling my whole hand around it, dirtying my palm. When I lifted it above my head, bending my arm back, she went still, taut as a string drawn back with its arrow, her eyes on the ball a distillation of desire. And then she became the arrow. I couldn't throw as far as I'd have liked but it was far enough, in her enthusiasm she overshot the ball, she tried to scoop it up in her mouth as she ran past it but she missed, she had to bring herself to a stop and double back. But that didn't temper her pleasure or her pride, and once she had it she shot toward us at full speed, muscular and lithe, her long ears streaming back, her brown flanks gleaming. Pure life.

ACKNOWLEDGMENTS

This book was written with support from the Guggenheim Foundation and the Iowa Arts Council.

The novel references, sometimes quite freely, several poems without attribution:

"The blown / aorta pelting out blood" is from Geoffrey Hill's *The Triumph of Love*, collected in *Broken Hierarchies: Poems 1952–2013* (Oxford University Press, 2013).

The Bulgarian poem described in the second section is Valeri Petrov's "Vik ot detstvoto." Richard Wilbur's translation, "A Cry from Childhood," can be found in Wilbur's *Collected Poems 1943–2004* (Harcourt, 2004).

"That they are there!" is from George Oppen's "Psalm," in *New Collected Poems* (New Directions, 2002). "Stranger's Child" is also included in this volume.

"Outside // time. Nail it." is from Frank Bidart's "Injunction," collected in *Half-light: Collected Poems 1965–2016* (FSG, 2017).

The lines beginning "Las rocas, mucho más, / los castaños bastante" are from Luis Muñoz's "Ilusión de permanencia," from *Guadarrama* (Papeles mínimos, 2023).

"Love set you going like a fat gold watch" is from Sylvia Plath's "Morning Song," collected in *The Collected Poems* (Harper Perennial, 2018).

"The pistol-shot / laughter" and "Bared body is not equal ever" are from Les Murray's "On Home Beaches," from *Subhuman Redneck Poems* (FSG, 1997).

"Earth was given to me in a dream / In a dream I possessed it" is from Louise Glück's "The Seven Ages," collected in *Poems 1962–2012* (FSG, 2012).

My life was changed by two great teachers who recently passed away. David Brown, at the Youth Performing Arts School in Louisville, introduced me to opera. James Longenbach, at the University of Rochester, made me feel that a life devoted to poetry would be the noblest possible life. No discharging the debt I owe them.

Garth Greenwell is the author of two previous works of fiction, *Cleanness* and *What Belongs to You*. The recipient of honors including a Guggenheim Fellowship and the Vursell Memorial Award for prose style from the American Academy of Arts and Letters, he is currently a Distinguished Writer in Residence at New York University.